THE SPACE BETWEEN

THE WALSH SERIES, BOOK TWO

KATE CANTERBARY

VESPER PRESS

COPYRIGHT

Editing provided by Julia Ganis of JuliaEdits.
www.juliaedits.com/

Cover design by Sarah Hansen of Okay Creations.
www.okaycreations.com

Coach Eric Taylor – this one's for you.

CHAPTER ONE

ANDY

SOMETIMES I HAVE THAT NIGHTMARE WHERE I SHOW UP AT WORK or school naked, on display for everyone to stare and laugh. I never studied psychology or sociology, or whichever -ology that fit into, but I could say with some confidence it more than likely related to feeling vulnerable.

Exposed.

Everything I wanted to guard from the outside world was illuminated, offered up for judgment. Then again, maybe it was from eating questionable Chinese food before going to bed.

Meeting Patrick Walsh was exactly like that: a waking naked-at-work dream.

"How would you adapt the roof geometries of a Queen Anne for maximum rain water catchment while keeping it historically accurate?" he barked.

It didn't matter that the ink on my Master of Architecture degree from Cornell University was barely dry. It definitely didn't matter that I wasn't quite twenty-five, or that I was a woman in a field where men outnumbered me four to one. I was good, and I knew it.

"What's your approach to handling conflicts between strict preservation guidance while also meeting LEED Green specifications?" he asked.

I'd been fantasizing about this for years—Walsh Associates was the ultimate apprenticeship and interviewing was my jam.

But Patrick wasn't nearly as excited about the interview. No, Patrick interrupted before I offered any substantive comments, glowering from across the rectangular conference table. He squinted at me while I spoke, stripping away the artifice of interview and openly dissecting my words. His lips twisted into grimaces while his eyebrows quirked and furrowed. He even rolled his eyes when I discussed my passion for original Bostonian masonry.

Everything about Patrick was assertive. Staring into his hazel eyes, I immediately knew it wasn't limited to architecture.

"Walk me through your approach to construction waste management. Specifically, CFC-based refrigerants."

I left my friends' apartment this morning pleased with my edgy-conservative outfit that avoided all manner of architecture school chic—no corduroy, no khakis, no ponytails, no wrinkles. My confidence was swinging high when I arrived at the hallowed halls of Walsh Associates, though I never noticed how frizzy the dry winter air turned my long, raven curls until I felt Patrick's eyes cataloging every errant strand.

He made little effort to manage his reactions and he clearly took issue with my appearance. I was unapologetic about my wardrobe and its shades of black simplicity—I was a charter member in the 'selective pops of color' cult—yet he repeatedly drank in my black skirt suit, pearl gray shirt with delicate beading around the neck, and black knee-high boots, with an arched eyebrow and blatant scowl.

I wanted him to glance at my résumé, leaf through my portfolio—anything to take his piercing hazel eyes off of me long enough to regroup and strategize. Something about his fierce gaze—how he'd stare, scowling, his jaw rigid—made my thoughts freeze and words dissolve into a fumbling, garbled mess.

Missing out on this apprenticeship was not an option. I didn't work my ass off for the past five years, fighting for every tedious assistantship, internship, and design fellowship, to blow it when I finally got my shot. I wasn't surprised when Shannon Walsh's assistant called to schedule my interview; I was perfect for their firm. Now it was just a matter of getting this interview back on track and them believing it as much as I did.

Despite the fact Patrick was annoyed that I was taking a second of his time, I would happily pluck my eyelashes if it meant learning from him. He didn't have any National Preservation awards—yet—or much more than a decade in the industry, but he transcended it all with his talent. It wasn't every day that early thirty-somethings received the type of acclaim Patrick earned from the start. No one bothered to tell him or his siblings —his partners in this work—it should have taken them longer to achieve this much success.

He could have turned out to be a bridge troll, and I probably wouldn't have noticed. I was prepared to endure an endless supply of his surly attitude if any fraction of his greatness rubbed off on me. Maybe I was a little infatuated, but plenty of my grad school friends geeked out over the reigning industry legends. I was fine. Definitely not over-the-top, boy-band obsessed.

The truth was his work got me fired up about historical preservation and its place in sustainable design. His master's thesis was my favorite bedtime story through undergrad and I pulled it out whenever I needed inspiration.

His siblings were equally brilliant—shockingly so—Matt, the structural engineer, Sam, the sustainable design guru, and Shannon, the grand master of it all. I heard rumors of the fifth Walsh, Riley, who recently joined the family business, though my research yielded limited information about him or his background.

I admired all of the Walshes but the love of the craft spoke to me in Patrick's thesis, grabbing me by the throat and demanding I believe in his philosophy. I wanted to fangirl all over him.

He sat back in his chair, minutely swiveling while his finger-tips drummed against the arm. I didn't expect him to be so...big. At five-eight, I wasn't short but I knew he'd tower over me. None of the online photographs accurately portrayed his presence. His harnessed intensity brought the walls closer and thickened the air. His stare was cool and observant, and I experienced a profound sense he could slough away my layers with one glance.

"Where do you see yourself in five years, Miss Asani?"

Time for the Hail Mary response, the one I prepared with my mentor, Charlotte, but never expected to use. My chance to put it all on the line was in front of me, and if I didn't appeal to Patrick as a visionary craftsman, I might as well pack my drafting kit and start designing rural fishing lodges back home in Maine. God knew I couldn't accept any of the commercial real estate design apprenticeships waiting in my inbox. I'd be happier working on Barbie dollhouses.

I wanted Patrick to train me. Teach me. Shape me. Infuse the unique spirituality of his craft into my marrow. Pour his wisdom into me until I overflowed with the muscle memory necessary to bring history back to life.

Fine, so I was completely boy-band obsessed.

"I see myself as a partner in a sustainable preservation firm, and I'd like to spend several years learning under you—"

"Thank you for coming, Miss Asani. Shannon's assistant, Tom—"

I held up a hand. "I wasn't finished, Mr. Walsh."

His icy stare turned molten, his eyes narrowing as if trying to assign a name to my defiance. I suspected he didn't hear 'no' very often. He lifted an eyebrow in challenge, and a smile pulled at my lips.

"I want to learn everything from you. I don't get coffee or copies, and I don't do busywork. Your philosophy on the role of sustainability and efficient design in preservation shaped my entire approach as an undergrad and beyond, and I've spent the past five years absorbing every field experience possible to prepare me for *this* work. With *you*. At *this* firm. I want to learn from *you*, Mr. Walsh. I want to learn the soul of preservation. I want to learn everything you have to teach me because your work fascinates and enthralls me."

On top of Patrick's vision seeping into my blood and bones, his family was gaining legend status in their corner of the architectural universe. In an age when architecture had more to do with erecting sterile filing cabinets as lifeless boxes for work and home, and sustainability was being co-opted as a hollow branding strategy, the Walsh family was proving boutique firms could run with the big dogs.

Their successes weren't accidental. It was clear they ran a

tight ship, and I knew much of the credit belonged to Shannon Walsh. Talking to the petite redhead was like being caught in a tornado—she yelled, exaggerated wildly, cursed like a frat boy, and walked faster in four-inch stilettos than physics should allow. The aggressive click of her heels coupled with the fifteen hair-thin jingling silver charm bracelets on her wrist meant everyone knew when Shannon was coming, and they made sure to pass inspection.

"Is there anything else, Miss Asani?" Patrick asked, his voice taking on a thick, gravelly quality that tickled the hairs on the back of my neck.

I didn't want to talk about architecture anymore. I only wanted that voice. And it was all wrong.

"This is the only apprenticeship I want," I continued, my eyes zeroing in on Patrick. "I know everyone you've interviewed. Zemario? He's only interested in checking off the historical box so he can get started on his doctorate and teach undergrads how to hold a ruler. Heywood? He wants residential—McMansions —and he's going to leave the second something opens up in the Sun Belt. Morton-Myers? He's smart, but lazier than most house-cats. I'm the one for you, Mr. Walsh. You're not going to meet anyone else as eager to learn from you or as invested in sustainable prez."

Patrick ran his thumb and forefinger along his chin, his stubble rasping against his fingers and filling the silence with a slight grating sound. He stared at me, and I held his gaze while curiosity replaced his chilly indifference.

"You know a lot about the competition."

"I make it a priority to always know what I'm going up against," I replied. "And as I'm sure you know, there's no shortage of gossip at Cornell."

"Do you always succeed? Do you always know what you're up against?"

I offered a slight shrug.

"All right. Andy, it was amazing to meet you," Shannon interjected, an eye trained on her brother.

The articles I read about Shannon suggested she knew her shit and enough of everyone else's too—real estate license at eighteen, first seven-figure sale at twenty, business degree at twenty-one, law degree at twenty-five. Everything I read pointed to her real estate savvy as the kick-start Walsh Associates needed to survive and thrive through the housing market crisis, though she insisted that success was a product of their team.

And fuck me if I didn't want to be on that team more than I wanted warm blood pumping in my veins.

"We expect to finalize our candidate pool this week, and you'll be hearing from me. Can I give you directions to South Station, or call you a cab? Do you have a sense about town?"

"No need," I replied, my eyes locked on Patrick while I responded to Shannon. "I'm here a few more days."

Standing, Shannon extended her hand across the table. "In that case, enjoy the week and stay out of the cold. Not too different from Ithaca, I know, but I think we have better restaurants."

"More variety," I offered. "I'll take Boston over Ithaca any day."

"Funny," Shannon said as she rounded the table and gestured toward the door. "Patrick says the exact same thing." Shaking her head, she smiled. "My assistant, Tom Esbeck, will show you out. Again, so fantastic to finally meet you." She leaned out the door and bellowed, "Tom!"

I nodded, taking in the pristinely preserved Beacon Hill offices. Working here would be a dream come true.

I glanced back at Patrick. He didn't offer any parting words or acknowledgement, but the inquisitiveness in his eyes seemed to grow with each moment I held his gaze. I felt his stare on me as I exited the conference room, and a subtle toss of my hair told me he was still staring when I walked down the hallway.

CHAPTER TWO

WHAT *WAS* THAT? WHAT THE ACTUAL HELL WAS THAT?

A long curtain of dark, wavy hair caught my eye through the conference room windows. I stared after it, half expecting to develop X-ray vision to see through brick walls, half hating myself for noticing it in the first place.

Shannon leaned against the door and squealed, "She is freaking awesome!"

Andy was nothing like the other candidates with their nervous tics, obvious immaturity, and shortage of authentic interest in this type of work.

She radiated cool confidence. Her gestures were measured and meaningful, her speech deliberate.

How she could sit there while I hit her with impossible scenarios and answer as if she expected the goddamn questions, cool as a fucking cucumber, was beyond me. I dug in with increasingly outlandish questions—problems *I* was trying to bend *my* brain around—with the perverted hope I'd break that cool.

Didn't happen, and I couldn't explain why I was determined to shake her. See her ruffled. Get her flustered.

I scrubbed my hand over my face, a feeble attempt at slowing my galloping heart rate. Nothing prepared me for Andy. I knew I'd be interviewing one of the most accomplished and focused candidates to apply for our fledgling apprenticeship, but I didn't anticipate an unflappable spine of steel *enthralled* by my work.

It got even more interesting when she wouldn't let me shut her down. She wanted to learn from me. She was demanding it. I knew it was inappropriate but the moment those words passed her lips I started drowning in fantasies far filthier than anything my mind had ever produced.

Oh, yes. I could teach her plenty.

My head and my dick wrestled for control in ways I'd never before experienced when Andy told me she wasn't finished. But noticing attractive women never fucked with my mind. Was this it? Was my sanity on its way out?

People didn't usually take me on, yet I had the distinct impression Andy would provoke the shit out of me with her poignant commentary and patronizingly dismissive "hm." I could see her sitting back and allowing me a tiny smile while I went ballistic over that "hm."

I barely noticed Shan's babbling.

"...perfect for you. She's taking her licensing boards in June but if this works out, we could bring her on long term to build your capacity. She said she's in town the rest of the week. I say we get her back this afternoon and make an offer."

No. *Hell* no. Not with her maddeningly unfazed responses to my brutal questions. Not with her steady gazes and precise expressions. Not with those dark eyes that were altogether too wise, too perceptive for her age. Andy needed to take her eyes and that smile far away from this office. Mentoring her was out of the question.

"No. She's like a...a feral cat, Shan."

"What?" She dropped into a seat across the conference table, her face twisted in irritated confusion. I loved Shannon in full-on Black Widow ass-kicking mode unless she was aiming her *Avengers*-style wrath at me.

"All that hair and her voice. She seemed annoying." Both of those things were very real problems. I'd never seen so much hair in my life. Thick, dark, uncontrollably curling. It was mythical. Odysseus would have had something to say about that hair.

"You're annoying. This whole process is annoying. I want to find a freaking apprentice for you and move on with my life. Is that so hard? We're talking about six months, Patrick. I don't see why you can't handle working with someone like Andy for six months. We've been searching since November. It's time to nut up, man."

"She acts like she knows it all." I shook my head. "I can't see her cutting it at a jobsite, Shan. Doesn't look like she can lift more than a latte."

I couldn't help it; lame responses kept spewing out while my brain fixated on that voice. If aged whiskey had a sound, it would be Andy's voice, all heady and rich, with a slow burn as it went down.

"Did you notice those fancy boots? I'm not about to wait on some girl because she tiptoes around in heels and is afraid of messing up her nails."

I noticed the boots. I noticed them and the long legs encased in them about four seconds after I ripped my eyes away from her hair. They went all the way up to her knees. All I could think about was wrapping those legs around my neck and feeling those ridiculous heels digging into my back while she writhed against my face.

Yep. That was a normal thought for the start of an interview.

Shannon rested her forehead against the table alongside her flattened palms. "The universe needs to help a bitch out."

"And there's her complete lack of originality," I continued, pulling at any thread possible to weaken Andy's candidacy. "She wants to learn from me? No design vision of her own? That's weak. I can't work with that."

Mentoring Andy would be the cruelest form of punishment.

Shannon lifted her head, leveling me with a patented Black Widow death stare reserved for moments when I was epically fucking things up.

"As your counsel," she started, her voice ripe with loosely restrained anger, "I am advising you to evaluate Miss Asani on her credentials rather than her shoes or hair. I am advising you to read her résumé, specifically where it lists her extensive jobsite experience as well as hands-on experience with Habitat. She's built fucking houses with her manicured hands, asshole."

She slammed her hand on the pages in front of me. I glanced at the name streaming across the top of her résumé: Andy A. M. Asani. I never liked people with two middle names.

"As your sister and a professional woman myself, I am advising you to get your head out of your ass and recognize that she is the most exceptional candidate you have met—by far. Please keep in mind that people come to interviews looking their best. They don't show up in tromp-around-a-construction-site clothes." She sighed and folded her arms over her chest. "I'd also love to know when you became such a raging misogynist. It's quite surprising to hear after all this time you evaluate a candidate's competency on the height of her heels."

"I don't think of you as a girl. You're more of a honey badger."
I lifted a shoulder. I could not mentor Andy. I didn't care if
Shannon was right. "Can't get around the originality issue. I
want someone with thoughts of their own."

Shannon fisted her hands and banged them against
the table.

"Last week you said no on Robert because he had too many
of his own ideas, and you wouldn't be able to teach him a
fucking thing. Which one is it, Patrick?"

Her screech brought work outside the conference room to a
momentary halt. It wasn't Shannon's first and it wouldn't be her
last today. Shrugging, I met her narrowed eyes.

She was my best friend and confidante but I couldn't tell her
I spent the past hour looking at Andy's mouth because I had
never seen such fuckable lips, or that looking at those lips on a
daily basis would drive me to alcohol dependency if they didn't
give me an aneurysm first. I couldn't tell Shannon that, while
listening to Andy's responses, I spread her across the table, tied
her hands behind her back, and fucked her six times in
my mind.

"She's not the right candidate, Shan."

"How is that fucking possible, Patrick?" Shaking her head,
she stood and opened the door. "Samuel Aidan! Get in here."

We stared each other down until Sam strolled inside. His
eyes swept between us, lighting with amusement as he digested
our standoff. The runt always took her side.

"We're in full first and middle name mode today, Shannon
Abigael? Shall I fetch Matthew Antrim or Riley Augustin?"

She handed Andy's résumé to Sam with a nod. "I want your
gut reaction."

He skimmed the document, his eyebrows lifting and his

head bobbing while he read. I sank deeper into the seat, knowing I was dead in the water.

On paper, Andy was the picture of perfection for us. Unlike most candidates, including the ones she mentioned, she wanted to work in our preservation-meets-sustainability niche, and came with the experience to prove it. She was competent enough to dive into the projects specifically earmarked for this role, and would require less handholding than the majority of recent grads.

But if I had to inhale one more ounce of her light flowery scent, my head and dick would simultaneously explode.

"Hire. Immediately." Glancing between us, he asked, "What exactly is the nature of the debate? Unless he kicked—"

"She," I interrupted.

"Unless *she* kicked a puppy in front of you, I'm unclear as to why we'd wait. It is mystifying that a candidate of this caliber isn't already slated for an apprenticeship, and you should know that, Patrick Arden."

I glared at him and his fussy gray suit with his pink shirt and pink tie. And the goddamn matching pocket square. He couldn't look more the part of a sustainability specialist if he bought a Prius and started wearing feathered fedoras.

"She only wants this apprenticeship. She's holding out for us, amazingly, but Patrick doesn't seem to know what he wants anymore."

I knew exactly what I wanted and I knew it in achingly precise detail. It was also ridiculous to think it would ever happen.

She snatched the résumé from Sam and slid it across the table to me.

"I'm giving you until the end of business today to figure out your issues. In the meantime, I'm writing a contract for Andy. I'll call her at five to offer her the job unless you come to your senses or find one hell of a convincing argument to dissuade me."

Looked like I had a long road of silent suffering or alcoholism ahead. More than likely both.

CHAPTER THREE

"To Andy's new job!" Jess squealed over the clinking of our shot glasses.

"Andy's new job!" Marley echoed.

They knocked back their shots before turning their attention to me. Offering a weak smile, I downed the contents of my glass but couldn't control the shudder of disgust shaking my shoulders. Jess and Marley high-fived and whooped, interpreting my reaction as an indication of the alcohol content rather than the artificial cinnamon and almond flavorings.

I hated mixed shots and the silly names attached to them—apparently this was a Cocky Motherfucker—but I intended to put that aside for the night. I was riding such an incredible high I wasn't even going to comment on the severely elevated douche factor at the bar Marley selected either.

Shannon's call came while I was admiring the brownstones along Berkeley Street. I didn't want to go back to Jess and Marley's apartment in Brighton after the interview, and decided to get my fill of Boston architecture while the January sun was shining. I was studying the panes of glass in double-hung window sashes on a gorgeous brick Georgian—I got that my hobbies tended toward weird—while we spoke, and her words still rattled around my brain.

So impressed with your work.

Clearly devoted to restoration and sustainability.

Perfect for our firm, perfect for the scope of Patrick's work.

Such a strong base of experience.

We want you on board as soon as possible.

So many opportunities to grow here.

Definite possibility of extending your work past June.

Patrick will be an amazing mentor.

I accepted a pathetically watered-down vodka gimlet from a bustier-ed waitress, and savored the loose feeling of inebriation slowly seeping into my body. I earned some drunkenness after the interview from hell. Spending the afternoon telling myself I nailed the interview and they'd be fools to choose someone else didn't prevent Patrick's chilly disinterest from rattling my confidence right to the edge.

"Enough thinking," Marley yelled over the thundering house music. "More dancing."

We danced as a trio and ignored attempts from men in awkwardly tight t-shirts to splinter our group, instead allowing them to admire us from the perimeter. I drained a few more gimlets while we tried to yell-sing along with the music, and found myself pressing into the large hands and firm chest that appeared behind me.

Holding my drink aloft, I tossed my head to the beat, closing my eyes when my partner's hands curled around my jean-clad hips. I didn't glance over my shoulder to check him out since I had no interest in leading the Tight T-Shirt Brigade's foot soldier to believe he had a chance.

His hands moved with me while I danced, and I imagined different hands on my hips, a different broad chest pressed against my shoulders. My backside swayed against my partner's crotch and I recognized the ridge of his arousal bumping against me. He squeezed my hips and urged me closer. Letting myself believe those hands belonged to someone else, I rolled my hips over his erection and covered his hands with mine.

"Let's get outta here," he grunted.

His accented voice dragged me back to reality and I shifted out of his hold. Taking in his v-neck t-shirt and hair that looked styled to the point of crunchiness, I shook my head. There wasn't enough alcohol in the bar to make it happen with Tight T-Shirt. Not even close.

"No thanks."

I offered my best attempt at a gracious smile. I did grind on the boy for at least four songs, and was leaving him in an unpleasant condition.

"Fuckin' cock tease," he murmured, his eyes coasting up and down my body.

I shrugged and walked away. I'd heard worse, and he wasn't entirely wrong in that moment. That didn't mean I was required to experience any remorse.

"I'll be right back," I yelled to Jess and Marley, both moving with the beat and ignoring me.

I hit the bar for another drink and guzzled a gimlet from the relative quiet of the white leather seating area. If wine was my rabbi, vodka was my therapist, and I needed some sorting out.

It didn't escape my notice that Patrick was attractive.

Okay, I can be honest: Patrick was strikingly hot.

He possessed the build and authentic masculinity of a rugby player. It was an observation I noted and discarded when we met this morning, and months ago when I read a feature about his work in *Architectural Digest*, complete with several photographs of him. I refused to allow a chiseled jaw or broad shoulders to kill my focus then; I wasn't excited about allowing it now.

Accepting another tumbler of vodka with lime, I nodded to the waitress in thanks.

Considering those observations were manifesting themselves in the form of dance floor daydreams, it was possible I hadn't discarded them at all. More than likely, I'd tucked them high on a shelf in the back of my mind and waited for a properly uninhibited moment to take them down and play. If my reaction on the dance floor was any indication, I really wanted to play.

And lest we forget, I hadn't *played* in a few months.

I spent years admiring Patrick's work from afar without once admiring him as a man. Becoming his apprentice meant immediately returning those observations to that shelf. It was an uncomfortable thought to swallow.

I frowned at the bar's faux Miami seashell-and-white-leather décor. As much as I loved my high school friend Jess, growing up and going to college in rural Maine meant she fell on the wide-eyed and naïve side of the lobster trap. In addition to finding a place to live, a hardcore yoga studio, and the farmers' market, better nightlife options were in order.

"Hey, hey, hey!" Marley shouted as she shimmied toward me. She collapsed on the sofa, panting and drenched with sweat. "Where'd you go?"

"I'm right here," I replied, muffling another sarcastic comment with my cocktail.

I wanted to like Marley, but I was content with simply tolerating her. Thirty minutes wasted explaining the difference between architecture and construction to Marley didn't help that tolerance.

"I thought you left with that Hottie McHotpants, but then I saw you over here."

"Hm." There was nothing to say to that.

She aggressively fanned her face, and I gnawed a chunk of ice to keep from explaining she was not going to cool off by waving her arms. If anything, she'd expend the same energy as bouncing around the dance floor, though getting that point across in a bass-thumping bar was not a challenge I wanted to accept.

It wasn't that I was a bitch. Sometimes, talking to people wasn't easy for me, especially idiots, and Marley was an idiot. And I didn't mean deep discussions of literature or politics, either. I know it sounded terrible, but the girl struggled to rub two thoughts together without setting her hair on fire. But she was a warm, sweet idiot, and she was an incredible friend to Jess.

Growing up along the coast of Maine, I did not have many options when it came to friends. I wasn't slamming Jess—there were only forty-six other kids in our graduating class. We've always had an easy relationship where we could go months without seeing each other yet pick up where we left off without a shred of awkwardness.

But the fact remained, close friendships were not my strength and I was exceptionally picky about the people in my circle. I possessed enough self-awareness to recognize that keeping people at a certain distance was a measure of preservation formed from years as an outsider. I've always been a little out of the ordinary.

I didn't have the opportunity to meet others who embraced

me and shared my interests until arriving at Cornell, and when faced with the option between people who could hold an intelligent conversation and people who grew up on the same frozen tundra, I'd chosen conversation.

Jess accepted this about me, and I accepted that she believed a billionaire would see her across a crowded bar, decide he couldn't live without her, fuck her in an alley or the back of his limo, and demand she move into his mansion to be his wife and sex slave.

She spent a lot of time fucking skeezy guys in alleys. It wasn't particularly reasonable, but at least she was upfront about it.

Patrick, should he choose to speak in more than a few words at a time, had the makings of an incredible conversationalist. His thoughts on architecture, history, ecology—all of it interested me, and I was comfortable saying he'd enjoy talking to me, too.

Getting a drink and chatting with Patrick after work would cross an entire quartile off my bucket list. While I'd initially pegged Patrick as a beer drinker by virtue of his rugby player looks, I'd guess his tastes ran closer to rich wines and whiskey or scotch. Sipping some fifteen-year Macallan, we'd bitch about the minimalistic modern craze and speculate about those early craftsmen who built a city on a hill.

His hand would stroke my leg, squeezing above my knee when he laughed at my pithy takedown of all things laminate. As the night wore on, his fingers would tease under my skirt while he debated the value of preservation legislation. He'd argue that, while well intentioned, much of current regulatory guidance prevented preservation from being in line with sustainability as his fingers slipped beneath my panties and into my wet heat. He'd make his point while he brought me to the edge, his eyes sparkling with the secret knowledge that he was wrist-deep and getting me off in a crowded bar. He'd press himself against me when I found my release, swallowing my cry with a smoldering kiss and a promise for much more when he got me alone.

"What was that?" Marley asked, her hands frozen mid-wave.

"What was what?"

"You made a sound. Like...like a sex sound. Did you see a hot guy?"

Oh, shit. Oh, *shit*.

I needed to lock that shit down. No more mixed shots.

I gave Marley a confused shrug, clearly indicating I thought she was hearing things. When she resumed fanning herself, I pressed my glass to my forehead in an attempt to temper the Patrick Walsh as Sex God fantasy playing behind my eyes.

And I thought vodka would sort me out. This called for stronger liquor. What was the right potion to quell spontaneous sexy fantasies about an off-limits man who spent more time scowling than speaking?

Absinthe, my voodoo priestess.

Maybe Jägermeister, my favorite frat boy.

Probably a lethal combination of the two with a chaser of tequila, my Mexican medicine man, followed by a good, old-fashioned stomach pumping.

"So where are you from?" Marley shouted.

I glanced at Marley, her fanning slowing. "Wiscasset. Jess and I went to high school together."

"Yeah, I know," she said, nodding quickly. "But like, where are you *from* from?"

She squinted at me, and I groaned inwardly. I got the 'you don't look completely white but I can't tell whether you're something else, so what *are* you?' question more than I should.

Every time I avoided an explanation of my genealogy and opted for vague responses that illuminated the inappropriateness of the inquiry. A backhanded quip was on the tip of my tongue but I swallowed it, remembering Marley was one of two friends I could currently name in Boston, and she was letting me stay at her place.

"My dad was Persian."

"Where is that? Is that a country?"

"He was from Iran, but lived in London and Istanbul." Marley didn't seem to notice my tone was beyond condescending.

Her eyes widened then narrowed, and I wondered which part she was struggling to understand. "Was? He's not alive?"

"No. He died when I was young."

"Oh my God, that's awful. What happened? Wait. I've heard about Iran. Wasn't there a war there? Aren't there a lot of terrorists over there? Was he like...involved with that?"

And there it was.

My raised eyebrow offered Marley an opportunity to backtrack and revise. Sensitive I was not—but assuming every Middle Easterner was a terrorist wasn't a matter of sensitivity. It came as no surprise that she continued gaping at me, waiting for my response to a question she considered reasonable. I'd prefer a scowly conversation with Patrick to another round of 'so how many virgins did your dad get for being a suicide bomber?'

"No," I responded, the word sharpened to a point. "He was not a terrorist."

"Oh." Before she could continue, Jess wedged between us and wrapped her arms around our necks.

"Where my ladies at?"

"Woohoo!" Marley replied. "I am going to be so hungover tomorrow!"

Jess stood and pulled us with her, smiling. "Then we better enjoy it!"

We occupied the center of the dance floor, and I redirected every guy who approached me to Marley. The attention thrilled her, and I couldn't risk another Patrick Walsh daydream at the hands of Tight T-Shirt.

IT WASN'T POSSIBLE FOR MY ARMS TO CAUSE ME ANY MORE DISTRESS than they were causing right now.

I leaned against the mantel above the fireplace in Shannon's office while she walked Andy through paperwork and handed her an armful of documents, equipment, and a fleece vest embroidered with our logo while I wrestled with my limbs like a newborn giraffe.

I crossed them over my chest, and Shannon stopped her explanation of our underground garage access system to tell me I looked 'angry' and 'intimidating.'

I shoved my hands in my pockets, and then clasped them behind my back. Both seemed wrong.

I was trying Matt's 'one arm across the chest, chin on the fist' thing and feeling like a moron when Shannon turned to me.

"Patrick, why don't you take Andy upstairs? Get her settled before the meeting?"

Shannon glared at me, her eyes fiery and lips pursed, silently willing me to get my act together. I held her stare as long as possible to avoid eye contact with Andy. If I didn't look at her, I wouldn't think about her hair, and how I wanted it in my hands. Or her eyes, and how I wanted them wide and hungry. Or her mouth, and how I wanted it on my cock.

I glanced at the ground, my eyes landing on her feet. Steel-toed boots. Seemed appropriate for the girl with the spine of steel.

And I wanted them over my shoulders.

"Now?" When I didn't move, she pivoted to face Andy. "I'm sorry, Andy, my brother is a bit of a bear in the morning. Especially when he hasn't had his happy pills or a swift kick in the ass. I'll make sure he gets an extra dose of both today. If there's anything you need, please feel free to ask Patrick's assistant, Marisa. She's right upstairs."

Marisa. It was probably too late to worry about all the times I called her Melissa.

"No worries," Andy replied, effortlessly juggling the laptop, tablet, cell phone, keycard, and vest. She was the picture of composure while I struggled with the existence of my arms. By all accounts, a fantastic way to start a Monday.

In the week since her interview, I never stopped to consider where she would spend the majority of her time or how we'd work together.

I spent a fair amount of time thinking about her naked in every conceivable position, and if this morning's erection from hell was any indication, I was enthusiastic about all of them.

She'd be a meter away from me all day, every day. What happened with that case of gin in Sam's office? Was it too early to start asking?

"This way," I grumbled, striding out of Shannon's office and up the stairs to my office.

I took the stairs two at a time and she was on my heels with her lavender scent. We stood in the middle of my office for a long moment while I crossed my arms, uncrossed them, tucked my hands into my pockets, and then propped my fists on my hips. She stared at me, that tiny smile tugging at the corner of her lips as if she knew exactly how she shredded me.

There were tons of stunning women out there, but it wasn't her beauty that tipped the axis for me.

Andy was exotic and mesmerizing, but she revealed nothing. She moved with aloof confidence and it was clear she gave not a single fuck about anyone's thoughts of her. Since the moment I met Andy, I wanted to know what she was thinking under that unapproachable shell.

I gestured to the redwood conference table and drafting desk. "All yours."

I also wanted to see how quickly I could destroy that cool reserve when my head was between her legs.

She blinked at me before moving and my stomach lurched when I realized I needed to give her something to do. Mind blank, I called up the calendar on my computer and glanced at the week ahead. Five minutes together and my head was already fucked up. Squatting beside the milk crate holding the on-deck projects, I selected twelve canisters and dropped them on the table.

"These are work-in-progress. We'll walk them all at some point this week, and these," I grabbed three, "today." Andy nodded, and our eyes met when she accepted the canisters. I didn't immediately let go, and we stood frozen in a tug-of-war.

Before I could continue with instructions, a quartet of voices rang down from the attic conference room. "Seven thirty!"

"Jesus Christ," I murmured, releasing the canisters and

darting to my desk to snap my laptop shut and tuck it under my arm.

"Should I go with you?"

"No," I stammered, and though I was far from certain about my response, I did not possess the strength to run a staff meeting with her at the table. That prospect heightened the brain-dick explosion probability, which was already quite high. "Figure out the plans."

I leaned against the wall at the landing, sucking in a deep breath to clear the haze from my mind before climbing the stairs.

Some of my favorite memories in recent years were seeing three—four, since Riley finished school—heads bowed around laptops and bluelines at seven thirty on Monday mornings in the attic conference room. The stress of managing a small business kept me up most nights, and spending an hour with my partners every week brought me a few kernels of sanity, especially when our work took us in so many different directions we barely saw each other outside of this time.

The familiar scene should have been a calming force, though the lavender-induced chaos in my system left me more impatient than ever. Most days, impatient was the best word to describe me. I didn't have Matt's tolerance for the unexpected, and I never managed to captivate anyone with talk of solar panels like Sam. I was impatient and intimidating, and there wasn't an easily accessible memory of when it was any other way.

Shannon rolled her eyes when I slipped into my seat, and she leaned to my ear. "I don't know what the fuck your problem is, but you need to fix it. We are not losing Andy because you're a moody son of a bitch."

"I didn't want to hire her in the first place."

Not entirely true. I didn't want to spend the next few months working alongside a gorgeous woman who pushed all my buttons when I knew damn well I shouldn't touch her.

"You need to have your head examined. Learn to know a good thing when you see it." She leaned away and sipped her coffee before returning. "Why didn't you bring her with you?"

"Isn't this a partners' meeting?"

She waved her hand dismissively and glanced at a new email on her screen. "Sure, boss, whatever. As if that means anything around here."

"If we don't start these goddamn meetings on time, there's no reason for me to be here on time, and I'm gonna start sleeping an extra ten minutes," Riley loudly whispered to Matt, who mouthed something back to Riley that I didn't catch.

It was good to see them working together, and Matt keeping Riley in line. God only knew what I would have done if I had to put up with his computation errors and inability to keep coffee off his clothes.

"Nice to see you all again. I'm super happy today because Andy Asani started this morning," Shannon announced. "She'll be working directly with Patrick as we try this apprenticeship model on for size. Please be nice to her. She's very smart and I think she'll add tons of capacity for Patrick because he really, really needs it, but he insists on being a dick to her and I'm concerned he will ignore her and she'll quit before Friday."

"That sounds about right," Matt murmured.

He looked tan and more relaxed than usual, if that were possible. The love of a good woman suited him, and a trip to Mexico to meet Lauren's parents during their winter RV trip didn't hurt either. It was especially nice that her father,

Commodore Halsted, didn't dropkick Matt's ass into the Pacific Ocean for touching his one and only baby girl.

"Is there a specific issue that you have with her, or are you just being an inveterate ass?" Sam asked.

I ignored them both while I called up my master workflow spreadsheet to track progress against milestones. "Riley. Bunker Hill. Make it fast."

He flipped his head, tossing his shaggy hair away from his brow. "We were on fire last week. Banged through hardwood refinishing, moldings, and plaster on all properties, and interior paint is on deck today."

"When should we expect to be down to punch lists?"

"Two weeks. Maybe three, depending on inspections." He shrugged and glanced to Matt, who offered an approving nod. Matt was good at mentoring, taking Riley from a useless heap of disjointed architectural skills to managing four concurrent builds with success.

"Fine." I turned to Shannon and glanced at the Multiple Listing Service map of Charlestown's active properties on her screen. "Put the word out. Get some traction. I want to unload those properties the minute we have the green light on occupancy. I don't want these on the market more than a week past a clean CO."

"Yeah," she murmured as she typed. "Riley, let me know when they start on punch lists and I'll go check it out. Let's not have realtors walking through construction sites again." She glanced pointedly at Matt and he held up his hands in surrender.

Working around the table, I tracked updates and flagged issues in my spreadsheets. For the moment, Andy wasn't in the forefront of my thoughts.

We were in a strong position despite a freak Thanksgiving blizzard that brought progress to a standstill for over a week, not to mention our father's fatal stroke. We bounced back from all of it as best we could, but Angus's shadow lingered over us.

I counted seven investment restorations that would be hitting the market within the next six weeks, plus a full slate of client projects launching in March, and three dozen new queries for our services in the past week.

"So when are we going to read Angus's will?" Riley asked.

Shannon minimized her open screens, leaving a picture of the five of us after we finished last year's marathon. The envelope arrived from Angus's attorney by messenger last week during my standing budget meeting with Shannon. We stared at each other and the delivery for longer than logical before she stowed it in her safe. We didn't say a word on the subject.

"I have it in my office." She looked up. "Sealed."

"Isn't there a timeline or something?" Riley continued. "It's been over a month since the miserable bastard shook hands with Satan."

Shannon rolled her shoulders as all eyes turned to her. "Yes, but...I think we need to be suitably drunk before that envelope opens. And set a few ground rules."

My sentiments exactly. It was anyone's guess what Angus had in store for us, but I knew he wasn't finished fucking us over. For all we knew, he left his assets to a stray Jack Russell terrier he befriended at the Alewife T station, leaving us with a few bags of rusty nails.

"Does Erin need to be here for this?" I kept my eyes on my screen to avoid withering under the glare I knew Shannon was shooting at me. My attempt to end the feud between my sisters was proving more complex than anticipated.

"No. Not when she couldn't be bothered to show up for the funeral." Shannon's eyes swept the table, inviting a word of dissent. We all knew better than to go there. "I'll FedEx her copy to her in Spain or Morocco or wherever the fuck she is now."

"Friday," Matt offered. "At the house."

"No. I'm not driving out to Wellesley and getting drunk in the Haunted Mansion. That's how the *Blair Witch Project* started." Riley shook his head. "And I won't ride the commuter rail back in, not drunk, and especially not since a goddamn python went missing on one of those trains."

"Now that's a coherent argument if I've ever heard one," Sam deadpanned, twisting the titanium ring on his thumb.

"My place," Matt said.

We nodded quietly but didn't meet each other's eyes. We were better when we lived in the present, in the lives we created for ourselves. We struggled with the lingering gore of our history, and true to form, we coped by ignoring, avoiding, and evading.

And alcohol. Lots of alcohol.

"Only if Miss Honey's going to be there," Riley said. "And she orders me some paella."

Matt shook his head as he turned to Riley. "My fiancée lives there, and I'll order paella, but do not call her that or any derivative of that."

"You call her that," he retorted.

"Right. She's *my* Miss Honey. It's part of the deal when I put a ring on it."

"All right," Shannon muttered. "Enough. We'll figure this out on Friday. I'll put Tom on catering duty. You all go do what you do, and be wonderful at it."

"Damn straight, sister," Riley hollered. I continued typing notes while my siblings shuffled out.

I had at least two major issues to handle at jobsites and a short lifetime's worth of prep for the next wave of projects, but I reviewed emails from my general contractors and tweaked four bids before sending them to clients.

Twelve stairs and a landing separated me from Andy.

I was stalling.

"THOUGHTS?"

Patrick approached me when he was finished discussing the terrace excavation necessary to fix the main drain issues with the plumber, welder, and mason. I learned more about managing subcontractors from Patrick's twenty-minute conversation with his team than in any other field experience.

It was equal parts humbling and horrifying. I was tempted to write a letter to Cornell requesting a refund.

Standing in a brick Greek Revival off Newbury Street, I bit the inside of my cheek to prevent a monologue of questions and ideas from exploding out of my mouth and onto Patrick. I turned in a circle, taking in the Quincy brick fireplace and built-in shelving niches with ornate carvings and imagined walls where the studs stood bare.

"The ceilings," I said, gesturing above my head. "They're low. Too low for this style. Off by three, maybe four inches yet the plans don't call for an adjustment."

Patrick's eyebrows lifted and he fought a smile. "Yeah, that's right. You saw the plans?"

"Yes."

I walked past him into the kitchen, and he narrowed his eyes at me. "I don't remember giving you this one."

While Patrick was in his partners' meeting, I furiously studied the bluelines. I scribbled pages of notes and sketched drawings, and listed important design elements and preservation techniques. When Tom dropped by to say hello and warn me about Patrick's revolving door of assistants, he mentioned their Monday meetings often ran closer to ninety minutes.

I took it upon myself to flip through the other plans nestled beside Patrick's desk. I might not have been a Girl Scout, but I knew a few things about preparedness.

Since my interview, I cleared out my apartment in Ithaca— no more lake effect snow for me, thank you—and devised a plan to keep all thoughts about Patrick strictly PG while moving into my new place. Although the plan was limited to 'don't think about Patrick as Sex God or hot, sweaty rugby player,' I was determined to succeed.

I attributed most of my X-rated thoughts to the extra time on my hands since graduating in December. Once work consumed my time, I'd forget all about Patrick's narrow waist and muscular arms. As soon as I got my hands dirty with projects, I'd forget about getting dirty with Patrick.

I'd definitely stop looking at his ass, too.

"Hm," I murmured, measuring the distance between the countertops. "You didn't give it to me. I read this one, and all the others, anyway. Can we talk about extending this island six more inches? Is that something you're open to considering?"

"You read them all anyway?" His voice rang with disbelief and he continued squinting at me.

"Yes."

"You didn't know we were coming here today."

"Hm." I shook my head. "The island. Six more inches?"

He stared at me before studying the empty shell of the kitchen. It materialized in his eyes—the keen awareness of space and dimension that allowed him to see the form and function of design before him—and it was exactly as magical as I hoped it would be. It was what I spent years imagining and it didn't matter that I wanted to lick his entire body because I finally knew how design looked in his eyes.

"I would agree with you, but I see this," he gestured to the spaces marked off for cabinetry, "as a stress point in the flow."

Crossing the kitchen, I stood beside Patrick and tried to see the shapes.

"If this is the primary route in from the mudroom," he pointed between us, "and there is a breakfast bar coming to here, imagine barstools backing up to here."

While he described the kitchen, a picture formed in my mind and I saw everything. Three-dimensional shapes sprang from the ground, and I felt their presence in the room. It reminded me of the fuzziness between dreaming and waking where I was aware of my dreams and they still made sense.

"Do you see it?" he asked, his voice deep and rough in my ear.

I didn't realize we were standing shoulder-to-shoulder until tilting my head to look up at him. I smiled, nodding, and his eyes brightened. My 'no fantasizing about sex with the boss' project was doomed if I had to stare into his eyes at this range every day.

"What do you want to do about it?"

Dismissing the sensuality in his voice and the sense he

wasn't referring to the island anymore, I stepped away from Patrick's force field. I stared at the floor for several minutes, yanking my measuring tape from my belt and testing a few hypotheses before responding.

"Half-moon. It would cut down the bottleneck over there while still providing the seating and increasing the functionality of the room."

Patrick considered my suggestion and strode into the front room and up the stairs. "Since you've already rifled through the plans," he called over his shoulder, "make the changes to the development drafts this afternoon and we'll reprint tonight."

"Why aren't you blowing out the ceilings?"

He stopped at the landing and faced me with his hands on his hips. Afternoon sun shone through the two-story window and illuminated the shades of red and brown in his hair. "You tell me."

I cycled through reasonable explanations while he gazed me. His phone alerted several times, but he never tore his eyes away from mine. It was fantastically unnerving: my dream apprentice-ship was exactly as ideal as I hoped and being this close to Patrick was nearly overpowering.

"Windows," I answered slowly. "The only reason you'd leave the ceilings intact would be the windows on all the other floors. You'd have to reposition them or they'd be oddly low, and that would mean destroying the stone façade."

"Not bad." His eyes flashed with surprise. "I'll buy you lunch if you can solve that problem and make those changes."

"THIS IS THE BEST TACO TRUCK IN BOSTON," PATRICK SAID,

gesturing to the van parked between Harrison and Concord in the South End. "The best. No pickled beets or arugula. Real tacos. You like tacos, right? If you don't, this isn't going to work out."

"Haven't met a taco I don't like," I replied from the passenger seat of Patrick's Range Rover.

"If you tell anyone about this, or put it on Twitter, and then everyone and their uncle shows up and I can't get a taco? You'll be pulling permits at City Hall for the next six years."

"I can handle that."

With a nod, we headed toward the van. We ordered the day's special, barbacoa de costilla, and he inclined his head toward the park across the street. It was cold but the late afternoon sun seeped through my skin, and I turned my face toward it when we settled on a stone bench.

The tacos were delicious, and when I told Patrick as much, he grunted in agreement. It was a raw, beautiful sound that annihilated Operation Don't Think About Patrick Walsh Naked.

I wanted to hear that sound again. I wanted to *cause* that sound. I ate my tacos, staring at a bronze statue of a rider on horseback, reminding myself to stop thinking about sex.

"Any other food trucks you'd recommend?"

Patrick nodded as he chewed. "Plenty. There's a Vietnamese truck that I could hit every day. The best banh mi ever, and there are a few awful banh mis in town. And this one truck that only does grilled cheese, but wicked amazing grilled cheese."

I offered him an appreciative smile. Patrick was speaking in complete sentences *and* we were talking about the only thing I liked more than architecture: food. "You're quite the foodie."

"Nah," he laughed.

"Anyone who can distinguish banh mi quality is a foodie," I said, directing a raised eyebrow at Patrick.

"There's a sriracha fried rice and braised beef dumpling truck I've been meaning to try," he said, his hazel eyes hard and reserved despite his light tone.

"Sign me up for that."

Taking the last bite of my taco, I nodded enthusiastically while he stared at me. I needed sriracha fried rice in my life, and it sounded like Patrick did, too. Sauce dribbled over my lip, and his eyes darkened when my tongue scooped it up.

"All right, Asani." He stood and started toward his car, his steps urgent. "Back to the office."

He navigated traffic while I made notes about each jobsite we visited, recording unique characteristics of each home and specific restorations I wanted to observe. Though I was comfortable with the silence, I felt Patrick glimpse at me every few minutes and I caught his scowl in my peripheral vision.

I was growing accustomed to the scowling. It appeared to be his default setting and I didn't let it bother me. Considering I didn't feel it was necessary to smile all the time, my default setting wasn't much better.

We rolled to a stop in the underground garage. I loved this garage. Parking my MINI Cooper alongside the row of black Walsh Associates Range Rovers induced a squealing giggle this morning.

And those were *not* a regular element of my repertoire.

When we approached his office door, I reached out at the same time as Patrick. His hand covered mine, his fingers layering between my fingers. He was warmer than I expected, his large hand simultaneously soft and rough as we held the antique glass knob. Pale freckles dotted his skin, and I doubted ever seeing such freckled fingers before. Electricity coursed from his touch into my veins, and despite every voice in my head, I couldn't pull away—I didn't want to pull away.

I lifted my eyes from the knob to look at him, and his face was inches from mine. If I rose to my toes, our lips would meet. His expression was tight and I couldn't read beyond the seriousness in his eyes. A shiver built between my shoulder blades when his fingers rubbed over mine, our eyes locked on each other. The shiver rolled down my arms and shook my fingers, and Patrick blinked, breaking our connection with a step backward.

"Sorry," he stammered, shaking his head quickly. "I have to go find sin—I mean gin—uh, *fuck,* I mean Sam." He paused, both hands running through his hair. "I have to talk to Sam. About something. You should...make those changes we discussed. Head out when you're done."

Inside Patrick's office, I softly banged my head against the door. I needed a mild headache to distract me from the fact I embarrassed the hell out of my boss by gazing at him like a smitten teenager wanting nothing more than her first kiss.

Project No Sex For You needed an overhaul. Fast.

CHAPTER SIX

PATRICK

"Do you still have that case of gin in here? From the people with the Chestnut Hill project?"

Sam pulled his glasses down his nose and propped his elbows on the drafting table, frowning at me as I burst into his office and slammed the door.

"Sure. I don't often drink entire cases of liquor inside a season."

"I need some."

I hated the desperate, breathless sound of my voice, and I especially hated that she affected me so much. Andy fucking Asani was turning me into a madman. Not your run-of-the-mill madman, either. The kind of madman who dedicated half of his brain space to concealing erections.

"Yes, it appears that you do." He stood, staring at me for several beats. "I presume you'd prefer it on the rocks, so..." His voice trailed off as he rolled his eyes at me and left his office. I dropped onto his tufted leather sofa with a thud.

It was an accident. I apologized. Simple as that. It's not as if I grabbed her ass or put her hand on my throbbing cock. I just rubbed her fingers while every cell in my body tingled with awareness and unquestionably perverted thoughts inundated my mind.

And I smelled her hair.

Honest mistake.

"G and T?" Sam asked upon his return, gently closing the door behind him. I knew he was making a point about me being a noisy bastard and clambering around the office like a Neanderthal, but I didn't care.

Scrubbing my hand across my face, I tried to wipe the memory of her intrigued expression but it appeared every time I closed my eyes. She wanted to know why her creepy boss was touching her, and she definitely did not give me that face because she felt anything other than supreme discomfort. Creepy was the only sensible explanation.

"G hold the T," I groaned. She didn't watch me with those dark eyes because she enjoyed any part of my assault on her slim hand or my proximity to her mouth. "We should build a liquor cabinet."

But God almighty, those fingers were like satin.

"Yeah, I'll get right on that." Sam busied himself at the built-in cabinets behind his desk while I stared at the ceiling. "Did Larry bust your balls over St. James Avenue again? I can send Alberto out there to consult on the—"

"No, no. Definitely not Larry. Not an inspector."

Just an incredibly hot apprentice who was spending altogether too much time saying "hm" and solving irreconcilably difficult problems in eight seconds flat and licking drops of salsa off her lips.

Fuck. My. Life.

It wasn't bad enough her legs were actually a mile long, but her tight little ass demanded an altar in its honor. Did she not know how she looked in those pants? How could she *not*?

Or that every time she knelt to measure or inspect something, the fabric pulled across her slender backside and exposed a sliver of skin above her waistband? Growing old staring at that inch of skin sounded like my new retirement strategy.

Sam handed me a tumbler, and I sucked the liquid down in three gulps. I coughed, instantly regretting that decision and feeling the spicy tang of the barbacoa sauce bubbling up my throat.

"Are you going to be okay?" Sam sat across from me in a club chair, his legs crossed while he angled his head in confusion. "You just shotgunned straight gin."

"Fine," I coughed, mentally negotiating with my stomach to keep its contents from coming back up. Sam would hire a crew to strip his office to the studs in the event I vomited in his pristine space, and send me the bill.

"Are you going to read me in?" He picked at a speck of lint on his trousers and arched an eyebrow. "Is this about the new girl?"

I shook my head vigorously and leaned forward, propping my elbows on my knees and running my fingers through my hair. I probably looked like I escaped from the asylum. "I'm fucked, and I'm a fucking asshole."

Bemused, his gaze darted around the room before stopping to study me. "Has something occurred that you'd care to share with me?"

Sighing, I flopped back against the sofa and rested my head on a burlap pillow printed with names of T stations. "No, dude. Definitely not unloading any of this shit on you. Safer that way."

It really was safer if all the insanity lived in my head and mine alone.

"Reasonable, if not a tad cryptic," he murmured, pushing out of his seat. "I have two projects teed up, and I'm finishing them before the game tonight. I have box seats, and I'm not missing that. By all means, make yourself and your issues comfortable."

"Thank you," I murmured.

"Anything else you need before I get back to drafting? A blanket? Some Xanax? A priest?"

"Some fucking willpower wouldn't hurt."

I closed my eyes, only to have a vision of Andy's face greet me while her tongue brushed across her full lips.

***

My mother always told me I needed to pay better attention to my hands and feet because I was too damn big for my own good. For the first time in my life, I heeded her advice.

It was too easy to brush against Andy while we leaned over plans at a jobsite or studied a model on my iPad, and it was even easier for my knuckles to graze the back of her hand when we reached for our drinks in the car.

Making it through the week without touching Andy was a greater accomplishment than finishing the Boston Marathon with a respectable time.

Thankfully, our work fell into an effortless rhythm. Routine made it easier for me to keep my hands to myself while delegating projects and overseeing Andy's work. Her willingness to roll with any rock in the road quickly earned the respect of my general contractors and their crews, and I was in awe of her enthusiasm when it came to demolishing those rocks.

Within the span of a few days, I trusted her thinking and relied on her to handle many of the issues arising from my GCs, which provided me the time to dive into long-abandoned strategic projects.

I didn't expect her to find a fix for the low ceilings on Monday, and I selected increasingly complex challenges for her each day. She solved everything I threw at her without so much as blinking. The prize was always lunch with conversation, and Andy ended the week having visited five of my favorite eateries and becoming my best foodie friend.

She was also intelligent and sexy and impossible to interpret, and I was obsessed with her. I preferred to think of our little problem-solving game as legitimate mentoring rather than a means to furthering my obsession. Before she arrived on Friday morning, I drafted a list of adventurous lunch spots for next week, eager to get her take on some new gastropubs.

She asked sharp questions and offered unconventional solutions to many issues that left me scratching my head, and her raw talent made itself known. Smart wasn't the word to describe Andy. Her work needed polish and she'd benefit from more experience, but she was gifted. Brilliant. She knew answers to questions before I asked them.

Inside five days, she became my left hand, and she loved it. It was a good thing she had no idea what I was doing with my left hand when she wasn't around.

She moved through complex structural geometry as efficiently as Matt, while her design aesthetic rivaled Sam's. Her brain was her sexiest feature, and working with her felt like the most bizarre, wonderful form of foreplay ever invented.

Through it all, my head overflowed with contradictory impulses, and it was driving me crazy. That, combined with the case of OCD I picked up from keeping my hands to myself, and Andy's scent permeating my office, my car, my brain...I was a loosely chained madman. A few pulls in the right direction and nothing would be able to stop me from unleashing myself on her.

"Patrick!"

Startled by the fist slamming on my desk, I shook my head and looked up from my laptop. Matt smirked before sitting across from me.

"I've been talking for five minutes."

"Mustn't have been very interesting," I murmured, rubbing my forehead. "Long week."

"They're the only kind. So...I've talked to the rest of the tribe, and we've decided to do this shit at eight thirty. That work for you?"

I glanced at the calendar on my screen, searching for an appointment. "Do what shit?"

Matt typed a message on his phone while he spoke. "The will. And the prerequisite drunkenness to read said will."

Shit. That was the last thing I wanted to do, and my subconscious helped me forget all about it until Matt banged my head back to reality.

My Friday night was going to feature a long run followed by quite a few beers, some red meat, and catching up on my industry reading while watching Premier League games.

I would *not* spend my Friday night thinking about Andy, trying to guess what Andy was wearing under her black pants and black sweaters, or inventing challenges for Andy to tackle so we could talk over lunch. There was no way in hell I was spending my night picturing Andy's hair draped across my pillows or her naked skin on my sheets.

Yeah, that was a complete and total lie. I'd be lucky if I remembered to eat between my Andy fantasies.

"Right," I groaned, standing and stretching my arms over my head.

We demoed a delicate Dutch Colonial today, one I wanted to do myself, and I was feeling it in my back. My shirt pulled free from my low-slung jeans and rode up my stomach. I reached higher, waiting to hear my joints pop while I arched back to stretch the tight muscles between my shoulders.

Andy walked into my office, hundreds of pages of new design plans rolled under her arms. She stopped, her eyes paused on my torso before lifting to my face. Her eyebrow arched and I noticed a subtle smile curling the corners of her lips.

Miss Asani was checking me out. The satisfaction I gained from knowing she liked my body was more than enough incentive to let Matt continue kicking my ass on the marathon training circuit.

If Andy liked what she saw enough for an eyebrow and a smile, maybe—

"Patrick!"

I lost it. I wanted this moment without Matt's involvement, and I just lost it. "Jesus Christ, Matthew, do you not have an office of your own? What the fuck are you doing here? Do I honestly need to be talking to you right now, or can you bother RISD with this shit? If it was important enough for me to hear, I'd be listening!"

"Play nice, Optimus." I nearly jumped over my desk to throttle him. Shifting to face her, he asked, "How'd it go this week, Andy?"

She offered Matt a warm smile, and I scowled. She never

smiled at me like that. I considered any reaction from her a victory. What would it take for her to look at me that way?

"Really good. I learned more in five days than the past few years. I think we figured out some interesting things."

Our eyes met over Matt's head, and she lifted her shoulders, asking for my confirmation.

"Lots of interesting things, Asani."

Though I was certain she was referring to the projects on deck, I started to catalog everything I learned about her this week.

She loved talking about food and it was one of my new missions in life to keep those conversations going. Eating with her daily was another mission.

Her water always had stuff in it. Mint leaves, cucumber slices, dried hibiscus flowers. I assumed it wasn't simply decorative.

She could produce measuring tape, Sharpies, and flashlights in the blink of an eye. I don't know where she hid them, but she whipped them out before I could ask.

She made nerve-wrenchingly sexy sounds when eating anything particularly delicious. I spent the better part of Wednesday afternoon at half-mast because she enjoyed the hell out of some pho and kimchi.

She wore a lot of black but it suited her. It was the ideal contrast to her rich olive skin and dark hair. She seemed altogether too serious for pink or yellow.

She was addicted to lip balm. She stored a quarter-sized pot of balm that smelled like cherries in her pocket, and retrieved it throughout the day. It was her most hypnotic ritual by far.

The tip of her finger would swirl over the pot before swiping her lips, and tasting the balm on her lips became another one of my life missions. Every time she did it, I spent at least five minutes reminding myself that sucking her lip into my mouth would probably result in a knee to my balls.

She always kept small glass jars filled with the most random shit in her Timbuk2 bag. Some days she'd have walnuts or figs. Other days it would be grape tomatoes or dried mushrooms.

I didn't even know dried mushrooms were a thing, or that anyone would choose to eat them.

"We need to take you out for a drink. Anyone who survives a week with this guy deserves a drink on me," Matt said. "Not tonight, but you need an official welcome to this madhouse, and to Boston. Next week for sure."

"I look forward to it." She gifted him with another smile.

My teeth ground together as I stared at Matt in irritation. He needed to stop bothering Andy and get back to his own office.

"You can meet my fiancée, too."

"Sounds great."

I wasn't sure what she'd make of Lauren Halsted, although I'd guess Lauren would happily embrace Andy. Everything about them was different, and imagining curvy, blonde Lauren with willowy, dark Andy bordered on comedic. Where Lauren was warm and sweet, and people tripped over themselves to make her happy—my brother especially—Andy was cool and calm, and more self-possessed than any other woman I'd ever met.

I spent a gratuitous amount of time theorizing how *I* could possess her.

"Eight thirty. My place." Matt stood, pointing a finger at me.

"Get the hell out of my office. Go text your fiancée. See if you can get your balls back for a few minutes."

I loved Lauren as much as I loved Shannon and Erin, but

someone needed to knock the grin off Matt's face every now and then.

Matt laughed and leaned over Andy's drafting table to catch her eye. "Andy, you're welcome to hang in my office with me and RISD when Optimus is being a pain in the ass."

The door closed behind Matt before I could call after him, and Andy's eyes were on me again. "You wouldn't like his office."

Another eyebrow lifted. "Why is that?"

"I can promise you'd want to beat the shit out of Riley inside five minutes. He isn't smart enough for you." I shrugged unapologetically. "Matt is, but his solution to most things is steel and that would drive you crazy."

"Hm." A thoughtful expression crossed her face, and she opened her mouth to speak but stopped herself.

I scowled. "What?"

She shook her head, shutting down my question as only Andy could.

I was tempted to stretch again, if for no other reason than seeing her reaction. I knew it was a terrible idea. Completely fucked up and begging for disaster. But the temptation was too powerful, and I craved her minute reactions. Even after a week spent in close quarters with Andy, I had no more insight into her thoughts than I did when I first met her.

If systemically stripping got a reaction, it would be worth it. I'd live to regret it, but I'd do it anyway. Those reactions, however small, were worth every consequence.

Staring at Andy, I bent my arm behind my head and pulled my elbow, and I felt cool air against my exposed waist. I waited for her eyes to dip from my face, the seconds ticking by in my head.

After holding my gaze for approximately five years, she blinked and dropped her attention to my skin. Her eyes barely widened before she resumed her study of the plans on the table —but they widened.

CHAPTER SEVEN

PATRICK

"And then he says, 'I've read all of John Lennon's work! I find it really interesting. Researching the political uprising and October Revolution put the sixties into a whole new perspective for me!'" Matt wrapped his arm around Lauren's shoulders, laughing.

"Riley, you are dumber than a sack of sand. What'd she say?" Sam asked.

Riley stared at his plate, an indignant smirk on his face. "I'm glad you find this so funny."

"Listen. I like pastrami as much as the next guy, but when it comes with a side of hot blonde doctoral student, there is no detail too minor. What did she say to your little synopsis?" Sam repeated.

Riley pursed his lips and continued gazing at his plate. "I hate you all. You're assholes. Every single one of you, except for you." He smiled at Lauren. "You know you like me better than this old man. Just look at him. He'll be bald in a month and I know about the erectile dysfunction."

"Don't even start," she chided. "You are too young for me."

I scratched my chin and estimated Andy's age. She couldn't be more than twenty-five yet she existed with confidence and maturity far beyond that. Andy wasn't preoccupied with figuring herself out or learning how to be an adult; she was already there.

"Tell us! When did she tell you about her...preferences?" Shannon banged her hands on the table.

Sighing, Riley rolled his eyes. "She said something about an honest mix-up of John Lennon and Vladimir Lenin, and the Bolsheviks and the Beatles, and she'd fuck me if she could tie me up and gag me."

"And naturally, they've been hanging out for three weeks," Matt laughed.

"This all went down in front of you?" I asked Matt.

"Yeah, they started talking while we were eating. I stepped away to take a call, and I came back to Sgt. Pepper and the Soviet Socialists with a side of bondage and submission."

"For your sake, I hope you have a safe word," I said. Riley shook his head, flipping me off.

"Amazing," Shannon breathed, brushing tears away from her eyes. "I had no idea you could find a dominatrix—one busy getting her doctorate in Russian history—at a deli. I just assumed it was more complex than ordering the same sandwich. Like a secret portal on eHarmony."

"Let me ask you something," Sam said, his laughter barely restrained. "In that kind of relationship, does she provide the strap-on, or do you have to get it yourself? And are you responsible for cleaning it, too?"

"Fucking asshat," Riley murmured while the table erupted into another round of laughter.

"I'm fascinated. Truly. I'm not ragging on you. Does she have her own ball gags, or does she just cram your boxers in your mouth?" Sam asked.

"You all think you're so fucking funny," Riley seethed.

"You're precious, RISD," Shannon said. "I can't wait to meet this chick."

"You can bet your balls that isn't happening, Shannon," he said.

"Think of it this way, Riley," Sam said. "They used to do this to me."

"And the difference between you and me," Riley retorted, waving his hands between him and Sam. "Is that you deserve it."

"All right..." Shannon pulled an envelope from her bag. "With that delightful story on the books, it's time to open these bad boys."

"Should we call Erin and put her on speaker, or try to Skype?" I asked.

Shannon sat back and twisted her lips into an angry snarl.

"Yeah...about that. Erin emailed me last night. She's back in the Azores and collecting samples of soil or rocks or something. There are a lot of volcanoes but not so much cell service," Matt said. "She said we should go ahead without her."

"Like I said," Shannon muttered. "If it was important to her..."

The humor lighting the room dissolved, and everyone looked remarkably more sober. Sensing the gravity of the moment, Lauren stood and refilled the wine glasses. I noticed full bottles of whiskey in their kitchen, and knew we'd at least have liquor to soften the blows.

Yeah, that sounded about as healthy and well adjusted as it felt.

Lauren shifted to leave the table, but Matt shook his head,

his arm wrapping around her waist while he hauled her into his lap. "Stay."

"Ready?" Shannon asked, her fingers primed on the envelope. We nodded in agreement, and the whistling rip of the paper punctuated the silence. Shannon glanced at the cover sheet before holding up six smaller envelopes. "We each get a copy. The last page requires a signature acknowledging you read and understood the enclosed documents, and they have to be filed within thirty days of receipt."

Once the envelopes were distributed, we continued to stare at each other, no one wanting to open first.

Sam tossed his envelope to the center of the table, sitting back in his chair with his arms crossed. In the two months since he and Angus had it out, he was no better at concealing his fury than he was in November. I studied him from across the table. This could be the night he cracked. It was going to happen. Sooner or later, Sam was going to unhinge.

All his life, Sam was a few degrees left of center. My mother said he'd be a late bloomer, and we all needed to look out for him, and she was right.

He was frequently sick and never strayed far from my mother's side. He was smaller than kids his own age, and was often mistaken as Riley's fraternal twin despite the two years between them.

He never fit in at school, and struggled with anxiety and crippling panic attacks after her death. He was a prime target for teasing, and kids loved to call him gay. He skipped a grade to avoid being stranded in middle school without Matt, but that only meant he wasn't bullied in front of Matt.

Kids can be evil, and they terrorized him.

Angus knew all of this, and he knew exactly which buttons to push that day in November.

First he attacked Sam's belief system: sustainability. To Angus, green design was a cheap fad attracting people who didn't have the chops to do the real work of preservation. Angus saw it as a parody of the craft, a mockery, and he ripped into Sam on that count.

Next he went for the sore spot: Sam's sexuality. Angus knew how much those taunts devastated Sam, and he exploited it. He went after Sam's attachment to Mom, his size, his health, his clothing. He was merciless, and it cut Sam to the bone.

That Sam wasn't gay was beside the point. He liked women. A *lot* of women. But when Angus hit him with that, he leveled Sam. The proof was sitting right in front of me.

"Shan..." I murmured, glancing at her fingers as they traveled over the edges of the envelope. "Could you read through the legal bullshit? Just tell us what it says?"

She nodded, and slipped her finger under the flap of the envelope. Holding the folded pages in her hands, she paused and looked around the table.

"I think we should agree, before this goes any further, that we're putting Angus behind us. He's gone. No matter what we find in here, he's gone, and we're not reliving any of it."

"Agreed," Matt said.

Shannon turned her attention to the legal documents, and I studied my siblings in the thick silence that ensued. Sam was still locked in his angry sneer, busy mounting arguments against whatever Angus left in the will.

I tried to look away from the wordless communication passing between Matt and Lauren, but I wanted to learn the private language of people in love. It felt voyeuristic to watch them, yet it occurred to me that I understood nothing about the inner workings of a serious relationship.

Matt's head rested on Lauren's shoulder while her hands stroked his fingers. I thought of Andy's fingers and their silken texture as my fingertips coasted over her skin.

Why the fuck was I still thinking about that?

From the corner of my eye, I saw Shannon lean back in her chair and drop her hands to her lap. "Holy shit," she sighed.

"I called it. Rusty nails for the win," I said.

"Don't tell me," Sam said. "He's leaving us a hoard of milk crates and bottle caps from the past twenty years that he expects us to transform into a monument in his honor, and he's leaving the house to a group of doomsday survivalists."

"No, I got it," Matt said. "He's left fifty grand buried in coffee cans all over the yard, and we have to find them. He left the rest of his money in a Cayman account and lost the number, and the house is going to self-destruct after we sign these papers."

"Wrong and wrong," Riley disagreed. "He's in debt at the dog track, and we have to cover his gambling losses unless we want some goodfellas to take out our kneecaps. And he burned all of our baby pictures and childhood mementos, and we each get a plastic baggie with the ashes. But they're all unmarked because fuck us."

"That one's good," I said.

"You're all wrong," she murmured. Pushing away from the table, Shannon grabbed the whiskey and glasses, quickly distributing them and uncapping the bottle with quivering hands. "Aunt Mae used to say 'There's a fine line between being an alcoholic and being an Irishman. Drunks are always assholes.'"

"That bad?" I asked when she poured three fingers into my glass.

"She also said 'What whiskey won't cure cannot be cured,' so bottoms up, boys."

"I never knew Aunt Mae was such a drunk, or a philosopher," Riley said. "I guess we have something to be thankful for after all."

"Oh yeah," I replied. "She took a drink upstairs with her every night. An alligator could have been spooning with her in bed, and she never would have noticed."

When the glasses were empty, Shannon nodded and passed the bottle around again. "Let me get this out." She glanced at the document, the liquid in her glass lapping against the rim as her hand shook.

I placed my hand on Shannon's shoulder and squeezed, and she responded with a patient smile. A Jack Russell terrier was definitely involved.

"Okay. Here goes. Assets were distributed in rather standard terms. Angus left two hundred and fifty thousand to Cornell."

"Figures," Riley said.

Cornell was the only family tradition that survived to my generation. Matt, Sam, and I studied at Cornell's architecture school, and Sam and I picked up our Masters of Architecture there while Matt went to MIT's grad program in structural engineering.

Riley attended Rhode Island School of Design's architecture program. On top of Riley's decision to stray from the herd, he frequently revealed shocking gaps in knowledge, forcing us to keep an eagle eye on his work. We suspected those gaps were more about Riley than RISD.

"His stake in Walsh Associates is to be divided between the six of us, and that stake can be cashed out or reinvested."

She took a deep breath, and I braced myself for the ax to fall.

"He invested five hundred thousand in Walsh Associates, with the earmark that it pays off the loan on the office."

"What?" I slapped both hands on the table in shock. My siblings wore the same stunned expressions.

"He decides to invest in us now?" Sam yelled. "Are you fucking kidding me? After we drained everything to start the goddamn business and mortgaged our asses off to buy that place?"

"And," Shannon continued, "he left the house in Wellesley, and all its contents, to us. We are free to sell it, although the will states he wants it restored first. He left money for that purpose."

"Which may still contain twenty years of milk crates and bottle caps," Matt said.

"And the ashes of my baby pictures," Riley added.

"Dude, you're the fifth kid. There were never pictures of you," Sam said.

"There's more."

We gazed at Shannon, all slightly terrified to hear anything else.

It shouldn't have surprised me. Everything Angus left would have fallen into reasonable territory if he had been a reasonable father. He wasn't. He was a demonic jackass who got off on abandoning us to raise ourselves while getting in regular jabs about us letting Mom die on our watch. We would have been more receptive to his final requests if they didn't sting like one last slap in the face, a reminder that he hated us.

"This is where the ass raping starts," Sam muttered. A sure

sign of Sam's intoxication was the slip in his vocabulary. He loved sounding erudite, yet never managed to pull it off drunk.

"He left two million to Brigham and Women's Hospital. It's only for research and treatment for preeclampsia. Anything left after the disposal of the estate goes into a trust for equal division among...his future grandchildren. It will be made available on their twenty-fifth birthdays, in addition to one hundred thousand already in the trust."

Holding the memories of Mom's death alongside a future generation was uncomfortable at best, unfathomable at worst. It didn't take much to relive the horrible moments of her death or the long road that followed, but imagining the possibility of our own children in the same thought felt wrong.

Even with five siblings, we were always somewhat incomplete. Angus's death didn't orphan us. We were orphaned the day my mother died. For us, family was far more fragile than it seemed at first glance.

One by one, we drained our glasses and darted glances at each other in bewildered silence.

"I was expecting something more demented," Matt said. "Why spend twenty-two years since Mom's death being the biggest cocksucker in the world, only to do this? It's not like he couldn't have funded that research a long time ago."

"He did," Shannon said. "According to this, he's been a major donor for about thirteen years now. Always anonymous."

"And he's suddenly concerned about grandkids?" Sam sneered. "We're talking about the person who referred to you as 'cunt,' Shannon, and routinely suggested that Mom was a whore and Erin wasn't his, so yeah, I'd say this is more than demented." He filled his glass again. "He knew what he was doing the entire time, and this is just another manipulation. I don't want a fucking dime of it."

"When was it written?" I asked.

"Two years ago," Shannon said.

"Two years ago?" Sam yelled. "Two years ago! Two. Fucking. Years. Two years ago, he creates trust funds for our nonexistent kids because he's such a caring guy, and two months ago he rips me a new asshole because he's decided I'm a disgusting queer. Unbelievable. No, actually quite believable, and we're the fools for expecting something different."

"We agreed," Shannon said. "It's the past. We're letting him go. We're not letting this screw us up anymore. We can't do that to ourselves. And we have to look at this as a window into his fucked up mind. Think about it—this tells us with great clarity that something mattered to him. He tried to explain it with this because all he had when he was alive was anger."

"Shannon, it is one big 'fuck you and the horse you rode in on.' I'm not going along with any revisionist history tonight. He was a demented son of a bitch, and I'm not remembering him fondly because he wants to pay off our debt and send his fictitious grandchildren to college."

"Refusing the money would let him win," I said.

"I don't think so, Patrick," Sam scoffed. He pushed to his feet and circled the table. "Taking the money would mean we think of him every time we look at our office space, or the children that we're all too fucked up to have." He stopped pacing and gestured to Lauren and Matt. "I don't mean you two. You'll have awesome, well-adjusted kids, largely due to Lauren, and we'll be the fucked up aunts and uncles who take your kids to Red Sox games. The rest of us are a little too damaged for anything normal or healthy."

"He loved Cornell, Sam. He loved the work, even though he had unusual ways of showing it in recent years. He loved that house. And he loved Mom—"

"Then he should have killed himself a long time ago, Shannon! It woulda been better," Sam roared. "And how can you even say that? If he loved her so much, how could he talk about her the way he did? How could he disown you, and me, and Erin? At least these guys look like him." Sam waved his hand at Riley and Matt. "It wasn't like he could pretend they weren't his."

"He loved her more than anything, and he couldn't live without her. I wish you could remember what it was like before she died, and the way they were together. But after Mom?" Shannon held out her hands and let them fall to her lap. "He existed. Just barely. He did everything in his power to drown it all out, and it made him a monster. In the end, he tried to make a few things right in the only way he could."

"He called you a cunt!" Sam ran his hands through his hair and bent at the waist, as if winded from the exertion. "How can you overlook that? How can you ever forgive that? How can you forgive everything he did, everything he said?"

"I'm not," she replied. "I'm letting it go. There's plenty to be angry about, Sammy. But it's his shit, not yours, and you have to let it go."

"I like how you think you're letting it go. I like that you think you won't wake up some day and realize he gutted you. He completely fucking gutted you. You don't even have a clue how much he ruined you but someday you'll figure it out."

Sam shook his head and shuffled down the hallway. The table descended into quiet again, the only sounds coming from the slosh of whiskey into glasses.

I thought about Sam's tirade, wondering if he was right—

were we too damaged? Taking over the business meant my time was devoted there, and not on dating. Marriage never figured into my thoughts. My interests centered on open relationships without the responsibility of keeping track of birthdays or holidays. Kids only crossed my mind when they screamed their demands from the middle of the grocery store aisle.

Lauren's engagement ring caught my eye when her fingers ran through Matt's hair. His eyes drooped shut and he whispered something into her ear that elicited a smile. That voyeuristic feeling returned and I wished away the unbidden thoughts of Andy that appeared every time I noticed Lauren's loving touch.

"We need to sell that house. Hire a crew to clear it out. Be done with it," Matt said. "But someone needs to make sure he doesn't have a pack of wolves roving the grounds first."

"I'm not going out there." Riley shook his head and reached for a bowl of paella. I watched as he picked through the dish with his fingers, selecting chunks of chorizo to nibble. We failed him on the table manners front.

Before I realized what I was offering, I said, "I'll go. It's my problem."

Four pairs of eyes snapped toward me in surprise. "We can do it together," Shannon said.

"No. You've got enough on your hands with the estate, and I really don't want to be involved in all the legal bullshit. I'll do this. You do that."

"Yes, boss," she replied with a salute. I grimaced at the title. "This officially makes you the CEO, you know."

"No," I said. "It means business as usual."

"What we need," Matt slurred, his hand sweeping over the table and narrowly missing a few wine glasses before Lauren steadied him. He was five minutes from falling face first into bed. I wasn't far behind him. "Is a party. Like the one they had in Oz when the witch died. The first witch, not the one chasing Dorothy."

"Not the direction I was expecting you to go, my friend. I was thinking something along the lines of engagement party, but please, proceed," Riley said.

"Yeah, that too," Matt said.

Lauren started clearing the table, and he smacked her rear end as she walked away. Their easy affection was unexpected and so arrestingly intriguing I struggled to tear my eyes away. Was that how couples interacted? Whispered words and ass slapping?

"We need to do that. We didn't do anything for the holidays, or our birthdays." Matt drew a triangle between himself, Shannon, and me. "We should. We deserve something good."

Shannon and I were born the same year, me in January, and her in December. Matt came along the following December. We usually picked one day as a communal celebration, but that ritual fell away this year. Taking Angus off life support and burying him the week before Christmas didn't leave much room for anything special or festive.

"You're right," I murmured, sipping my whiskey. Crawling would be an accomplishment tomorrow; running would be out of the question. "This all feels like a kick in the ass, but we'll own the Derne Street office outright. All the Bunker Hill properties will be off the books by the end of February. We get to do what we love and hang out with each other every day. We need to celebrate that shit."

"Good," Matt shouted as he stumbled into the kitchen. "But don't think I'm forgetting that you're thirty-three, and Black

Widow is thirty-two now." He pressed Lauren up against the refrigerator and kissed her. I looked away when he hooked her leg over his hip and his hand slipped under her shirt.

"They're fucking exhibitionists." Riley jutted his chin toward Shannon. "I've seen this show before. Want to a hit a frat party?"

"Why do you know about these things? It's not in Rhode Island, is it?"

"You're lucky I don't hit women," he replied. "No, it's not in Rhody, but you'd be in for something special at an Ocean State frat party. And don't ask questions you don't want answered."

"Won't I be the oldest person there by...ten years?" she asked.

"Yeah. Some guys are into that."

Shannon shrugged. "Good enough for me." She gathered her things before touching my forearm. "Will you check on him?" I nodded, and she bit her lip. "He drank a lot and barely ate. His insulin pump won't work as well."

"I know, I got it. Go."

She smiled and headed out with Riley while Matt articulated his unquestionably filthy intentions for the night with Lauren. Was *that* what love looked like?

"I'm takin' you to bed, sweetness," Matt said when he released her from the refrigerator, his hands deep in her back pockets.

"You're welcome to stay," Lauren offered as Matt marched her toward their bedroom.

"Thanks, Lauren. Let him sleep wherever he falls. A night on the floor never hurt him."

"If you only knew, Patrick," she laughed.

I stared at the ocean before turning off the lights and locating Sam's messenger bag. I grabbed his medical kit and headed toward the spare bedroom. Unsurprisingly, he was fully dressed and snoring. I rolled him over, expecting him to wake up and launch into a long-winded argument, but he went on snoring.

Opening the kit, I retrieved the supplies and knelt beside the bed, conjuring the last shreds of sobriety. He didn't flinch when the lancet punctured his skin, but after all these years with type I diabetes, I suspected he was immune to it. His levels were low, but not dangerous. I inserted a new canister in his insulin pump and waited for the screen to register it.

Sam grunted and turned to his side, and I pulled the blankets over him before flopping beside him. I set the alarm on my phone to wake me when he needed his levels checked again, and scrolled through my texts and emails.

The sight of Andy's name attached to six emails with updated designs brought a smile to my face. She worked hard and didn't call it a day until the work was done, and done well. I admired that and I wanted her to know.

The wine and whiskey left my brain muddy, not to mention Angus's shitshow will and unsolicited reminders of her soft skin against mine, but I fought it all off and typed a text message to Andy.

Exhaustion hit my body like an avalanche, and the phone slipped from my fingers when I tried to place it on the table. I reached out as it skittered away, only to grasp at air. Sighing, I rolled back and wondered what she was doing.

My eyes heavy, I thought about the shock of the will. Nothing would have changed the blunt force trauma of it all, but my arms wrapped around Andy and her head on my shoulder wouldn't have hurt.

CHAPTER EIGHT

ANDY

"Who's that?" Marley peered over my shoulder. Sugary lemon drop martini spilled from her glass and splashed down my shirt, a puddle dammed against the underwire of my bra. Sticking with my original plan of staying home and criticizing all the design shows on HGTV sounded heavenly right then.

"Girl, you need to watch yourself," Jess yelled. "That drink is everywhere but your mouth."

"Nice." I shook the droplets from my arms and wiped my phone on my leg. "I need to clean up."

"Sorry," Marley squealed, and I replied with a halfhearted smile.

My tolerance for Marley was still a work in progress, and her ability to find the douchiest bars in Boston was worthy of an Urbanspoon entry. An extensive conversation over dinner about a 'welpy' guy that she met on OkCupid—who she was considering seeing again primarily due to the fact he drove a 2004 Lexus—convinced me I needed to put more effort into finding friends in Boston.

The bathroom was vacant when I entered, and I wiped the syrupy alcohol from my body without an audience. Salvaging my silk shirt and bra, however, wasn't happening.

The pounding adrenaline of my first days at Walsh Associates was gradually subsiding, and lemon drop disaster aside, life was magnificent.

I was impressed with how quickly Patrick transitioned from wordless scowls to full, decipherable words and sentences—my mere existence wasn't wasting his time anymore, and I was beginning to think he actually tolerated me.

Learning from Patrick was more amazing than I expected, and I was blown away by the amount of responsibility he entrusted in me. I kept my inner fangirl in check, but she was primed for an explosion, especially when I discovered we were both starving foodies.

Leaning against a stall, I stared at the unopened text message from Patrick. Our texts were rare since we spent the majority of our time together during business hours. When we were separated, our messages were limited to quick questions about projects and contractors, and photos from jobsites.

Wanting to get lost in work, I spent my evenings combing the plans for weaknesses and issues standing in the way of true restoration, and researching techniques that might work for Patrick's projects. Though I loved the rush of solving unworkable problems, Patrick still engulfed my thoughts even after hours of poring over research.

My apartment was fortified with a wall of unopened boxes and I couldn't find a spoon to save my life, but my vibrator was unpacked and stowed at arm's reach. But after five days of concerted effort and nights spent draining my toy's batteries, I abandoned Project Don't Fuck the Boss when those abs entered my line of sight.

Resisting Patrick Walsh required an iron chastity belt, not a self-control initiative.

We could agree the first glimpse of his torso was accidental, but there was no doubt in my mind the second was premeditated. His demanding stare was too intense, his stretch too long.

I knew enough about him after a week as his shadow to know he followed his own playbook and answered to no one, but his freely offered abs were still shocking.

I didn't take him for the flirtatious type, what with all his scowling, growling, and intimidating glares, but that was as far as it could go. Just flirting. My finger hovered over the message for a moment, and a vision of his beautifully sculpted body entered my mind. The artful spattering of freckles across his abdomen was unlike anything I'd ever seen, and I wanted to play Connect the Dots.

"There you are! Is it ruined?" Jess breezed into the bathroom and brushed her hand over my shirt. "Holy moly. My dry cleaner might be able to help...or you can wear it under cardigans, if you button up."

"Hadn't considered the cardigan angle."

She turned to the mirror to wipe away some smudged mascara. Meeting my eyes in the mirror, she said, "Last call's coming up. Do you want to come back to my place for a sleepover? We have some salted caramel gelato."

I chuckled, remembering our fondness for Friday night sleepovers back home in Maine—the good old days when we didn't curse the deities after gorging on ice cream and sleeping on the floor.

"Tempting as that sounds, we're pretty close to my place. I'd invite you guys to stay, but..."

"But you live in a shoebox, I know. That's what you get for living on Beacon Hill."

Shoebox apartment, yes. Presentable apartment, no. Unpacking was climbing higher on my to-do list.

She turned, and noticed the phone in my hand. "Did you get a number?"

"That wasn't my objective," I laughed, wincing at the memory of the Tight T-Shirt Brigade's most recent appearance. "No, I got a text from my boss."

Jess frowned. "On a Friday night? What an asshole. I know you said he's intense and all, but slave driver much? What does he want?"

I shrugged, and slipped the phone into my clutch. "It's nothing. Should we close out the tab?"

We located Marley grinding on an alleged European prince, forced the dregs of the lemon drop down her throat, and huddled on the curb for cabs. I hugged them both, and savored the relative quiet of the cab as the highlights from the evening's Celtics game blasted, and the driver's radio squawked with dispatch alerts.

Back at my apartment, I discarded all of my clothes, removed my makeup, and slipped between the cool sheets of my bed. Reaching for my phone, I opened Patrick's messages.

Patrick: Really want to tell u that your grant and
Patrick: Shane was right your fucking awesome
Patrick: U work hard as I do and thirst great and year so smart
Patrick: I want too teach u so much

I laughed out loud. "Oh Patrick," I murmured. "What are you up to tonight?"

I typed a quick response and set my phone aside. I didn't expect to hear back from Patrick—his texts and emails were usually crisply written with pristine grammar, and I imagined his touch screen rebelling against his big hands after a few drinks.

Tom mentioned something about buying a case of wine for a serious dinner at Matt's place, though I was lost in concentration when he appeared in Patrick's office with documents from Shannon. He knew everything about Walsh Associates and the inner workings of the Walsh family, and his ability to sniff out office gossip was disarming. I figured his role as Shannon's taskmaster meant he was privy to all the juicy information.

I was still trying to determine whether Tom was wildly metrosexual or gay—I liked the guy either way, but I would not date someone who spent more time on eyebrow grooming than I did. He invited me out every day—coffee, brunch, dim sum, drinks. Tom could spare me the agony of another outing with Marley and the Tight T-Shirts, but a night with him didn't interest me.

My phone's screen faded, and my bedroom descended into darkness while the noise of cars on Storrow Drive and ambulances at Mass General offered a soothing soundtrack. Maybe it was a shoebox, but it was a gorgeous old shoebox, and it was mine. Patrick would understand—he knew the spirits of families past lived in the walls of these homes, and it was his responsibility to care for them.

Maybe it was our responsibility now and not just Patrick's alone.

Mouthwatering visions of his abdomen filled my mind, and I

longed to run my fingers along the ripples and indentations. His trim waist was a wonder to behold with all those notches and grooves, and I couldn't imagine a sight more sexy than his jeans hanging low on his hips.

I even got a sneak peek at the black band of his boxers.

It was one thing to know his body was as cut as I imagined, but it was another to watch him repeatedly cross those strong arms over his chest. Keeping my hands filled with tape measures and flashlights averted awkward bicep-rubbing incidents. It was worse when he rolled up his shirtsleeves, and it was an accomplishment if he made it to ten in the morning with his cuffs buttoned.

My legs drifted apart on a sigh, and my fingers brushed over my chest. My nipples hardened in response, the delicate fabric of the sheets offering the right amount of texture. Scraping my nails along my skin, I went straight for my aching core and groaned when my fingers dipped into my arousal. Two fingers swept over my clit and I could feel my pulse hammering there. The quiet shattered with a loud hitch in my breath.

Reaching to the bedside table without so much as a glance, I retrieved my vibrator and spread my legs wider. Every day spent with Patrick left me hungry, and knowing he wanted me looking at him made the hunger more oppressive than before. I wasn't in the mood for long, teasing play—not after a day filled with Patrick's perpetually crossed arms, bared belly, and late night texts.

The arousal pooled at my opening, and the toy filled me with one smooth thrust that had me clenching my inner muscles and pressing against my clit. My body was ready—all systems go for a devastating orgasm—and I needed it. Since meeting Patrick, I searched in earnest for the muscle-weakening, brain-clearing orgasm to relieve the ache in my body, but I only found shallow, limping mini-orgasms that left me frustrated and edgy.

Turning to the lowest setting, I groaned in satisfaction as the pulsations radiated from my core and spread up into my clit. My fingers circled my throbbing bud in time with the vibrator, and my hips started rolling to find an outlet for the pressure building in my nerves. Small gasps and moans passed my lips, and I clicked to a higher speed.

I felt the quivering inklings of an orgasm deep in my core, and closed my eyes to focus on the sensations traveling through my body. My fingers quickened in their frantic circuit over my clit when my knees lifted off the bed to offer better access, yet I struggled to find the tipping point that would bring me closer to warm, pulsing release. So close, yet so far.

As the minutes ticked by, I fought my body for more—alternately pinching my nipples while running the vibrator over my clit and swiveling to rest my feet on the headboard to get a new angle. I was always *this* close—and it darted away from me every time.

My elbow ached, and my fingers were numb around the toy's base when I finally deposited it on my side table. My other hand continued circling my clit—after a week of nightly self-love sessions, the last things I needed were raw, chafed ladybits. That and a bout of carpal tunnel syndrome, and I'd be the spokeswoman for crimes against orgasms.

I laughed out loud at the prospect of telling Patrick I couldn't sit down or operate a screwdriver because I tweaked my wrist and elbow after an hour of furious orgasm hunting. I could see him narrowing his eyes at me while he crossed his arms over his chest. He'd lift an eyebrow, letting the tension rise between us and waiting for me to explain myself.

Or he'd throw me on his desk and fuck me.

Groaning, I curled on my side and squeezed my eyes shut. My dreams would most certainly feature that new fantasy.

Two hours of Bikram yoga drained enough energy from my body to temporarily forget Patrick and his abs, though it also left me sweaty and starving. After a quick shower, I headed to the winter farmers' market with the hope of finding a co-op or CSA opening to keep me supplied with local fruits and veggies.

I preferred unconventional pastimes—reading Patrick's thesis and yelling at DVR'd HGTV shows came to mind—and farmers' market shopping was no exception. It's not that I didn't love shopping for clothes or shoes—I did—it's that I loved heirloom greens and discovering new produce from local farmers more.

Wandering through the stalls, my cloth bags rapidly filled with an assortment of goodies. I stopped at a table advertising community dinner parties to experiment with Persian recipes and practice Farsi. New town, new job, and maybe a new opportunity to explore my heritage. I added my name to their email list.

Only a few of the Farsi words and phrases my father taught me before he died remained in my memory, along with vague stories of his family and childhood. He loved Tehran yet preferred Isfahan, and promised we'd spend an entire week exploring the bazaar there. We were going to visit the ruins of Persepolis in Shiraz, and Qeshm Island and the Hara marine forests. We were going to go just as soon as it was safe for him to return to Iran.

Everything I knew about my dad's culture and family came from the internet—my mother stopped talking about him after a year in Maine. She said it was too painful, and I didn't want her to suffer.

When I buried my face in a bouquet of basil, I felt a hand squeeze my shoulder.

"I'd know that hair anywhere!"

Shannon Walsh stood before me, her arm linked with a petite blonde's, both beaming at me with bright smiles. For a moment, I struggled with her friendly familiarity, but soon remembered I now worked at a third generation family firm where only a handful of outsiders joined the ranks. Of course she was friendly outside the office. I realized I should figure out how to do that, too.

"You're so awesome...already found the farmers' market and everything."

I shrugged and gestured to her long, red waves. "They call to me, and I'd know that hair anywhere."

"Hi, I'm Lauren." The blonde offered her hand to me.

"Andy." Remembering to be friendly, I added, "It's nice to meet you."

"Andy is working with Patrick," Shannon said to Lauren. "And Lauren is my future sister-in-law."

It was impossible to keep their stories straight—they looked alike and talked alike, and were in and out of Patrick's office all day long. I vaguely remember hearing about someone's fiancée, but I couldn't remember which one.

I forced a smile at the blonde, and my fingers closed around the bunch of basil when it dawned on me: she was probably engaged to Patrick. I was a little embarrassed—I did spend the week lusting after him and sent a few overtly flirty texts last night—but I was a lot irritated. She wasn't right for him. I felt my eyebrow arch into my forehead while I studied her.

"Matthew," Lauren supplied with a bright smile. "Matthew's mine."

A wave of relief crashed over me, and I released a breathy laugh. I looked around the market, hoping to find the source of my rapid onset possessiveness among the kale, hand-churned butter, and purple potatoes.

"We were going to grab some lunch, Andy. I'd love for you to join us," Shannon said.

"Hm."

I glanced between them while scanning for appropriate lunch conversation topics with my boss's sister and my boss's future sister-in-law. It wasn't as if I could discuss my surging jealousy at the prospect of Patrick's engagement or my struggle to reach a decent orgasm.

"Don't worry, Andy. No business on the weekends, and lunch with us usually involves mimosas and a thorough examination of Shannon Walsh's men—the ones she dates, not the ones she's related to."

"As long as you're not reporting back to Patrick." It sounded ridiculous the moment I said it—he wouldn't care about me having lunch with Shannon and Lauren. Or would he?

This wasn't healthy. Must get my thoughts away from Patrick.

Lauren hooked her elbow through mine and, inexplicably, I was walking through the farmers' market with a blonde and a redhead. We must have looked like we were filming a shampoo commercial.

"He's probably still where we left him—begging for death in Matt's den," Shannon said.

"He just needed some food," Lauren replied. She looked up

at me—even in flats, I was at least five inches taller. I couldn't imagine such a small woman next to Matt. "He had a few cocktails last night—"

"A few? Honey, please, he was trying to put alcohol out of business. Between Patrick and Matt, I think they drained all the whiskey in Boston."

Lauren shrugged and steered us across the street toward a bakery cafe. "You were no better, and if anyone stumbled away with the first place medal, it was Sam. Besides, those boys have been drinking whiskey since they were two. As soon as they get him a new phone, I'm sure he'll be barking orders in no time."

"What happened to Patrick's phone?"

Did he remember texting me? Or see my response?

Shannon nibbled her lip while scanning the menu, her shoulders bouncing back and forth. "He smashed it."

"Smashed?"

"I think he was trying to put it down and, being the ogre he is, accidentally smashed it into a table, and then it flew across the room and hit the wall." Lauren layered her menu over Shannon's before looking at me. "So Matthew went out with him to get a new phone. I'm getting the brie and arugula with red peppers."

"Chicken with jicama and avocado," Shannon said.

They glanced at me expectantly, and I scrambled to skim the menu as the waitress arrived to collect our orders. "Grilled portobello and pesto."

Our mimosas appeared within minutes, and when our glasses clinked together, I noticed an enormous diamond ring on Lauren's hand. "Oh my God," I yelped, grabbing her hand and gazing at the sparkling stone.

"Right? It's a headlight. Isn't it amazing?" Shannon laughed.

"That bastard didn't even ask for my help. I want to be insulted but...he did good."

Lauren blushed and acknowledged my outburst with a gracious nod. "Do you have a date set?"

"We do," she replied, an undeniably gleeful smile pulling at her lips. "Late May."

"And she's not pregnant!" Shannon stage-whispered. "We all thought it."

"Hm." Not knowing how to handle Shannon's comment, I sipped my mimosa and contemplated my reaction to Lauren's ring. In all of my twenty-four years, I never expressed more than obligatory politeness at weddings and babies. I went so far as debating the purpose of engagement rings in a day and age where a man's proof of possession over a woman was illogical, and marriage no longer required down payments or dowries.

"Is it all planned?"

Lauren lifted a shoulder and paused to sip her mimosa. "We're taking a laid-back approach to the whole wedding planning thing. We just want friends and family on the beach and some good food and music. Nothing elaborate or formal."

It sounded glorious, and completely void of all bridezilla tendencies to which otherwise intelligent, levelheaded women fell prey.

"They also needed to get married as soon as humanly possible," Shannon snorted.

"We wanted to get married before things got crazy at my school, and yes," she sighed, "we want to be married soon."

"Are you a teacher?" Lauren looked like a teacher. Not in an ugly sweater, chalk on the seat of her pants way, but in a kind, patient way that she'd listen attentively to your story about shadow monsters in the library, then plot ways to scare them off.

"I used to be," Lauren said. "I taught third grade for six years, and I'm opening a school in September."

"Wow." I was officially finished hating her. Lauren was genuinely warm and sweet, and I felt drawn to her.

"Yeah, yeah, Lauren's amazing and incredible. Let me tell you about Hunter. Ohmigod. Disastrousness. Why do I think these guys are worth my time?"

"Where did you meet him again?"

"The Genius Bar at the Apple store." Shannon rolled her eyes and groaned.

"Was he a Genius?" Lauren asked skeptically.

"No. Just a dude who was there, waiting in line, but that boy had no personality, and—get this—he expected me to pay. Not 'hey, let's split this' but 'hey, you're picking this up, right?' He was just rude about it." She shook her head. "Then he decides to reconfigure my phone to optimize the memory or whatever. I told him I was pleased with its performance, and would like to hear more about him, and he said I would be really impressed with the difference."

"Are you?" I asked.

"No," she answered. "No. And I wouldn't be shocked to discover some pervy surveillance app on here. I ended up sitting there for half an hour while he dicked around with my phone. I couldn't even text Sam to call me with a fake emergency."

"Shannon," Lauren sighed. "No more boys for you. No more hook-ups. You've met every weirdo in Boston. You need to let the universe take over now. Accept that there is a plan for you and surrender."

Shannon opened her mouth to speak but paused when our lunches arrived. Once the waitress left, she removed all the avocado from her chicken, jicama, and avocado salad. She noticed me staring, and offered the plate of discarded avocado. "I like a tiny bit of avocado flavor but I don't like biting into avocados. The texture is weird."

"Sure," I murmured, accepting the plate. Getting used to that level of friendly familiarity would take some time.

Shannon pointed at Lauren with her fork. "I don't feel like I need a relationship to be happy. By no means. I'm totally happy in my skin right now. I like my independence. I don't want to get on a daily call-text-email program with some guy, and I really don't want him getting miffed when I can't hold up my end of that bargain. I don't have time for the off-the-deep-end kind of relationship you and Matt have." She sent a horrified look in Lauren's direction and shook her head. "But I don't want to miss out on someone really great because I'm not looking."

As the words slipped from Shannon's mouth, I wondered whether she hacked into my psyche to find them. Eating the avocado she picked out of her salad didn't seem quite as weird anymore.

"Well...neither was I," Lauren replied. "I certainly attempted to send him on his merry way a couple of times, regardless of whether it made any sense."

"Yeah. That. I don't have time for dramatic shit, or obsessing about the random things some guy said or did, or didn't do. I can't even start with that. And I don't want to wake up with fourteen cats when I'm forty-eight."

"I wouldn't let that happen to you, Shan. I'd intervene after two cats. Hell, we'd have a come-to-Jesus when the first one showed up." Lauren shook her head. "And let me remind you of something you said not too long ago—it just happens when you stop looking for it."

"You're saying I need to stop looking so I don't start hoarding cats."

"Yes," Lauren said.

"I can't make any promises, but...I'll see what I can do."

"So Andy, we were going to hit a few boutiques around town if you'd like to come along. We have a wedding dress to find. We are *choosing* to be happy today, and not letting anything drag us down." Lauren directed a pointed stare at Shannon, and she nodded in response. "I don't want a poufy dress, and not necessarily a white dress, so we're looking for something a little different."

"As if you could wear white anyway," Shannon laughed. "We're skipping the bridal boutiques, Andy, so this is the end of our champagne, and I doubt we're going to find any sparkly tiaras."

"Somehow I think I'll survive."

"Good," Shannon barked. "You're part of the family now, and you have a vagina so you're obligated to look at dresses with us. Sam's the unofficial vagina that we usually drag along and he's busy hating the world these days so we really need you."

I always knew I wanted to work at Walsh Associates as an architect, but it wasn't until they welcomed my vagina into their makeshift sisterhood that I knew I wanted to be part of their family.

RESTING MY CHIN ON MY CLASPED HANDS, I GLARED AT HER TEXT messages for the twentieth time that morning.

Andy: thanks. I appreciate this. I like learning from you.
Consider it a mutually beneficial arrangement.
Andy: But as a friend: you're drunk. Go home.
Andy: give me a call if you need someone to put you to bed.

I remembered everything about Friday night at Matt and Lauren's place. The paella. The whiskey. The will. Sam's freak-out. Shan and Riley crashing a frat party. Passing out next to Sam. Waking up clutching a pink velvet pillow. Everything except texting Andy and destroying my phone in typical Neanderthal fashion.

There were an infinite number of ways to interpret Andy's texts and my weekend was devoted to analyzing each one. I read her responses so many times that the words stopped sounding like words and all I could hear was her saying "hm."

I knew how I wanted to interpret her messages. I also knew I was an idiot for thinking she'd want those things, and a bastard for twisting her words into something very, very dirty. If she only knew the kind of mutually beneficial arrangement I was thinking about, she'd run fast and far.

Or maybe that spine of steel would stay.

"When did you get here?" Shannon asked.

Lifting my head from my hands, I glanced over my shoulder as Shannon rounded the corner from the attic staircase.

"Six thirty." At her surprised expression, I continued, "I'm in the field most of the day. Needed to wrap my head around a few projects. And I'll be damned if this meeting doesn't start on time."

I failed to mention I was camping out in the attic conference room to avoid Andy. It was easier to fantasize about her lips around my cock when she wasn't staring at me.

"Right, well...since I have you here, I'm going to pull the payoff amount for the note on this place today. I think it's in the mid to low fours. I'll need your signature to make the distribution from the estate once all the affidavits are filed."

"Sam's going to blow a gasket."

"That will happen regardless of whether we pay off the mortgage or not." Her lips folded into a grim line, and I nodded. "I don't want to pay interest on this loan a minute longer than I have to, and you need to get out to Wellesley this week."

Shannon's reminder found a home at the bottom of my to-do list. Having an open discussion with Andy about my desire to tie her to my bed and fuck her seven ways to the weekend seemed less daunting than visiting my childhood home.

Matt, Riley, and Sam trudged up the stairs minutes later, and I made a point of starting on time. Work was moving along as quickly as possible for the early days of February, though the deep freeze forecasted for the end of the week would slow a few projects. Shannon argued her pricing strategy for the Bunker Hill properties, and I enjoyed watching Riley disagree with her. It was good to see the kid getting his sea legs.

"In other news," she sighed, exaggeratedly flipping pages in her notebook. "The 'Witch is Dead' party will be next Friday evening at my place."

"The what now?" Sam asked.

"We decided we needed a party," Matt said.

"A party in the spirit of munchkins celebrating Dorothy's house killing the witch," Riley said with an eager smile. "Just my two cents, but we shouldn't refer to it as the 'Witch is Dead' party outside this room. You know, basic respect for the dead and other things we don't seem to possess. We might be thoroughly fucked up, but that doesn't mean we need to broadcast it to the world."

Matt frowned. "That's Valentine's Day, Shan."

"It's not like any of us have plans." She gestured around the table and my brothers shrugged. "It's fine. You two can go gather your rose petals afterwards."

"Where was I when this was discussed?" Sam dragged his hand through his hair while he peered around the table.

"You were busy pissing on the wall in my half bath," Matt replied.

"Oh." Sam frowned and rubbed the back of his neck. "Sorry about that."

"Apologize to Lauren. She made that discovery," he said with a smirk. "We're going out for drinks this Friday, for Andy. Like, normal office happy hour to make her feel welcome."

I groaned at the mention of her name, earning me a rapid

elbow to the ribs from Shannon while she addressed Matt. "Happy hour isn't legal in Massachusetts. The concept of bargain beverages at a specific, common time doesn't exist in this state." She turned toward Riley. "Bring your dominatrix. I'd love to meet her."

"You're tripping balls," he murmured. "Not gonna happen."

"What's her name again?" Sam asked.

Riley gazed out the window as he exhaled loudly, his head shaking. "Ma'am. She lets me call her ma'am."

Matt pressed his fist to his mouth to conceal a laugh. "Twenty-First Amendment, around six. I want Lauren to meet Andy."

"She didn't tell you?" Shannon asked. She closed her laptop and folded her arms on the table. "We had lunch with Andy on Saturday. Bumped into her at the farmers' market. Andy picked out Lauren's wedding dress."

"Really?" Matt murmured, his arm crossed over his chest and his free hand propped under his chin while an affectionate smile danced across his face.

"Don't ask. I'm not telling you anything other than it is gorgeous and ideal," Shannon said. "And don't even think about asking Andy. You won't get anything out of her."

Didn't I know it.

I tried to picture Andy shopping for wedding dresses with Lauren, her dark, fitted clothes a sharp contrast to the sea of white. An uninvited image of Andy's slim body encased in a delicate white lace wedding dress floated into my mind, and I choked on my coffee.

I sputtered and coughed while Shannon smacked my back, though I couldn't escape the vision of Andy's hair spilling over her shoulders, and the gentle rise of her breasts against the lace.

Yep. Losing my fucking mind.

They continued talking but my attention slipped back to Andy. She was turning me into a delusional maniac, and now I had a wedding dress fetish.

———

ANDY DIDN'T MENTION MY DRUNKEN TEXT MESSAGES ON MONDAY. I waited for her to inquire about my weekend, or offer anecdotes from hers, and found myself irrationally annoyed when we talked through design changes over lunch without a moment of small talk.

At one point in the late afternoon, I started babbling to myself about finding a case to protect my new phone because it cost more than most kidneys on the black market. She gazed at me from the conference table while I rambled, glanced at the phone in my hand, and turned her attention back to her laptop.

Fucking infuriating.

Tuesday passed without comment, and I repeatedly scrolled through my messages to reread her responses and confirm the exchange did in fact occur. Given the degradation of my sanity as a product of Andy's aloofness and pouty lips and ever-present "hm," it seemed entirely possible I hallucinated.

Her hair wasn't helping my mental state either. The gusting wind that came in with Wednesday's blast of arctic air sent her tendrils flying in spite of her earmuff headband.

I had the good fortune of getting a face full of her hair that morning. I felt hundreds of brain cells explode when I inhaled the lavender scent that was uniquely Andy. It happened three more times, and those moments when my fingers connected with her raven strands launched a new batch of fantasies.

Seated for a late lunch at a farm-to-table sandwich joint in Arlington, the curly mass was secured in a messy knot. I itched to loosen it, and feel her strands on my fingers again. The image of her hair wrapped around my fist as I took her from behind fueled my arousal, and if I didn't get this situation under control, my dick was going to be hard enough to hammer nails all night.

Andy sent me a concerned look when I groaned and missed the window for a decent cover-up. "The pork belly is...really good," I stammered.

"Hm." She continued dotting her roasted vegetable wrap with spicy mustard.

She met my every maneuver with chilly indifference, and it left me more rankled than before. It wasn't about the texts now. I wanted her attention, and I knew that was beyond fucked up considering I was her boss. I still wanted it, and I was long past worrying about professional boundaries.

"Any plans for the weekend?" Andy looked up, her eyes wide, and I plowed ahead to fill the silence. "I was thinking about getting out of the city. Maybe heading up to the North Shore, or New Hampshire. It's not far. Only forty-five minutes or so." I shrugged. "I think I've hit my limit of gray Boston days, and there are a few dives in New Hampshire with incredible seafood. Legit dives. And the best part is they're totally empty this time of year."

Andy nodded while she chewed, and I held my breath, worried than another "hm" was headed my way. "Have you been to that area?"

"Yes and no." Shaking her head, Andy sipped her tea. I wanted her to give me an opening. No matter how small, I'd run with it. "That is, I'm familiar with the region but probably haven't been to the dives in question. Seafood is...not for me."

I was going to make an opening out of seafood if it killed me.

"That's blasphemous. You're in New England. We take seafood seriously in these parts."

"Trust me, I know. I grew up surrounded by seafood worship."

Some Neanderthal part of my brain failed to register until then that Andy's life didn't start at Cornell, and there was more to her than the finer points of her résumé. "Where are you from?"

"Maine. Wiscasset."

"Shit, that is up there," I murmured.

I tilted my head and stared at the loose corkscrew curls escaping her bun. I heard no trace of the Down East accent in her voice.

Imagining such a sophisticated woman living on the rugged, barren coast of Maine wasn't an easy throw. I didn't doubt she could survive up there. I got the sense Andy was capable of turning an actual cave into a two-bedroom condo. Maine just didn't fit her.

"And you don't like seafood? That really is blasphemy."

"What can I say?" She dragged a brussels sprout through the spicy mustard and popped it in her mouth. There was nothing specifically sensual about it but I was adjusting myself at the sight.

Anything involving Andy's mouth turned me on.

"Come to the seacoast with me this weekend. I'll change your mind," I vowed, snatching a few pickles from her plate. "Think of it like a dive tasting menu meets pub crawl."

She shot me an unimpressed glance. "Maybe—"

"Do you have other plans?"

I looked away when she speared another brussels sprout.

Between her hair and the sprouts, my balls were on the verge of becoming a new shade of blue.

"Yoga and the farmers' market. And an advisor from the architecture school might be in town. We've been meaning to connect and get drinks."

"Yeah? Anyone I'd know?"

"Probably not." She smiled at her tea. "You could say that Charlotte is...new at Cornell."

"Fine, so you can get a lobster roll with me on Sunday," I said.

"Hm. We'll see."

Smiling, I nodded in agreement and finished her pickles.

FOR ALL OF MY SUCCESSES WITH KEEPING MY HANDS TO MYSELF, staring was becoming a problem. I found myself gazing at Andy while she ate lunch, talked about restaurants she wanted to try, and worked in my office.

She frequently caught me looking though it didn't seem to bother her. Nothing rattled her cool, and that made the challenge of ruffling her more enticing than ever.

I realized that made me a creepy bastard. Add it to my list.

I also realized everything I knew about Andy outside of architecture was the result of observation and foodie conversations. While food seemed to be a good discussion starter for us, I couldn't figure her out based on her enchilada sauce preferences alone. I needed to spend time with her away from work and our lunch routine. And I needed to finally apologize for the drunken texting.

"So my recommendation is tearing the joint down and building a laser tag arena," Riley said. "See? He's not listening."

"What?" I blinked, looking between Matt and Riley. I was on the cusp of figuring out what to say to Andy before Riley barged into my thoughts.

"We were going over the JP property," Matt replied.

I glanced at the plans on my screen, nodding. "It's fine."

"Are *you* fine?" Riley asked.

"No. Yeah. I mean, I'm just trying to figure something out," I muttered, snapping my laptop shut then jogging up the stairs to my office.

I was going to apologize for the drunken texting, and see where that took us. With any luck, a drive up the coast for some divey seafood, and conversation that didn't revolve around architecture.

The words melted on my tongue at the doorway to my office. I reached a steadying hand to the doorframe and stared at Andy. She was kneeling over a set of plans on the floor beside my desk.

Head bent and hair spilling over her shoulders.

Skirt riding up her thighs, exposing her long, stocking-covered legs.

She was the picture of sophisticated sin, and I was hard the moment she lifted her eyes to mine and parted her lips.

"This seems to have some chaotic roof forms—"

Gazing at her for a moment, I licked my lips before biting down. She looked obedient, docile. I needed to explain the texts and convince her good clam chowder could be life affirming, but more than anything else, I wanted to know if she liked that position and would consider spending some time in it at my apartment.

Staring at the physical embodiment of my recent sex-filled dreams would end badly for everyone.

"I can't talk about that right now," I snapped. "Figure it out."

After stumbling down the stairs and striding across the building, I stormed into Matt's office and slammed the door behind me.

"Told you he wasn't fine," Riley said. They regarded me from the drafting table and Matt slapped some bills into Riley's hand.

"Andy needs her own office."

Riley and Matt launched into individual, simultaneous arguments, and while being on the receiving end of their annoyance was one of my least favorite things, it was far preferable to thinking about the fucked up situation I had with Andy.

Matt waved at the office. "We don't have room for—"

And her kneeling at my desk.

Riley interrupted, "If anyone gets a goddamn office around here, it's me—"

And her full lips, open and waiting.

Matt held up a hand, silencing Riley. "I don't know where you want that to come from, but unless we're redrawing—"

And the skin of her thighs underneath those thick stockings. I just knew it would be soft and smooth.

Riley pushed Matt's hand away. "I've put up with both of you assholes since May—"

And the sounds she'd make when I wrapped my hands around her hair and pulled.

"Shut. Up," I yelled. "One. If we cannot figure out how to find some space, we aren't nearly as good at this as we think. That's a problem. Figure it out and don't bother me with the details. Two. Deal with it, Riley. Andy is ten times more capable than you, and she's been here for two weeks. Three. I'm going to work here for a few hours, and unless you have a solution to our office space problem, we're not talking about this. Or anything else."

I dropped into a chair at Matt's conference table and opened my laptop, staring blindly at my email program while Matt and Riley exchanged loaded glances. I still wanted to apologize for the texts, but the thought of Andy on her knees blew my control to hell.

"Challenge accepted," Riley murmured.

He started rifling through the long, wide flat file drawers along the wall before producing the plans for our office. He gleefully paged through the plans and scribbled notes. His murmurs helped me focus on the major issues in my inbox, and the afternoon slipped into evening.

She departed for the day before I emerged from Matt's office. The rough slap of disappointment at my inability to draw Andy out lingered while I walked home. It was my own fault, I knew that, but I didn't know how to interpret or manage the frantic energy that spiraled through my veins in her presence.

Climbing the stairs to my apartment, it hit me. This all started with a text, so why not keep it going with a text? The distance allowed me to construct my thoughts without her tongue or her hair or her scent overwhelming my system.

Stowing my cold weather gear and quickly changing into fleece-lined sweats, a thermal t-shirt, and dry socks, I grabbed a beer and turned on the recording of Manchester United's game. I drafted several text messages before selecting the most straightforward.

Patrick: I was drunk last Friday night when I texted you. Was I an asshole?

It felt like an eternity before my phone signaled a response, but the timestamp indicated it was only minutes. Yet more evidence a padded cell was in my future.

Andy: No

I sighed and typed another message. When she responded quickly, I felt relief surging through my veins.

Patrick: Do you make a habit of offering to put drunks to bed?
Andy: No
Patrick: Just me?
Andy: Recently, yes
Patrick: I managed to put myself to bed that night
Andy: I heard

Slamming the phone down on the couch, I stalked across the living room and stared out the doors at the snow-covered deck and icicles hanging from the pergola. Her painfully concise responses were fucking infuriating.

Was my game so rusty that she couldn't decipher flirting when it was ringing in her hands? What I wouldn't do to spank her ass until it was hot and pink, and she was all mine.

Patrick: Am I bothering you?
Andy: No.
Patrick: You don't give me much
Andy: How much would you like me to give you?

Eyes wide, mouth open, I stared at the screen. I felt my heart thumping up my throat.

Patrick: More than you think you can
Andy: That seems like a lot of responsibility for you

Patrick: If you haven't noticed, taking on a lot of responsibility is my thing. It's either an incredible strength or massive weakness.
Andy: Let's go with strength
Patrick: Let's

Getting up for another beer, I kept my eyes glued to my phone in anticipation of her response. The ball was squarely in her court, and I wanted her to take the next step.

Andy: May I ask why you're texting me tonight?
Patrick: You can ask me anything, anytime
Patrick: I realized that we spend 60 hours a week together and only talk about work
Andy: I like talking about work with you.
Patrick: Me too
Andy: We talk about food. A lot.
Patrick: Ok, so work and food. but I don't know much about you even though we spend all this time together
Andy: That would require you to ask me questions
Patrick: I can do that
Andy: So then maybe you should ask me out for a drink.

I finally understood why footballers ripped off their shirts and hugged each other like long-lost twins when they scored a goal: that moment when everything aligned and you seized the opening to sink your shot was fucking amazing.

Patrick: I'd suggest tomorrow...but I know you have plans
Andy: And how do you know that?
Patrick: I noticed a text on your screen when you were going over the Capriossi designs

Andy: You're very observant

Patrick: I try.

Andy: Some people might see that as early stalking symptoms

Patrick: But not you?

Andy: No...I just know you're thorough

Patrick: I can be very, very thorough

Andy: Promise?

Patrick: Swear.

Andy: Ok stalker, what about that drink?

Patrick: I could ask you questions over a drink and fried clams in NH

Andy: I've seen plenty of NH and I could do without the clams

Patrick: You haven't had the right clams

Patrick: What if we talked about the possibility of clams?

Andy: I would be open to that

Patrick: I think everyone's going to 21st amendment. At 6 on Friday

Patrick: It's near the office

Andy: That sounds like asking questions with everyone

Patrick: Doesn't have to be

Andy: I'd rather be alone with you when you're asking me questions

Gulping, I gazed at her message and felt the joy of another shot hitting the net high and right.

Patrick: As would I but I know Matt believes it's his duty to formally welcome you to Boston and the firm. He sees himself as a goodwill ambassador or something these days

Andy: Yes. He does.

Patrick: It's his new thing

Andy: I'll have a drink with Matt. Then you can ask me questions

Patrick: If I'm getting you a drink, what am I ordering?

Andy: That depends on a number of factors

I started typing out my recollection of the beers on tap at Twenty-First Amendment with the hopes of collecting another morsel of Andy knowledge. On a sigh, I erased it all when it dawned on me her response wasn't necessarily related to the menu, and I was a loser who memorized that sort of shit.

Patrick: Factors?

Andy: Yes

Andy: I'll tell you Friday night

Patrick: You're not giving me much

Andy: I've given you quite a bit

Andy: Probably too much

Patrick: I don't think so

Andy: That's just it, Patrick

Andy: I get the sense that there will never be enough for you

CHAPTER TEN

More than you think you can.

More than you think you can.

Patrick's words echoed over the throbbing techno mix, leaving me elated and edgy. I couldn't shake them last night, and they lingered in the back of my thoughts. I spent most of the day distracted and a couple steps behind.

A glance at our table informed me that Jess and Marley were deep in discussion—some drama at the dentists' office where they worked as hygienists had them and a few of their co-workers fired up tonight.

A quick drink was all I signed up for, not a late night out. It was easier for them—their offices didn't open until nine, while I was checking out my third jobsite of the day by that time. I didn't have the endurance for weeknight partying anymore, and figuring out how to back away from their drinking and drama routine was growing more crucial.

I edged closer to the speakers to drown out my thoughts, dancing with my companion for the evening: a limey gimlet.

The songs started blurring together and my muscles loosened. The combined effects of vodka and dancing made everything a little more mellow, and I didn't protest the hands that landed on my hips.

"Your friends have terrible taste in bars," a voice—*Patrick's voice*—rasped against my ear, and I actually moaned in delight.

I didn't dare look over my shoulder. I wanted to know why he was here, how he found me, and what he wanted, but those questions were going to wait. I needed to enjoy the way we fit together first. He enveloped me, his body curling around mine, wrapping me in sinewy muscle. Long fingers mapped my pelvis, pressing and pulling with the rhythm.

"And you were wandering around Lansdowne Street on a Thursday night, looking for overpriced drinks?"

"Something like that," he murmured. "Those texts on your screen are hard to miss sometimes. And then you looked up the reviews for this place when we were stuck in traffic. I...I couldn't stay away. I should, but...here I am."

"I never told you to stay away."

"You shouldn't have to, Andy."

Patrick's lips brushed across the nape of my neck, and I hoped the music swallowed my guttural sigh. Or maybe I wanted him to hear, to know what he did to me. His fingers pried the glass from my hand and he studied the melting ice.

"My therapist," I murmured, glancing over my shoulder for the first time. I smiled at his wrinkled brow. "Vodka. She keeps me in line. Usually."

Patrick set the glass on a passing waiter's tray. With a flick of his wrist, he spun me around and reclaimed his place on my hips.

"Running a couple miles along the Charles usually does it

for me," he said, ducking to my ear. "But it doesn't seem like anything's working for us right now."

I shook my head. My eyes dropped to his lips and the pale freckles there. Where else would I find freckles? "There's always tequila."

"No," he whispered, threading his hands through my hair. "There's a much better solution."

Stretching up on my toes, I captured Patrick's lips as a growl rattled in his throat. It wasn't like other first kisses. There was no hesitation, no patient exploration. This was the deep end. He knew what he was doing, and it was clear he intended to teach me something.

A distant voice reminded me that he was my boss, and this type of lesson from Patrick meant our professional relationship —the same professional relationship I dreamt of for *years*—was changing forever.

"We shouldn't do this," I whispered, our mouths a breath apart.

"Yeah," Patrick murmured, his hands moving over my hair and down my back until he cupped my ass. His lips mapped my cheekbones and jaw, leaving a fevered trail in his wake while his hands urged my hips forward. "And the fact we lasted this long is a fucking victory."

He wasn't wrong.

The ridge of his erection connected with my belly, low—just a few inches away from where I needed it. My grip tightened on his sweater. Patrick's hand slipped under my shirt, his thumb coaxing my nipple to attention. Weeks of fantasizing about Patrick and flirty chatting over lunch did nothing to prepare me for his hands on my body and his lips on my mouth.

"Do you want me to stop?" He studied me, his expression

even despite the rapid rise and fall of his shoulders while he caught his breath.

He was giving me an exit. Swallowing thickly, I stared at a patch of freckles on his neck while I brainstormed a list of acceptable reasons to make out with my boss. It wasn't a long list —'because I want to' was the first entry, and 'because he wants to, too' was the last.

I shook my head and framed his face with my hands. "No. Don't stop."

I didn't know how long we stayed that way—maybe it was minutes, maybe it was an hour. Our bodies tangled while we moved with the pounding rhythm, our lips parting for frenzied moments before reconnecting.

"Andy? Oh, hey." Jess's hand squeezed my arm and tugged it away from Patrick's neck.

"Hey." Her coat was buttoned and her purse folded under her arm. "This is Patrick—"

"We're going." Jess's eyes moved over us, and she spared Patrick an irritable glance. "Now."

His hand rested in my back pocket, and was all the confirmation I needed. "You go ahead. I'm good."

Jess pinned me with a fierce look. "Can I talk to you?" She sneered at Patrick. "Privately?"

With great reluctance, I stepped out of Patrick's arms and followed Jess to the side door. Emergency exit lights illuminated the alcove, bathing us in red.

"Why are you being hostile?" I asked, my arms crossed over my chest.

"Um, I thought you were here to support me. I didn't think you were here to get skanky in a corner. I had a really bad day, and I needed you on my side. Obviously that was too much to ask of you."

"It looked like it was under control with Marley and your dental people—"

"Is that Patrick, your boss Patrick?" Jess interrupted. "The one you talk about all the time? The one who's really anal about stuff?"

"Same."

Jess recoiled from my words. "If it were me, I wouldn't be getting into shit like that right now. I wouldn't want to go through that again, even if he does look like sex on wheels. I certainly wouldn't be whoring it up."

I glanced back at Patrick, his hands propped on his hips, his eyes fixed on me. I didn't answer Jess, but she did get me thinking.

What was next? Did I invite him to my place, or me to his? Did we spend the night together then conduct business as usual in the morning?

Could it ever be that simple?

"Okay, you're going to do what you want anyway. You always do." Jess held up her hands. "Just tryin' to help. This has been a wicked bad day and I need to go home now, so whatever."

She stomped away, and I watched her go. I felt Patrick's eyes on me, and met his gaze. He approached, reaching out for my waist.

"I have an early morning," I said.

"Yeah. Me too."

I laughed at his wry smile. My hand wrapped around his wrist, bringing his watch into view. "And it's late."

He shrugged. "We should do this again. Maybe at a decent

bar, or a fish dive. I hear there are some great ones in New Hampshire."

"Maybe both."

———

I SLEPT FITFULLY WITH THE MEMORY OF PATRICK'S LIPS AND HIS hand under my shirt on heavy rotation in my dreams. Eventually, I surrendered to my insomnia with an unfocused hour of Pilates before sunrise.

I showered and dressed in black wool trousers, black Merino turtleneck sweater, and black leather boots that laced up to the knee. Even by Maine standards, the cold was brutal, and I piled on the layers before heading out.

I loved keeping my car in the Walsh garage and living within walking distance of the office, but these days made me long for door-to-door driving. Checking the time on my phone, I noticed a missed call from Patrick and played the voicemail.

"Hey Asani, pipes froze and burst overnight at Foster Street. It's a block away from my place so I got here as soon as the GC called. I need you to check on our other sites while I try to salvage the hardwood here," Patrick shouted over the rush of running water. "Call me with any floods."

I grabbed a few supplies and swapped out my outfit for flannel-lined jeans, two thermal shirts, and royal blue Wellies, and mentally cataloged our properties by pipe age. An 1806 farmhouse would require the lion's share of my attention.

The day flew by in a blur of cold and wet. The subzero overnight temperatures froze delicate plumbing systems all over town, and while the majority of our jobsites suffered no damage,

I spent my day aiming a hair dryer at old pipes in cold, wet basements to keep them damage-free. I lost contact with my toes a little before noon.

Patrick and I exchanged a few brief texts during the day to update each other, but I couldn't get a read on his mood. I wanted him to remind me about drinks tonight, make another attempt at a road trip to New Hampshire, or suggest we finish what we started last night.

It meant arriving at the bar after seven, but stopping at home to change into dry clothes was a necessity. Thick socks and lace-up boots took the edge off the bone-deep chills, and I hoped Patrick was interested in warming up the rest of me.

It wasn't hard to find the Walsh table, especially considering a chorus of voices that yelled "Andy" the minute I stepped through the door. If nothing else, Shannon's hair was a bright beacon drawing me to the back corner. I quickly inventoried the table—Shannon, Matt, Lauren, Sam, Riley, Tom, and someone I didn't recognize next to Shannon and Matt.

A flare of disappointment hit me—no Patrick. He was probably tied up with his share of issues. I fixed a smile on my face and headed for the table.

"Hey, girl," Lauren yelled, standing to welcome me with a hug. "Good to see you."

"Any more water damage?" Matt asked.

Riley and Sam sat across from Matt at the table, their heads bent in conversation. Riley shared the same dark hair and slate blue eyes as Matt, though Sam was leaner with a lighter complexion and Patrick's auburn hair. There was no doubting they shared a bloodline.

Lauren gestured to an empty seat facing away from the door

between Sam and the stranger with thick, tousled dark hair. "Some leaks, thankfully no floods. I did some intensive pipe triage to keep it that way."

"What can I get you?" the waitress asked over my shoulder.

"Shiraz. Whatever the house bottle is," I replied. "Any news on Foster?"

Matt nodded slowly, and my attention turned to Lauren's hand on his knee. He layered his hand over hers, his thumb brushing across the ring on her finger as he spoke about the flooding and restoration efforts. The gesture was simple but said so much. The love between them was palpable, and I got the distinct impression they were an eye-blink away from climbing all over each other.

"Hello," the stranger said, angling his head to face me. I noted a slight southern accent.

"I'm the worst," Shannon groaned. "Sorry. Andy, this is..." She scowled at him. "What are you? This is Nick Acevedo, and he's the guy who hangs around with Matt. It's kind of a problem, actually. He's a level five clinger, so definitely don't pay any attention to him or you'll never get rid of him. Nick, this is Andy Asani, and she puts up with Patrick."

"The next time you think your headache is a brain tumor, don't call me, Shannon," Nick drawled with a laugh. "It's good to meet you, Andy."

I shook his hand, soon releasing it to accept my drink. He started to speak again, but Sam pivoted and draped his arm over the back of my chair.

"I tried that Night Walker juice. With the beets and kale and jalapeño?"

"And?" A smirk tugged at my lips. Few possessed the constitution of will necessary to drink raw beet juice.

Sam laughed and patted his stomach. "And it put a little hair on my chest. How can you drink that?"

"You get used to it. Once you're off processed sugar, it is fantastic." I shrugged. "It gives me a ton of energy."

"Don't get him started on banning more foods," Shannon yelled down the table. "He only eats spinach and seaweed as it is, and he's a little more than borderline OCD about it."

Sam rolled his eyes. "I haven't touched processed anything in years, and I still gagged. It looks like blood," he laughed. "The subcontractors gave me some strange looks when I rolled up with a bottle full of dark red juice."

"They give you strange looks regardless."

A tingle ran down my spine when Patrick's voice boomed over my shoulder. I smiled when he jabbed his brother's arm, knocking Sam's hand from my chair and dragging his fingers between my shoulder blades.

It felt lusciously possessive and I was perfectly fine with a little possession. I sipped my wine, waiting until he pulled a chair between Nick and me to meet his gaze.

"Hi." His voice was low and eyes sparkling with an uncharacteristically warm twinkle. Such a wonderful departure from the irritable scowl.

"Hi." I waited for him to reply, lifting an eyebrow while he stared at me.

"If not the Night Walker juice, what do you drink every day?" Sam asked, oblivious to the silent conversation spoken between Patrick and me. "Or do you only juice occasionally?"

I held Patrick's gaze another beat before shifting back to Sam and our discussion of pressed juices—another one of my random hobbies. Our conversation soon shifted to several other unconventional interests—part-time vegan eating and power yoga and arguing the fidelity of *The Lord of the Rings* movies to the books—and I discovered a mountain of things Sam and I had in common.

Around us, Matt, Lauren, and Nick were pumping Riley for information about the woman he was seeing, while Patrick stayed quiet.

I noticed him nursing a beer and I felt his eyes on me. It wasn't enough for Patrick to spend the majority of his time staring at me as if he were inspecting every thought in my head —he stared with an intensity I expected to leave singe marks on my skin.

"Try a mix of raw local honey, cinnamon, and apple cider vinegar," I said. "That always clears up my sore throats. Honey is my go-to."

"I will," Sam murmured, sending himself an email with the proportions.

"We need to do this more often," Shannon said while Matt stood to help Lauren into her coat. "It's like I never see you people unless it's Monday morning."

"That might not be a bad thing," Riley muttered under his breath.

"We're headed out for sushi, and we're heavy one Texan so a few more won't hurt if anyone wants to come along." Matt glanced around the table.

Sam and Riley joined the sushi group, and Tom departed after I declined his offer of more drinks elsewhere. Following a round of goodbyes, I was left with Shannon and Patrick. She slid down the bench to sit across from me, and Patrick angled his seat between us before glowering at his sister.

"You love Oishii."

"I do," she admitted, rubbing the bridge of her nose. "But I saw Mackay and Brewster from the Planning Board walk in and I owe them a drink. Or nine. And I went out with the general manager at Oishii and..." She held up her hands and shrugged.

"You're racking up a long list of spots where you're *persona non grata*," he said.

Under the table, his knee brushed against my thigh and my skin reacted with a series of tiny sizzling shivers. I liked him pressing against me. I shifted my leg to slide against his knee in encouragement, and concealed my smile with a sip of wine when he cleared his throat.

From the sound of it, he liked me pressing against him, too.

"You're going to have to move to Vermont soon. Start corrupting the shepherds."

"Fuck you." Draining her beer, she narrowed her eyes at Patrick. "Did you get out to Wellesley?"

Patrick turned his head toward me and rolled his eyes, his knee pressing more firmly against my thigh. I shifted, the spiked heel of my boot rasping against his jean-clad leg. His muscles tensed under my touch when the leather passed over his shin and around his ankle.

"No, Shannon, not this week."

"Why the hell not?"

"I spent the day knee-deep in literally freezing water." He consulted his phone before slipping it into his pocket and dropping his hand to his leg. Pointing at Shannon with his beer bottle, he continued, "I'll get to Wellesley when I get a chance."

"If you don't have time, you shouldn't have volunteered." She glanced to me. "Andy, make sure he gets to the Wellesley site next week. It requires Patrick's immediate attention."

"No, it doesn't."

"And what if the pipes burst there?" she demanded.

"Then we tear that motherfucker down like we should have in the first place."

Under the table, his palm covered my knee and my decision to wear pants instead of a skirt turned into a serious regret—living out fantasies trumped frostbite any day of the week. I nibbled the inside of my cheek to keep my expression mild while his hand warmed me through the denim and his thumb brushed across my thigh.

"What's the story with Nick?" I asked.

Patrick cleared his throat and aimed a critical gaze at me, his hand clamping down on my leg. "Marathon training friend of Matt's. Brain surgeon at Mass Gen. Texan. Matt and Lauren's official third wheel. I hear they've met Nick's parents."

"And hotter than Houston in July," Shannon said. "I've wanted to get my teeth on his ass since Christ was a cowboy."

"Really?" Patrick asked.

"Oh yes. Yes. He's not into me, not at all, and it's not from my lack of effort. Are you interested?"

Patrick's stare could have cut glass, and his grip on my leg tightened. "No," I said. "Just curious."

Shannon consulted her watch. "All right. I'm dragging these Planning Board boys to Last Hurrah. Time to grease some wheels."

She talked to herself while she collected her things, and Patrick's hand inched above my knee. I shifted, increasing the pressure against his leg. He squeezed in response. Five more minutes of soundless pressing and squeezing, and I'd have a blazing orgasm in the middle of the bar. My gaze boring into Shannon, I silently begged her to hurry the hell up.

"And don't forget, Patrick," she called over her shoulder. "You're picking up the tab."

Patrick watched Shannon for several minutes, his hand alternately stroking and squeezing my thigh. Not wanting to turn around to follow his stare, I responded to texts from Jess and Marley inquiring about my plans for the evening. Jess was over her snit from last night, and she wanted me to join them at a new club, but there was a hand on my knee and I intended to keep it that way.

"You seem to have a lot in common with my brother," he commented.

"Sam? Yeah, I'd say that's accurate."

Patrick gestured for another beer and kept his eyes trained on the crowd. "Maybe you'd rather have drinks with him. Or Nick."

"If I wanted to be somewhere else, I would be. I don't think I need your permission for that."

"What factors led to...cabernet? Pinot noir?" He lifted the glass and sipped my wine.

The intimacy of his gesture floored me. I felt my chest compress and my breathing quicken. Slanting a glimpse at Patrick, I finished a message to Jess inviting them to yoga with me on Saturday. His gaze wrapped around me, intense and unyielding. "Shiraz."

Patrick balanced an elbow on the table, his fingers tightening on my leg as he leaned in. "When I say you don't give me much, this is what I'm talking about."

"What would you like me to give you?"

"Everything." He laughed when I lifted an eyebrow, and glanced at my glass. "But let's start small. What led to shiraz?"

"I think of red wine as my rabbi." It felt exceptionally

dangerous to invite Patrick into my unfiltered thoughts—a place where I allowed so few to tread.

"I can see that," he murmured. "Spent the day praying over pipes, too?"

"Yeah," I answered, shocked he understood. He reached under the table, dragged my chair to face him and angled my legs between his. Everything around us faded away. We were in our own bubble, just like my fantasy.

And goddammit, I should have worn a skirt.

"What do you think about minimalistic modern?"

"You want to talk about minimalistic modern?" he asked, his brow furrowed and his lips curling into a smirk. "Aren't I supposed to be asking you questions?"

"Yes, but I want to know what you think about minimalistic modern," I laughed. "I've spent some time hypothesizing about your preferences."

"What else have you hypothesized about?" That quiet, rough tone did awful things to me. If he asked me to caulk his tub with that voice, I'd eagerly do it.

"Lots of things. I've been hypothesizing about you for a long time," I said with a shrug. "Especially about this minimalistic modern thing."

"Sounds like a lot of thinking when you could have asked sooner. Maybe we both ought to ask more questions," he suggested, his hand running through his hair. "I'm not coming out against it or saying it needs to die like McMansions do, but it isn't my preference."

"What is your preference?"

He hesitated, and I pushed my knee against his inner thigh. "I like what we do," he replied simply, his hands planted on my thighs. "I like preserving things from the past, and making them better, more efficient. And I don't mind some modern and maybe some minimalist on the inside, but not too much."

"I like what we do, too," I said. "I want your honest opinion of preservation legislation."

We drank—I saw how the Walsh boys could put liquor out of business—and talked for nearly three hours—all architecture and design. It was better than the fantasy, even without an under-the-table orgasm.

Being with Patrick wasn't what I expected. He was always intense and serious, but he was funny and sweet, too. It was easy. His big hands warm on my legs certainly didn't hurt.

"Can we talk about other things now?" Patrick asked, his voice husky and low. I would caulk the shit out of that tub.

We stared at each other for a few long moments, and I studied the freckles riding along his nose and cheeks, noting a few on his eyelids. Some were dark and others were light, and they were both adorable and masculine. I wanted to taste each of those freckles, and I leaned forward.

"Like what?" I asked, my eyes fixed on his lips.

"Like you coming to New Hampshire with me," he whispered, his fingertips rubbing over my knuckles. "Preferably this weekend."

Laughing, I sat back. In my book, traditional New England seafood ranked right above fried grasshoppers popular in the Oaxaca region of Mexico, but husky and low were persuasive, and I surrendered. "Maybe." When his eyes brightened, I pushed his hands off my legs. "I'll be right back."

I walked through the bar in search of the restrooms with his eyes trained on my back, marking me with hot, prickling sensations. I needed a reprieve from Patrick's gaze, his touch. I needed to think. Was it escaping anyone's notice that we shouldn't keep this up because it was rapidly spiraling far beyond flirtation? Did he think we'd have some fried fish and a quick fling and go about our business?

But I didn't want to think about those questions, the consequences, the rights or the wrongs. I didn't care about anything beyond feeling his hands on me again. Exiting the restroom, I barreled straight into a wall of hot, solid Patrick and my wish was granted.

"Get over here," he growled, his hands clamping around my biceps and dragging me against his body. His hands skimmed up my arms and over my shoulders to tangle in my hair. He walked me backwards into the restroom until I leaned against the wall, his eyes focused on my lips.

Patrick's head dipped, and I fisted my hands in his shirt as his lips connected with mine. He was hesitant for a split second, but when I angled my neck back, he devoured me. He kissed as if it was an Olympic sport and he was the defending gold medalist.

Patrick caught my tongue between his teeth, and I squealed at the tiny bite. His touch was urgent, his fingers digging into my skin and communicating every ounce of his desire. My hands went to his neck, and I felt every string of his restraint pulled tight.

He was holding back.

He was holding back while his all-consuming presence obliterated me. Nothing compared to Patrick, and with the bitter flavor of beer lingering on his tongue, the pressure of his fingers on the seat of my jeans, the way he canted my hips to connect with his erection confirmed my initial designation of him as Sex

God. Only his grip on my ass prevented me from sliding to the floor with a kiss-drunk grin.

Somewhere outside our heated embrace someone suggested we get a room, and I started estimating how quickly I could get him back to my apartment. Minutes. Probably less than ten.

His kisses slowed, and I sighed when his mouth traversed my cheekbones. His lips were phenomenal, and as I gained the strength and presence of mind to tell him, his teeth scraped across my earlobe. The sensation erased all thought—everything stored in my brain was gone, and I doubted it would ever return if more earlobe scraping was in my future—and my body pitched forward, my arms tightening around his neck.

"Does this change anything?" he murmured, his mouth brushing against the shell of my ear.

He pressed his face against my hair, inhaling deeply. I wanted to know the right answer but all of them were tinted with shades of wrong. I wanted Patrick just like this, but I also wanted Patrick the craftsman, Patrick the mentor, Patrick the visionary. I shook my head. "No."

"What? No?" He pulled back, studying me while the fog of arousal cleared from my eyes. "No? How—why?"

When I didn't respond, he kissed me again but he was completely different—soft, restricted, tentative. No longer demanding or instructive, Patrick was retrieving the emotions his kisses communicated, shutting down under my hands. The fire in his eyes cooled to embers and his hands slid from my backside to rest on my elbows—the least sexy part of any body and a clear indication he intended to let me off and not get me off.

"You're right. We shouldn't...I don't know what I was thinking."

He turned and walked out of sight while I leaned against the wall in a poorly lit bathroom. My feet weren't ready to carry me forward, and my brain was still obsessing over that earlobe scrape—it wasn't ready to assess the whining, achy desire pooled between my thighs or the turn of events that extricated Patrick's hands from my body.

CHAPTER ELEVEN

PATRICK

THE CEILING FAN ABOVE MY BED WAS AN EVIL BITCH.

She saw everything: the tossing and turning, the suffocating regret, the unsatisfying self-gratification, the dreams that bordered on nightmares because they existed just out of my reach. She saw it all, and kept right on spinning and staring as if she decided my turmoil wasn't worth her time.

Or maybe I was a delusional bastard.

Why did Andy have to feel so good against me? Couldn't it have been awkward and bland? Couldn't we have just laughed about our ridiculous, misplaced attraction and my occasionally stalkerish behavior?

No. No, no, *fuck* no.

She had to taste like tart cherries and her body had to be as taut as I imagined. If that annoying friend of hers hadn't dragged her away, I would have taken Andy home with me and it wouldn't have been to watch *Top Chef*. If I hadn't been a giant idiot, and left her swollen lips and flushed cheeks in that bathroom, well...I was giant idiot.

Fuck my life.

Even if getting my hands on her body wasn't a sneak preview of heaven itself, the smart, witty conversation with Andy rivaled the best of my life. She thought about architecture in such a passionate manner I couldn't help getting lost. If restlessness hadn't ejected me from my seat and sent me in search of Andy, we would have talked through last call.

I kept reliving the moment when her façade melted. I saw her, really saw her, with aroused vulnerability in her eyes, her fingers clawing and begging for more contact, her disheveled breathlessness.

I spent more time replaying those memories, while simultaneously cursing myself for leaving the most complex, alluring woman I ever touched, than was healthy.

She said it changed nothing, and that sounded like a tray full of glasses hitting the floor, each crash louder and more jarring. Though I knew blurring the lines with Andy was quite possibly the riskiest move I could make, I wasn't interested in a quick fuck in a bar bathroom. Touching her, kissing her—it changed things.

It changed everything. At least for me.

Somewhere in that bathroom I found it in me to walk away because she wasn't giving me exactly what I wanted. And that was it: she never gave me quite enough.

It was my own personal Bermuda Triangle.

I spent the week breathing fire and raising new sorts of hell.

I threatened to block new projects until someone discovered more office space. I took on Shannon during the Monday meeting, and found new ways to dig myself deeper in that pit each day. Marisa—or was it Melissa?—the newest in a long line of short-term solutions and hiring errors, quit when I kicked the habitually jammed copier and requested she get a technician to replace it by end of day.

Naturally, Shannon and I went a few rounds about my inability to keep an assistant for more than two months, and she refused to find a new one until I handled my alleged rage issues.

Through it all, Andy regarded me with the same unaffected calm that made me want to bind her wrists and ankles to my bed and lick her until her eyes rolled back in her head and the "hm" was nowhere to be found.

She was completely cool and impassive, and while I didn't expect anything less from Andy, a small part of me wanted to see her flailing in the sea of awkward formality that developed between us.

In a moment of supreme weakness, I started stalking her Facebook and Instagram pages to fill my sleepless nights. It was a special variety of punishment, and I resented Andy for leaving her privacy settings open. As if she wanted me to suffer.

I scrolled through years of photos, fully expecting to find things I didn't want to see. There were the obligatory girl group line-ups before a night of partying, rueful commentary attached to pictures of epic Ithaca snow banks, several happy years of Cornell's Slope Day festivities, and I counted at least six different guys in various forms of embrace with Andy. I noted, with some disdain, they reminded me of Mumford and Sons: all hipsters who represented a broad spectrum of beardedness, favored plaid, and were in the range of seven to ten years younger than me.

I was also pretending my recent shaving hiatus was related to the obscenely cold weather rather than a fucked up attempt at gaining her attention.

She went to the Bonnaroo music festival in Tennessee last

spring, and wore a few scraps of fabric meeting the loosest criteria of a bikini.

As if I could pretend I didn't see that.

Her most recent Instagram post was from one our properties on demo day, and captured a sledgehammer as it connected with a wall. The caption read, "hammer time" and like the deranged fool I was becoming, I laughed hysterically when I saw it.

She traveled extensively during her school breaks, and filled entire Facebook albums with photos of architecture and food from all over the world. By Thursday, I was itching to ask about her travels, but I didn't want to reveal my creeptastic tendencies.

"Didn't peg you for a matzo ball soup guy," she said, pointing at my bowl with her spoon. "I learn something new about you every day, Patrick."

"Really?" I asked, glancing across the table. "What did you learn yesterday?"

She sat back in her seat and crossed her arms. "You hate traffic circles."

"You're in Boston, Asani. They're called rotaries. And they're only acceptable when traveling by horseback, and even then, I bet they were a pain in the ass. And everyone hates them."

"Okay," she said. "I know you refuse to accept *Top Chef's* awesomeness because you can't try the food, and I know you like fish dives."

"You would like them too, if you gave them a chance." It was rocky territory, but I continued, "Offer still stands. And no, I'm not getting into another *Top Chef* argument with you right now."

She spooned a bite of vegetarian lentil soup into her mouth while staring out at Sullivan Square. After a long pause, she said, "Maybe."

I rolled my shoulders and studied my soup, waiting for the flare of adrenaline in my system to slow. "Maybe you'll consider the possibility that fish dives aren't terrible, or maybe you'll take a ride with me this weekend and actually try one?"

Andy leveled an even gaze in my direction, an eyebrow lifted subtly as if she knew exactly how much her prolonged silence tortured me.

She knew. She knew, and she liked it.

"Maybe I'll go with you. But I reserve the right to eat nothing, criticize everything, and drink a lot of beer."

I always knew the serious, composed woman working beside me each day was only one iteration of Andy Asani, and along the way, getting past her poised veneer turned into another one of my missions. It also seriously threatened my mental health.

"That's exactly what I had in mind."

Just book the padded cell for me now.

WE WERE IN AN ODD LULL WITH MANY OF OUR PROJECTS, AND Friday was miraculously free from site visits that would put us side-by-side in the car all day. It was no surprise to find Andy seated at the drafting table when I arrived, her long legs tangled around the stool like dark, sexy vines.

We exchanged silent pleasantries, and I knew enough about Andy's concentration to know she needed quiet. I admired her preference to go all in when she was designing on paper, shutting everything else out and allowing her instincts to guide her. It was tempting to offer constructive criticism while she worked but my obsession was too deep, and I couldn't focus on the lines without wanting to touch her.

And kiss her.

And breathe in her scent.

And feel her body against mine.

I stayed away, promising myself I would get my Andy fix over the weekend, and as usual, email beckoned. An hour passed before putting a sizable dent in my inbox. Andy was lost in her focus, and didn't notice when Matt's chime sounded on my phone.

Matt: Widow, incoming.
Matt: She's locked and loaded.
Matt: Bunker down.

Glancing up, I saw Shannon's hair flashing in the doorframe. "You haven't been to Wellesley."

Shannon stormed into my office, slamming the door behind her. Andy roused from her headspace but kept her eyes on the table. Though I knew she heard most everything, Andy excelled at seeming to ignore the endless stream of visitors into my office.

"Good morning, Shannon. It's nice to see you too," I replied.

"If you're not going out to Wellesley today, I'm going," Shannon said. "But I've looked at your calendar, and you have time. I'm scheduled to meet with our accountants to make sure everyone gets paid on time. Would you rather I do that, or go to Wellesley?"

"Fine." I closed my laptop and tucked it into my messenger bag. "I'll go."

"Take Andy. I don't want you going alone in case there is a pack of pit bulls, or something."

"Right. Better for us both to be attacked by the pit bulls." Andy looked up, our eyes met, and I shrugged.

"I hear pit bulls can be quite friendly," she offered, shrugging in return. "All depends on the upbringing. My mentor at Cornell, Charlotte, used to foster pit bulls and none of them killed her. A few attacks, maybe, but she's alive."

Andy delivered with the sardonic banter. Every time. Her dry wit ran to the bone. It came through in our lunchtime chats and long discussion of all things architectural at the bar, and her social media posts commenting on pop culture, politics, and mundane things offered a covert glimpse.

"Exactly. These would be the worst pit bulls imaginable."

"No," Shannon replied, drawing the word out. "You can go in, fight off the pit bulls, and Andy can call 911 from the car if you lose a leg. Andy, we'd like to keep. You, we can do without." She pointed her finger at me. "Do it today, and don't think you can be all disgruntled later and skip the party."

Shit. The party.

"Fine," I repeated. "Anything else, Shannon?"

She crossed her arms over her chest, her lips pursed as if she was holding back on the stinging commentary.

Lifting her chin in challenge, she replied, "Yes. A plan for a two hundred and fifty thousand dollar rehab with milestones, materials, and approved subcontractors."

She exited, the door slamming behind her. I hated fighting with my best friend, and though Shannon and I never carried an argument for more than a couple of days, I knew she was capable of completely shutting me out if I pushed the wrong way at the wrong time. If her years-long feud with Erin was any indication, Shannon was ruthless when it came to holding grudges.

The thirty-minute drive was quiet while Andy flipped through her notebook and I tried to remember my last visit to

Eastern Pond Road. It was probably around the time Angus kicked Erin out, and that was seven or eight years ago, maybe more, and it wasn't a pleasant visit.

The memory of him leaning out her bedroom window, tossing books and clothes to the lawn while raging about our mother screwing every man in town and winding up pregnant was hard to forget. Erin sobbed on the porch steps while he screamed unimaginably horrible things about our sweet little mother, the mother she didn't know long enough to remember. Forever the peacemaker, Matt eventually convinced Angus to leave Erin's room, enticing him with a fresh bottle of scotch and the promise that Erin was leaving.

Erin cried herself to sleep on Shannon's bed that night. Matt, Shannon, and I figured out how we'd collectively care for a teenager while struggling to get the business off the ground.

Stopping at the rusty wrought iron gates, I leaned over the steering wheel, taking in the rambling expanse of land.

"We're looking for dogs?"

"It's a mystery," I murmured, and rolled down the window to enter the access code. The gates moaned and creaked when they swung wide, and I bit back a groan as I drove up the winding driveway.

"Oh my God," Andy whispered when I pulled to a stop in front of the house. "That's an 1880s Arts and Crafts. These are incredible."

A quick scan of the property told me Angus kept a landscaper on the payroll, and part of the chimney looked new. Of course. It was all about the façade. Appearances were the only things that truly mattered to Angus.

I was more than a little relieved angry dogs were not descending upon us. That, of course, left rusty nails, burned baby pictures, and bottle caps, but I could handle those. It was the energy radiating off the property, the lingering sadness speaking volumes about the sorrows the house knew, that I wasn't prepared to handle.

"I love this style," she breathed, running her hand over the stone wall surrounding the front porch. "This is a rehab? Do we have any other information?"

The scent of lemon cleaning products slammed into me when I stepped through the front door. Andy was busy caressing the bench carved into the side of the staircase, and didn't notice me wander through the sparsely furnished living room and dining room.

For a house receiving only basic maintenance over the past two decades, it wasn't in bad shape. Trees growing through the windows and raccoons nesting in the pantry were my worst case, yet likely, scenario. We could thank the housekeeper for not only finding Angus after his stroke but also keeping the flora and fauna at bay.

Staring out the family room windows at the blue slate patio, garden, and pool, I searched for good memories. They were there, in the far back, and most of them were tainted with the knowledge my mother would die before my eleventh birthday and Angus was a miserable bastard who would ruin everything good and pure that we knew.

"I walked every room and captured some rough dimensions," Andy announced as she approached the wall of windows. I stared at her, startled that my thoughts led me far enough astray for Andy to study the entire house. Examining six thousand square feet over three floors plus a basement meant I spent more than an hour in my own head. "This place is incredible. Lots of dated energy systems but—"

"Any evidence of water damage?" I interrupted. "Or animals?"

"No water, no woodland creatures. I checked all the crawl spaces."

"Good," I murmured. "What are you thinking? Walk me through your plan. Start with fundamentals and then go through preservation."

She paused, her brow furrowed as she paged through her notebook. "I'm thinking a lot of things. This place has amazing bones, but...what's the story? Is this a client property or an investment property? It's almost completely empty, but it looks like someone still lives here."

"It's a little of both," I replied.

"Hm. Well...I'd start with energy systems, then deal with exterior—"

"Actually, no. I don't want to hear this." Turning, I retreated to the library, my fingers skating along the built-in bookcase until I found the lever. Pressing down, the structure glided away from the wall, revealing a narrow set of stairs. The wine cellar held a few dusty bottles and a small colony of spider webs, and the best look at the foundation.

A flashlight landed in my palm before I could ask, and I scanned the foundation for cracks and leaks. "Thank you. Budget of two-fifty, focus on shoring up the structure and systems as needed. Turn it green. Draw it up and get started. Keep me out of it unless you hit a wall. And do not mention anything about this to Sam."

"Hm."

I squatted to study a dark corner while Andy walked through the hidden rooms. I wanted to find a major foundation issue, anything that would give me the green light to level the property, sell the land, and never come here again.

"Patrick?" she called. When I found her, she was inside a small root cellar, and her focus was on the door where our ages and heights were recorded each year on our birthdays. "Where are we?"

I glanced at Erin's name, and the short increments marking her height. It stopped after her second birthday, and I immediately remembered her bobbling around as a chubby baby, wailing for mama every single night for months after my mother died. We took turns holding her, walking her, singing to her, making bottles. None of it worked. Eventually, she started falling asleep with Shannon and refused to get into bed unless Shannon was right there with her.

My stomach twisted. I didn't want to think about the past. The lost childhoods. Angus's drunkenness and gambling and rage. I didn't want the memories of Sam's hysterical screams when the paramedics tore him off my mother's lifeless body. I didn't want to remember making the call to 911 or how long it took me to wash away all that blood.

The first towel soaked all the way through until I couldn't see any white, just red, so much red. Then the second. Then the third. I piled six towels in the bathtub that night.

It stained the wood and spilled into the crevices between the planks. Smaller puddles marked the path from the bed to the bathroom, and to the place where she collapsed. Handprints lined the sink and walls.

The bleach burned my eyes but I didn't know what else to use in my quest to put things back in order. My mother would have scrubbed on her hands and knees until it was clean, and she wouldn't have wanted people seeing her blood spilled all over the bedroom. She was proud and private, with her stiff Irish upper lip, and that wasn't what she would have wanted.

Blood covered my clothes, my arms, and my legs. My aunts Mae and Carole were busy making arrangements. That's what they called it, as if my mother was planning a trip to Fort Lauderdale.

They stayed away from the bedroom. They knew what happened in there but they didn't want to see it. No one saw me in my mother's bathroom, surrounded by her oatmeal soaps and flowery perfume, with her blood all around me.

I should have checked on my brothers and sisters but I knew they were safe in the nursery with Shannon. She knew what to do. She always did.

The water was too hot but I didn't feel it, not really. I focused on the pink water sluicing off my body. In the shower, it looked harmless.

The stained bedding and towels went into thick black garbage bags, along with my clothes. It was late when I brought the bags to the latticed enclosure behind the garage, probably after midnight. No one noticed me or the oversized bags.

When I closed the lid on the dented metal barrel, I sat in the dirt and cried. The panic, horror, pain, confusion—they took over for the first time since finding Mom on the floor. They won, and I cried it all out. Hiccupping, hyperventilating, and eventually vomiting, I left it all in the shed.

That was the last time I cried, if we ignore the incident where I ran a jigsaw across my thigh. I left my childhood in those barrels with the bloodied towels.

I found an oval rug in the den and moved it into the bedroom, covering the planks discolored from blood and bleach. No one asked where it came from or why it was there. They never asked where the bedding went, or who cleaned the blood.

But the reminder was always right there. Everyone knew and no one wanted to talk about it. It was easier that way.

Shannon took care of my brothers and sisters, and I took care of everything else. And that hadn't changed in over two decades.

Andy's hand passing vigorously between my shoulder blades jerked me out of my memories and I turned to face her. Her eyes crinkled in concern, and she didn't stop rubbing my shoulders. "Patrick?"

And this is why I don't come here, I reminded myself. This is why I can't live in the past.

Exhaling, I stared at the door. "I grew up here."

She was doing it on purpose, and of that, I could be certain. She was trying to kill me, and damned near succeeding.

Why else would Andy wear jeans resembling a second skin, a long, slim black v-neck sweater, and knee-high boots straight out of Catwoman's closet? And that hair. God help me, that hair. It was always the same style, with an abundance of thick raven curls tumbling over her shoulders and midway down her back, but it hit me like a fist to the gut. Something about that hair begged to be pulled, then written into fables.

"Is there something preventing you from interacting with all humans, or just me in particular?" Sam asked.

I glanced at him before refocusing my attention over his shoulder to where Andy leaned next to Shannon's dining room table. She was talking with Tom, offering bright smiles and nodding eagerly, and he seemed to be describing something she found fascinating. Probably his willingness to grow a wiry beard and go to music festivals.

In the two hours since her arrival at Shannon's apartment, she spent all of her time close enough for me to see her yet far enough away that I couldn't eavesdrop. She also spent her time talking with every unattached guy at the party, starting with Nick, who seemed to have substantially more time outside the operating room these days, a few lawyer friends of Shannon's, a skinny marathon friend of Matt's, and now Tom.

It was fucking excruciating.

"All humans," I said, gulping the Newcastle in my hand.

"Right," Sam murmured. "That is splendid news, Patrick. I'm not sure where you get the idea that it's appropriate to be an asshole to people. Running around the office like an angry bear isn't kosher. If possible, I'd recommend you pry your head from your ass this weekend. This is getting old."

Sam stepped away and joined a conversation about an upcoming trip to Arizona to see some spring training games, and I continued my covert study of Andy.

I was tired from a week of sleepless nights, wrung out from the morning at Wellesley, and teetering on the edge of sanity after watching a handful of guys hit on Andy, but I wasn't leaving until she was. If she decided to leave with one of them, I wanted to see it.

Shannon edged next to me on the window seat and wordlessly watched the party. I knew she was reaching out for a truce, and she was waiting for me to make the first peace offering.

That was how it worked: one of us fucked up, the other spent an irrational amount of time pissed off about it, and then we talked around the original fuck-up. The Walshes weren't especially familiar with the words "I'm sorry."

"Wellesley was in good shape," I started, receiving a quick nod from Shannon. "No dogs, either, but let's get real. Andy probably would have whipped them into shape within five minutes while I hid in the backseat. She's working on the proposal."

"I like her a lot. She's good for you, really good. She's good for us," Shannon said, her eyes still focused on her guests. "Is there anything left?"

Tilting my beer back, I drank it down in slow sips. She already knew the answer; she was hoping to hear something different. "No. Some furniture. His closet. Everything else..."

"Yeah," she sighed, swallowing loudly. "Let's not bring that up to anyone else for the time being. Or maybe we don't say anything at all, and they figure it out."

I knew she wanted a thread of redemption for Angus. As much as I wanted it too, redemption never interested Angus, and it never mattered to him that he destroyed our history when he purged the house. With the exception of a few closely guarded snapshots, there were no pictures of us as kids and no evidence of my mother.

Minutes passed before Shannon turned to look at me. "Okay, so now that the heavy shit is out of the way, what the hell happened to you this week? Marisa? Office space? Monday's meeting? Do you actually doubt my investment strategy, or are you a massive dickhead?"

"Massive dickhead." I studied Andy's movements as she spoke to Tom, following her precise gestures and eager nods that encouraged him to continue speaking. He was definitely growing a beard for her, and chances were high that he'd be Instragramming photos of oddly shaped radishes at Whole Foods by Monday.

"I'd rather not hire another assistant, considering the past five have walked out claiming PTSD. I mean, seriously, dude. I don't have time for that shit. Do you think I sit around all day looking for combat-tested personal assistants?"

"I know, I know," I sighed. Andy was sipping a mixed drink, and the desire to find out what it was and hear all about the factors leading to that decision struck me. "Maybe I don't need an assistant. Andy's running a lot of projects now. I need someone to handle my calls and calendar. And manage my expenses."

"Maybe Tom can—"

"No," I interrupted. By my watch, Tom had five minutes before I was firing him and his beard. "I...I think Tom's busy enough with you. Maybe Theresa can help."

"Sure," Shannon said. "She handled Angus, after all, and Matt's a field of daisies in comparison. But you have to know—she doesn't take any shit."

"Yeah, that's because she knows what she's doing. She wouldn't have let that copier jam for four days, and she wouldn't have let me try to take it apart. She's the only reason Angus wasn't a homeless bum."

"All right," Shannon said, indicating the conversation was over. "I'll handle it Monday. But if anyone else walks out because you're a massive dickhead, I cannot be held accountable for my reactions, and my reactions will involve taking off my shoes and beating you with them."

She nodded and walked away from the window seat, leaving me to continue watching Andy. After fetching a fresh beer from the refrigerator, I returned to see Tom leaving the apartment alone. The thrill of getting him out of the picture was short lived when I realized I didn't see Andy, and without much consideration for what I intended to do, I went looking for her. Shannon's home office and guest bedroom were both dark and vacant.

Back in the hall, I stared at the closed door to Shannon's bedroom. She didn't like me going in her space as a kid, and I sincerely doubted she would be happy to find me there now. As I weighed my desire to locate Andy against my fear of Shannon and her sharp heels, a hand shot out from the bathroom, hooked my elbow, and dragged me inside.

"You've been staring at me for two hours." Andy crossed her arms over her chest as she leaned against the sink. It was an observation delivered with the same tenor she used to order an iced green tea. Lemon, no sweeteners.

God, I wanted her. I wanted all of her, and I knew at that moment I'd give up most anything to get out of my Bermuda Triangle and have her.

"Yeah, I was wondering...did you decide if you have room in your weekend for fried clams?"

"I don't know yet."

"When will you know?" I asked.

"When you tell me why you have me under surveillance."

I glanced at the expanse of bare skin from the plunging neckline of her sweater up to her jaw, and I remembered the way her body reacted to my teeth on her ear. Setting my beer bottle down, I pushed away from the wall and approached Andy until we were a breath apart.

I shrugged. "I stare because you don't give me much else." My knuckles grazed her upper arm and I waited for her to push me away or tell me to stop.

"You walked away from me," she said hotly, her head cocked.

That was how she saw it? Fantastic.

I lifted my hands to her face and kissed her, pouring all of my frustration and misery and desire into the tangle of our lips. I tasted the tart cherriness of Andy. My hands went to her hair, angling her head to take more, taste more, tell more. I needed her to know everything I wasn't able to put into words, all the things I couldn't explain or understand myself.

It wasn't enough to weave my fingers through her hair and consume her mouth. I wanted her skin in my hands. Her waist was slim and silken where my fingers kneaded her beneath her sweater. She must have craved the same contact because her fingers slipped between my sweater and shirt. As she pried open the buttons of my shirt, her touch was a searing reminder of what I missed this past week.

Breaking our connection, I gazed into Andy's heated eyes and smiled when I saw her beautiful and flustered. She was different, at once dark and light, and a warm flush hinted at her cheeks.

"There you are," I whispered, my hands framing her face, my thumbs stroking her delicate cheekbones.

"I've been here the whole time."

"No," I murmured. "No, you don't let me see you."

Andy's lips pulled into that tiny smile, and she wrapped her hand around the nape of my neck, drawing me to her and capturing my mouth in a hungry kiss. Her lips communicated more in one kiss than any combination of words. She wanted this.

She wanted *me.*

My hips pinned her against the sink, but it wasn't enough. I needed her to know how much I wanted her. I palmed her ass and Andy roped her arms around my neck when I lifted her off the ground and backed her against the wall. Her legs coiled around my waist and she flexed against my erection, and we groaned at the sensation sparking between us. Her nails bit into my neck, unleashing a fine tremor of pleasure over my nerves when our lips met again.

"Patrick," she sighed, her fingers scraping over my scalp.

"I want you making that sound while I'm fucking you. When you're coming for me. When you're begging for more, for me."

I kissed down her throat and over the rise of her chest, licking the valley between her breasts and savoring her concentrated flavor. It still wasn't enough, and I nipped and sucked at her skin, leaving angry welts in my wake. Setting her feet on the ground, I dropped to my knees and stroked my hands up the back of her legs. She was solid and strong, and lean like a ballerina.

Pushing her sweater up, I kissed every inch of skin I could reach. I pressed my lips to her body and inhaled her scent. I wanted to consume her and I would flatten anything that stood in my way, though I was keenly aware this didn't change anything in her book.

Shoving Andy's jeans down, I held my breath in anticipation of her panties. I was an expert on her ass. I studied it while she was kneeling at jobsites and each time her shirt rode up her back, I expected to catch a glimpse of her underwear. Each time, I was disappointed. I was also half-convinced she didn't wear any.

When the string bikini came into view, I exhaled, and stopped abruptly to tilt my head and study the tattoo centered on the rise of her right hipbone. My urgent desire to explore Andy warred with my fascination at her tattoo. I hooked a finger around the black bikini strings to better visualize the tattoo, and I blinked at the thin circle circumscribed by a square, with smaller shapes circumscribed within the circle. Of all the things

Andy could have imprinted on her body, it shouldn't have surprised me to see rational geometry.

Andy was watching me, smiling when I met her gaze. "Is this Lauweriks's compositional theory?"

"You're quick."

"You're strange," I muttered, and she laughed. "And such a geek."

"If I'm geek for having it, you're a geek for knowing it."

The scent of her arousal hit my senses, redirecting my attention away from Andy's ink and back toward Andy's panties. I wanted to rip them off and keep them like a secret trophy, and I knew a psychologist would have a field day unpacking those urges. I instead focused on her narrow triangle, catching my tongue between my teeth as the fabric gave way and revealed her flesh.

I saw the wheels turning in her mind, her eyes clouding with uncertainty. "What," she started, her voice shaking with need, "why are you doing this?"

"Because it's Valentine's Day and you deserve something special," I replied, our eyes meeting with blistering heat. "And because you want me to. That's why you brought me in here. This is what you're getting. Deal with it."

With her jeans and panties finally pushed to her knees, Andy was bared to me and I wasted no time running my nose through the tight thatch of curls above her glistening slit. My hands snaked around her thighs and cradled her ass, opening her stance for me. She was breathing hard while her hand gripped the towel bar, her knuckles white.

"Hold on," I ordered with a smirk, and dragged my tongue through her slit.

A soft wail when my tongue circled her swollen nub was my

reward, her cries intensifying as I increased the pressure and slipped two fingers inside. Her free hand fisted in my hair, her nails scratching and biting into my scalp until I groaned against her. Arching against my mouth, Andy moaned and hesitantly shifted her hips.

"That's right, kitten," I said. I twisted my wrist, my fingers thrusting deeper, harder while I sucked her clit. I wanted to see her unravel. It wasn't enough for the aloof veneer to dissolve; I wanted her flushed, panting, and begging me to let her come.

Tightening her grip on my hair, her hips undulated against my face and I was drowning in her. Pleas and whispers slipped from her lips between breathy moans. She begged and swore and sighed my name while she tried to find the rhythm that would bring her to release. She faltered, and I increased the tempo of my fingers as they shuttled through her slippery center. I drew her folds between my teeth, biting gently before returning pressure to her clit.

I wanted her remembering every last moment of this tomorrow, and thinking about me. Hopefully she wouldn't also be thinking about resigning or filing a restraining order. Or both.

"Come on, kitten. Get it," I growled, renewing my assault on her clit. I licked and lapped, feeling new rushes of arousal dripping down my wrist as my fingers pushed her higher.

"Oh fuck, Patrick," she moaned. I was thankful the music coming from Shannon's speakers would muffle Andy's sounds. But I also wanted her screams. "Please. Please. Please, Patrick, please."

I thought about dropping my pants and sliding into her right then, knowing I could get us both there within minutes. But this wasn't about me. This was about seeing Andy raw and primal, and begging for my attention as much as I begged for hers. It was about proving to her that she wanted me, and I could give her what she wanted.

"What do you need?"

I pulled her clit between my lips and sucked hard while my fingers continued rocking into her center. Releasing her tender nub, I glanced up and regretted not stripping her before starting this wicked game. I wanted to see her flushed with heat, her breasts swaying in time with her hips. I wanted more of her. I wanted everything I could get, even if it changed nothing. Even if I hated that.

Her head lolled against the wall with a low moan. "How... how did you know...?"

"How did I know you wanted this?" Andy bit down on her lip while her eyes closed and she nodded. She was beautiful, and completely at my mercy. "The sweater, for one. You wanted me staring at your tits, thinking about tasting them."

My tongue teased over her and I felt her walls spasm around my fingers.

"The flirting, for two. You let me watch you with all those guys, knowing you'd torture me until you got me alone. You're evil like that, kitten."

Gently biting at her folds, I twisted my wrist and increased the rhythm.

"The drink, for three. You knew I'd want to know what and why. And finally—"

My tongue circled her clit, and I felt her pulsing against me.

"You wanted me staring. You like keeping this dirty little secret from them." I smiled against her wet center. My tongue swirled over her clit again and I was rewarded with a shuddering moan. "But what you really want is me taking you back to my place and tying you to the bed. You really want me fucking you all night."

"Fuck, fuck, fuck," she groaned, her hand pulling at my hair. I was on board with a bald spot if it meant feeling Andy come on my fingers. "Don't stop, Patrick."

I wanted to respond to her demand, and insist a flaming asteroid slamming through the building wasn't stopping me, but her hand held me in place as the tremors rippled in her core. Latching onto her clit, I sucked greedily when the spasms rolled through her body and she chanted unintelligibly, mumbled pleas and curses mingling with my name. Andy's fingers twisted in my hair when her release finally arrived, her inner walls surging and contracting for minutes while my tongue traced her clit and she panted my name.

I wanted to hear my name, just like that, for the rest of my life.

Andy's knees threatened to give out, and I reluctantly pulled my fingers away. I stood, anchoring her to the wall. After half an hour of worshipping Andy, my belt was strangling my cock, and the rush of blood to my brain dulled my senses. A wide, lazy grin spread across her face when our eyes met, hers slightly unfocused and soft. Exactly as I wanted her.

Andy's plump lips brushed against my neck and jaw, finally reaching my mouth for a slow kiss. I always knew she had a filthy side. I just needed to invite it out to play.

"That was...incredibly thorough," she sighed against my mouth, and I was ready to respond with an offer to spend the night at my place but she shook her head, pressing a finger against my lips. "But we shouldn't. This is such a bad idea. No more of this. We *have* to stop."

Her voice trailed off and I released her from my hold. It hit me while she was righting her jeans and fluffing her hair into place: she was politely dismissing me.

Drinking in one last look at Andy, the emptiness blindsided me. Her rejection, my day reliving family bullshit, my agonizing week. It all slammed into my chest, and I couldn't get out of that bathroom quickly enough.

CHAPTER TWELVE

ANDY

IF BAD WAS SPILLING A PIPING HOT LATTE OVER A LAPTOP, subsequently frying thirty new designs without backing them up, and if very bad was ordering fifty grand's worth of the wrong marble slabs, then very, very bad was letting my boss go down on me in his sister's bathroom.

As much as I hated to admit it, the facts weren't lying. Patrick gave me the best orgasm of my life. I'd be willing to argue it was the best orgasm known to womankind. If there was a contest for that sort of thing, I'd happily write up my entry.

His hands scrambled my thoughts, chasing rational decision-making out of town. He turned my body into a needy, achy ball of want, and with each passing hour, I wanted him twice as much as I did the previous. And he was my *boss*—the man I idolized from afar for years, the man in control of my future as an architect in the sustainable preservation field.

Facts. I hated every single one of them.

The only option was to keep it professional. I thought it was the right thing, the smart thing. But after a week, I was ready to make an offering to the gods in exchange for another stolen half hour in a bathroom with that same boss.

Very, very bad was quickly turning into worse.

Those ridiculous words were out of my mouth and Patrick out of the bathroom before I comprehended what I said. I wanted him—more than anything. I wanted to flirt with him over drinks, kiss him in bathrooms, let him tie me to his bed. I also wanted to learn and understand preservation from his perspective and grow under his guidance.

I didn't see how I could admire the bite marks he left on my skin while being his apprentice, and I wasn't good at navigating messy relationship waters.

If that didn't bring me all the way to worse, he was avoiding me.

Initially I accepted his disappearance, and relative to my body's all-consuming addiction to his tongue, a little breathing room wasn't a bad thing. But the entire week? It was a giant signal that our flirtation stopped being harmless when I dragged him into the bathroom and my pants came off.

Not that I regretted dragging him into the bathroom, of course, but five days without Patrick left me feeling unsettled and a little lonely.

I was also hungry—my Mason jar salads were dreadfully bland in comparison to the eclectic mix of hidden gems Patrick picked for lunch.

He spent Monday and Tuesday out of the office with Shannon, and aside from a quick discussion of priorities after the partners' meeting that morning, I didn't see or hear from him. He spent Wednesday and Thursday with Matt and Riley as they handled issues at jobsites, and though I understood those issues to be serious, I knew Patrick didn't spend his days micromanaging his siblings. He told them to "figure it out" and they always did.

He was inventing reasons to dodge me. No amount of hot yoga would untie the heavy knots of tension in my body—sexual and otherwise.

Patrick delegated walk-throughs without any overbearing, control-freakish backstory on each site or an insistence I apprise him of the progress. Regardless, I emailed him detailed notes from all of my visits and conversations with contractors, and attached extensive slideshows to keep him updated on our projects.

Even though Patrick wasn't one for chatty or overly formal emails, his "thanks—patrick" responses smacked of reticence. I didn't have the words to explain why it hurt so much, but every time I thought about that one-word reply, it was like a rubber band snapping the fleshy part of my wrist—not exactly painful, but surprising and unpleasant.

I reveled in the knowledge Patrick trusted me enough to let me fly solo, but his absence meant I couldn't think through problems with him, and my lunchtime conversations were radically less instructive. We traded a few curt texts and emails each day, but I missed seeing him, talking to him, being near him. The amount of time I spent each night typing out texts I never sent was shameful.

After spending nearly every working moment of the past month with Patrick, I felt adrift without him—and I promptly hated that emotion just as much as I hated the way my apprenticeship was turning into a slow-motion train wreck asterisked with a life-altering orgasm and a curiosity about being tied up.

I expected to see him Friday morning, but a pre-dawn text informed me that he and Shannon wouldn't be in until the afternoon. I pouted over that message for a full five minutes and packed my reply of "ok" with loneliness, frustration, lust, and fear that I was losing an incredible mentor and friend.

"Did you hear the good news?" I glanced up at Tom as he sauntered into Patrick's office and deposited several files on his desk. Setting my phone aside—willing it to produce a message from Patrick wasn't working—I shook my head. "All four Bunker Hill properties sold this morning. There was a crazy bidding war last night. Ended up with a cash deal and it was far over asking price."

"Is that where Shannon and Patrick have been all day?"

Tom nodded and started organizing Patrick's desk. "Yeah, apparently the people buying those properties wanted to discuss some changes, and Shan didn't like the idea of sending Riley, for obvious reasons, and Matt's away for the weekend with Lauren, and Sam won't set foot on those properties, so...they've been doing that. She just texted that they're headed back from the title agency and she wants to go out for drinks." He chuckled. "Her exact words were 'It's time to get rowdy.'"

That sounded exactly like Shannon—the woman was comfortable in Christian Louboutin heels and preferred to drink cheap beer from the bottle.

Tom continued straightening Patrick's things—he either didn't know or didn't care that Patrick preferred some chaos on his desk. Was Patrick's home like that too? Slightly disorganized yet completely logical to him?

I shook my head. That wasn't helping the current situation.

Tom's knowledge of all things Walsh was deep, and it was time to tap into that well despite the fact engaging him in conversation would result in more invitations. I was still unclear on Tom's sexuality, but it was obvious he wanted a girl—one to dress up or one to date, I couldn't be sure—and I didn't want to be her.

It was misguided and terrible and foolish, and even though I fought like hell to avoid it, I wanted Patrick.

"Is that why they were busy earlier in the week?"

"No," he murmured, flipping through documents on Patrick's desk and relegating a few to the recycling bin. "They were in Maynard on Monday and they bought a farmhouse that's going to fall over on the next breezy day, and paid off the loan on this building. Then they were in Boxborough and Acton on Tuesday and bought two more old places. Then they went to the old Walsh homestead, and according to the Widow, they yelled at each other and didn't talk until the Bunker Hill buyers asked for a consult. They've both been hell on wheels this week, if you ask me. I'm thinking of getting a Taser."

"The Widow?"

"Uh-huh," he replied, shifting his focus to Patrick's bookshelves and carefully lining up the spines. "Shannon's nickname. You know, from *The Avengers*. The hot redhead who kicks a lot of ass? They all have nicknames. Mostly superheroes and comic book stuff. For all the time they spend screaming at each other and slamming doors, they're really tight in non-sentimental ways."

"Tom, you've let me work here for a month and not mentioned this? I'm hurt," I said, pressing a hand to my heart. Getting information from Tom required some theatrics on my part—before the Orgasm to Rule Them All, I spent half an hour charming the details on the Wellesley property out of him, only to discover he didn't know much or wasn't willing to share.

"That is what a coffee date is for," he teased with a wink. "It kinda makes sense, the nicknames." He shrugged and continued organizing the bookshelves. "They're like a little band of misfit street toughs. Shannon's the Black Widow. Riley's RISD because he went there and not Cornell like the rest of them. Sam's the runt and that's my favorite thing in the world, but he's usually Tony Stark—not Iron Man. Appropriate in so many ways. They never agreed on one for Matthew, although I'm still rooting for Jugger. And Patrick is Optimus Prime. Obviously."

The *Architectural Digest* feature on Walsh Associates neglected those details. "Why were they arguing about the Wellesley property?"

"He wants to get rid of it and she wants to rehab it because she's a sadist." Tom adjusted Patrick's diplomas to right angles and turned to me. "You *have* to come out tonight. You're the only one who can keep me from carbo-loading," he said. "I just reserved half of Pomodoro, which isn't saying much because it's literally the size of a broom closet, but the food is the best."

"He's right, it is," Patrick said from the doorway. "You should come. And she's definitely a sadist."

How Patrick always managed to sneak up on conversations, I will never know, but there he was, delicious as ever with his top button opened and his tie loose. I glanced at his dark trousers and instantly recalled his narrow waist and carved muscles, and salivated at the memory.

His eyes locked on me for a long moment while I studied him, and my body immediately betrayed me—my cheeks and neck flushed, my lips parted, and my nipples hardened—and Patrick noticed the subtle changes, smirking.

He dropped to his desk chair and motioned to Tom. "Are these it?"

I studied my plans—anxious to direct my thoughts away from crawling into Patrick's lap to taste his scruffy jaw, and the way his eyes gazed right into me—and ignored their quiet discussion. They paged through the documents, pausing every few moments when Tom pointed, repeating "and sign here" until Patrick snapped that he could see the lines without Tom's help.

"Any emergencies today, Asani?"

Looking up, I discovered we were alone and Patrick was skimming his email. "No," I replied. "Everything's fine. I sent you some notes, though. Updates."

"Great, well..." He swiveled away from his screen to stare at me. "Thanks for taking care of everything. It's been a long week. Head out for the weekend." I nodded, overwhelmed with disappointment.

I wanted to go back in time, back to Shannon's bathroom. There was the added benefit of reliving Patrick's mouth on me, but I only wanted to retrieve my thoughtless, knee-jerk words.

Tucked into layers of outerwear, I waved goodbye and was at the threshold when he spoke again. "You really should join us tonight. Pomodoro, on Hanover Street. Eight."

———

BETWEEN THE FOOD, WINE, TOASTS, AND TOM'S INCESSANT chatter, there was barely time to notice Patrick at the opposite end of the table. That wasn't to say I didn't notice—I did.

And Patrick noticed me.

I knew every time his eyes landed on me, and it wasn't long until I started matching his gazes. They were momentary, and in the excitement of the celebration, no one picked up on the building tension. Shannon and Sam were busy gushing over the new properties while Patrick pretended to listen, and Riley invited himself into the kitchen to talk basketball with the servers. Tom regaled me with tales of Patrick's endless string of assistants, and I indulged in his random questions about my interests.

"You need to try this," Tom said, pushing a plate of tiramisu to me.

My eyes flicked to Patrick while my mouth closed over the tines of the fork. The warmth of his gaze did something to me—something electric that awoke every cell and nerve and muscle in my body, and made my insides feel delightfully restless.

At the sound of Patrick's throat clearing, I slid the plate back to Tom. "Thanks. I'm not really into desserts." Tom sent me a dubious look, and I drained my wine. I think it was my third but after a few hours at the table and an eager server, I lost track. Glancing around the tiny restaurant, I spotted the restrooms. "I'll be right back."

I felt Patrick's eyes follow me from the table and down the narrow hallway. I wasn't surprised to feel his hand wrap around my arm when I reached the cramped bathroom, and I was even less surprised when he locked the door behind him and turned to me, scowling.

While his gaze pinned me to the wall, I realized something. *None of it mattered.* The wrong, the inappropriate, the out of line. I invented all of those things, and maybe there were good reasons for them at time. None of it mattered *now*.

It only took one step to be in Patrick's arms, his mouth pressing against mine with an urgency that matched the need screaming through my veins. His hands were in my hair, fisting around it and pulling, and I moaned against him.

Like clockwork, Patrick's hands landed on my backside and lifted me, wrapping my legs around him. It was my favorite kind of predictable. When my fingers met his soft hair, I felt the remnants of my long-held tension liquefying and draining out of my muscles. He kissed my throat and jaw, and I arched into him with a whimper.

There was no denying there was something between us, something potent. It was bigger than us, and it was pulling us deeper as each day rolled by. It was intense and real, and I was finished trying to push it away.

"I want to know what you're thinking," he demanded.

My thighs squeezed around his waist and I brought his attention back to my mouth. Tasting and breathing him in sent tingles through my system. "I'm thinking I've missed you."

"What else?" He pulled back, his head banging against the door, and stared into my eyes. "I want to know exactly what's in your head right now."

"And..." I studied the tendons of his neck while I attempted to bring order to my thoughts. "This is the worst idea I've ever had, and it is beyond irresponsible and unprofessional, but..."

"But what, Andy?"

I licked my lips and met his eyes. "I'm risking everything here... You know that, right?" He held my gaze, finally nodding and dropping his eyes to my throat. "I have sex with you in my mind. Frequently."

Patrick angled his head and I watched him absorb the weight of my words. Eventually he asked, "Is it any good?"

I nodded vigorously. "Incredible."

Patrick blinked twice, his eyes searching mine, before locking his arms around my waist and kissing me. The tension between us was shifting—one form of pressure released while another started building. His mouth was hard and demanding, and I dug my fingers into his shoulders to feel more of him.

"Why doesn't this change things?" he asked against

my mouth.

"You tell me what this changes," I murmured, my lips leaving wet kisses along his neck and throat. "You're in control here, Patrick."

"If you only knew." A humorless laugh escaped Patrick's mouth, and he dropped his forehead to my shoulder. "Everything," he breathed into my hair. "It changes everything."

"Then it has to stay between us," I said, my nails scratching along the nape of Patrick's neck. "They can't know."

"Whatever you want. I'll give you whatever you want." His nose and lips teased the corner where my neck and shoulder met. "I've missed you too, fuck, so much, but we don't have the best track record with bathrooms. Or Fridays."

I laughed against him, and pressed a series of kisses to his lips before dragging his bottom lip into my mouth and biting. He wasn't the only one with teeth. "Tell me what you want to happen next, Patrick."

"I'm going to leave, and you can come with me, or you can stay. I'll text you my address. I live three minutes away. I want you, but you have to decide how it's going to be. I want you to come to me."

Patrick brought his hand to my hair and crushed his lips against mine, our mouths moving together until I started unbuttoning his shirt. He pulled my wrist away and folded it behind my back with a pointed look, and set me on the countertop.

"It's your decision."

He slipped through the door, and I was alone. Glancing at my reflection in the mirror, I saw out-of-control hair, swollen lips, and the faint redness of stubble rash riding along my neck, all complemented by a wide smile that represented exactly how I felt.

IF I HADN'T RACKED UP ENOUGH POINTS TO EARN A PADDED CELL yet, leaving Andy in another bathroom surely put me over the edge. After sprinting to my apartment, I killed time picking up dirty socks, filling my dishwasher with the wreckage in the sink, organizing my refrigerator, and sorting the industry journals piled on my kitchen table.

I spent weeks believing I was a pervy creeper who leered at his young apprentice, and her admission in the bathroom felt like absolution. I wanted to celebrate the removal of my creeper status, and I wanted that party in my bed with Andy.

My pulse pounded against my temple while the minutes ticked by, and I glared at my phone as I begged for some confirmation Andy received the texts with my address and door code. More than an hour passed before I flopped to the sofa, dejected and doubly miserable.

I was fast-forwarding through the most recent Premier League games and devising a plan to transfer Andy to Matt's projects and bring Riley back onto my projects when her chime sounded from my phone.

Andy: I once heard someone say that if something is equal parts amazing and terrifying, you should always pursue it.

Rolling my eyes, I stopped the game and scowled at the phone. She was a never-ending trail of breadcrumbs.

Patrick: I've said it before and I'm saying it again: you don't give me much.
Patrick: And you are beyond confusing when
Patrick: A) you go radio silent for 2 hours
Patrick: B) you send me wildly ambiguous texts that require several more questions to understand when you could have just told me what you're trying to say
Patrick: And C) I can't read you at all unless your legs are wrapped around me and my tongue is in your throat
Patrick: And believe me, I'd like to do that ALL fucking day, but I can't so you need to give me a little more if you're going to keep dragging me into bathrooms
Patrick: Please, save me the trouble of interpreting your commentary, and tell me what the fuck you've decided because I'm two seconds away from an aneurysm

A sharp knock echoed from my door, and I glanced back and forth between my phone and the door, knowing that I'd either find a sibling too drunk to make her way home and looking to crash, or Andy.

Patrick: If you're not on the other side of that door...

Andy: You'll never know until you look

A ripple of joy mixed with absolute panic flowed over my body when I found Andy leaning against the doorframe, her head bowed over her phone.

She gifted me with a small smile and raised eyebrow. "You seem angry."

"You're impossible to read."

"I didn't know you were interested in reading me," she countered with a shrug.

I pursed my lips and closed my eyes with a tight groan. She was going to drive me to a new level of insanity, and I'd be arriving there very soon.

"Get your ass in here," I said, and she rewarded me with another smile as her shoulder brushed my chest.

She lifted her phone. "I'm here. Even though it's amazing and terrifying."

"I see that," I said, leaning against the door. Her words started feeling mischievous, almost like a flirty game that we were playing except I didn't know any of the rules. "Would you like to tell me why?"

Andy rolled her shoulders and tucked her phone into her bag. "You invited me."

I paced toward Andy, my frustration and arousal blurring together until I couldn't separate the two. "It took you two hours to decide."

"But it's not Friday anymore, and as you pointed out, we're tragic on Fridays. I was chatting with your sister. She's hilarious, and we had some wine, and we're going to yoga next Saturday."

"She's afraid I'm going to scare you off."

Unbuttoning Andy's coat, I tossed it to the sofa before

plucking her gloves from her fingers and unwinding her scarf. Taking layers of clothing off of her, even outerwear, was an exquisite seduction, and I barely restrained my desire to throw her over my shoulder and charge for the bedroom.

"Hardly." Her fingers brushed down the row of buttons on my shirt and settled on my belt buckle. "A few weeks ago, at the bar?" She glanced at me, and I nodded for her to continue. "I've been thinking about it. I wish I had worn a skirt."

"Other than the fact your legs are amazing, and I would have spent the entire night staring at them, why is that?"

"Well," she whispered, her fingers releasing my shirt's buttons. "I've had this...fantasy."

Her eyes met mine when the word 'fantasy' rolled off her tongue, and they were wide, dark, and deviously twinkling. I swallowed a growl and fought to keep my expression flat. It was stay serious or fuck her where she stood, and I was doing my best to be slightly more evolved.

Slightly.

At least for a few more minutes.

"I'm expecting you to start explaining that comment, kitten."

Andy tugged my shirt loose, and let it hang open with her hands stilled against my chest. The flame in her eyes brightened and she licked her lips. Maybe bearded hipsters weren't her type anymore, which was good news because I really wanted to get rid of the overgrown stubble, and I did not want to start shopping for skinny corduroys.

"I had this fantasy about having drinks with you, and talking about minimalistic modern and preservation legislation—"

"You are so weird," I interrupted. Only Andy would have talking points in her fantasies.

"Maybe." She smiled, slipping my shirt from my arms. "But

we didn't get to my opinion of laminate, and we didn't have an aged whiskey, and I would have liked your hand up my skirt, making me come under the table."

My eyes widened, my mouth hanging open in stunned silence. The oxygen seemed to vanish from the room. She was in my apartment, telling me about her public orgasm fantasies for fuck's sake, and we both knew the gray area between mentor and apprentice long ago faded to black.

"Have you been thinking about that all this time?" I asked, dropping to my knees and unzipping her boots. My hands stroked up and down the backs of her slim legs while I vacillated between my love and hate for her tight jeans.

"Longer." She glanced down at me with a smirk.

She thought I was in control. If she knew anything of my misery in the past weeks, she would know the inaccuracy of that sentiment, and gazing at her from my knees only cemented reality for me.

Her effect on me was profound, and it terrified me. I didn't understand Andy. I couldn't explain what she wanted. A small part of me knew she'd never truly reveal herself to me. It would always be breadcrumbs.

"How long?" Standing, I anchored my hands to her hips and narrowed my eyes at Andy. Her hands dropped to my belt and my pants hit the floor.

"Since the day I met you. When you interviewed me." Her fingers scratched down my chest, and the predatory smile playing on her lips had me hard in a matter of seconds.

I nodded, and yanked her soft black sweater over her head while I attempted to recover from her revelation. Her breasts came into focus from their seats in her smooth graphite bra, and my need to free those beauties and bury my face between them eclipsed my attempts to figure Andy out.

After tossing the gray fabric over my shoulder, I cupped her breasts, my thumbs circling her small, mocha nipples until they hardened against my palm. She arched forward into my hands, her fingers clawing at my waist as her breath hitched. Another wave of her soul-stirring lavender scent hit me when my nose coasted over the rise of her breast.

I groaned against her nipple when her flavor seeped into my senses. She tasted like warmth, honey, sex, and tart cherries. Her fingers tugged at my hair while I sucked that hard little gem into my mouth and I was dizzy with want.

"Bite it," she hissed. "I want your teeth."

My tongue traced her nipple before my teeth skimmed over her skin, scraping the tender flesh repeatedly while my hand mimicked my actions on her other breast.

"I said *bite*."

Whatever the opposite of docile was, Andy was it. If I believed for a second that she'd obediently take my directions, I was further along in my insanity than I initially thought. She was aggressive in her concise, pointed way, and she was content to make demands and argue about my technique while standing in the middle of my apartment, half-naked.

I fucking loved it.

Releasing her nipple with a sharp pull that elicited a throaty moan, I turned to meet Andy's eyes. "You're a dirty little kitten, aren't you?"

"Maybe. Is that a problem?"

"It's fucking fantastic." I met her dark eyes. "I knew there was something very naughty about you the second I laid eyes on you."

"Hm."

Gripping her hips, I pulled her forward and my hand cracked against her ass. Her eyes flashed in surprise while a deep purr escaped her lips. "Oh, hell no. No. There is no 'hm' here. You have something to say, you say it."

"I was just thinking...if that's what you thought, you've been thinking about me, about this...for almost two months."

"Yes," I said quickly. "It's been complete and total torture."

"Good," Andy breathed. She dragged her hands through my hair and brought my lips to hers for a hurried, impatient kiss. "So we're on the same page."

I rolled my eyes and pivoted Andy in my arms, propelling her into my darkened bedroom while I unbuttoned her jeans and shoved them down her legs. I was confident about a few things, and one of them was that Andy and I were not on anything resembling the same page.

With her jeans and black bikini panties balled on the floor, my eyes skimmed over her body. She reminded me of a Renaissance painting, all flawless skin and rosy lips. Her hair tumbled over her shoulders, cloaking her small breasts.

That is, if women in Renaissance paintings wore red knee socks embroidered with miniature owls. Perfectly random. Perfectly Andy.

She noticed my head inclined toward her legs and my furrowed brow. "I'm all for naked," she said with a laugh. "But it's four below out there. I'm cold. I'm keeping them on. You can, too."

Her fingers slipped under my boxer briefs and pushed them down, and in typical infuriating Andy fashion, she avoided my straining erection. My palm smacked against her skin, lower on her backside this time, closer to her legs. I knew she felt the jolt deep in her center when she moaned into my chest and sank her teeth into my skin.

And that was the end of my control.

In a blur of movement, she was sprawled on the bed, her knees bent to her elbows while my hand dug through the bedside table drawer for a condom. Kneeling between her legs, I rolled it down and slammed into her with one demanding motion. I couldn't resist a smug smile when her eyes rolled back and her lips went slack.

"Oh, *fuck* yes, Patrick," Andy groaned, her nails clawing into my back.

I withdrew slowly as my eyes moved away from her closed lids, over her firm nipples, down her taut abdomen to where I lingered inside her. I noticed the stark contrast between her dark olive skin and my light, freckle-ridden skin. Captivated, I stared at my cock as it slid into her, and repeated the motion. A whirlwind of errant thoughts whipped through my mind, leaving behind ideas of possession and rightness and all-consuming desire.

Glancing away from our union, I found Andy leaning up on her elbows, watching as I pushed in and pulled out, her chest heaving with shallow pants. She gulped, and met my eyes. "Faster," she commanded. "And harder."

"Dirty and demanding?" I asked, adjusting my stance to hover over her.

"Complaining?" Her eyebrow arched and her lips edged upward into an inkling of a smile.

Gripping the backside of her bent legs, I hammered into Andy with the singular mission of bringing her a colossal orgasm that would drop every one of her defenses. I wanted to know Andy at her most uninhibited and vulnerable. "Not at all," I grunted.

Wanting more, wanting deeper, I pressed Andy's knees to her chest and thrust forward with her sock-covered ankles bouncing over my shoulders. A chorus of "oh" stuttered from her lips, and I felt tingles signaling my rising orgasm all over my body. Her heat was like a live wire, all fire and unbound energy that coursed into my veins and electrified me.

"You are so beautiful," I stammered, my breath shuddering when her inner muscles clamped around me. And she was; from her wild hair spread over the blankets, and round, perky breasts, to her strong legs, she was magnificent and wholly addictive.

My hips crashed against hers, and when I drove my fingers into her legs, it called up memories of my fingers gripping her ass in Shannon's bathroom. I was suddenly aware even a defenseless, post-orgasmic Andy could very well reject me.

"Patrick...yes, please," Andy whimpered, her body jerking beneath me as her nails dug into my sides.

Bowing my head to her neglected nipples, I sucked one of the tips into my mouth, my thumb circling the other. The hard suction sent her arching off the bed. The exposed brick walls absorbed most of her shriek when I slammed into her again. I released her nipple with a loud pop that afforded her the pressure of a bite, and shifted her legs to wrap around my waist. A wave rippled through her muscles, and I felt her body tense in anticipation of her release.

"Patrick...oh, Patrick, I'm so close."

"That's cute. As if I need you to tell me." I tilted my hips to hit her clit, and we groaned at the new depth. Breathless and teetering on the edge of my own long-overdue orgasm, I murmured against her ear, "Let go, Andy, just let go."

I ducked my head to her chest and captured her nipple between my teeth, tugging and biting while Andy bucked beneath me. She was primed to explode. Her nails scratched up my sides, sinking into my shoulders until I recognized the faint sting of punctured skin. Andy's answering thrusts were erratic and frenzied. Her inner walls contracted around me, sucking me in and demanding more. She was right there. She just needed to stop holding back.

My lips landed on the valley between her breasts, and I licked up and down her skin. I delivered quick bites to her nipple while her body dissolved into a quivering, moaning bundle of restrained sensation beneath me. Lasting this long was an epic accomplishment, and in another minute, I would be down for the count.

"Get it, Andy," I growled against her skin. My teeth closed around the side of her breast, and I soothed the bite with soft kisses. "I want you coming all over my cock. *Now.*"

My hips rolled against her, and she rocked against me in response, her eyes locking on mine and begging me to go over the edge with her.

An airy moan heralded Andy's orgasm, and I felt the spasms flowing through her, surrounding every millimeter of me and demanding reciprocity. I erupted with a stream of unintelligible babble about how good it was, that I wanted her all night, and how much I wanted her, and I kept my eyes trained on Andy while my hips slowed.

A warm, sated grin broke across her face. She looked open, calm, and unbelievably sexy. Mission accomplished.

I disentangled our limbs and rolled to the mattress, discarding the condom and dragging Andy to her side to face me.

"I think...I think I'd like to do this again. I don't want just one night with you," she said, her fingers gliding through my hair. "If that's all you wanted...tell me now."

I eyed her, wondering where the woman who repeatedly shut down my advances went. How did she go from 'we shouldn't do this' to 'I want to do this again'? What changed for her?

"As if one night would have been enough." I pulled her closer, weaving our legs together and stroking my hand up her thigh, over her spine, through her hair, and back down again while I let her words sink in. It wasn't enough to look at Andy anymore; touching was a necessity on par with breathing.

"But I don't want anything to change between us at work. You have to promise me, Patrick. Just sex. Nothing else."

The word 'just' knocked against every competing urge in my body until I was bruised. Her fingers threaded through my chest hair while my hand continued mapping her every rise and curve, and I would have happily given Andy the frontal lobe of my brain if she asked for it in that moment. For a second, it felt like I did.

Andy looked up, her hand paused on my chest. Her espresso eyes, the darkest brown I'd ever seen, gazed into mine. Her teeth scoured her bottom lip, and she blinked, her unapproachable veneer stripped away and abandoned alongside her panties. She was vulnerable and open in my arms, and without that spine of steel, she suddenly looked young and delicate.

"Patrick?"

I wanted her as mine. Nothing about that belonged in the 'just sex' category, but I knew what it was like to let her go, and I wasn't about to walk that road again. Not unless it led to a padded cell stocked with enough whiskey for me to float away.

Regardless of how impossible her request was, I wanted Andy and I was taking whatever she offered. "I promise, kitten, anything you want."

Her lazy smile returned, and she planted light kisses on my lips before staring at me as if she was trying to communicate something words couldn't say.

Those eyes...they fucking owned me.

I needed to rewrite my submission for the Orgasm of the Universe contest. I wanted to do that quickly—while the memories were fresh and muscles sore—but my thoughts scattered like marbles down a staircase.

Patrick touched me with a skill I couldn't comprehend, and my body was still reveling in the aftershocks, but the quiet was most fascinating. It was a strange feeling, really, to have everything fade away. It wasn't entirely welcome, and I didn't know how to handle the newly placid lake that was my mind.

The tips of Patrick's fingers brushed over my back, and I shivered. With a deft movement, Patrick engulfed us in thick blankets and tucked my back against his chest.

"Better?" he murmured, his lips pressed beneath my ear.

I nodded, my eyes falling shut when his fingers resumed their trail along my body. The light pressure compounded the looseness of my muscles while I debated the appropriate course of action. It was the middle of the night, and Patrick wasn't sending out any hints for me to hit the road, but having sex with my boss muddied the etiquette waters.

Patrick's fingers traced the back of my knee, and I wiggled away from him with a squeal. I sat up, dragging the sheet over my chest, and shook my head at him. "Tickling is unnecessary after the age of five."

He levered up on an elbow, his eyes trained on my side. His fingers passed over my ribs, and he asked, "Is that Arabic?"

I glanced down at the narrow strip of black ink running vertically down my side. "It's Farsi."

Patrick laughed, and brought me back to the center of the bed with an eager sweep of his arm around my waist. "Of course it is."

My defenses flared to attention, and I narrowed my eyes at him. "What does that mean?"

He shrugged, his hand stroking back and forth over the ink. "It means that you, the most complex, mysterious creature I've ever met, would tattoo both rational geometry and Farsi onto your gorgeous skin." He bent to kiss the marking, and I bit my tongue to restrain a moan. My ribs weren't particularly sensitive but something about his lips on my skin was illogically erotic. "Is speaking Farsi one of your secret talents?"

"No," I sighed, leaning back against the pillows while Patrick continued studying the characters. "Barely at all."

"But some?" He peered up at me from where his head rested on my stomach. I nodded, wondering if he'd inquire further. I didn't divulge information freely, and I knew he wanted more, but he was patient. That's how Patrick was different—he never acted as though he was entitled to my life story. He respected boundaries. Most of the time. "What does it say? Where does it start?"

I pointed to the spot adjacent to my breast. "It starts here, going right to left. It says, 'If you have to ask, you'll never know. If you know, you need only ask.'"

"Of course it does." Patrick's eyebrows lifted, and he smiled at the tattoo as if he were trying to unlock the riddle. Minutes passed but he continued studying my skin. He glanced at me and asked, "Is that from something?"

I blinked at him, waiting.

"You really aren't going to tell me."

I lifted an eyebrow. "I'm sure you'll figure it out."

"I'll work on that," he murmured, shifting to kneel over me.

His eyes swept over my torso, stopping to study the bites and bruises left by his teeth. The conflict in his eyes was evident. For a moment his brows would knit together and his lips would flatten into a grim line, and then he'd remember I asked—let's get real: I begged—for it, and he'd relax perceptibly. I ran my hands through his hair as an extra layer of reassurance.

"Do you have any others?"

"Maybe."

Patrick's head dropped to my sternum, and he released a long, rumbling sound that vibrated through my body and put my ladybits on high alert.

"You...you drive me fucking crazy," he growled, his hands flexing on my hips. "Completely. Fucking. Crazy. I should spank your ass red for your little stunt last week, or you should get on your knees for letting me think you weren't showing up tonight."

Lust swamped my blood and swelled my center, and I was speechless. I had plenty of sex in college and grad school, but never sex like this. Never desperate, frenzied sex that involved spanking or biting or my ankles over anyone's shoulders. This was exceptionally new to me, but I didn't want it to stop.

"Can I have both?"

Patrick's head snapped up, his eyes shining with the same heat that was flooding my thighs with arousal. Clamping his hands on my waist, he flipped me over and pulled my hips up.

"Fuck yes," he growled, his hand connecting with my bare backside.

I yelped, and his hand rubbed away the light sting. It didn't hurt. Part of me loved the smarting tingle, and the way it heightened the throbbing, clenching sensations building inside me. I didn't know what that said about me, and I didn't want to examine it closely.

The other part of me wanted to be horrified. What kind of woman lets a guy—her boss, no less—throw her face down on a bed with her ass in the air and spank her? And because of something I did last week? Nothing about that sounded right to me, and I inched away from Patrick's hold.

"Baby, get back here. I am *not* done."

His hand pressed against the base of my spine while another spank landed low on my backside, nearly connecting with my thighs. It was different—better—and I stopped plotting an escape. Two more landed in the same area, and between wildly unrestrained moans, my thoughts were spilling out of my head so quickly I lost track of the issue I wanted to take with spanking.

I decided to make my case some other day.

Patrick dipped two fingers inside me and stroked slowly while a hand continued caressing my backside. I was shivering with anticipation, hoping Patrick would deliver the next spank with his fingers inside me—better yet, he'd get a condom and really join the fun.

His hands froze in place, and I looked over my shoulder at him. "What was that 'hm' about?"

My eyes dropped to his erection where it jutted out from his body, standing proudly at attention. "Mmm," I sighed. "Just wondering when you were going to stop chatting and fuck me again."

"You are such a demanding, dirty girl," he growled, his hand connecting with my skin inches from where his fingers moved inside me. I moaned into the pillow and pushed back against his fingers, craving a little more friction. He retreated, and I cried out at his departure—he left me with a snarling, frustrating need, and while I knew he wasn't leaving to make a sandwich, I was too worked up to be anything less than outraged.

Patrick folded himself over me, dragging his teeth up my neck, and I quivered when he reached my ear and spoke softly against my skin. "What did you expect would happen, when you decided to come here?"

I rolled my eyes and pressed my hips against him, feeling his erection nestled between my cheeks. My body protested, over-come with a discomfort light stroking would not assuage. "I have the *New York Times* crossword puzzle app on my phone, and you never did get to hear my position on laminate."

"Let's get a few things straight. First, you hate laminate. That doesn't require discussion. Second, when I'm finished with you, a crossword puzzle is about the only thing you're going to be able to do. And third, don't doubt that I'll fuck you senseless and those snappy little comments will fall right out of your head."

My back arched and I rocked against Patrick's erection. "You make a lot of lists, Patrick. Do you intentionally speak in bullet points?"

Patrick leaned away from me and I heard the rustle of a condom. I sighed in relief.

"*Andy*," Patrick growled.

I loved that sound. I wanted to record it and use it as his ring tone. It would require some explanation in mixed company, but I'd live with that.

"Soon enough, kitten, the only thing you'll have to say is 'thank you.'"

"I told you I had enough talking ten minutes ago."

"You also told me you've spent the past month thinking about me fingering you in a bar."

He tucked my knees under my body and anchored my wrists on the small of my back before positioning himself at my opening. Being pinned down offered an unexpected thrill, filling me with breathless desire. I wiggled against him to express my impatience.

"You know how to wait for what you want."

"Patrick," I whispered, desperation wrapped in each syllable. I twisted my fingers in Patrick's hold, lacing them with his. "Fuck me. Please."

"I'm not stopping you," he murmured, and I turned his words over and over before backing against him. He filled me completely, and responded with a sharp thrust. "Andy, fuck, yes."

A stinging spank landed low on my backside as he pulled out, and I shrieked as the reverberations bounced through my throbbing core. My fingers clenched around his, wordlessly begging for more while his cock lingered at my opening. He answered with a squeeze to my fingers and a hard thrust that inched me farther up the bed.

His competence was impressive, though reminiscent of the fact Patrick was older, evidently much more experienced, and wise to his preferences. His erection brushed over my clit and through my folds, and though the sensation wracked me with shivers, I needed to remind myself this would most likely crash and burn, leaving me to pick up the pieces alone. Memories of stellar orgasms wouldn't save me then.

"I can actually hear you thinking, kitten." Patrick leaned over me, his teeth running along my shoulder as he eased out of me, and ever so slowly slid in again. He released my hands, but pressed them against my back in silent command. His fingers crawled over my belly and down to my clit, moving in rhythmic circles that had me moaning into the mattress. "Let. It. Go. Whatever it is, let it go, and focus on what you feel right here."

I hummed in agreement, banishing thoughts of disaster with a pledge to protect myself no matter what, and I turned my face to press a kiss to the corner of his mouth. "That voice of yours is hypnotic. You could be reading your grocery list and I'd still be on the edge of the best orgasm ever," I panted. "But I'm not a delicate flower, Patrick. Save the narrative and fuck me."

"You know, you could just do what you're told." Laughing, he delivered a teasing slap to my ass. He was unhurried and thorough, and my body loved the decadent fullness of him buried inside me while his fingers tended to my clit.

"I could." He continued with deep, protracted strokes. I met his thrusts, once again begging for more. "But you don't really want that. You want much more than that from me."

Patrick paused before his hips snapped against me and he launched into a furious rhythm that brought about my complete surrender—my mind was blank to everything but the orgasm building low in my core.

"If you knew what I really wanted," he murmured, his words

punctuated with guttural moans and gasps. "You would...ah, fuck, Andy, you're right there."

His teeth gnashed into my shoulder, and I exploded—every inch of my skin tingled while my orgasm multiplied with Patrick's continued thrusting. He kept talking, but it wasn't what I wanted to hear—it wasn't an explanation of what he wanted or what I would do with that information.

"God, Andy, tell me you feel that." He spoke around my shoulder, his breath soothing the sting of his bite. "I feel you coming all over my cock and my fingers, and yes, yes, keep going, don't you fucking stop." Kisses rained across my shoulder blades, and I shivered beneath his touch. "Oh fuck, the things you do to me, Andy. Fuck, *fuck*, I'm close, so...so...so close."

Lingering in that hypersensitive post-orgasmic phase while Patrick chased his release, I focused on flexing my internal muscles around him—thank you very much, yoga—and it was a win for us both. I got my first-ever double orgasm, which was a lot like a bliss-filled near drowning.

"Oh God, Andy. I'm gonna fuck this hot little pussy until you forget that anyone else has ever been here. This is only for me."

Patrick yelled a long, filthy soliloquy when he came, collapsed over me, and wrapped his arms around my body to roll us to our sides.

Disappointment washed over me. I wanted to see Patrick's orgasm roll through him, to feel that bone-deep connection—the one that had the power to ignite the air, the one that convinced me I needed to protect myself for the day this ended—again. I wanted to see the intensity behind his promises of possession.

For once in my life, I yearned for the simple comforts of face-to-face missionary.

Patrick nestled his face against my neck and breathed deeply. "You were right."

Glancing over my shoulder, I slanted him a look. "About what?"

He smiled against my neck—that one gesture broke through the heavy gates I was using to keep him from trampling my heart —and he chuckled softly. "Terrifying and amazing."

———

PATRICK'S DOOR CODE WAS BURNING A HOLE IN MY BACK POCKET. IT was a hot, constant reminder that my Sex God was a text away, and relative to the wannabe-Vegas club Marley insisted we hit, that reminder sounded better and better.

Yeah, he was *my* Sex God now.

"What'll it be?"

I glanced up at the bartender and rattled off our drink order. When he returned, I threaded the martini glass stems between my fingers and elbowed my way through the crowd, cursing each time the drinks bobbled and liquid sloshed over the rims. I needed to teach Jess and Marley how to drink without all the flavored sweetness.

We toasted to not needing men to make us happy—Jess and Marley were swearing off men after another Valentine's Day spent alone.

No need to mention I was exceptionally happy with the man in my life or that there was a man to mention at all—sort of. It wasn't like that with Patrick because I asked for something different, and I could lie and convince myself I was content with that.

I'd be a little more content if I was in his bed instead of a crowded club in the Back Bay, and I'd be a lot more content if I wasn't compelled to continue inventing boundaries so that I consumed Patrick in measured doses.

The sex was...amazing, and up until that night when I showed up at Patrick's door, I lived in dim ignorance of the kind of amazing it could be, but that wasn't why I needed to keep our time in check. I didn't trust myself to see Patrick outside of work more than once a week.

Spending the night was dangerous—without a clear exit strategy, we were getting fresh mango-papaya pastelitos for breakfast and that always led to Patrick licking something off my lip, and we all knew where that led.

If I wasn't careful, an entire weekend evaporated before my eyes. Not that I didn't want Cuban pastries or sex-filled weekends with Patrick—I did, and more than I was comfortable admitting. But he didn't sign up for that, and if I had any hope of walking away unscathed at the end of my apprenticeship, I needed to keep it tidy. And tidy meant parceling out our time into bite-sized chunks, and no pastelitos.

"Okay, so I know I said I don't need to be in a relationship," Marley said, a hand gingerly touching her hairspray-frozen waves. "But I'd be happier with one, and it's not wrong to admit that. It doesn't make me any less strong or independent."

"Yeah," Jess agreed. "If that man was good enough for you and took care of you. You deserve someone who treats you like a princess."

The words were out before I could rein in my annoyed tone. "Meaning what?"

I witnessed some version of this conversation every time I went out with Jess and Marley. They always wanted to be princesses, and though I didn't know enough about my heritage to speak with authority, I knew some princesses lived a life very different from Marley and Jess's imagination, and they often met with tragedy.

Marley's eyes turned dreamy as she leaned her head toward me. "Someone who surprises me with romantic dinners and flowers at work. He has to hold the door, and get angry when he sees other guys checking me out. I love those guys who go apeshit when they see someone hitting on their girlfriends. And he goes crazy on guys who treated me bad in the past."

"And gets mad when you offer to pick up the check," Jess added. "I want someone who makes a bubble bath and brings me wine when I've had a hard day, and I want him to spend the whole night talking about what we should name our kids. I want him to want me to stay home and iron his shirts or bake brownies, or paint murals."

"Yes!" Marley agreed. "And he picks out sexy couture dresses right from the designer for me to wear on special nights out, and has them messengered right from the shop. Oh! And he sends me to the spa for a day of pampering, just because I deserve it."

I focused on my drink to keep my attitude in check. As far as I could tell, they wanted generous, selfless men stuck in the 1950s who also ran up against anger management issues. I wanted to tell them they watched too many cheery rom-coms, and their version of a princess's life sounded boring, but I was working on being friendly. "Let me know when you find him."

My back pocket jolted with a series of vibrations, and I excused myself to the ladies' room—the list of people who texted me after midnight on a Saturday was short. Leaning against the stall door, I opened the message.

Patrick: I haven't seen your socks in a couple of days.

Patrick: Am I going to find out what color you have on tonight?

I laughed and bit my lip, ready to escape for my morsel of Patrick time.

Andy: I didn't know you were interested in my socks.
Patrick: Very interested. Starting to think you're hiding webbed feet, but very interested.

Exhaling, I tucked my phone in my pocket and returned to our table. Jess and Marley wedged a tray full of shots between them, and several Tight T-Shirts cheered them on—as if Patrick's texts weren't enough reason to leave. I caught Jess's eye and gestured to the door, mouthing that I was leaving.

"No!" she yelled. "We're doing shots!"

I didn't want to lie, and I wasn't about to describe my weird arrangement with Patrick. I knew where she stood on that. "I'm tired, and I have some work to do tomorrow..."

"Just two!" Marley cried, and the Tight T-Shirts surrounding her started chanting.

I grabbed a glass in each hand, knocked them back—whatever they were—slammed the glasses down, and walked through the club without a word. Within moments, I was in a cab headed toward the North End.

Going out with Jess and Marley felt necessary—even if it was awful and I spent the entire time thinking about Patrick. Working with Patrick and sleeping with Patrick added up to a lot of Patrick, and though I struggled to find fault with either, blowing off my only friends not connected to him seemed shitty.

Aside from Jess and Marley, all of my friends belonged to

Patrick: his sister, his brother's fiancée, his brothers. They were his and they'd stay with him when this ended.

Climbing the stairs to Patrick's apartment, the alcohol hit me hard and the horizon swayed. Goddamn shots. Either I was convincing Jess and Marley to try less douchey clubs or I wasn't going out drinking with them anymore. I wanted a cheese plate and wine instead of bassed-out music and kitchen sink-style shots, and I didn't care if that dropped me smack in the middle of spinsterdom or aged hipsterhood.

I leaned against the wall near his door to collect my equilibrium, and typed out the first thing that came to mind.

Andy: You said you wanted to tie me up. Is that the sort of thing a girl has to request in advance, kind of like how you have to call ahead for Peking duck?

His response was instantaneous.

Patrick: Tell me when you're coming and I'll get your order ready

Pushing away from the wall, my line of sight teetered again and I braced my hands on the doorframe before knocking. There was a muffled crash inside Patrick's apartment, and I laughed when he opened the door with a pleased, if not startled, expression.

"Come to think of it," I said, leaning forward to wrap my arms around Patrick's neck while his hands settled on my waist. "Peking duck sounds really good right now. I bet you know a place."

"Mmm," he murmured against my lips. "You sound better."

My hands dove under the hem of his shirt and spread up his back as he kissed me. Huge improvement over the noisy club and smarmy guys and shots. It was always like that—when my hands connected with his skin, everything else seemed irrelevant and I wanted to lose myself in him.

Patrick leaned back, his brow furrowing. "Is that...peppermint schnapps?"

A laugh bubbled up from my chest, and I stepped out of his arms to remove my coat and boots. "I think so. I was at a bar with some friends and they got shots, what kind I don't know, but drinking some was the toll for leaving even though I really hate shots."

Patrick leaned over the leather sofa and turned off the soccer match on the obscenely large flat screen. Folding his arms over his chest, he watched while I discarded my winter layers. "You were out with friends?"

"Yeah, but," I sighed, struggling to free my foot from my boot and nearly toppling over in the process. The room was swirling around me. "They're good friends but sometimes hanging out with them is dreadful, and I've been waiting for an opening from you all night, and we were at the douchiest place in the entire world."

"You're adorable unfiltered," he said. "Whatever was in that shot was totally worth it." He approached, stilling me with a hand to my stomach while he unzipped the boot I was fighting. That explained why it wasn't coming off. "Where were you?"

"Um, I think it was Undertow."

Patrick snorted, and turned his attention to my other boot. "I can't picture you there."

"Try picturing me tied to your bed," I said, my hand running through his hair. He glanced up, his hazel eyes hard. Patrick paused, and I had the distinct sense he was debating with himself. When I hiccupped—another graceless moment added to the evening's tab—Patrick laughed, wrapped his arms around my thighs, and tossed me over his shoulder.

I yelped, and started to protest his barbaric stunt, but a quick slap across my backside ended my commentary. God, what I wouldn't do to feel his palm on my skin. He was created with the sole purpose of giving me all the things I never knew I wanted and never found the courage to request. I flipped through memories of the past few weeks—our feverish bathroom encounters, that first night after dinner at Pomodoro, last weekend. He was intense and powerful and dark, and I'd swear he was built especially for my enjoyment.

"Your enjoyment, huh?" he asked when he set me on the bed. I stared at him in confusion, and he laughed. "You were thinking out loud just then."

"Hm." I shrugged and stared at the ceiling, and hoped my embarrassment didn't show. Patrick didn't prepare bubble baths or send evening gowns, but I was more than happy with innuendo-laced texts and good old-fashioned spankings.

He busied himself with stripping my clothes and muttering about my jeans being painted on when I registered that he wasn't my boyfriend, and it didn't matter what I was happy with because I forced him to agree to sex, and sex alone. The way I wanted it to be. The way I needed it to be.

"Doesn't have to be."

"What?" Our eyes met, and he looked away, shaking his head.

"Cute," Patrick murmured, his fingers tracing the bands of color on my rainbow knee socks. "Cold?"

My eyes swept over the dark bedroom, and I startled, realizing that, aside from my socks, I was naked and a silky fabric tied my hands to the headboard. A wave of heat started in my core, and spread through my body. I spied Patrick's sweater hanging off the edge of the bed, and noticed he was naked, too. Either my walk down memory lane was more extensive than I thought, or Patrick was The Flash.

And perhaps I was a little drunk, and not altogether aware of the events around me. I blamed the peppermint schnapps; I could handle my vodka.

"Can I take these off?" Patrick's fingers dipped beneath the band of my socks, and I shook my head. His eyes narrowed, and he crawled up the bed to cage his arms and legs around me. His erection bounced against my mound, and I fidgeted for more contact. "How much have you had to drink?"

"Hm." Thinking backwards, I attempted to recall the entire evening. When I didn't respond, Patrick caught my attention by scratching a thumb over my nipple and I jerked on my restraints. His hands covered my breasts, and though I knew my B-cups were hardly remarkable, the rumbling growl from Patrick's chest and glimmer in his eyes made them seem worthy of a spot in the Victoria's Secret runway show. "There were two shots of something pepperminty, two dirty martinis, a few vodka gimlets, and some vodka tonics."

"I'm surprised you made it up the stairs. Are you sure you want to do this?" He gestured toward my hands.

"Patrick, let me bring you in on a little secret." He nodded, his fingertips trailing over my skin so lightly I couldn't stop the shiver. "I haven't stopped thinking about this since you said it when my pants were around my knees in your sister's bathroom, and yes, I'm drunk, but I probably wouldn't have the balls to ask without a sensible concentration of vodka in my blood. So please, fuck me now or get me some Peking duck."

Patrick's head vibrated against my sternum as he shook with laughter. "Shit, I need to get you drunk more often. You are adorable."

Shifting my knees, Patrick settled between my legs. I was too hungry for his touch to complain that he didn't restrain my ankles as promised. One swipe of his tongue, and I was convinced I'd break the headboard. There was no way I could survive Patrick's tongue swirling around my clit or his teeth scraping across my folds without some damage.

"You will be just fine," Patrick murmured, and I bit my cheek to keep my thoughts from sliding out of my mouth. Too much dangerous information in there.

Patrick knew the magical ratio of intense suction to teasing strokes. The smooth slide of his tongue put my nerves on edge, and the muffled vibration of his words against my body sent tremors through my core.

He babbled about how wet I was, and that I was beautiful, and this was exactly where he wanted me. With his lips sealed around my clit, my heels dug into his back and my hips lifted off the mattress, and I was *this* close. A glance at the clock told me it took him less than three minutes.

"You really are a sweaty rugby Sex God," I slurred, my breath coming in halting pants.

He broke away with a laugh, quirking an eyebrow at me that clearly indicated he had no idea what I was talking about before leaning over to fish a condom from the bedside table. The shiny evidence of my arousal painted Patrick's mouth and chin, and I wanted to drag him to me and lick it away.

"You can lick it in a minute, dirty girl."

I groaned in frustration when the smooth fabric around my wrists refused to budge. Somewhere along the line, I failed to recognize that being tied down meant losing the use of my hands. Illogical as it might be, I always imagined touching Patrick while restrained, and though the absence of control ratcheted up the anticipation, I missed the feel of his skin on my fingers.

Once sheathed, Patrick knelt between my legs and positioned his hands on my hips. I heard him speaking, asking me questions, but the ceiling was spinning and his words blurred together, and I nodded absently. Note to self: mystery shots are off-limits.

He started to shift my body, and understanding hit me. "No, please don't."

Patrick stilled, his hands gently rubbing my hips while concern flashed in his eyes. "What's wrong, baby?"

"I want you like this," I insisted, my voice more petulant than Veruca Salt herself. "Please. I need to see you and I want you close."

Patrick studied me for a long moment, and I fought the torrent of thoughts threatening to slip from my lips. I wanted to explain I liked it—uh, no, I loved it—from behind, and I knew I'd love it even more with the excitement of the restraints, but I hated being cut off from the raw, unrefined reactions on his face. I needed to see every emotion burning in his eyes.

I needed to know this was dragging him under, too.

Even if it was the worst possible idea in the history of terrible ideas, I wanted to believe I meant something to him, something more than sex, and watching him gave me that.

Shifting to lie beside me, Patrick dragged his fingers over my hair and kissed me, his lips patient and generous until my heart stopped racing. The hand in my hair cruised up my arm, and with a blind flick, he freed my hands. I was immediately annoyed I hadn't found the escape hatch, but that was replaced with the relief I could touch Patrick again, and frustration that I failed to fully achieve yet another fantasy.

I started to shift toward Patrick, but he gripped my wrists. "Don't move yet. Your arms are numb. Your joints will be sore and the blood flow will come back in a minute," he whispered against my ear, his hands gently massaging my skin. "Are you sure you're all right?"

"Yeah."

Patrick nodded, and his teeth scraped across my earlobe until I understood the meaning of the word boneless. His kisses rained over my lips and cheeks and nose and eyelids before he dipped his head to my chest where he sucked my nipples into dark little pearls.

"You taste so good," he groaned, his hands spreading over my breasts. "I've wanted to tie you to this bed and lick you for so long...and now I just want to do it again."

My hands found their way over Patrick's shoulders, and I steered him on top of me. "I want you. I need to feel you."

My arms wrapped around his shoulders when he filled me and his hips started rolling against me. I saw another side of Patrick—a side I doubted the existence of after he left my ass covered in beautifully tiny bruises outlined by the imprint of his teeth last weekend. I didn't mind—rough, growly sex with Patrick made me realize what I'd been missing all these years—but the smooth thrusts of his hips and calm caresses were special.

His body covered me entirely, his warmth chasing away the lingering chill while his mouth attended to the sensitive juncture of my neck and shoulder. We rocked together, our hushed sighs and moans filling the air around us, and I could feel the heavy ache of my orgasm as it waited to unravel.

"Faster?" I asked, my mouth sweeping over Patrick's jaw.

"No," he gasped, his body tensing as he thrust into me and stilled. "This is...perfect."

And it was. If staying like this forever were an option, I'd take it in a heartbeat.

Patrick wrapped my legs around his waist, and the depth he discovered pushed me to the edge. I was coming with soft whimpers, my fingernails gripping Patrick's waist and hips for a little more friction to keep the tingles going.

He whispered into my ear, "So deep, right like this. All I feel is your pussy squeezing me, fuck...how do you do that?"

"Wouldn't you like to know," I laughed.

"Mmm. Andy." Patrick's eyes drifted shut and he smiled. "God, you're incredible. And you're mine."

I flexed my inner muscles until he shuddered and moaned before going slack.

His heart pounded against my breast—was it normal to like someone's heartbeat so much?

The thought didn't get especially far—I was on the edge of consciousness when Patrick tucked me against his chest.

I USED TO THINK WORKING ALONGSIDE ANDY WAS TORTURE, AND I spent the greater portion of those days obsessing about the ways she drove me crazy and wanting to get her naked.

As with most things, I didn't have a fucking clue what I was talking about.

Torture was sharing an office with a woman who seemed oblivious to the fact that, for the past three weekends, we had hot, wild sex for hours straight. It was wanting to throw her on the conference table and fuck her because her hair was everywhere and she smelled like flowers and her lips did terrible things to my imagination, all coupled with the newly acquired knowledge of precisely how good it was with her.

Torture was falling asleep with Andy in my arms only to wake up and discover her on the opposite side of the bed. It was spending the whole day in her company without seeing a single flicker of recognition in her eyes.

It was fucking agonizing.

Drumming my fingers against the edge of my laptop, I

invented ploys to steal time with Andy. She wanted to try tons of restaurants, and I still owed her Peking duck. I kept my grandfather's designs in my apartment, and if Andy was anything, she was fanatical about old architecture. We could always get a drink and see to that fantasy of hers, the one with the talking points. Or I could stop being a giant pussy and just ask to see her, even if it was a weeknight and she always created reasons to wait until the weekend.

"Dude, I know. This afternoon has been like ten years. I'm tired too, but let's get this done," Shannon said.

"Sorry." I inclined my head toward Shannon's list. "What's next?"

"One big item and some smallerish-slash-personalish items." She hoisted a folder. "We need to redraft our strategy and partnership structures because we're no longer a sole proprietorship. Angus changed things when he and Uncle Seamus went their separate ways, and while it isn't a huge deal, I think we need to clarify our partnership structure. I can totally handle that, but there are some big questions."

I glanced at the clock on my screen and figured Andy was still elbow-deep in the next round of Wellesley plans, and wasn't leaving until she solved whichever problem was vexing her. That's how she was; it wasn't done until it was done, and she never walked away from a challenge.

That's probably why she tolerated my brand of impatient bastard so well.

"Okay. Let's knock them out."

"I think you need to acknowledge that you're the managing partner or CEO or principal."

A huge sigh burst from my chest and I leaned back. "Only if you're a managing partner, too."

She threw her pen across the table in frustration. "If it's you and me, why not Matt? Why not Sam, too? We'll leave out Riley for the time being, but the four of us for sure, right?"

"Shannon," I groaned. There was no right answer to this question, and more wrong answers than I could shake a T-square at. "We need to be a small firm with a small table of partners, and that's it."

"You're wrong. You're wrong." She pushed out of her chair to pace. "Just sit there, stewing in your wrongness." Shannon dropped her hands to the windowsill and stared down at the alley below. "I'm going to draft a few org structures and we'll decide on them as a team," she hissed. "You'll spend a lot time being wrong then."

"Outstanding." I held up my hands in surrender. "What else?"

She plopped into her chair with an exaggerated sigh, and flipped through her dark purple notebook while her bracelets jangled. "The leases end on our Range Rovers next month, and I decided to upgrade to hybrid models. We can't exactly roll with this sustainability thing and drive around in gas-guzzlers. Is it time to add a car to our fleet for Riley?"

"No. I told you that in October. He shouldn't be allowed out of Matt's sight."

Shannon nodded and consulted her notes. "Andy's managing Wellesley?"

"Yep." I checked my project spreadsheet for notes on her progress. "She's working through some inconsistent plans from the original build to the work Angus did on the house when he and Mom moved in. Once she nails that down, I think we'll be ready to move forward. Already replaced the water heaters and solar panels are going in next week."

"You're good with her managing such a big project?"

"Yeah." I shrugged, frowning in confusion. Didn't I tell Shannon about Andy managing most of my projects, solving every random problem I threw her way plus making my life equal parts magnificent and excruciating?

"Totally fine," she replied quickly. She sounded placating and that was tremendously weird for Shan. "I'm delighted to hear it. Do we need to have a crew empty the house?"

"Depends on what you want to do with that furniture," I said. "A lot of what's left was built for that house. But other than that, anything that might have been there before is gone now. As far as I can tell. There's his room, but that's it."

"We have to tell everyone else at some point." We stared at each other for a beat, waiting for the other to take on that task. It wasn't going to be me.

"I'll have Tom arrange for the furniture to be donated to a shelter unless you think there's something crazy valuable that we should keep or sell with the house, and I'll ask Matt or Riley if they want to go through Angus's things."

Tense silence settled between us, and I toggled to my email to avoid thinking about that house. I hated the emotional toll it took, and that after all these years of being on our own and redefining ourselves, that house had the power to bring us right back.

"Last thing: I'm going to give Lauren a bridal shower. She's not having bridesmaids, and both of her closest friends are busy being pregnant all the time, but I still want her to have a party."

I blinked at Shannon. "And you need my help with that?"

"Yeah, asshole, I was hoping you could bake a penis cake," she snapped, but her irritated eyes quickly crinkled with humor. She giggled, and soon my shoulders were shaking as laughter took over.

"What the fuck is a penis cake, Shan?"

"It's a cake!" she squealed between laughs, her face and neck flushing bright red. "Shaped like a penis, with a puddle of tapioca pudding and some chocolate shavings for—"

"That's enough! I don't want to hear another word." I closed my laptop and folded my arms on the table. "I love Lauren but I don't want to imagine her—or you, or anyone—eating dick cake. I never want to talk about this again."

"Dude, you're so easy," she giggled. "I just wanted to know if you were good with me inviting Andy."

"Of course. Why wouldn't I be?" I scratched my head. "Doesn't she hang out with you and Lauren?"

Shannon lifted a shoulder. "Well, you aren't super-positive about her, and you get super-annoyed when I bring her up, and you freaked out when me and Lauren went dress shopping with her. So I wanted to check with you first." She twisted her bracelets and considered me. That placating voice was back. It was as if she didn't trust me around sharp objects. "Are things getting better with you two?"

It was the day of no right answers. "I mean, yeah, she's... smart. And people like her."

"'People like her' but not you?"

"I...I, I like her," I stammered. I didn't think it was necessary to clarify my appreciation for Andy had many facets. "She's smart. She was a good hire."

"Impressive. You're evolving." She glanced at her watch, and her eyes widened. "Shit. I have to go."

She swept her laptop and phone into her bag, and slipped on her outerwear while I gathered the paperwork on the table.

"Don't think the cake conversation is over," she yelled from the doorway.

The lights were on in my office, and though her things were still there, Andy wasn't. I dropped my laptop and files, and headed out to search the building for her. I wandered through four levels, turning off lights as I went, and eventually found her in the materials room. I watched her from the hall, admiring the way she cocked her head while she studied the paint color bridge over the stone finish samples.

Straight-up creeper, but that was nothing new.

Careful to keep my steps quiet, I positioned myself behind Andy, and wrapped my arm around her waist. "That one." I pointed over her shoulder to a dark gray paint chip. Once I swept her hair to the side, I pressed my lips to her neck. She gasped, her body stiffening in my arms. "We're alone. I checked."

"What are you still doing here, stalker?"

"Looking for you," I said, my nose running along her neck. Over the past few weeks, I learned only her hair smelled like lavender, and though it left perfumed traces in her wake, Andy tasted slightly different.

"I had to walk away from those plans. I threatened to shred them a few times but they haven't learned their lessons yet."

Seeing Andy frustrated was a new experience for me. It felt special, like another secret treasure she was offering. My cache was limited to her mood-driven alcohol choices, the tattoos, and the adorable way she completely lost her shit when she was drunk. "What's wrong?"

Andy exhaled, and rested her head against my shoulder. "There are some strange variations in room dimensions between the two plans. In some places, it's insignificant—an inch or two. But in others, it's substantial."

"We should talk about this over dinner," I said against her skin. "I'm sure I can figure it out."

"If there's anyone who could, it would be you."

I squinted at the screen, and swiped the image to zoom in further while scribbling numbers on a cocktail napkin. Looking between the screen and the numbers, I shook my head. As far as I could tell, Angus turned the Wellesley plans into something incomprehensible in one of his final ass-kickings.

"Fuck if I know."

"That's what I'm screaming about." Andy lifted her wine glass in salute. "I need to go out there and measure the entire property myself. So that's great."

As much as I hated trips to Wellesley, she was right. The numbers didn't make sense, and she couldn't get new plumbing or electrical underway without clean plans. "We should have time tomorrow or Friday."

"You don't have to go with me."

"No, I really do." I grimaced. "I told Shan I'd make some decisions about the furniture."

Andy shook her hair over her shoulders, and I started wondering how long I should wait before asking her to spend the night with me. I needed some Andy time. Weekends weren't enough. I was certain she'd say no for any number of bullshit reasons, though I hoped none of which included her doubting her decision to see me these past few weekends. Was it even possible? Her insistence that weeknights didn't work, and that she couldn't miss a Saturday yoga class seemed bizarre, even for Andy. The mocking reminders that she pushed me away before were never fully retreated.

"Okay, but you're not allowed to spend the entire day in the bell jar," she said.

The original visit wasn't my finest hour, and spending the afternoon snarling at everyone in my path wasn't especially mature. But she noticed, and tracked my mood to the house rather than my general irritability.

"You'll have to keep me in line."

Andy's eyes narrowed and she leaned across the table, her lips twisting into a smirk. "Does that mean I get to spank you?" she whispered.

Andy never mixed business and pleasure; an armload of icy glares over the past few weeks taught me that. I swallowed, my fingers tightening on the stem of the glass as I set it down. I sensed a door inching open.

"Definitely," I laughed, my hand darting out to caress her wrist. She gave a pointed stare to my hand and a brief frown crossed her face, but she didn't pull back. "You can do anything you want to me."

Andy offered a suggestive smile, and there was nothing sexier. I was in big trouble, and considering the way her pulse was hammering under my fingers, I wasn't alone.

"Come home with me."

Looking disappointed, she broke my gaze but didn't pull her hand away. "I can't. I have work to do."

Did she forget that I knew exactly which projects were under her care and which milestones were on deck? I scanned all of our current projects, plus the random queries that I frequently sent her way, and still couldn't come up with a single item that required her attention on a Wednesday night. Grabbing her hand when we exited the restaurant, I tugged her toward Hanover Street. A few fluffy inches of snow blanketed the cobblestone streets and there was much more to come.

"What work? You can't do anything on Wellesley until we get out there, and that's your only pending project."

Andy stared at the sidewalk and fought to restrain a smile. That got my attention. "I can't tell you."

"Yeah...that's the perfect thing to say if you want me to ask a million questions and not give up until you answer. What are you working on?"

"This must be what multiple personalities feel like." Rubbing her forehead, Andy released a rueful laugh before meeting my gaze. "My boss—I might have told you about him before—he always makes up these pop quizzes for me. Every morning, he picks the most unworkable problems from the projects we have —sometimes, when he's annoyed with the world, projects that other people have—and he tells me to figure it out."

Okay. We'd deal with me being a giant prick some other time. If this was what she needed, this was a game I could play. "Sounds like an insufferable bastard."

Andy laughed, nodding. "That's one way to put it. So he gives me these problems in the morning, and I have to figure them out like...on the spot. And if I get them wrong, he won't eat lunch with me."

When she described it that way, I was the odds-on favorite for Boston's Top Douche.

"I really like eating lunch with him. He finds the best places, and he's funny and radiates megawatts of knowledge. I've told you my goal in life is to learn everything I can from him. So...I started reviewing all the plans the night before, and trying to figure out what he'd ask, and doing a lot of research to be prepared with the right answer. That's what I have to do tonight."

I laughed, thrilled to discover I was blocking my own cock.

"I seriously doubt that your boss radiates anything, but I'm guessing he's giving you problems he hasn't figured out, and then taking you to lunch because he likes the way your brain works. He's also trying to get into your pants." Andy licked her lips and gifted me with a quick smile from under her thick lashes. "Maybe if you told him you like having lunch with him, you could take a night off."

"Trust me—he radiates. I spent years waiting to work with him. You're going to think I'm a major geek, but...his thesis was kind of like my bedtime story all through college."

Holy fuck. My grasp on her hand tightened. "You read my —wait. What?"

I remembered Andy insisting the only apprenticeship she wanted was the one we were offering, but I filed it away as standard interview-speak.

She lifted a shoulder. "Yeah. At the end of my second year. I read it and...it spoke to me. Whenever I was uninspired or unmotivated or confused, I'd read it and remember why I wanted to do this. It always brought me back to what I loved about preservation."

Apparently, I wasn't the only creeper. It shouldn't have been sexy to imagine Andy reading the least interesting thing I wrote in college, but images of her poring over my thesis in nothing more than funky knee socks inundated me.

Clearing my throat to suppress a growl, I squeezed Andy's hand. "I have it on good authority that your boss wants to take you to lunch tomorrow, and you should come home with me tonight. I might have an inside track on those pop quiz questions."

"Say no more," she laughed, a bright, uninhibited smile breaking across her face.

I WAS BLAMING IT ON BEING PAST MY FRIENDS-WITH-BENEFITS phase. There was also the whole issue of her showing up all sweet, babbling, and sloppy drunk on Saturday. And she read my thesis. Repeatedly and for comfort, though it certainly called her idea of comfort into question.

I wanted her body, but I also wanted her conversation, her bent eyebrows worth a million words, her sharp, dry humor. It was gradually ripping me apart, and it was all foreign to me.

Somewhere between the creepy staring and finally tying her to my bed, I developed an affection for Andy that made every minute she wasn't in my arms feel wasted. Saturday night wasn't 'just sex' with every word of her inner monologue on display and quiet mentions of wanting to see me, or waiting for me to invite her over, or me being made for her. It was no more 'just sex' than her uncharacteristically shy description of her boss, and how much she liked lunch with him. Or with me. Or whatever.

I was done with 'just sex.' It was never just anything. I knew that when I agreed to it, and I knew it when Andy thought I was breaking our treaty by touching her in the office. I wanted to respect her parameters, but I also wanted so much more of Andy.

My fingers skimmed over the curved characters of the tattoo clinging to her ribs. The sight of Andy's exposed skin lit only by moonlight while she was tucked against my chest was staggering, and part of me recognized that she would always affect me this way.

"Andy," I murmured. She hummed in response, and pulled my arm under her breasts. The simple gesture was a giant billboard reminding me I passed the exit for 'just sex' many miles back. "Tell me something about you. Something I don't know."

Her nails scratched up and down my forearm for a few minutes, and I figured she was tuning out my request until she replied, "My father died when I was seven."

I tightened the arm around her torso while I kissed her shoulder and rummaged around my memory for mention of Andy's family. I only knew she was from a town far up north Maine's coast.

The cold, heavy ache of understanding landed in my gut, and I pulled the blankets up. My mother's death ended childhood for me and my siblings. When it broke us, it wasn't the kind of break that healed neatly. It was the quiet shattering of a frozen-over pond protesting too much weight, all tiny fissures racing out from the impact site until the ice dropped out and chilled emptiness rushed in.

Some of the broken places made us stronger, and some healed over time, but not all.

Andy glanced over her shoulder. "You're not going to ask what happened?"

"No." My mouth continued mapping the sharp jut of her collarbone. "My mother died when I was ten and I hate when people ask. If you want me to know, you'll tell me."

Minutes slipped by, and the rasp of her fingers against my arm combined with city noises to occupy the quiet.

"He was shot, in South Africa. Some militant group wanted him dead. His family was exiled during the Iranian Revolution, and he ended up in Egypt, and then London. That's where my mom met him. I was born in Istanbul, and we lived between there and London until he died." She released a long sigh. "I never talk about that. Ever. People know he died, but they don't know why, or that I didn't always live in Maine, or that I'm even Persian. They just think I tan easily."

Holding her closely, I searched for the right words but I knew all too well nothing eased the loss. It shrouded even the best memories in sorrow. "After my sister Erin was born—you haven't met her—my mother was pregnant again, and there was a complication and she bled to death. She and the baby died in that big room on the second floor at Wellesley, with the six of us there. We never really talk about it, and like you said, people know, but they have no idea."

The blueprint of that bedroom appeared in my mind, and within white space bound by thin black lines, I saw my mother crumpled on the hardwood floor, and the puddle of blood around her. I saw the paramedics working on her while Sam refused to let go of her hand. I saw the ambulance spitting gravel as it skidded down the driveway, leaving us and our blood-stained hands behind.

Andy rolled over, her brown eyes boring into mine before she wrapped an arm around my neck and pulled me in for a kiss. Her lips soothed, and communicated that she understood, and knew the limitations of words. She pressed her forehead against mine with a smile.

"Tell me something. Something else. Something that's really off-limits."

"'Really off-limits?' I don't even know what that includes. Hell, Andy, I've never seen what's hiding under your socks."

"Not hiding anything. My toes just get really cold." She laughed, though her expression rapidly sobered. "Something that scares the shit out of you to say."

Unless I was completely misreading her signals and she was expecting me to ask for a threesome, she wanted me talking about this. It wouldn't be the first time I completely misread Andy, but something she let slip on Saturday night told me to push forward.

"I have a crazy idea." I gazed into her eyes, and she nodded in encouragement. Her eyes dropped to my chest and she studied my freckles, her teeth clamping the edge of her lip. "I want...I want to stop pretending this is 'just sex.' This isn't 'just sex' for me, Andy, and I don't think it is for you either."

After a long, painful pause during which I invented at least nine ways to play off my comment if her response wasn't the one I needed, she shook her head. It was always her little gestures. The eyebrows, the tiny smiles, the 'hm,' and now her slight head shake.

"I like you," I confessed. "A lot. As in, miss you when I don't see you, need to talk about your Facebook privacy settings, want to find out how you found my thesis, rearrange my schedule to eat lunch with you, ready to see what's under your knee socks, like you."

"Hm." Andy nestled her head against my chest, and I inhaled the rich lavender scent of her hair. "I like you, too. Even if you're a growly, bitey stalker, and always rolling up your sleeves and stretching so I have to—" Her nails scraped low over my stomach and I was ready for her again. My hand rubbing deep circles on her hip, I urged her body closer to mine. "—look at this."

I used to think hearts only skipped beats in near-death experiences, but often enough, Andy's words had that effect on me. "Sounds like we have a lot to talk about."

Andy's leg hooked over my hip, and our bodies were flush together with her breasts pressed against my chest, my erection digging into her stomach, and our hands gliding over warm skin. "Maybe I should stay over."

"I like that plan." Armed with the best possible outcome from my crazy idea, I plowed into the most dangerous territory without a shield. "I get that your boss is Captain Douchebag, but would it be so bad if he knew about this?"

"No." She laughed and glanced up at me with a wince. "But it would be bad if his partners knew."

"Why?" I cupped her breast, the flesh heavy and heated under my fingers, and my thumb brought her nipple to attention.

Her forehead pinched into fine wrinkles while her finger traced paths between the freckles on my chest. "Hooking up with the boss isn't usually a good idea, and you're in each other's lives so much..."

Rolling Andy to her back, I bracketed her hips with my legs and balanced my hands on either side of her head. "I don't give a fuck what they think," I said, and sucked a nipple into my mouth.

"Easy for you to say," she ground out, her body quivering beneath me. "You run the place. You're forgetting that I'm just an apprentice. I can't be that cavalier, Patrick."

Her nipple shone with moisture when I released it from between my teeth, and I promptly shifted to the other. I needed the distraction of her skin in my mouth. I was too close to giving her the keys to the firm, or offering to fire any number of my siblings if they gave her so much as a side-eye. None of that would help, either; she'd gut me for suggesting it.

In many ways, Andy was nothing like the other women I'd known intimately, and above all else, it was obvious that she didn't need me. I admired her strength and independence.

Guiding her career was part of my responsibility as her mentor, but I knew she wasn't about to let me stand in her way or set her course. Part of me loved that she wouldn't be calling me to unclog a drain anytime soon, yet another part of me wanted to be much more than a dirty little secret.

My teeth grazed over her nipple, and I moved my way down her breast before biting at the underside while her nails dug into my scalp. The time I could reasonably allot to this discussion without coming all over her belly was nearly up.

"Fine. Here are your options. One—we don't tell them until June when you've passed your boards. I hate that option, by the way." Andy started to comment, and I pressed my thumb over her lips to keep her quiet. I didn't count on her sucking me into her mouth. I felt the wet suction all the way in the base of my cock. I needed to talk faster.

"Two—you work with Sam or Matt, but I'm telling you right now you'll hate that option and be on your knees begging me to take you back before lunch. I mean, that doesn't actually sound terrible," I murmured, and she bit down on the pad of my thumb. "Ow. Behave."

The wicked gleam in her eyes nearly pushed me right over the edge. Grinding against her center, I felt her heat coating my cock, and I snatched another condom from the table.

"Three—decide you don't give a fuck because it's never been 'just sex' and aside from the fact I spend most of the day wondering whether you'll let me fuck you in the printer room, we've managed to make it work." Reluctantly removing my thumb from her mouth, I gestured for her to respond.

"Is that what we've been doing? Making it work?"

I groaned and my head fell back against my shoulders. She wanted the secrets. "Kitten, let's just make it work right now and hammer out the details later. My brain might explode if I don't get inside you in the next four seconds."

Andy's knees pressed against her shoulders, and she glanced at her kelly green and pink polka dot knee socks. "You can take them off," she said while the head of my cock pressed into her wet folds. "But you have to keep me warm."

She eased the socks down her legs, nodding for me to complete the job, exposing her slender feet tipped with shiny black toenails to me. I brushed my fingers over her skin, hooked her ankles around my waist, and laced our fingers together, pinning her wrists to the mattress. Andy squeezed my hands, her fingertips gently rubbing against me.

For a moment, the offering stunned me. For whatever reason, socks were a hard limit, and now they weren't. It meant something I didn't understand, but my dick was not concerned with deconstructing the symbolism.

Lavender tinted with the aroma of her arousal permeated every breath while her fingers communicated her desires against my hands, alternately squeezing and stroking and scratching. She met me, thrust for thrust, and demanded more until I was drenched with sweat and pistoning into the hot clench of her center.

"Oh fuck yes," she moaned. I knew she was close, and a few more deep thrusts would send her right over the edge. "More, Patrick. I want more of you."

She had no idea how right she was. I realized I wanted more of her too—more than I understood. I wanted her hands in my hair, on my skin. I wanted to watch her orgasm shatter through her body and listen to her quiet moans. I wanted to hold her while she slept and wake up with her in my bed. Whatever it was before this night wasn't enough anymore and the recognition I could never be content with so little left me reeling.

I sank into her heat, groaning at the sensation of her body engulfing me, drawing me in. We fit together perfectly. Our bodies anticipated each other's moves and I felt the ghost of release tickling the base of my spine. Bracing our clasped hands beside her shoulders, I dragged her lip between my teeth and nibbled while my hips rocked into her, offering barely enough friction to turn her body feverish.

I wanted to convince her we could be open about our relationship without compromising her career. I needed her to know that, despite her heroic attempts at avoidance, she did something to me I couldn't comprehend, and whatever it was, I liked it. There was more to say, more to confess but Andy still wanted secrets. She thought she needed them, and nothing I said would change that yet.

I'll never know how I managed to hold back.

When Andy went over the edge, her body melting beneath me, I saw that rare openness take over. So captivated by her unrestrained smile and wide, hazy eyes, I barely noticed my orgasm charging through my veins until heat filled the condom. My lips found Andy's and my hands were in her hair, and she was the only woman I wanted.

For that moment, she was raw and beautiful and mine.

Patrick: Where did you go?
Andy: Home
Patrick: Why?
Andy: Clean clothes
Patrick: Tell me if you're leaving. or, keep your ass in my bed until I get back from my run, because I wasn't finished with you.
Andy: I'm going to Roslindale this morning and you're going to Medford, so...
Patrick: grr
Andy: ?
Patrick: I'd like to know who scheduled us on opposite sides of town
Andy: My boss.
Patrick: I need to have a few words with that asshole.

I SLIPPED MY PHONE INTO MY POCKET—THIS LINE OF conversation was going nowhere good—and headed for the early Gothic cottage. Studying my clipboard, I forced all sexy-time thoughts from my head and ignored the repeated vibrations inside my pocket. A narration of his plans for me wasn't going to fast-forward the time before lunch, and it wasn't magically depositing me into his bed.

My only option was supervising some demo and thinking about anything other than the thin grasp I had on the storm brewing between Patrick and me.

"THIS DOESN'T MAKE SENSE," HE MUTTERED. I NOTED THE measurements while Patrick's hands skimmed over the surface of a pale yellow wall. He pivoted, and gestured for me to join him. "Does this feel like the original plaster to you?"

I spent the early morning hours figuring out how things would be different today. We never agreed upon a more-than-sex plan, and I didn't know how I'd handle it if Patrick wanted to be all cuddly at jobsites. I was down for a quick, silent fuck in a closet on special occasions but I drew the line at holding hands in front of our general contractors—those boys would die laughing if they knew I was with the boss, and any credibility I had built would them would be lost.

Relief did not even begin to describe how I felt when we met up for lunch and things felt normal—or, as normal as they could be when you're sleeping with your boss and revealing basically every private thought you've ever had.

My hands pressed against the wall, and I concentrated on the smooth, seamless texture beneath my skin. "No. This feels like drywall. Drywall with...some kind of faux finish, or a few layers of oil-based paint. It's too flat for one-hundred-and-thirty-year-old plaster."

"Exactly," he murmured, and stepped back from the wall. "But those—" Patrick gestured to the other walls, "aren't. It's just this one."

I shrugged. "A lot of walls are redone when there are electrical or plumbing issues."

"There are no major junctions here, though." Patrick took another step back and crossed his arms over his chest, and I seriously considered stroking his bicep. Just for a minute, and just because I could, even though it contradicted everything else in my head. "Let's bust it open."

"Patrick. That's ridiculous."

He stared at the wall for another moment then strode into the hall. I found him standing in the doorway of the neighboring room, his hands fisted at his side. That was the room—the one where his mother died—and this time, I let my hand rest on his arm.

I always resented that my father died alone on the street, in a sea of strangers, and the opportunity to say goodbye was stolen from me, though I never considered being there—powerlessly watching his final breaths—might have been worse in ways I couldn't begin to fathom.

Resting my head against Patrick's shoulder, I squeezed his arm. I knew something about Patrick's grief. He kept it hidden away, but I saw it. I knew it.

We stayed that way for a few moments, and he covered my hand with his before charging toward the wall adjoining the yellow room.

"It's the same. This isn't the original wall. Do we have a sledgehammer around? I might have one in the trunk."

"No." I shot him a bland look. "I don't want a sledgehammer

in here until the floors are protected and the original moldings and baseboards are appropriately handled."

"This doesn't make sense. He did this for a reason. He wouldn't put up new walls to fuck with us...there's a reason."

Patrick was quiet on the drive back to the city and didn't say much while we returned to his office. Something was bubbling around in his brain, but he immediately turned his attention to design plans when he reached his desk.

The afternoon quickly faded to evening while I updated my plans with the corrected measurements and printed new copies for the contractors.

He glanced up when I returned with a reel of new designs hot off the printer. "Matt and Riley are downstairs. They want to check out what you have. I told them about the room dimensions and new walls."

It was a full house in Matt's office. Shannon, Matt, Riley, and Lauren occupied the seats around the conference table, and the hungry vultures dug in the minute I put the plans down. Patrick nodded toward the small sofa on the other side of Matt's office, and we sat there while they debated. I listened attentively for comments on my designs, and was pleased with the stray remarks.

Patrick's knee bumped mine and he whispered, "Your phone."

Grabbing it from my pocket, I glanced at the unopened text messages. I shot him a confused expression. He nodded toward my phone, his knee rubbing against my leg again. "Why are you texting me?"

"Because you don't want them to hear what I have to say," he replied with an irritable wave toward his siblings.

Growing up in a family firm, planning for his career trajectory was far different from someone who wasn't an heir apparent. It was easy for him to dismiss my issues with making our relationship public. He never needed to defend his choices in interviews, and whether industry people talked about his personal life probably didn't cross his mind.

My mind skipped ahead to June, and my licensing exams. Once my apprenticeship ended, things would be different—he'd still be running a firm and I'd still be a young architect, but maybe...could we make it work? Would I stay at Walsh Associates? Would they want me to stay? Would they want me to stay because I was with Patrick? Could we stay together if I moved to a competing firm? Were there competing firms that interested me?

Patrick's knee firmly nudged me out of my thoughts, and he growled, "*Andy*."

Questions about the future spiraled through my mind while I tried to focus on the screen of my phone.

Patrick: Those pants make thinking very difficult for me.
Patrick: I'd very much like to get you out of them.
Patrick: Can we arrange that?

Turning my head, I met Patrick's smirk and narrowed my eyes in response. There was nothing exciting about my black wool wide-leg trousers.

Andy: I like these pants. I'm sorry you don't care for them.
Patrick: Trust me, I like them. so much that I want to take them off and get a better look.
Andy: At the pants?
Patrick: No. Not even a little.

Patrick: Are you coming to my place? I want to take you to bed.

Patrick: Maybe you could wear those boots. The ones you wore to 21st. and nothing else.

Patrick: And maybe I could wrap your legs around my neck and lick your sweet pussy for an hour

Patrick: And maybe then I'd fuck you so hard and for so long that you can't move a muscle without thinking about me tomorrow

Patrick: And maybe after you've come 16 times, you can suck my cock until I come in your mouth

"Hey."

Startled and blushing a dark shade of crimson, I fumbled my phone. Patrick caught it before it bounced to the floor, a loosely restrained smirk on his lips. I smiled at Lauren as she dropped into an armchair beside us.

"What's up, Laur?" Patrick asked. He pressed the phone into my palm, his fingers brushing slowly over my wrist.

"It sounds like aliens might be to blame," Lauren laughed, looking over her shoulder at Shannon, Matt, and Riley as they argued and gestured wildly at the plans. "Up for a pedicure? Shannon and I usually go for pedis on Thursdays but she's focused on this. We go to this great place that serves margaritas but I don't like drinking alone. I mean, I will, but...I'd rather go with friends and not be that lonely drunk lady talking to herself."

"Yeah, and someone needs to keep your drunk ass from tripping into oncoming traffic," Matt called over his shoulder.

"Oh would you be quiet?" she said. "I can handle my liquor just fine, thank you."

I laughed. "Margaritas and pedicures?"

"Yeah. It's been forever since we talked, and I never get to see you when I swing by. I'd love to chat with you again."

I looked at Patrick expectantly. Claiming to need me working on Wellesley would be believable—and keep me in pocket. Patrick's eyes flashed with disappointment but he quickly schooled his expression.

He nodded at me, and said, "Go. They're just dicking around. I doubt they even have notes on the design." As we turned to leave, Patrick called, "Keep your phone on, Asani."

A FEW MARGARITAS AND A THOROUGH LEG MASSAGE WERE MY NEW Thursday night requirements. Wonderfully absent of bros in tight t-shirts, shots, and electronica, this was exactly how I wanted to spend my time. I adjusted the pressure on the chair's massage settings and swallowed a groan.

"I know, right?" Lauren sighed, clinking her glass to mine.

"Yeah. This is going in the rotation."

"So worth it," Lauren said. "Especially when you don't have time for anything and you're running around with your hair on fire."

"Speaking of hair on fire, how's the wedding planning coming?"

Last we spoke, Lauren was the picture of chill but altogether too many of my college and grad school friends went from completely calm to completely batshit crazy while planning their weddings. I continued wondering when Lauren would drink the bridezilla Kool-Aid.

"Good. Really, it's all good, and the biggest variable is whether my brothers will be able to make it." She signaled to the young man pouring refills, pointing to our glasses before flicking her gaze over her phone. "They're deployed, and it's up in the air whether they'll be back. Sometimes their missions are...unpredictable. But I'm sure it will be fine."

I studied her, watching her teeth sink into her bottom lip and her head bob as if convincing herself.

"So anyway," she continued. "What's new with you?"

Hm. There was a lot of new in my life. I nodded to myself, and drank my margarita, thinking about all this newness. Amazing apprenticeship where I was learning more than I thought possible. Great colleagues who were smart, funny, and swore like sailors. A new city to explore, and more good eats than I could consume in a lifetime. A few more pairs of tall boots added to the collection—as if I didn't have enough Wellies or riding boots to wear a unique set each day.

And one incredibly hot architect with the most expressive hazel eyes I ever encountered and entirely too much talent in and out of the bedroom.

"Mmhmm. Yep, about that dreamy look you have right now. So how is Patrick?"

Holding my breath, I slowly swiveled my head to face Lauren, and found her smiling at me with her chin propped on her fist. There was no way she knew. Not possible.

"What?" I asked, struggling to keep my voice steady.

"I knew it! I knew it that night we all met up at Twenty-First."

She knew and the tequila started rebelling against my stomach. Despite the alcohol warming my blood, a cold sweat broke out across my skin. If Lauren knew, Matt and Shannon knew, and that meant everyone knew. Everyone knew and they were going along with this little act to pretend they didn't and I was the apprentice who slept with the managing partner. Where was the cheesy soundtrack for that cliché?

"What?" I repeated.

My stomach roiled. I tried to calculate an appropriate tip for vomiting in the footbath.

Lauren smiled and nodded patiently. "There's something going on between you two."

This wasn't happening. This was a hallucination bred of tequila and sugar scrubs, and it wasn't happening. I leaned forward and focused on my breathing to keep my stomach contents in place. "Who—I mean, where did you hear that?"

"I didn't hear it anywhere, I just noticed things. Though you confirmed it all with that deer-in-the-headlights look, my friend."

"No one said anything to you?"

"No," Lauren replied. "Sweetie, we're friends, right? This is between us."

A breath I didn't know I was holding whooshed out, and I slumped back. "What do you mean, you 'noticed things?'"

Lauren frowned, gesturing toward me with her margarita glass. "The way you were sitting tonight. You were leaning toward each other. And you kept looking at each other, and having little talks with your eyes. I've never seen Patrick do that. And he kept trying to be all smooth and touch you when he thought no one was looking."

Mr. Smooth's ears must have been burning, because he decided to text me at that exact moment.

Patrick: Still want to take you to bed. I'm back at my place. come over whenever

Patrick: Or I'll go to you

Patrick: Do I know where you live?

I pocketed my phone, electing to concentrate on the issues at hand instead of the issues in Patrick's bed—as if they were different. "Did anyone else notice?"

"No. And no one noticed the sneaky looks you were giving each other at Twenty-First." Lauren sipped her drink and placed a soothing hand on my arm. "It's obvious you're a little frazzled, and I'm sorry for doing that to you. But it sounds like you need to let it out, so let it out on me. Just between friends."

The story tumbled out in a tangled, frantic mess, and I told her everything—the flirty texts, the lunches, the fangirling, the bathrooms, the dirty fantasies, the anxiety I felt over the future of my career, and the secrecy—and she listened as if I was reciting some Emily Dickinson rather than describing the most wild experiences of my life.

None of it surprised her, and that surprised *me*.

Lauren was right: I felt better getting it out, and I felt substantially better when she swore up and down she wasn't peeping a word to anyone. Not even Matt.

"I gotta say," Lauren laughed. "I love that you have this perfect storm. You're so in sync at the office and it sounds like that carries over in bed. Too perfect. And the fact you held him off for so long blows my mind. I did *not* have the same success."

"Success with what now?"

Lauren licked her lips while a broad smile spread across her face. "So...I met Matthew on a Thursday, and went home with him on a Friday. Of the same week." She lifted her hands. "And somehow managed to spend the next four days attached to his side, even though I was full-tilt obsessed with my work and not letting a guy get me off-track. I might have been a little crazy back then. And by 'back then,' I do mean a couple of months ago."

That was the last thing I expected to hear from Lauren. I spent very little time piecing together her relationship with Matt, but I didn't expect it to start with a glorified hook-up. She seemed altogether too innocent, too by-the-book.

"So, Andy, let's get down to it. What do you want out of all of this?"

I watched the technician as she applied warm oil to my foot before digging her fingers into my tendons. She was getting an earful—I bet she could eat out for weeks on the stories she heard from her vantage point. My phone buzzed again, and I studied the screen.

Patrick: Yeah I don't know where you live. You don't make a habit of telling me things like that.

"I don't know," I said. "I'm just trying to enjoy Patrick, and not kill my career in the process."

I typed a quick response while Lauren chuckled at a message streaming across her phone.

Andy: Patience is one of the strongest warriors. The other is time.

"Yeah. I tried that too," Lauren muttered. "Turns out you can do both. Who knew?" She shifted her attention from the sunny yellow color on her toenails, and gave me a serious look. "It's been a rough couple of months for them, and they've been through a lot. I think...I think Patrick needs a soft place to land. They all do, but Patrick needs someone who will ride out the storm with him. He rides them all alone, and he can't do that to himself anymore. Not now."

I couldn't tell whether she was warning me off or giving her blessing, and I decided not to ask, as I didn't know what to think about either. "Rough couple of months?"

"Honestly, it's been a rough twenty years for them." My eyebrows arched and Lauren held up a finger to shut me down. "Do not misinterpret the Ivy League educations or *Boston Magazine* covers or the fact they're generally put-together, functional adults. They're little orphans in nice clothes who know how to use big words."

Lauren skimmed through the Walsh family highlights, and I started to see my colleagues in a new light. My eyes fixed on the first coat of polish as it went down, studying the brushstrokes instead of Lauren's soulful expressions. The Patrick I knew was funny, and generous, and a great mentor—he wasn't an abandoned child who rebuilt a family business from rubble and kept it going despite his father's destructive ploys.

While two more coats of black cherry paint covered my toenails and our glasses were refilled with another round, Lauren recapped their history. Angus Walsh's hate-filled blowout with his sons, and his subsequent stroke and death. The grenade attack will. The blame Angus levied on his children for their mother's death. Their collective dedication to the business that left them without an ounce of free time. Their loyalty to each other. Their refusal to quit when all of the odds lined up against them. Their warm acceptance of her in their circle.

We eventually parted—after Lauren insisted that we meet for lunch and shopping over the weekend—and I hiked through the snowy streets of Beacon Hill toward my apartment. It was a lot to digest, and I knew a little something about growing up with an adequate degree of dysfunction to know that Patrick *was* riding out a storm. It was a lot to process, and if I knew what was good for me, I'd back away.

Without thinking, I tossed a few items in my bag and headed straight for the North End. Icy slush and snow crunched beneath my boots, but I didn't hear it while I reorganized everything I knew about Patrick, his siblings, and the firm.

I couldn't explain why I was going to him. I only knew I needed to be with him, put my arms around him, and hold him tight.

I wasn't the girl who paid attention to sad stories. I had my own, and I wasn't waiting for anyone to pat my head and make it all better—no, I found my big girl panties a long time ago, and I expected everyone else to do the same. In fact, I steered clear of all sad stories unless we were talking solutions. The last thing I was qualified for was comforting friends in their times of need. I never knew what to do and empathy wasn't my strength.

It's not that I was a coldhearted bitch—I wasn't. I knew sitting around and being depressed wouldn't make a damn thing better, and if I wanted to stop feeling broken, picking up the pieces and gluing myself back together was the only way to do it.

Patrick glued himself back together, too. All the signs were there, waiting for me to add them up. He was a survivor, and he saw to it that his siblings made it through, even if it crushed him a little more along the way. He avoided asking personal questions because reciprocating led down a path few cared to explore. He kept a small, tight group of friends who knew enough to keep history in the past. Though he never brought it up, it was obvious serious girlfriends were few and far between. But when he let himself connect with someone, he gave *everything*.

I memorized Patrick's building code the night he gave it to me, and barely noticed my gloved fingers moving over the keypad when I reached the door, or the climb up three flights of stairs. He answered within seconds.

"Was that a Tolstoy quote?"

"Yes, now come here." My bag and coat dropped to the floor, and I sighed when my arms wrapped around him. My palms pressed against the corded muscles of his shoulders, absorbing his warmth. There was something charming about Patrick's low-slung fleece pants and thermal shirt. It was a younger, less intimidating look than the dress trousers, Oxford shirt, and tie combo that he frequently paired with v-neck sweaters or half-zip pullovers, or suits. God help me, those suits were devastating.

Patrick's fingers tangled in my hair—they were always in my hair—and his lips swept along my neck. "Texting with you gets really complicated. You make Google work for it."

"Let's not talk," I murmured, pulling him toward the bedroom. "Not right now."

Patrick's bedroom was fast becoming my favorite hideout, and even I could admit the old exposed brick and beams balanced nicely with the contemporary closets and bathroom. The high ceilings and angled windows at the roofline avoided the harshest morning sunlight while always providing the perfect amount of darkness and moonlight at night.

Getting Patrick naked and then feeling his skin were the only priorities, and I threw his shirt over his head and pushed his pants and boxers down without ceremony. His hands were busy unfastening my pants when I backed him to the edge of the bed. Patrick sat, observing while my clothes and boots landed in a heap, and I stripped to bra, panties, and socks. He summoned me closer with a hand on my hip.

"I don't know why these are so fucking sexy," Patrick said, his fingertips grazing my knees and circling the blue and white striped socks embroidered with tiny Eiffel towers. His fingers stroked higher, over my thighs and along my torso. One quick flick released my bra, and my panties soon hit the ground. "Can they come off?"

"As soon as I warm up." I stalked him back against the pillows, and pulled the blankets around us. His clean scent was at once sedative and stimulant.

"For a Mainer, your blood's thin," he laughed, his hands coasting along my back to diffuse my body heat.

My teeth nipped at the thin layer of skin stretched over Patrick's collarbone, my tongue soothing the miniscule bites. "Don't call me that."

His hands clutched my backside, scooting me closer to his erection. "Fine, but you spent five and half years in Ithaca with seventeen feet of snow. It's not like you've been in Miami."

Against Patrick's growling protests, I levered up and glared at him. Every time we were naked—without fail—he launched into a game of twenty questions. "Would it be possible to reserve this topic for another time?"

"Of course," he retorted, gripping my forearms and pulling me closer. "But you're more forthcoming like this. I take the opportunities I get."

'You don't give me much' and 'you don't make a habit of telling me things' echoed in my thoughts, and I shuffled away from Patrick long enough to peel my socks down, cast them to the ground with a harried look, and tangle my arms around his neck. I wanted to give him more—even if his methods were maddening.

Our lips met for a long, torturously slow kiss that summed

up exactly what I wanted with Patrick tonight. *Slow.* Spanking and hair pulling and fast, demanding sex hung the stars in my sky, but tonight was going to be different. Every part of him was strong and hard, and I wanted him unraveling under my hands. I wanted those hazel eyes to soften and glow with pleasure, and I wanted to feel his heart pounding against his chest.

The kiss ended and I crept away, my fingers raking through his light chest hair, down his beautiful belly, and around his swollen length. Of all the cocks I had encountered, Patrick's was the nicest—all the right proportions, appropriately manscaped, and reliably responsive.

I pumped my hand over him, squeezing the base and twisting my wrist at the crown while my other hand loosely cradled his balls, and Patrick's hips lifted in response.

"*Fuck*, Andy, get up here and let me fuck you."

"No," I replied, my tongue sweeping over my lips in preparation. "Not yet."

If there were words to describe the taste of Patrick's cock, I didn't have them—he just tasted *good*. That first swipe over the flared head was always the best, followed closely by Patrick's shuddering moan when I sealed my lips over him and sucked. His hips shot up when I took him deeper, and his fists were balling in my hair when my lips closed around the base. My gag reflex warned, and my eyes watered as he pumped against the back of my throat, but I maintained the pressure and Patrick starting spewing curses.

"*Andy*, your mouth is...fucking amazing. I want to fuck your mouth and come all over you. Fuck, I've wanted that for so long."

It felt very wrong and very dirty to admit, but I liked the sound of that.

A firm shove to his sternum sent him falling back against the pillows, but his sighs and moans continued. My tongue swirled around his head, teasing at the underside ridge and tentatively squeezing his balls.

"Fucking Christ, *Andy*," he yelled. "Get on my cock right *now*."

My mouth stroked over his length with soft, easy suction that pulled him off the frantic edge of release. With a condom in place, I backed Patrick up against the headboard and settled on his hips, his erection throbbing over me as I slid against him.

"God, you are so beautiful," he murmured, his lips fusing with mine.

"Slow," I insisted, my hands cupping his strong jaw as I shifted, taking Patrick inside. He filled me, stretched my tissues, pushed deeper, made me arch and cry out. My hips canted back, dragging my wet flesh over him until only the head remained inside, and I gradually pushed over him again, feeling every ridge and sensitive spot come alive around the weight of him. "I just want to feel you, okay?"

Gone was the secretive fucking. In its place was a soul-deep desire that multiplied by the minute. In that bed, he wasn't my boss, and he wasn't an orphan, either. Patrick was the one the universe made for me, and in that bed, I was going to be his everything—the one the universe made for him.

"You say that as if there is anything I can deny you," Patrick growled.

His hands were on my backside, pulling me closer as he moved in me. He set the measured rhythm, and powers far greater than mine commanded me to follow. My arms twined over Patrick's shoulders, and I started moving my hips, feeling him invade me in the most magnificent ways and leaving tiny, pinprick sensations exploding over my skin.

We clung to each other's bodies, holding and pressing and

grabbing for more contact, kissing necks and shoulders and lips. Breathless and covered in a light sheen of sweat, quiet words passed between us, begging for more and deeper and *now*.

"Andy, kitten, I'm close," Patrick stuttered, his hips lifting up to match my downward stroke. "I need you with me."

He waited for me, always. I saw the muscles pulled tight across his shoulders, felt it in the way his fingers dug into my ass. He denied himself—refusing to let go until I was coming apart —and that realization left me disorientated, suddenly seeing my relationship with Patrick from a new vantage point.

I nodded, and flattened Patrick against the pillows with my hands on his chest and my knees squeezing his hips. The angle was new, rasping against my clit in the most incredible ways and hitting right where I needed him, and it unleashed a flood of arousal as my hips fell into a rolling motion. He let me set the pace for several minutes, moaning and cursing and sucking my nipples until I swore they could conduct electricity, but an impatient snarl ripped through his chest, and I knew there was a limit to how long he could hold back.

Patrick's hands landed on my hips with a growl, grinding me against his cock. Suddenly he was harder and deeper than ever before, and I almost felt him throbbing inside me. His hands held me in place, his fingertips claiming me and marking my skin with small welts while forcing my clit over his pelvic bone as we moved together. The slight edge of pain cut through the waves of pleasure crashing over my system.

My eyes were half-closed, mouth hanging open while unintelligible babble leaked out, and I probably looked ridiculous, but slow and hard was quickly shutting down the majority of my brain—and I didn't want it any other way. Would it always be this way, this intense, with Patrick? Could it?

Close. We were close. It was new for me—unfamiliar—yet for the first time, neither uncomfortable nor unwelcome.

Patrick surged up, driving deeper inside me, and I screamed —actually screamed, surprising myself to no end—doubling over while my orgasm ripped me apart like a fucking tornado tearing through my body. Patrick's arms folded me against his chest while he thrust, and I heard the growl—that primitive, predatory sound announcing his release and commanding my inner muscles to clench around him just a few more times— rumble up through his diaphragm before it filled the room. Patrick's body tensed for a long beat before collapsing against the pillows.

"*Fuuuuuck,* Andy," he groaned into my hair. He rolled us to the middle of the bed and drew the blankets around us. "Fuck."

Patrick's arms twined around my waist and he settled his head between my breasts. My fingers tugged at his hair, his smiling eyes drifting shut. I wanted to remember him this way forever—my Sex God.

All of a sudden, he stopped being the larger than life visionary who steered my architectural philosophy and taught me to how preserve history one cobblestone at a time, and he turned into a flawed, precious man who preferred speaking in bulleted lists and leaving love notes on my skin in the form of teeth marks. It wasn't the sad story that made him mine—the sad story made him real.

As I stared at him, I started to understand what he meant when he said it wasn't just sex. That's how it seemed to be with us: he was one step ahead, figuring it out, taking it to the next level, asking for what he wanted. He might be waiting for me to come, but he wasn't waiting for me to move this—*us*—forward.

CHAPTER SEVENTEEN

PATRICK

I BROUGHT A SHAKING HAND TO MY MOUTH, PASSING IT OVER MY lips to catch any drool that slipped free.

Wrecked. I was totally fucking wrecked.

Andy twisted out of my arms with a promise to return soon, and I tested the strength of my limbs while she was in the bathroom. Even my toes felt languid, and the effort required to discard the condom was equivalent to lifting a Volkswagen.

I didn't know much about slow sex. My skill set ran to quick, hard fucking, and I assumed everything else was reserved for the sad fools who still couldn't find the clit.

But this, with Andy? This proved I knew exactly jack shit, and while I definitely wasn't the fool who couldn't find the clit, I was fast becoming the guy who wanted to talk about feelings after sex. That's the special treat built into asking for more than 'just sex.'

Andy returned wearing black panties and a thin gray camisole, and reddened patches scratched over her breasts.

Logically I knew it was weird to want to see my mark on her, but *fuck*—it looked so good.

Dishes of pistachios and blueberries teetered in one hand when she nestled beside me, her long legs crossing in front of her. "Are you going to kick me out for eating snacks in bed?"

I tore my eyes away from the stubble rash on her chest to tuck a wayward curl over her ear. "The only reason I'll ever kick you out of bed is to fuck you on the floor."

"Good, good," she smirked. "Glad we had that talk."

Andy balanced the dishes on either knee, alternately sampling from each while my fingers traced the smooth expanse of her shin. I wanted to ask about the troubled look in her eyes when she appeared at my door, to understand what transpired between us just now, to know she was staying the night in my arms, but my eyes landed on twin markings on Andy's inner ankle bones.

"You *have* been hiding something under those socks," I murmured, sitting up and dragging an ankle to my lap.

It blended flawlessly, and without the close study that I intended to give her body, would go by undetected. Craning my head to follow the tiny words circling the bulge of her ankle-bone, I read them several times before meeting Andy's eyes in question.

She smiled, nothing revealed in her expression.

The other ankle was less straightforward, and I felt Andy forcing back a smile while my finger traced the bisected circle enclosed by an equilateral triangle centered on her bone. It didn't resemble a geometric principle I used with much regularity, and I would be far from surprised to hear Andy rattle off an ancient theorem. There was no way it was an ordinary inscription of shapes. It meant something to her.

"Tell me about this one," I requested, my finger following the words. "'The ones that love us never really leave us.' I like that."

There were moments when Andy beguiled me, and then there were moments when I was stunned by our similarities and similar yet separate experiences. Those moments opened my eyes to the reality I knew her soul.

The meaning was obvious, and I didn't need to know anything about the quote's origin to understand the importance. I turned the words over in my head a few times, testing them out.

"It's from *The Prisoner of Azkaban*," she said, and I blinked, wondering if I was supposed to know what that meant. "Sirius Black? *Harry Potter*?"

"Okay," I said, grasping for a link between Andy and a movie about...was that the one with sexy vampires? "And...you like that movie?"

"It's a good story. I'm partial to the books, but I usually am, and I was hooked when they came out."

Erin liked those books too. I was home before my last year of undergrad, and she conned me into standing in line with her for a short eternity to get the newest release. Some quick calculations confirmed my suspicions: I went with Erin because she was twelve at the time, and needed a ride to the bookstore, and Andy was approximately the same age as Erin. My baby sister. The one who was nine years younger.

Talk about pervy cradle robber. Surely, someone would be happy to tie my ass to a weighted lobster trap and send me to a burial at sea for thinking about young Miss Asani the wrong way.

"How old are you?"

Andy frowned and swatted my hand away from her ankle.

"They aren't kids' books. They're great stories about the triumph of good over evil—"

"No," I interrupted, stilling her gesticulating hand. "How old are you?"

"Twenty-four," she breathed, and a hysterical giggle slipped past my lips.

"My sister's twenty-four," I said, my hand tangling in her hair and sweeping it off her shoulder.

"Is that a problem?"

I shrugged. "You don't look twenty-four. You look...exotic. Mysterious. Brilliant."

"Age is what you make it, Patrick." She offered a blueberry, and I sucked her fingers into my mouth to eat it. I wasn't ready to give up the pervy. "I'll be twenty-five in May if that helps, but seriously, why bother worrying about that when it isn't about to change?"

She was right. Not uncommon. "And this one?" I tapped the triangle.

"You have to ask? Really, Patrick? Oh honey, you don't get out enough," she laughed. "It's the Sign of the Deathly Hallows."

I glanced between Andy and her ankle while I itched to Google yet another one of her references. It wasn't enough that her primary mode of communication was eyebrow arching; she needed to add some riddles and obscure references, too. More breadcrumbs.

Fucking fantastic.

"You're going to have to unpack that one for me, kitten."

"Have you been living in a cave?" When I shrugged, she shook her head and pointed to the tattoo. "It's also from *Harry Potter*. This is the Elder Wand, that's the Resurrection Stone, and this is the Cloak of Invisibility. When combined, they form the

Deathly Hallows. If one person gets them all, that person is the Master of Death."

"Does that have something to do with those kids who try to kill each other for sport?"

"That's *The Hunger Games*!" she exploded, her hands waving furiously. "You honestly don't know anything about *Harry Potter*?"

I shook my head, and Andy looked up at the ceiling. Over the past few weeks, I determined being with Andy meant getting a few boxes checked off. It was unclear whether she kept a list of these requirements, or even thought about them as requirements, but they were the things most salient to her, and I wanted to be on the right side of them. I knew she was obsessed with food and sustainably preserved architecture, preferred natural solutions to everything but happily allowed vodka to solve a fair amount of problems, too, and she used dry humor with such frequency it was difficult to parse her real opinions from the ironic. Apparently, a mild fixation on *Harry Potter* was part of the deal, too.

"Is that because you've been busy getting the firm off the ground, or because you object to the idea of *Harry Potter*?"

"No objections to *Harry*, and busy is something of an understatement. If he earned two permanent positions on your body, I want to know a lot more about this guy. I should be so lucky. That's why I keep biting you."

"Three." I frowned, and Andy pointed to her flank, drawing up her camisole to point at the Farsi inscription. "Three," she repeated. "And please don't stop biting me."

"Yeah, this kid's gotten enough of your skin," I said, pulling Andy down to the mattress. "Where's my spot?"

Andy's hand brushed over her chest. "How about 'Patrick' here?"

Fuck me running, that dry humor was going to be the death of me. I snorted, and trailed kisses over her chest. "That might be a bit much, and I'm really not into possessive assholery. But you know I can't say no to you."

"Mmm," she purred, and as the sound invaded my brain, I stopped dissecting her suggestion of inking my name into her skin as serious or satirical. "Okay. What about a little shamrock, right here?"

Andy pointed to her inner wrist, alongside her pulse. The sarcastic glint was missing from her eyes, and replacing her lopsided smirk was that tiny smile. Nodding slowly, I stared at her wrist, imagining the tiny flower against her olive skin.

Shamrock tattoos. Slow sex. Socks. It came down like an avalanche, and I shifted Andy so her back rested against my chest. One look and she'd see the panic in my eyes. I was supposed to be in control while she was the one who backed away. Those roles worked for us, and I wasn't ready to give her the impression that anything was changing.

I held her for a long time, my heart hammering against her spine while we watched thick drifts of snow accumulating on my balcony.

"You should stay," I mumbled, sudden exhaustion weighing down my words. "If it keeps snowing like this—"

She shifted, running her fingers through my hair. There was something new in her affection, something comforting, something dissolving my panic. I arched into her touch.

I nuzzled her neck, inhaling her lavender scent, and melted against her warm body.

"I'm staying," Andy said. "I'm not leaving you, Patrick."

ANDY DIDN'T LEAVE THAT NIGHT, OR THE NEXT.

She stayed in my bed and by my side through the snowy nights of winter, and memories of life before Andy slipped into the dark recesses of my mind. When April rolled around, some of Andy's clothes shared space in my closet, and her random glass jars of mushrooms and chia seeds and assorted oddities took up residence in my refrigerator.

She made pancakes. Not normal ones, but healthy apple-sauce pancakes that were surprisingly tasty, all while standing at my stove in tiny camisoles, panties, and the ever-present knee socks on Sunday mornings. My DVR housed all of the *Harry Potter* films, and I acknowledged the appeal of the boy wizard and his crew.

I expected my hunger for Andy to diminish by small degrees each day but it was exactly the opposite. Before the first day of spring, we were intimately acquainted with every flat surface in my apartment. I was hornier than any teenage version of myself, and I turned into a pissy bitch if Andy wasn't within an arm's reach. Her Saturday trips to the farmers' market and yoga with Lauren left me climbing the walls, and I was no better when she met her friend Charlotte for drinks every couple of weeks.

She claimed I growled in my sleep whenever she rolled out of my hold, and on more than a few occasions I found all two hundred-odd pounds of me completely sprawled over her sleeping body. Andy didn't mind. She was always cold and I was merely making good on my promise to keep her warm.

It all felt right, so fucking *right*.

With some minor exceptions.

We worked hard to keep it professional in the office, though the comforts of intimacy whittled away our cover. Anyone paying attention would have seen us holding hands as we walked up Cambridge Street each morning, or leaving the office together in the evening. We seized every unnecessary opportunity to touch, whether it be brushing against each other at the copier or me pressing a hand to Andy's waist while I studied her designs. I chose to believe my siblings were too wrapped up in their projects to notice I brought her an iced green tea with lemon every afternoon, or the fierce, heated way my eyes lingered on her.

Part of me wanted to get caught. A big fucking part, and my sanity frayed a little more each time I ignored questions about my weekends or omitted the most important details. Nothing would make me happier than Sam walking into my office while Andy talked through designs with my hand conveniently fondling her ass. It was a matter of time until we ran into one of them at the grocery store, and there was no mistaking the meaning behind a Saturday afternoon Whole Foods trip. I knew exactly what I wanted to say, how I'd tell them Andy was mine, and she accepted every dark, dusty part of me, and I belonged to her.

Sheltering our relationship from my siblings wasn't without its costs, and I paid the highest price with Shannon. It wasn't long ago Shannon and I met for dinner or drinks most weeknights, talking through everything from project problems to her latest disasters in dating. Nothing was off-limits: she knew my morning runs doubled, tripled, and occasionally quadrupled in distance when I needed to get laid, and I knew more than enough about the trials and tribulations of finding a birth control pill that kept her periods regular but didn't make her intermittently crazy.

We still connected a few times each week, but our discussion of personal topics centered around disposing of the estate, Shannon inserting herself into Matt's wedding, marathon training, and Sam's impending meltdown. I padded my stories with highlights from European soccer. After an extended analysis of Chelsea's defense intended to distract her from the fact I ignored all of her texts that weekend because I was buried in Andy the entire time, Shannon gave me a long, contemptuous glare and stopped asking altogether.

All told, I needed Shannon. I wasn't equipped to confront the emotions stemming from an increasingly serious relationship, and though Shannon sure as shit wasn't either, I knew she would understand and get me through it. If there was anyone who knew a few things about helping me make sense of myself, it was Shannon.

I wasn't going to be settled until they knew.

Wondering about life post-apprenticeship replaced most of the time I previously dedicated to obsessing over Andy. Most. Her hair was still everywhere, she still drove me crazy with her 'hm,' and springtime meant there were fewer black layers between me and the body I knew better than my own.

We never discussed the next step. It was a delicate détente, and it was easier to joke about keeping my siblings in the dark than addressing the reality that was closing in around us. I watched Andy in those in-between moments when she wandered around the apartment in a bra, panties, and knee socks, when she gazed at her designs and twirled the amethyst studs in her ears, when she read new restaurant menus as if she was looking at the Rosetta Stone. I tried to decipher what I wanted. What she wanted.

I wanted this, but *more*, and that scared the living shit out of me.

That 'more' was a giant fucking question that kept me kicking copiers and yelling at Shannon's herd of support staff whenever their atrocious grammar made it into client emails, or they applied whimsical organizing principles to the materials room.

'More' always translated to Andy dumping her apartment. I'd never seen it and she lusted over my wide balcony and restored hardwood. I wanted to be open with my siblings and have a shared address, and every combination of possibilities beyond that consumed my thoughts like a spectacular case of flesh-eating bacteria.

Andy's exams couldn't come soon enough, but I needed every minute of the next few weeks to get my shit together.

———

"YOU WANT TO GIVE ME THE FIFTEEN-SECOND UPDATE ON Wellesley?" I pressed my fingers against my eyelids to clear the fog. I never regretted late-night indulgences in Andy's body. I only regretted the amount of time it took caffeine to hit my brain cells the next morning.

Andy's rapidly expanding expertise meant she was able to manage the majority of my projects, the Wellesley project in particular. I checked in once or twice each month, and we all gave up on the wall issues after she talked us out of tearing into it. She might have said something about being a human barricade if my crazy ass even thought about coming at the wall with a sledgehammer, and not being afraid to drop Riley and Matt with one swing each if they tried.

"Hm." She paged through her notebook before glancing up. "Still on the timeline. Once electrical wraps this week, floors are scheduled for refinishing and a saltwater pool pump is going in, and I told you that taking advantage of me at two a.m. would turn into only three hours of sleep and a day full of surly."

"I wouldn't be surly if you let me take advantage of you against the wall in the printer room, or," I rolled away from my desk and gestured underneath, "you could take care of my mood down there."

"It's seven twenty-eight." That tiny smirking smile appeared, the one I thought of as the smile she reserved for me, and there was no stopping the flood of heat to my crotch. "Wouldn't want you to be late."

"You're evil. You know that, right?" Groaning, I collected my laptop and coffee, and rounded my desk to stand behind Andy. I leaned over her shoulder, and, always keeping up appearances, I pointed to something on her screen as if we were discussing a project. "When I get you home tonight, I intend to take advantage of you. Multiple times. You might want to stretch."

"I'll keep that in mind." My lips passed over her jaw, and before I could change my mind, I sprinted upstairs to the attic.

"Hit any good keggers recently?" Shannon asked. "That's why you look like death warmed over, right?"

Withholding information from my siblings turned the dial way up on my paranoia, and Shannon's assessing gaze when I settled into my seat put me on alert. I shook my head and sipped my coffee, hoping the right explanation was mixed in with the milk and sugar. "Nah," I replied. "Up late watching a few games, and Matt's a demented bastard who thinks wind sprints are good fun on a Monday."

"Uh-huh," she murmured, her eyes narrowing over her iced latte. "Let's get this show started."

The business was in good shape. After all these years of busting our asses and hanging on by threads, our plan was working. Listening to my partners detail the progress on their projects only reaffirmed that for me. We accomplished everything we set out to, and we weren't white-knuckling it anymore. For the first time in forever, there was space in my life for more than our business, and filling that space with Andy was the only thing I wanted.

"There are some other things on my list," Shannon said after we walked through updates and strategy for new properties.

I shot her a surprised look; we usually worked through her list before discussing them with the group.

"I also have a few things, so get ready for me to drop some knowledge," Riley added, and four pairs of confused eyes landed on him. "Don't look at me that way, you assclowns. Stop being so superior."

"Enlighten us," Shannon said.

Riley produced several blueprints and unfurled them in the center of the table. "It took a few months, but I found two more offices. It means subdividing the biggest offices with some strange geometries. Matt's office here," he pointed to the document, "and Patrick's office here, but that just cuts some of the space wasted on conference tables. And for real, people, we have three conference rooms we never use, so it's no loss. The new offices are smaller, but at least Princess Jasmine and I won't have to be squatting like bums on the street."

"'Princess Jasmine?'" Sam snickered. "Isn't that a little...inappropriate or...insensitive, or infantilizing, or something?"

I thought about my dark-eyed girl and smiled, betting she'd

start assembling the Halloween costume today so long as it was an ironic exploitation of her culture's misappropriated icons, and not a benediction on cartoon princesses.

"Ask her. She'll tell you what she thinks. I think she'd be down for a nickname." I gave the plans a quick study and glanced to Matt. "You've looked at this?" He nodded, and I thought about a permanent office for Andy. An office right next to mine.

So fucking *right*.

"Draft a budget," I ordered, and Riley allowed himself a subtle fist pump. "Let me see it as soon as you have it."

"What?" Shannon snapped. "We built existing offices around the original footprint when this was a house, and we didn't want to fuck with that. And, shouldn't we determine where Andy fits in after her apprenticeship before building office space?"

What the actual fuck? 'Where Andy fits in?' How was that even up for discussion?

Yelling at Shannon in Black Widow mode in the middle of a team meeting was a bad idea, and it always ended with a ball beating but I was ready to take those licks if she didn't cut the shit. It seemed like she was intentionally goading me into a reaction.

"We need to keep Andy," Matt said gravely. "Whatever it takes, she's fucking gifted and GCs eat out of her palm. She can have my entire fucking office if she wants it."

"Seconded," Sam added. "The building integrity won't suffer because we break up a few rooms."

"No disagreement from me," Shannon replied, holding up her hands in surrender. "I've always advocated for this. I was the one who insisted on hiring her, and I opened the door to keeping her on longer so Optimus could get some sleep at night. It's obvious he isn't, so that experiment failed."

I stifled a laugh. If only she knew what was keeping me up these nights.

"I agree with all of you, but no one brought me in on any of this, so I apologize that I'm out of the loop."

"I don't think that's accurate, Shannon," Sam said, leaning back in his chair and circling his hand around the table. "I think we've discussed it in some fashion every week since January. Perhaps we haven't articulated 'Andy needs an office because we want her to be a permanent fixture' but we've discussed her as a transformative member of our squad, and we've made it clear that if she can handle Optimus at his worst, she's earned her stripes."

Shannon clasped her hands in her lap and pursed her lips. I held my breath, waiting for the explosion. It was either an explosion or she stopped recognizing my existence.

"Okay, moving on. Cornell invited us to a special breakfast next week. Next Friday." Shannon pulled up an email with the details. "The architecture school's dean wants to personally thank us for Angus's donation. I took the last meet and greet for Angus's charitable giving at Brigham and Women's. If I had to go to the vagina shop, someone else is doing this."

"Well I'm out," Riley said. "Last thing they need is RISD representing up in hill country."

"I would have to believe they'd rather see Patrick," Sam said, his attention fixed on straightening his cufflinks. "Fitting for the SMP, wouldn't you say?"

While Andy was busy running the shit out of every project on deck, I was coming to terms with my new title as senior managing partner. My partners outvoted me on that measure, but I succeeded in elevating Shannon to managing partner and adjusting titles for Matt and Sam to reflect their respective specialties.

For me, the changes lived in legal paperwork and on our website, and though it didn't imply anything new, it felt different to me. Theresa dropped three boxes of freshly printed business cards on my desk last week with a purposeful cluck. I immediately shoved them in my bottom drawer. Although I spent more than a decade at the helm, making it official required some adjustment. It was a reminder of everything that changed.

Shannon nodded and glanced at me. "I would agree. So Tom will book you at The Statler?"

"Fine," I ground out, struggling to contain my irritation. We didn't do this to each other. We figured out shit out before coming to these meetings.

"Awesome," she chirped. "Now. Matty's wedding is only a few weeks away, woohoo, and we need a plan for when he's out of the office."

"I got you, bro," Riley said, dousing his pants with coffee as he attempted to slap Matt's back. It was refreshing to see the spill in action. I was beginning to think he was buying his pants pre-stained. "I'm all over it."

Matt started to speak but stopped, snatching Riley's coffee as it teetered toward his keyboard. He met my gaze with a small shake of his head, and we knew there was no way in hell Riley was rubber-stamping anything structural. My irritation flared again. I glanced at Shannon, my eyes asking why she didn't come to me with these issues first. Shrugging, she looked away and I added 'deal with Shannon's shit' to my list for the day.

I tapped my coffee cup against the table, and said, "I need someone on engineering. Someone who understands physics."

Looking up, I met Riley's irritated grimace.

"Could be good for Andy," Sam mused.

I inhaled sharply, immediately wondering whether we'd be able to keep up our daily rituals if she shifted gears for a few weeks. Spending a couple of nights in Ithaca was bad enough; the prospect of loaning Andy out to Matt's office for three weeks was heinous.

Riley stopped blotting the coffee and scowled. "And where the fuck does that leave me? You don't think it would be better for me to take over Matt's projects since I know what they are and work on them every day?"

I needed to have a serious talk with Riley. In all fairness, that talk should have happened ten months ago when it became clear that his skills required extra levels of supervision. He was making progress, but I occasionally doubted he'd be able to manage anything independently.

"With me," I replied. "I have a lot of design projects coming up, and I need your eye on those."

Riley rolled his eyes, and with a lifted shoulder, the topic was dismissed.

"Look at us, on schedule and everything," Shannon said with a glimpse at the clock on her screen. "I want everyone to know that Lauren's shower is Saturday evening, and there are no boys allowed so I expect you all to keep Matt occupied."

"Can I renew my objection to this?" Matt asked. "Lauren wants me there."

Shannon crossed her arms over her chest and gazed at Matt. "That's horseshit, and what part of 'no boys allowed' are you struggling with? Go drinking with these idiots, and have a big, bloody steak, and leave us girls alone for once!" She shook her head and slammed her notebook and phone on her closed laptop. "Christ on a crutch, Matthew. I'm leaving. Figure out your Saturday."

Sam and Riley launched into a point-by-point comparison of the city's best whiskey bars and steakhouses, and Matt rolled his chair away from the table to type a message on his phone. He smiled at the screen, replacing it with a tolerant grin when he returned to the table and offered his opinions on Grill 23, Abe & Louie's, and Boston Chops.

I knew exactly what that look meant. He was going along with this obstacle course, and he'd probably have a stellar time with us on Saturday, but he would spend the evening counting the minutes until he could get home to Lauren. She would always be his first choice.

I knew all about that.

I told the boys to make the decision without me and moved 'deal with Shannon's shit' to the top of my list for the day. I was prepared to breathe some fire. My legs ate up the two flights of stairs between the attic and Shannon's office, and she waited a full ten seconds to look up from her documents after the door slammed behind me.

"What the fuck was that about, Shannon?"

She carefully peeled a sticky note from its decorative dispenser and marked a few notations before lowering the lid of her laptop and meeting my eyes. "I'm not sure what you're referring to, Patrick."

So that's how we were going to play? Fantastic. Fucking fantastic.

"All right, Shan. I'll break it down." I deposited my laptop on her round conference table and approached her desk. "Your little list? We never bring up topics that we haven't run through in advance, especially not big things like coverage for Matt. You need Riley losing his shit about as much as I do, and it was not the time to figure that out."

"I'd be happy to do that, Patrick," she replied with enough sweetness to rot teeth. "But that only works when we check in before meetings and you don't bother to do that anymore. You don't even talk to me unless I corner you in the stairwell."

I winced, thinking about the stolen moments with Andy in the shower this morning and the assumption Shannon would have chased me down if there were something important to review before the meeting.

"And Andy? How is it not obvious that we need to keep her? Do you need a fucking billboard?"

"You know that I like her. Hell, Patrick, I go out for pedicures and drinks with her a couple times a month, and she's one of Lauren's best friends, and I think she's awesome, but you don't communicate with me anymore." Shannon rolled her Starbucks cup between her palms and lifted a shoulder. "You're in your own head, and you're not talking to me, and I don't know what else you want me to do."

"So you decided to throw down in a team meeting? Is that the smartest thing you could come up with?"

"I'm sorry that meeting didn't go the way you wanted but... I've tried to talk to you about these things for weeks, and you either ignore my texts, or tell me to schedule a meeting but there's never time on your calendar, and you don't want to meet for dinner anymore. What am I supposed to do? I know you're having a hard time with this SMP thing—"

"It's not the reorganization," I murmured, and my control over the riot in my head faltered. I wanted to sprint upstairs to my office and convince Andy to bring our relationship into the light of day.

She'd probably beat the shit out of me with her Perspex ruler.

"Okay, I guess that's good to know, but...what is going on? I thought we were doing well, Patrick. We finally have cash reserves to cover a few *years* of investment projects, and we haven't worried about making payroll in ages. And do you know how it's been since I've had to clean up a single Angus disaster? Five months, two weeks, and six days."

My head was swimming with too many competing thoughts to keep still, and the idea of Andy wagging a ruler at me was more than a little arousing.

"Things are finally good, really good, but Patrick, how the fuck am I supposed to know that we're creating a post-apprenticeship role for Andy if you don't tell me? And yes, I know we've talked about how amazing she is, but you're also a fucking ogre when it comes to her. If you hate working with her so much, maybe this isn't the right firm for her. I was expecting you to come in here one of these days and tell me you needed her gone."

That sucked the air right out of my chest. I gripped the ornate mantel to catch my breath. "This is the right firm for her."

"Patrick. Talk to me. You look like you're giving yourself a hernia. Please, whatever it is, just talk to me."

I paced between the bank of windows facing a roof garden in bloom, and the windowed wall separating Shannon's office from the bullpen where Tom and her support staff were staring at us. "Do something productive," I yelled at them, and they snapped into action.

I was thankful Shannon had the sense to stop speaking while I wore the rug thin. I paced for at least ten minutes, repeatedly building and disassembling evasions as I walked, and constantly finding myself at impossible junctions. There was only one solution that prevented me from going to war with my business partner, best friend, and sister. That same solution would probably have Andy abandoning me in a bathroom somewhere, too.

But Shannon didn't betray confidence. She never trafficked in rumors, she took trust seriously, and that unyielding bond made us good together. I pivoted to face Shannon. It was the only solution. It meant we could go back to being open and talking to each other, and we could get the house in order.

"If I tell you something, can you swear on your life that you'll keep it between us?"

"Does this need to be an attorney-client privilege conversation? Is there a warrant out for your arrest? Who did you kill?"

"Don't joke," I warned. "This is serious, and yeah, consider yourself my attorney right now."

"The fact you even have to ask if I'll keep something between us, and then invoke privilege, makes me realize that something went down and it wasn't good, and I need you to be honest so we can figure out a path forward. I won't run a business with you if you can't be upfront with me."

I searched for my perfectly crafted speeches, but they were lodged in a sticky part of my mind and wouldn't form on my tongue. I met Shannon's concerned gaze, and as adrenaline borne from months of secrecy jolted my blood, the words tumbled out. "I'm in love with Andy."

The rush of admitting my relationship with Andy throbbed in my veins, and it felt real. With that clandestine weight lifted from my shoulders, I allowed realness to wash over me until an infatuated grin replaced my fire-breathing snarl. It was then that my confession echoed in my head, and 'in love' started playing on an infinite loop. I loved her, and it was finally real.

"What?" Shannon screamed, her palms slapping against the desk when she surged to her feet. A flick of my wrist sent the audience back to their computers and phone calls. The glass was thick enough that they heard only raised voices. This kind of attention would draw my siblings in a few minutes, but nothing was wiping that smile off my face. "What! What? You're *what*?"

"I'm. In love. With Andy," I replied haltingly, the words feeling foreign as I repeated them. "Be quiet. Your minions are trying to listen."

"Wow, that wasn't even on the short list of what I was expecting," Shannon panted, dropping into her desk chair. "I am experiencing this at a rate of several hundred what-the-fucks per minute."

"Shannon," I warned, realizing her disapproval could rock me to the core.

"Where do I even start? Did you not care that she's your apprentice? I thought you didn't like her. No offense, but is she in your league? Do you even talk or is it a lot of silent scowling at each other? And isn't she a lot younger than you?"

"Shannon, you have to swear you're not going to say anything to anyone. Not Sam, not Matt, not Lauren. No one. And you definitely can't say anything to Andy."

"Does she know?" Shannon asked incredulously. "Is this like...unrequited love? I didn't think you even talked to her."

I chalked that up to successful avoidance tactics. If Shan didn't think we talked, she certainly wasn't thinking we were groping each other in any empty corner we found. The bathroom. My office. Garages. Stairwells.

"She sort of lives with me," I said, my hand grasping the nape of my neck. "She stays with me four or five nights each week, but no, I haven't told her that I'm in love with her yet. I didn't really process that until just now."

"What! What?" Shannon was on her feet again, and her bony fist slammed into my chest. "You're in love and living with some-one? When the fuck did that happen? That explains...you know what, that explains so much of your dickish behavior."

Sinking into a wingback chair to avoid looking at Shannon's overly interested assistants, I scratched my head. "March. And sit down and be quiet before the runt finds a reason to run in here."

"Are you fucking kidding me, Patrick? You've been living with a woman and you didn't bother to tell me until now?"

"Come on, Shannon. Think about it from her perspective. I'm just trying to protect her."

Shannon sighed and sat across from me in a matching chair. "When were you planning on telling me? Or were you?"

"Of course! Do you have any clue how hard this has been for me? How much I've wanted to tell you? How much I need you to help me figure my shit out? I'm losing my fucking mind right now. I didn't ask for this, and I'm in love with her, and I don't know what to do with that."

"Are we talking 'I really like you and the sex is awesome,' or 'I really like you and want to get a Maltepoo that we raise together and put on a joint Christmas card' or 'I really like you, and want you and only you forever, and here's a sparkly ring' or something else?"

I didn't want to stop at a shared address. I needed Andy, and I was planning on needing her for a long time but of all the things I expected for myself, marriage was a few notches above learning Portuguese, and I knew Andy was in a similar boat. In those dark, quiet moments when we held each other, skin to skin, and all pretenses came down, we bared it all. We were the poster children for fucked up childhoods.

Andy's parents never married. Her father's traditional Persian parents didn't approve of her casually Jewish, wandering artist mother, and they refused to acknowledge Andy as their grandchild, even when her father was murdered. They barred Andy and her mother from the funeral, and to this day, Andy didn't know where her father was buried.

Her mother married Bob, an accountant, shortly after Andy left for college, and they had two girls who Andy referred to as the Bobbsey Twins. Andy visited on holidays, but the Bobbsey Family didn't include her, not genuinely, and staying away was safer than being an outsider.

I watched my parents adore each other for the first ten years of my life, and then I watched my father destroy every shred of that happiness in the cruelest, most vengeful ways for the subsequent twenty-two years.

I glanced at Shannon's impatient stare, her crossed legs bouncing furiously beneath the table.

Fuck the history. Fuck the dysfunction.

It was all bullshit. None of it held any power over us, and if we survived months of secrecy while in the trenches with my siblings, we could survive anything.

I stared into Shannon's green eyes, and knew my answer. "Forever."

"Holy shit," Shannon gasped.

CHAPTER EIGHTEEN

ANDY

SCROLLING THROUGH PAGES OF CUT CRYSTAL GLASSES, candlesticks holders, and cheese boards left me disheartened. It was possible I might not find a worthy gift for Lauren. They didn't have a wedding registry to guide my search, and she spent our entire pedicure last week detailing the excessive and unneeded cookware and towels and vases descending upon their loft—of course, she never mentioned what she did want.

Beyond the occasional club hopping with Jess and Marley, Lauren was my only real girlfriend in Boston, and over the past few months, she became an irreplaceable part of my life. We shared more than a few bottles of wine discussing our growly, bitey boys, and always met for hot yoga and lunch at the farmers' market on Saturdays. The hunt for wedding goods—a hair band, cute guest book alternatives, lacy lingerie—kept us busy.

I even started a secret Pinterest board to archive my wedding ideas. I had no idea when I turned into one of those girls who had recurring thoughts about weddings.

Not that I was planning a wedding. Or thinking about

getting engaged. Or even sure where things stood with me and Patrick, or what I wanted for us as my apprenticeship popped the landing gear on its final descent.

For now, it was simply a place where I noted lovely things that caught my eye, and absolutely nothing more.

The idea that women could spend time together without devolving into insecure squabbling was foreign to me, and Lauren taught me that strong female friendships were critical to my mental health—especially considering I was semi-living in full-blown sin with my secret boyfriend who was also my boss.

She taught me the power of a few carefully selected pieces of lingerie, too.

Shannon bowed out after one foray into hot yoga, arguing that no amount of calories burned was worth covering her body in an angry, raspberry-red flush for hours. Such was life for a redhead. She maintained her presence for our regular pedicure dates though my footing with her always felt a little off. Don't get me wrong—she was open and hilarious and wonderfully uninhibited, but her allegiance was very clearly with Patrick, and I'd be old and gray before that changed.

Patrick spent the morning shut up in Shannon's office, and the better part of the afternoon back and forth between our office and there, and his continuous stream of under-the-breath babble had me concerned. He was on edge, and being weird about it. I wanted to know where my Patrick went.

And that's exactly what he was: mine. At least for the time being. The future was vague...at best.

Plan A was—and always had been—sticking around Walsh Associates. We ambled around discussions of an implied future —whether it be a shared interest in an Oktoberfest tasting menu event or taking on projects that wouldn't break ground until

August—as if there was no question I was staying. Patrick sweetened that deal, but he also added a layer of complexity that made banking on Plan A tenuous.

Things were good—I had a freaking Pinterest board for our hypothetical wedding, after all—but the minute they stopped being good, I stood to lose everything.

Instead of tackling the realities of Plan A, I resorted to a well-developed Plan B that involved sending out dozens of résumés and portfolio samples to sustainable preservation firms throughout New England and the mid-Atlantic. With the exception of a measly handful, they were dreadful operations that misinterpreted the most basic principles of sustainability, preservation, or both. I was more interested in chewing glass than relocating, though it was possible that Plan A's cozy perfection dimmed the appeal of everything else.

It all felt deceptive given the walls between Patrick and me were long demolished and the rubble swept aside. Hiding behind late yoga classes as my prime motivation for staying at my apartment rarely sounded believable, but it was the best cover available for phone and Skype interviews—that, and I was still paying rent on an apartment I graced with my presence once or twice per week.

It was misleading, and I hated myself a little more after each interview, but Plan B was non-negotiable. Protecting myself was always the first priority.

I watched Patrick's index finger stumble over book spines until finding the volume he wanted, the overhead lights illuminating his auburn hair against the darkness outside.

My spy informant Tom—sexuality still unconfirmed—reported that Patrick and Shannon spent an hour yelling at each other post-partners' meeting but failed to provide intel on the topic of said yelling. Patrick didn't mention anything over lunch, and it was evident he was still slogging through it while he absently studied a technical manual on rainwater collection systems.

"Fucking hell," I groaned, scrolling through another page of prosaic home goods. It was easier to bulldoze a historical landmark than find the right bridal shower gift.

"What?" Patrick snapped back from the bookshelf.

He looked startled—maybe a little bewildered—and I pushed away from the conference table to approach him. It was after eight, and knowing we were alone in the office, I laid my hands on his chest. Feeling his thundering heart under my palm, I looked up with alarmed eyes. Residential rainwater collection wasn't that exhilarating.

"Hey," I murmured, my hand snaking up to wrap around the back of his neck. "You're a little twitchy."

"Yeah," he breathed, his forehead pressing against mine. "I feel a little twitchy."

I stared into Patrick's eyes, waiting for an explanation while my fingers teased apart the bunched muscles in his neck and shoulders. I was not holding the same man who warned me to stretch in advance of my evening with him.

"Are you coming home with me?" he rasped, his voice heavy with stress and exhaustion. He sighed, his eyes drifting shut. "Do you know how much I hate asking that?"

I blinked, studying the jumping pulse along his throat. "No, Patrick, I don't know, but I don't think that's why you're twitchy."

"Andy," he sighed. "There are at least five other things we need to talk about right now, tonight, but goddamn it, my head is going to explode if you're not with me tonight. So please, tell me you're staying."

I vacillated between wanting Patrick's confessions—the ones his eyes and hands and body openly communicated—and knowing I required a career path independent of hot sex and a hotter man.

"Your head is going to explode," I started, backing him toward his desk chair, "because your heart is beating as if you just ran ten miles uphill, and you haven't taken a cleansing breath since you walked in."

He sat, and I climbed on his lap, my fingers continuing their work on his shoulders while his hands gripped my waist.

"You didn't answer my question," he murmured into my hair. "Don't torture me right now. Today has been...overwhelming, and I need to know. Are you coming home with me?"

Patrick grunted as my knuckle dug into his shoulder. "Of course."

Lifting his head from my shoulder, Patrick smiled. "Good," he growled, and his lips fused to mine, his hands tangling in my hair and diving beneath my shirt. "I want to wake up next to you every single day."

I'd like to say it took more than one kiss, one touch, one look, but that's how it was with Patrick. The instant his lips brushed over mine, I was lost to him and the magnetic pull drawing us together. Every touch magnified that pull, and as his mouth pressed against mine, I shifted to roll my center over the erection straining behind his fly.

Patrick's fingers tugged at the ribbon knotting my poplin wrap shirt at the side, loosening the ties until it hung from my elbows and his chin scratched over my chest. His arm snaked under my thighs, and with one deft movement, I was staring at the hand-carved plaster medallion surrounding the chandelier. I didn't notice the edge of Patrick's laptop digging into my ribs, or the mechanical pencils snagged in my hair. My legs anchored Patrick to me, towing him closer until I felt him pushing against me.

"This isn't how I expected the night to go, but I'm not complaining," Patrick murmured against my lips.

"If you were complaining," I replied, my hands fisting in his shirt to free it from beneath his belt. His warmth, his weight, it was breathtaking, and I didn't want to let go. "There'd be something wrong."

"And this is not wrong," he laughed, his teeth capturing my bottom lip as his fingers fought with the button closure of my pants. He slipped beneath my waistband, his fingers passing back and forth over the spot of arousal dotting my panties, my thighs quivering with each stroke.

"Yo, Patrick, here's the updated budget for the new offices that you asked for, with the floating wall between Andy's office and...oh shit."

Riley's upside-down frame froze in the doorway. His eyes bulged as he drank us in, our tangled arms locked around each other for a slow motion second.

My first thought: could he see my boobs?

Second thought: was my underwear still on?

Third thought: why the hell was Riley in the office after five?

"Fuck," Patrick hissed. He jerked me off the desk and shoved me behind his back, wrapping a hand over my hip.

A quick survey of the state of my clothes answered my first two questions—boobs: out; underwear: riding below my hips.

"Yeah, so I'm gonna go," Riley said, his voice trailing off as he backed away from the door.

And by 'go' Riley meant he was probably calling his siblings to spread the news. His slow wit was the only winner in this situation—if he were faster on his feet, he would have snapped some photos to illustrate the group text that I expected to blow up the Walsh family phones any minute.

The snarky Facebook post practically wrote itself: Who has two thumbs and just walked in on his brother rounding third base with the apprentice? This guy.

Patrick bent to meet my eyes, his hand covering the fingers that attempted to fasten the ties of my shirt. "I'm going to talk to him. Fix this. Are you okay?" I murmured and Patrick squeezed my fingers. "I need you to give me more than 'hm,' Andy. Are you okay?"

Somewhere between resenting that Riley interrupted some scrumptious petting and recognizing that our cover was irrevocably blown, I met Patrick's eyes with a shaky exhale and stiff nod. My turn to be twitchy. "Yeah."

"Here." He slipped his keys into my pocket and dropped a gentle kiss on my mouth. "Go home. Eat. Have a drink. I'll be there soon."

He was gone, and I was on autopilot. I stuffed most of my things in my bag, but in the back of my mind, I remembered contracts, designs, and notes I intended to review tonight littered my drafting table, plus an open jar of pecans and dried papaya.

I didn't want to imagine the deal Patrick was brokering with Riley, or the changes inherent in taking our relationship public, instead focusing on the path to Patrick's apartment. Left on Cambridge Street. Right on New Sudbury. Pass through Haymarket Square. Cross over I-93. Pass Bread+Butter, Neptune Oyster, and L'Osteria on Salem Street. Left on Prince Street. Fourth building on the right. Enter the code, up the stairs, unlock the door.

The vodka cranberry poured itself, and despite the evening

chill, releasing the pressure building in my chest with some fresh air was mandatory. The hard structure of the teak chair was a welcome sensation, and I felt the initial shock of Riley's appearance gradually subside.

In my ideal world, our relationship was the best-kept secret in town. In the world where I actually lived, I knew it would get out. The fact we made it to May without any real notice from Patrick's siblings was worth celebrating—and examining closely, as we stopped being covert around the same time the daffodils started blooming, and their involvement in each other's lives tended toward ridiculous levels.

I sat back, knees tucked to my chin and empty glass dangling from my fingers, expecting the panic to knock me flat on my ass. My bared breasts aside, I was experiencing a complete shortage of screeching angst and anxiety over the presumed shards of my career, and it was confusing as hell.

Halfway through my count of the pergola's beams, the chair swiveled and Patrick's hands gripped the arms.

"Everything's fine, kitten. Riley's not saying anything to anyone," Patrick promised. "Come inside, you're freezing."

"Would it be so bad?" I asked, my eyes still studying the pergola.

Patrick frowned, and leaned against the edge of the teak dining table, his arms crossing over his chest. Something about those rolled up shirtsleeves knocked my train of thought off course every time. "Would what be so bad?"

Lowering my gaze to Patrick's eyes, I hugged my arms around my legs. "You said you wanted to wake up next to me every single day."

Patrick nodded, the muscles in his jaw pulsing. "Yeah."

"What does that mean?" My hand swept out, gesturing between us. "What happens at the end of my apprenticeship?"

"What do you mean, what happens? You're staying right here. We're tearing up half of the office space in a few weeks because I'm building you your own fucking office, Andy, six and a half feet away from mine, because I can't function without you."

My own office.

At Walsh Associates.

"When did you plan on mentioning that? I've spent the past three months trying to figure out what to do when this ends. You could have spared me two dozen phone interviews and some of the most ludicrous performance tasks ever conceived."

Patrick stared at me, irritation and sadness and confusion passing over his face. "You've been interviewing?"

"Yes," I cried, my hands slapping the wooden seat. "Life beyond June hasn't been a popular topic of conversation."

"But you're leading Mahoney and Castavechia, and Wellesley is far from finished," he replied, his hands spread wide in front of him as if that evidence proved his point. "Plus the other nineteen projects you have going through June."

"Right, and though those are late summer projects, you've never said 'Andy, we're hiring you at the end of your apprenticeship, so don't waste your time interviewing with morons.'"

Patrick returned his hands to the armrests and leaned forward. We were a breath apart. "Andy. We're hiring you at the end of your apprenticeship. Don't waste your time interviewing with morons." His lips brushed over my jaw and down my throat, then up, finally stopping at my lips. "I spent all day finalizing plans for your office with Riley—"

"Did he see my boobs?"

"Not that he's admitting." Patrick laughed, and dropped his head to my knees. "Andy...We need to talk about...a lot of things. Let me take you inside."

"You said there were at least five things. You can sit," I pointed across the table, "over there. Where you can behave."

"Not happening," Patrick murmured, and he dragged an ottoman in front of my chair. Sitting, he wrapped his hands around my ankles and rubbed small circles along my calves. "We start construction at the end of the month, and we're sectioning my office to create space for you. I changed the design to put a glass wall between us, so it feels like one room and I can always see you. Deal with it. That's one. I need you in that office because you've earned it. I also don't have the patience for Mahoney or Castavechia, and you know my position on Wellesley. Don't even think about taking another interview because you're incredible and fucking gifted, and everyone agrees with me. And I'm beyond pissed that you were looking, and didn't tell me. That's two."

My hand reached out, weaving my fingers through his hair, and he leaned into my touch. "What else?"

"How do you feel about covering Matt's projects while he's away?"

"That's mostly structural?" Patrick nodded. "Hm. I may need to dig out a few textbooks, but yeah. Sure."

"I'm not worried about it. The fact that you know which textbooks to dig out proves you can handle it."

"That's three."

Patrick groaned, and turned his face to press a kiss in the center of my palm. "I'm going up to Ithaca next week. Fundraising photo op, basically. Thursday into Friday."

"There's no reason to be grumpy about that, Patrick. There's nothing better than Cornell in May. I'd love to go back for a few days."

His eyes brightened. "Come with me."

My thoughts darted to Charlotte and some of the prevailing campus gossip. "I'm supervising demo on those rickety little windows in the attic at Wellesley next Thursday, and considering how it went with the windows in the sunroom, I'm expecting problems."

"Then I'm sticking with grumpy."

My hand moved to his neck, and I waited for the next item on his list. His wry humor was gone, and in its place, cords of tension tightened beneath my fingers.

"Shannon knows. We had this huge argument today. She called me on a lot of superbly accurate shit, and...I'm sorry. For what it's worth, she had no idea, and she'll take it to the grave."

I waited for the wave of panic, but it never crashed. "Lauren knows."

"Lauren, what—*what*?" Patrick's eyes burned with uncertainty when he gripped my wrist, stilling my fingers. "Since...how?"

I gulped loudly and concentrated on the thin, jagged scar on my right knee earned from a rusty nail on a jobsite three years ago. Focusing on the fine white line was easier than analyzing the frustration in Patrick's voice. "Since she figured it out a couple of months ago. She's very perceptive."

"So Matt knows?"

Shrugging, I met Patrick's eyes. "She hasn't told him, no."

"So we're going to all this trouble to keep Matt and Sam in the dark? Two people who adore you and would give approximately zero fucks about what we do?"

"That's one very linear way of thinking about it."

Patrick released my wrist and his hands fell to his lap. His narrowed eyes scanned the neighboring rooftops for several minutes before he spoke again.

"I want this. You. Us. I want the language that your eyes speak and all of your quirks, even if they drive me fucking crazy. I want you to live here with me, I want you working next to me, and I want everyone to know. I want us to be like we are now, but...I don't want any more secrets."

I stared at him in the bright city darkness, blinking while his words caught fire in my belly. "I want that, too."

A dazzling, childlike smile filled Patrick's face, and he laced our fingers together. "Good. Now if you don't mind, I'm taking your sweet ass to bed because you need to stop thinking and have some rough sex. Let me just get those paper clips out of your hair first."

"OH, ANDY," LAUREN WHISPERED, TUCKING THE CARD INTO THE envelope. She stood, stretching out her arms in my direction, and I squeezed her shoulders. "Thank you. This is perfect."

"Tell me, tell me!" Shannon demanded, her neck craning to see between us.

"It is a book all about the Swiss Lakes District," she replied, brushing tears from the corners of her eyes. "For the honeymoon. And she included ideas for boat tours and hikes, and restaurants and everything, it's wonderful. I can't wait, and Matthew is going to love it."

Returning to my seat, I adjusted the waist on my navy blue skirt and fiddled with my hot pink bib necklace—I couldn't get away without some brightness at a bridal shower—while

Shannon gazed at me with a fond smile. It was her new thing, and I smiled in response before turning my attention to Lauren's next gift.

Shannon created reasons to swing by Patrick's office or casually chat while I refilled my water bottle in the kitchen. Her pretenses were always sensible: she was thinking about placing a furniture order for the new offices, and wanted my thoughts, or she heard about a new farmers' market by Northeastern University for my Saturday ritual. Implicit in all of it was her closely guarded approval mixed with a fierce warning that she was keeping an eye on me.

I begged Patrick for two more weeks of semi-secrecy but I was more than ready to drop the act with Shannon. I didn't dare tell him that. I wasn't about to see him bust a capillary over my shifting feelings. Two more weeks brought us up to the day Riley and I swapped places so I could get up to speed on Matt's projects and engineering processes. It seemed like a clean transition point, and while I wasn't looking forward to relocating to the second floor, I was ready to go public.

Lauren plowed through a dense pile of pristine white gift wrapping to uncover more wine glasses, serving trays, and silver picture frames than any couple could ever put to good use, but she graciously complimented each gift and thanked the giver. Once the gifts were opened and cake served, the guests trickled out of Shannon's apartment. It wasn't long until we were alone.

Together with Shannon and Lauren, we finished the dregs of eight champagne bottles. Shannon regaled us with another round of tragic dating stories: the guy who made his own deodorant, the guy who didn't mention he was engaged until they were naked, the guy who kept an awkwardly large collection of stuffed animals, the guy who wanted to be a lactation consultant because he was really into boobs. For a beautiful, successful woman, Shannon tapped into a special crop of Boston's most eligible bachelors.

Later, I found myself shuttling stray champagne flutes into the kitchen when Lauren wrapped her arm around my waist. "Hear from your boy tonight?" she asked, her finger swiping a dollop of frosting off the cake.

"I assume he's the one blowing up my phone, considering it hasn't stopped vibrating, but I haven't looked. Yours?"

She sucked another dollop of frosting from her finger and nodded. "Yep. It's amusing that he's spending his bachelor party texting. I'm thinking about wandering down Berkeley Street soon. I wouldn't be surprised to find him chatting up an oak tree or passed out in Park Plaza."

"I thought Nick was supervising," I whispered as Shannon approached.

Lauren shrugged. "He was on call, and something came up."

As much as I enjoyed Patrick's drunken texts, I was more interested in getting him home.

"That's the last time I order a cake this size for twenty skinny bitches," Shannon muttered. "We probably could have shared a single cupcake."

"Speak for yourself," Lauren said. "This cake and I have plans. There's nothing better than cold cake for breakfast."

"It's all yours."

"Thanks for such a wonderful night, Shan." Lauren folded Shannon into a tight hug. "You're the best non-maid of honor this girl could ask for."

"You're the best sister-in-law," Shannon retorted, her eyes meeting mine over Lauren's shoulder. "You make my brother happy, and you take care of him, and that's more than I could ever ask for."

I held her loaded gaze for a beat before excusing myself to the bathroom—*that* bathroom—to apply a fresh coat of lip balm and check my phone. Three texts from Jess inviting me out for drinks and dancing—declined with the promise of catching up later in the week. One from Charlotte showing off a cute new sundress. Twelve from Patrick.

Patrick: What time is your thing finished?
Patrick: Tell me when you're done and I'll leave
Patrick: Three good reasons why you'd hate this restaurant
Patrick: 1. Waiters in white jackets.
Patrick: 2. There's pot roast on the menu. It claims to be epic but...
Patrick: 3. All kinds of raw bar up in here
Patrick: But you'd be all about the beet salad
Patrick: I actually think you'd like a few things on this dessert menu
Patrick: Is there a cake at this party?
Patrick: How long has it been since I touched you? It feels like 400 years and I hate that
Patrick: When I get you home, you're mine.
Patrick: Here's the thing about whiskey: its great

I chuckled, and typed out a quick response.

Andy: On my way out soon, glad I missed the raw bar, you saw me this afternoon, and I'm always yours.
Andy: Where are you?

Emerging from the bathroom, I found Lauren belting a light raincoat while Shannon reclined on a tufted chaise. "Don't worry about this stuff," Shannon said, her hand waving toward the mountain of gifts. "I'll keep it in my guest room until Matt can drop by."

"Yeah, he'll love doing that when he's too hungover to blink tomorrow," Lauren replied. She glanced toward me, a questioning look in her eye. "Walk with me?"

I nodded, and we departed after another round of hugs. "Any idea where they'll be?"

"They ate on Berkeley Street, and I'm guessing they either went to M at the Mandarin Oriental or Eastern Standard. Sam's probably the ringleader, and I bet he's all about M. That boy is hooked up at all the VIP spots."

Thankfully, Shannon's apartment on the southern slope of Beacon Hill was only a few blocks from the Common and Boylston Street, and the trek in nude heels wasn't treacherous but it did force me to shorten my steps. I gazed at gorgeous brick homes as we strolled, thinking back to the snowy day in January when I hiked these streets after my interview with Patrick and Shannon.

At the edge of the Common, Lauren grabbed my wrist and pointed across the intersection. "Do you see what I see?"

And there they were: four well-dressed, strikingly handsome hooligans stumbling and shoving each other, howling with laughter, and looking like trouble. They crossed toward the park and nearly walked right by us.

That whiskey must have been fabulous.

"Dude, dude, it's Princess Jasmine and Miss Honey!" Riley yelled, his fist landing on Patrick's shoulder for emphasis.

Lauren and I glanced at each other, quickly shaking our

heads. "I don't know what it is about these kids and nick-names," she muttered, "but you're an official member of the club now."

"Miss Honey?" I asked.

"You know," she shrugged. "From *Matilda*? That sweet, inno-cent teacher?"

"Oh yeah," I replied. "They don't know you at all."

"Nope," Lauren giggled.

Riley wrapped his arm around my shoulder. "You're like really high priced call girls."

Patrick squinted, studying me as if he didn't believe I was standing five feet away before grabbing the neck of Riley's shirt. "Did you just call her a hooker?"

"No," Riley replied, drawing the word out. "It's just funny that they're standing here, on the corner. And they're really hot. So hot."

"Come on, Matthew," Lauren commanded, grabbing him by the belt and waving for a cab. "Time to put you to bed. And I have cake. Andy, text me tomorrow."

"Whatever you do, do not eat that cake," Patrick yelled. "It's perverted!"

Lauren and I exchanged another confused glance as she poured Matt into a cab. Patrick maintained his hold on Riley's collar, his gaze dark and unfocused. Against my better judgment, I pried his fingers away and wrapped my arm around his waist. "Enough of that," I murmured, and he dropped a sloppy kiss on my mouth.

Sam wagged his finger between Patrick and me, a puzzled look crossing his face. "What...?"

Riley clapped Sam on the back and pointed down the street. "Are we going to M or what, man? The night's young and so are we. And you said you'd introduce me to those actresses who were shooting that film in Southie."

"Are you going to tell me what's—"

"Nope." Riley towed Sam toward Boylston Street. "Classified information." They walked away, Sam glancing over his shoulder repeatedly before they detoured down a side street.

"Whiskey, huh?" We wandered through the park, my arm anchored on Patrick's waist to minimize his wobbling.

"Whiskey is great," he slurred. He was silent for a few moments, the sounds of my clicking heels echoing around us. "My aunt, my father used to say she was a tough old broad, she used to drink whiskey in bed with an alligator every night."

"Yeah, I'm sure she did," I replied.

"After my mother died, she came over with casseroles. So many casseroles. Chicken divan. Chicken à la king. Chicken cacciatore. Chicken pie. Chicken and dumplings. Fuckin' chicken. One time, Shannon left it in the oven too long, Jesus, Shannon should not be allowed in a chicken."

"You mean a kitchen?"

"That's what I said. It is a fucking public health crisis when she tries to cook. And she left it in too long, and when she tried to get it out of the pan, my hand on the bible, the dish slipped off the counter and popped Sam square in the eye. That son of a bitch had a black eye for a month, and no one believed it was a casserole. They just assumed a girl beat the shit out of him. But that was a meatloaf."

My apartment was closer and as we made our way to my floor, it was obvious that Patrick was in no shape for steep, narrow stairs, slipping and knocking his shins against the risers every few steps. "Fuckin' stairs," he groaned.

He leaned against the wall while I fished my keys from my clutch, his eyes sweeping back and forth across the landing.

"Andy," he whispered. "Where are we?"

I pushed him through the doorway, propping him against a wall while I stepped out of my heels. "My place."

"No shit?" he murmured. "Final frontier. There's probably something else I don't know about you though, but I don't know what I don't know. You don't give me much, Andy. I don't even know your long name, like your *real* name, not Andy."

"Andriel Ava Mazanderani Asani. You can see how I'd need to shorten that." I glanced at him while he listed precariously to the left. "And you only have to ask, Patrick."

"'If you have to ask, you'll never know.'"

"Not sure that quote applies to this situation." With the hot pink necklace returned to its peg in my closet, I padded into the kitchen. Patrick followed and pawed through my refrigerator.

"I can't find any roast beef...or anything from the deli."

"I keep a vegan kitchen here."

Patrick slammed the refrigerator shut and stared at me, shocked. "There're so many things wrong with that statement. You're not a vegan."

I shrugged. "Sometimes I am a vegan, and...you're not going to remember this conversation tomorrow, so let's not argue about it."

His hand waved toward the wall of boxes. "Packing up already?"

We didn't reach a clear agreement on my move-in date because I couldn't get out of my lease within Patrick's timeframe of right-that-second.

"Never unpacked," I murmured, my fingers flying over the buttons of his shirt.

"Lauren used to live a few blocks away. Chipmunk Street. Wait—no, Chestnut. Fuck, Andy, she makes him so fucking happy. He used to be so, I don't know, cold. Like he didn't care about anything. He didn't want to care. But now? Happy. Not like double rainbows every day happy, or some bullshit, but he's...I don't know. Loved. He's loved, and he loves her, and for a coupl'a kids who wouldn't know how to love a leprechaun if it fucked us in the ass, he's working at it, and doing it, and it's working."

"A leprechaun, huh?"

I stared at Patrick, a glass of water with a cucumber slice for extra hydration in my hand, and waited—I didn't want to interrupt his diatribe. It was illuminating and hilarious, and keeping my laughter in check was testing my abdominal muscles.

"Bed. Now," I ordered, and Patrick complied. "Drink this."

Knowing his track record with cell phones and whiskey, I retrieved his phone, keys and wallet from his pants and set them on the other side of the room. When I turned around, the glass was empty and Patrick was sprawled across my bed with his eyes closed. I retreated to the bathroom to remove my makeup and change, and found him flopped on his stomach when I returned.

Apparently, he was a wiggly drunk.

Smoothing the covers around us, I pressed my hand to his back. He was right: a few hours apart felt like a short eternity, and his skin against mine was all I needed to recharge.

He rolled over, scooping me into his arms. "Do you love me?" Patrick asked, his voice thick and quiet.

I brushed his hair back, my fingers moving through his soft strands. "Yes."

"Mmm," he sighed, his eyes drifting shut. "'If you know, you need only ask.'"

CHAPTER NINETEEN

PATRICK

I PROBABLY DIDN'T APPRECIATE COLLEGE WHILE I WAS THERE. I didn't value self-replenishing dining halls, schedules that conveniently avoided Fridays and anything before noon, or the seemingly endless excuses college kids invented to throw parties. I knew I didn't appreciate it, and the three hundred and thirty-mile drive to Cornell was a definite reminder. Once I was deep in the rolling hills of western Massachusetts, the gilded memories of a responsibility-free youth crept into sight.

Nonetheless, college was a messy time for us, and it was the first and only time in my life that I was separated from my siblings for more than a few days. All told, I spent two solid years alone at Cornell before Matt showed up.

Shannon should have been a year behind me like always, but Angus went to war with her during my first semester away. Before I made it home for Thanksgiving break, he emptied her college fund. He justified his behavior with his breed of fatherly wisdom, insisting Shannon was attending college with the intent of finding a husband, and he didn't deserve the tab for that.

It didn't deter her. She picked up her real estate license and cleaned up during the condo and loft boom, went nights to Suffolk University in the city, and proved Angus very wrong.

Good old Angus. May his ornery, angry soul rest in peace... or the eternal fires of hell. Whichever.

Smiling and nodding while the university lavished praise on his generous gift and visionary approach to preservation arts were preferable only to wading through a septic tank explosion. After six rounds of stiffly posed photographs and four requests for comments on my father's commitment to developing a robust crop of young sustainability architects, my forced smile started to crack.

"That's a great question," I replied, my eyes darting across the ballroom in search of the closest exit. "He believed...it was important...to put new architects through their paces. Learn the craft. And what better way to learn than by doing?"

That was a nice way of saying he was a massive douche who taught us by making us figure it out ourselves.

"I'm curious, Mr. Walsh, what propelled your father to embrace sustainability when the preservation field was slow to get on board?"

I glanced at the student reporter and withheld a snicker. Angus never embraced sustainability; he seized every opportunity to criticize our decision to move in that direction, and harped on our every misstep as evidence of our foolish strategy. Sam was still bruised from Angus's final beating on that topic.

"Well..."

"Just the man I wanted to see!" A strong hand clamped over my shoulder, and I was face-to-face with David Lin. Never was I so relieved to see my undergrad roommate, and I clasped his hand in a firm shake. "How the hell are you?" He glanced at the reporter. "Mariella, I need a few minutes with Mr. Walsh here. If you have more questions, forward them to his office. Give the reporter your card, Walsh."

She accepted my card—with my new title—and moved on to get comments from other university leaders.

"Thanks for that," I said, inclining my head toward the reporter. "How long's it been, Dave?"

He shoved his hands in his pockets and bobbed his head from side to side. "At least three, probably four years since I've seen your pretty face." He looked around the venue and leaned forward. "I'm sorry about your dad. Can I buy you a cup of coffee? Catch up?"

"Lead the way."

DAVE MENTIONED SEVERAL RECENT ADDITIONS TO THE AREA, BUT I was compelled to stick with something I knew well: Stella's Café. Cornell was always the kind of place that lived untouched in my memory, and I preferred the old haunts.

"Is it true that Mr. Disinterested is getting married?"

"True. The big day's coming up. Next weekend." I sipped my iced coffee and smiled. "He couldn't have found a better girl. Such a sweetheart, but she doesn't take any of his shit. It's awesome to watch someone put him in his place, seeing as he likes to think he knows everything."

"Never thought I'd see the day. He was my back-up, you know," Dave said. "I need to revamp my long-range relationship strategy if he's off the market."

"Off the market," I confirmed. "And, I don't doubt you, Dave, but I don't see him playing for your team."

"Well, shit."

"What's this new gig you've got?" I asked.

Dave passed a hand over his forehead and adjusted his glasses. "Associate Dean. Never thought I'd be The Man. Definitely not The Man in the suit," he laughed, gesturing to his gray three-piece. "But I'm more interested in what you're doing. Hell, we used to talk for hours about the shops we were going to open and the shit we were going to do, and you're the only person from our graduating class who went out and did it all. We were going to change the world, one brick at a time. I give you a lot of credit. We all do, up in the Ivory Tower, that is."

I sipped my iced coffee and shrugged. Shannon was better at handling the praise. "Not without its challenges, Dave. My girlfriend likes to remind me I haven't been inside a movie theatre since the nineties and I've missed major elements of culture because my head has been in building code for ten years straight."

"So you're not taking the girlfriend to the movies?"

My fingers were itching to message Andy. I wanted her to know how exquisite the word 'girlfriend' tasted on my tongue, and how I was beyond ready to tell everyone about us on Monday morning. Less than four days. "She's in the business, so...it's easier. Are you still with Jerome?"

Dave's lips pursed and he broke his biscotti into several pea-sized pieces. "No. Didn't want the same things. You think you know someone after six years..." He sighed, and looked up with a hollow smile. "Didn't we send you an apprentice? How'd that go?"

"Andy Asani, and she's fantastic. Incredible, really. We just offered her an associate position, and if she's the kind of graduate you're turning out, this program got a lot better after I left."

"She's a smart kid," he said, his brow furrowing. "Good to hear she's finding her niche, but, uh...keep an eye on that one."

I laughed, thinking about any number of ways Andy could put Cornell through its paces. I couldn't wait to tell her about Dave's comments. "Anything in particular?"

Frowning, Dave spun his straw through his sweating iced coffee. "I'm not sure how much to say, and most of this is second-hand information, but..."

"But what?" I asked, my blood chilling. His tone was too serious, and I wanted to hear what he had to say while retaining the right to scrub every word from memory immediately.

He lifted a shoulder, his frown deepening. "She was close with the department chair, Dr. Batista. He picked her up for quite a few research assistantships, and she TA'd for him. Rumor had it that Batista left his wife for Andy, and then she blew him off when she moved to Boston. He spent this past semester on personal leave."

Aggravation teased at my nerves. No way in hell that was Andy and my patience for Dave's bullshit rumor was slim to nonexistent. No. Fucking. Way.

"That's a heavy accusation, Dave."

He held up his hands. "No accusation from me. There was a lot of talk, and when he dropped his courses three days before the semester resumed, there was a lot more talk. I heard he spent some time in Boston these past few months, trying to reconnect with her."

Gossip. It was all gossip. I refused to believe she was capable of that kind of manipulation. She definitely wasn't the kind of woman who left a man's life in shambles.

Except for when she told that man a few passionate moments in a bathroom didn't change anything.

I shook my head, ridding her cool, dismissive words from my mind. "That's not the Andy Asani I know. The Andy I know is focused and talented, and she doesn't need to sleep with anyone to get..." I swallowed, and the coffee went down like a handful of gravel. "To get ahead. Her work speaks for itself."

"Like I said, getting graduates placed in the right firm is the priority, and it sounds like Andy's in the right spot, and so long as she stays out of your trousers, it shouldn't be problem for you."

I glimpsed at my watch and estimated the amount of traffic I'd hit by leaving Ithaca at noon. The Mass Pike at rush hour on a Friday was the last place I wanted to be but I needed to talk to Andy.

THE SECOND FLOOR CONFERENCE ROOM WAS A SAD SUBSTITUTE FOR
Patrick's office, primarily due to its complete shortage of Patrick,
but the small, alley-facing window was part of the problem, too.
It was slightly disturbing that less than twenty-four hours away
from him left me discombobulated. I didn't sleep quite right, my
Mason jar salad was a depressingly dull lunch, and I missed him
—his scent, his touch, his eyes. All of him affected all of me.

Boston was experiencing its first hot day of spring, and I seriously contemplated a move to the State House courtyard to
brighten my mood and soak up some sun. It seemed like the
proper response to a winter dominated by permafrost snow
banks and several visits from the polar vortex—never mind a
solid month of April showers that looked a lot more like April
monsoons.

"Well this is a dark and dreary cave," Tom said as he strolled
into the crammed room. Boxes surrounded me—everything in
Patrick and Matt's offices was packed in advance of tomorrow's

demo, and teams were busy protecting the original elements in both rooms. "Is this where you and Patrick are camping until construction is finished?"

Mmm. That sounded nice. My rugby Sex God would make this room far less dark and dreary.

"I'm in here with Matt. Riley and Patrick will be upstairs."

"Right, right. Well, your boss told Shannon he would be back in the city around six tonight, and I need his signature on all of these." Tom hefted color-coded files and dropped them in front of me. "If you could get them into his hands, I will owe you an afternoon coffee."

There was no sense in reminding Tom I didn't drink coffee or that I handed the coffees he routinely brought directly to Patrick. There was always a snarky comment from Patrick about Tom compensating for his inability to grow a beard with coffee, or Tom's general inattentiveness to my beverage preferences. Patrick liked to claim he knew within a week how I took my tea and the minimum amount of hot salsa necessary for maximum taco enjoyment. "No worries, Tom. I need to run a few things by him tonight anyway."

By 'a few things,' I did mean some sassy new panties that laced up the sides.

Tom murmured his thanks and turned to go, soundly whacking his elbow on a tower of boxes. "Freakin' construction," he muttered. "I still don't understand why we're doing this to begin with. It's not like the firm's getting any bigger."

"How's that?" I called.

Tom edged into the room, his elbow cradled in his hand. "The firm isn't getting any bigger. It's right there in the partnership structure." He motioned to the blue folder on top of the stack. "Some possibility of future interns and apprentices, but five partners max. Don't take this the wrong way, but it floored me when they offered you a spot. It's not as if they were actively searching for associate architects. You should check that out. There's a lot of juicy bits in there."

I stared at the blue folder for a few minutes. There was no reason to believe Patrick was withholding information from me. He frequently mentioned the work he and Shannon were doing to adjust the organizational model. One particularly snowy weekend, we ate at least a quart of my red lentil soup while he bitched about the changes Shannon was pushing through. Trusting Patrick was a no-brainer, and digging through his paperwork felt presumptuous.

On the one hand, I knew they weren't looking for more architects—Patrick spent plenty of time bemoaning the number of résumés clogging his inbox on any given day. I knew Tom answered every single one with a 'thanks but no thanks but we'll keep your résumé on file' response. But they were also building an office for Riley, and it was no surprise he joined the firm after attending RISD. Right?

I weighed the evidence for a moment before snapping my laptop shut and shoving it in my bag along with the file. A sunny spot alongside the rose garden called to me, and I settled on the grass to read.

Hours drifted by and the sun moved across the golden dome of the State House. Stopping my hands from shaking was out of the question. When considered alongside the spectrum of awesomely bad decisions from the past few months, leaving the office to read the real story of Walsh Associates and hiding my tears behind sunglasses were the only smart ones. I never wanted to be the girl who cried at work. I wasn't letting any one of them see my humiliation or my hurt.

Tom was right: the firm had no intention of growing. They weren't looking for another principal architect, and they certainly weren't looking for another partner.

Unless I wanted to spend my entire career kneeling in submission at Patrick's side as an associate architect, there was no future for me at his firm.

PATRICK'S OFFICE—*OUR* OFFICE—WAS BARELY RECOGNIZABLE FROM my seat in his desk chair, surrounded by protective layers of cardboard and twill tarps. Without the drafting desk or conference table, it was as if I never inhabited the space.

I swiveled back and forth, my fingers drumming against the armrests while I stared out the window. There was no innocent explanation for the partnership structure documents, and I didn't misunderstand the legalese.

Patrick screwed me over. The plain black and white wasn't lying about it.

His text messages informed me he was hobbling through thick traffic on the outskirts of Boston. He didn't know my "ok" and "sounds good, meet me in your office" responses contained as much contempt, outrage, and betrayal as a text could hold.

The sad part was I knew better. All along, I knew better.

I heard him in the stairwell—his throat clearing and bouncing step on the stairs echoed through the empty building, and I hated the fluttering in my traitorous heart. It wasn't fair that at least one whole organ wanted me to lay my head on his chest and just breathe.

Ray-Ban Wayfarers propped on his head, and blue Oxford shirtsleeves rolled up to his elbows and travel-wrinkled, Patrick filled the office like a blast of icy air. With his collar wrenched open and the top buttons undone, his tie swung from his pocket, and he looked about as hurt as I felt.

"Hey, I need to talk to you," Patrick said.

Standing in front of me with his legs braced and arms crossed, his stance was defensive. Did someone tip him off to my study of the documents? What would be better? Catching him off guard or discovering that someone saw me crying over a partnership structure like a naïve, lovesick fangirl who was too busy pinning bridal bouquets to see her career going up in flames?

There was no 'better' in this situation. I was right back at worse and worst.

"Yes." The calm in my voice betrayed every emotion hammering in my veins. "We do need to talk." I tossed the file across his desk, its heft ringing out in the empty space, and I wrapped my fingers around the armrests to draw strength. "Care to explain this to me?"

The muscles in Patrick's jaw ticked and bulged, but he didn't spare a second to acknowledge the file. "Care to tell me about Dr. Batista?"

"No, Patrick, I'm not telling you a thing about Batista until you explain why I didn't know that I was never going to advance past an associate here."

We glared at each other, his rippling jaw to my white knuckles. Backing down wasn't part of my game plan, but I knew all about Patrick's style—he let his scowl do the talking and waited out his opponent with scalding silence. It worked like a charm on GCs and subcontractors, the entire office staff, and most of his siblings.

The scowl didn't bother me one bit, and if there was anyone who tolerated silence as well as Patrick did, it was me. Arching an eyebrow, I tilted my chin and forced my fingers to loosen their hold on the armrests.

When he finally broke his stare, he peeled back the folder with a snarl, his bunched shoulders dropping as he scanned the contents. "Where did you get this?"

"It doesn't matter, Patrick. What matters is you failed to mention at any point in the past few months that staying here meant hitting the ceiling at associate. You know that's not what I want, and you told me to stop interviewing. I've turned down partner-track jobs."

"None of this means anything," he said with a flippant wave toward the folder. "It's just...paper."

"That's bullshit and you know it. You know that you should've told me about this."

Patrick sneered at the file and slammed it shut. "These documents, they're meaningless. If I wanted to promote you to partner tomorrow, I could. If you read past the first few pages, you would've seen that I'm pretty much empowered to do whatever the fuck I want. These are meaningless. Totally fucking meaningless. It's the shit that lawyers like to do."

"Yeah?" I challenged. "What about the clause stating that partners must be family? Is that meaningless too?"

"No, actually, it's not meaningless," he shot back. "Jesus Christ, Andy, what do you want me to say right now? You want me to go back to Shannon and have her change the whole fucking thing because you've been here for a couple of months and think you know how this shop runs? You're not the center of the universe. You want me to change the operational philosophy because you want to be partner in a few years, and you happen to be fucking me right now? I'm not touching this document until you answer my questions."

His words bit into my flesh like a whip. "I'm thrilled to hear I'm simply the person who's fucking you right now. That's great, Patrick."

"Are you still seeing Batista? This guy left his wife for you?"

"Are you kidding me? Really?" I shook my head. "I'm going to assume that you're not suggesting that I'm some kind of slut. You spend forty-five minutes at Cornell and you've bought into every rumor mill in town. I thought you were smarter than that."

"I thought you were smarter than making a habit of fucking the people in charge."

"Wow," I murmured. I shifted in the chair and recrossed my legs to absorb the sting. "Wow. I really misjudged you. I was wrong about so many things."

"Apparently so was I." He shrugged, and gestured toward me. "I don't know why I thought you'd ever let me in, but I was really fuckin' wrong about that."

I shouldered my bag and stomped toward the door. Whirling around, I studied Patrick's rigid form and the spasming in his jaw. "Not that you deserve the truth or anything, but I do still see Batista, and I've told you about it multiple times."

Patrick turned his head to the side, but didn't meet my eyes. "What?"

"Yeah. You might remember me talking about my friend, Charlotte. I see her when she's in town." Patrick's eyes narrowed, the tension in his jaw easing slightly. "She didn't leave her wife for me, you bastard. Her wife left her because she's transsexual, and going through reassignment surgeries and the wife couldn't hang anymore. *Charlotte* Batista confided in me about it. We're friends. So no, Patrick, I don't just fuck the people in charge, and I definitely don't fuck you anymore."

MY APARTMENT WAS TOO SMALL, TOO HOT, TOO EMPTY, AND AFTER a ninety-minute whirlwind cleaning session interrupted by periods of ugly crying, I needed to escape. I changed into jeans, a black t-shirt, and silver flats, and charged out of the apartment with nothing more than my keys and wallet.

A cell phone was bound to cause trouble.

People-watching on the Red Line was adequately distracting, and the trip to Brighton ebbed my tears. Ringing the buzzer, I prayed that Marley and Jess were at home rather than pregaming—they upheld the college tradition of starting the weekend off right with startling fidelity.

"Andy, hey." I whirled around to see Jess leaning against the doorway in her favorite clubbing dress with half of her hair curled in loose waves and a mascara wand in her hand. "What're you doing here?"

"I'm sorry I didn't call," I sighed, feeling the rush of tears prickling my eyes again. "I had a huge fight with my boyfriend, and it's been an awful day, and I just need to talk to someone."

"Yeah, so, about that," she said, pointing at me with the wand. "You didn't bother to tell me you were seeing someone."

"Oh, I know, I'm sorry—"

"Can you just wait?" She held up her hand to stop me. "Let me finish. I haven't seen you in two months, and you blow us off every single time we make plans. You have this big dramatic problem right now, but you're never there for me when I go through a bad breakup. I can't even...you literally never ask about me, or my life. I mean, I thought that since we were living in the same city again we'd be friends, but it's obvious to me that you're just a selfish bitch."

I should have checked the weather this morning. It would have advised me to stay in bed to avoid the shit storm coming my way. "Jess, I'm sorry—"

"Let. Me. Finish," she said, ticking off her points with her wand. "So it's fine if you want to have your own life or whatever. I'm not sitting around and crying because you don't want to have sleepovers with me anymore, but you've been a complete bitch since you showed up here in January."

Marley tiptoed past the door, and when I tried to catch her eye, she made a beeline for the other side of the apartment.

"You don't think I notice that you hate the clubs we go to, and the guys we hang with, and you think you're too fuckin' smart to even talk to us. Marley's too nice to say anything, but you treat her like she's dog shit, and I'm done with you. We were friends in high school, and that's it. You need to find new friends to deal with your little boyfriend dramas."

I didn't have the strength for a counter-argument, and it probably wouldn't have amounted to much. Wrapping my arms around my waist, I nodded, and stepped away from her door.

"And if I had to guess," Jess called, her words landing on my back. "That boyfriend probably figured out you're a cold, self-centered bitch and you're too busy admiring your own asshole to give a fuck about anyone else."

The door slammed behind me.

I debated skipping the subway and wandering along Beacon Street until I reached my apartment, but shouldering the weight of the day alone was starting to crush me. One more step seemed like too many. I watched the city stutter by with my head pressed to the Red Line window.

Emerging at the Park Street station, I squinted toward Beacon Hill and knew wallowing at my apartment wasn't a wise choice. Not in the bed where I told Patrick I loved him. Not that he remembered, of course.

I stumbled toward the Theatre District, and found myself at the only dive bar divey enough to handle me: The Tam. I took up residence at the far corner of the bar, ordered three shots of vodka, and put on my best 'don't fuck with me' face. I craved some communal anonymity but I wasn't above backhanding the first bro who sidled up next to me.

Turning over my palms and forearms, I studied my skin, expecting to find myself bloodied and bruised from the blows levied by Jess and Patrick. Bruises would have been better, and part of me craved a physical representation of the pain inside. I knew how to heal bruises. I didn't know how to recover from this.

It was a slow night at The Tam—anyone with a shred of sense was outside enjoying the weather, and not wishing for open wounds to appear on their body.

The bartender leaned against the bar with a nod toward my empties. "'Nother round?"

"Um, vodka gimlet," I replied, my head braced in my hands. I hoped my vodka therapist was answering calls at this hour. A thorough sort-out was in order since I was complete shit as a friend and girlfriend, and patently incapable of holding either title. That, and I was utterly alone in the world.

"Comin' up."

I wanted Jess to be wrong—grossly wrong—but she wasn't. I was a terrible friend to her. I treated Marley like an imbecile. I hated going out with them and faked my interest in all of their conversation topics. Badly. I expected them to be waiting with open arms when I needed them, and had the balls to be surprised when they weren't.

And Patrick...oh, Patrick. He wasn't without fault, but he wasn't entirely wrong either. Pain radiated through my chest at the memory of his words.

You're not the center of the universe.

I thought you were smarter than making a habit of fucking the people in charge.

I don't know why I thought you'd ever let me in, but I was really fuckin' wrong about that.

Patrick rewriting the partnership agreement was exactly what I *didn't* want—special treatment based on our relationship. But why couldn't he have told me sooner? Why did I have to find out from Tom, and his suggested snooping? Why did Patrick let me look like such a fool?

"Vodka gimlet," the bartender announced, and I fisted the tumbler before it touched the cocktail napkin. "I know that look."

"Listen, dude. This is a beautifully made gimlet, and for that, I thank you. I promise to tip generously. A few more of these and my day won't look like such a monumental clusterfuck anymore, but I'm in no shape for bar banter."

"My bar, my banter," he quipped. "Like I said, I know that look. Either your boss is putting you through hell, or your boyfriend is. Am I close?"

Snickering, I set the empty tumbler on the napkin, and after I sent a purposeful glance toward the glass, he started fixing another. "They're putting me through hell, that's for sure," I mumbled. "They're the same person."

"Shit."

"Amen." I lifted my glass in salute. "While you're here, you should also know my oldest friend just told me that I'm a self-centered bitch, and my only other friend is my boss-slash-boyfriend's future sister-in-law."

"In that case, this one's on me. Start talkin', sister."

CHAPTER TWENTY-ONE

I was in lavender withdrawal, and though I didn't know much about heroin withdrawal, I couldn't imagine how that could be much worse. Andy, and all of her lavenderness, lived in my cells, and I suspected detoxing required the assistance of a witch doctor. Maybe leeches.

When I finally scraped my jaw off the floor Friday night, Andy was long gone. I gained an unhealthy amount of satisfaction from calling Dave Lin and ripping him a new asshole over the bullshit he was spreading. I stalked her apartment for hours, eventually giving up around one in the morning. All of my calls went to voicemail, and I ignored the possibility that fiendish texting was overkill. Convinced she'd show up at my door or text me in the middle of the night, I spent the entire weekend awake, watching a Spanish language soccer channel while the phantom scent of lavender mocked me from every corner of my apartment.

Eating, sleeping, and bathing took a backseat to staring at

my phone, although there was the ancillary benefit of picking up some conversational Spanish.

There was no getting around that I was a steaming bowl of douche stew and there was no need to examine my failure to mention the firm's partnership structure to Andy. It wasn't a master plan to trick her into staying. I was willing to rewrite those documents when it was her time, and that time wasn't coming until she spent a couple years at the firm and my siblings embraced the idea of her as a partner. It was an idiotic omission and I let it turn into a landslide of jealous, insecure bullshit.

Monday morning felt like a joke. We were going to be an official, legitimate couple—finally. All that rightness was now a pile of wrongs.

My bed earned a baleful stare when I shuffled toward the shower, and I hated the smooth blankets and neatly stacked pillows staring back at me. I remembered her making the bed while I bitched about my trip to Cornell last Thursday morning, and her wry comment that I had more separation anxiety about a night apart than most toddlers.

Sleeping there without Andy didn't interest me. Hell, sleep in any location without Andy didn't interest me.

Stepping into my closet brought me face-to-face with an assortment of dark-colored clothes, and a pile of absurdly random knee socks. My fingers stroked over a yellow pair with green bullfrogs, and I ached to go back in time. If it weren't for the certainty I'd soon be able to lock Andy in an office and talk this shit out, I would have spent the day scowling on my sofa.

Taking the long route around Beacon Hill to the coffee shop Andy loved on Tremont Street gave me time to evaluate my precise depth in the insanity quicksand, and the route from

Tremont Street to the office reminded me the quicksand was of my own design.

When I reached the office, I headed straight for the attic, grateful for the distraction of talking shop. At the top of the stairs, I rounded the corner into the small, safe room that always renewed my faith in my siblings and our work, the one room in the office free from any tint of Andy, and I froze in my tracks.

She was the last person I expected to see seated between Riley and Matt at the round table. But then I remembered: she was Matt's apprentice now.

She didn't belong to me anymore. If she ever belonged to me at all.

Laughing at a story Riley told, she didn't shift her focus from him for a moment, and not a single trace of sadness over the state of us was evident.

I just needed a breadcrumb.

"Anytime you're ready, Patrick," Shannon whispered.

Clutching my messenger bag to my chest, I sank into my seat and turned to Shannon. "Can you get this started?"

She frowned. "Are you okay? You look...a little green."

Andy was glowing. Her skin was sun-kissed and her dark eyes shone brighter than usual. She wore a thin gray v-neck blouse, the trendy kind that was a little too big and a little sheer, and I wanted to trace the edges of the fabric, feeling her smooth skin against my fingers.

"Run the meeting, Shannon," I snapped. She recoiled at my tone, and I hated myself for it.

"It's a lovely morning to see you all. We're living in the middle of our own jobsite right now but I'm sure Riley can tell us about the progress on that in a few moments. If we can survive the next few days without injury or incident, I will gladly pick up the bar tab Friday night. But right now, no time to waste." Shannon snapped her fingers and pointed toward Sam. "Go."

I kept my shoulders hunched and eyes on my screen, typing nearly verbatim notes without listening. Their projects were not my primary concerns. They probably didn't crack my top ten.

Her thin beaded bracelets and matching necklace caught my attention from across the table. They looked new.

Andy felt my eyes on her necklace, and her hand went to it. It *was* new, and before I got worked up over her spending the weekend shopping for jewelry while I was decomposing like a discarded banana peel on the couch, I remembered the farmers' market. Andy and Lauren did yoga and organic vegetable shopping every Saturday, and she liked to pick up handmade scarves and bowls and random shit at the farmers' market.

For a heated second, our eyes met over the edge of my laptop, and I was instantly deaf to Sam's report. Andy's gaze dropped to my coffee cup. Her eyebrows inched up, knowing I passed at least nine perfectly good coffee shops before arriving at her favorite. She knew I went there with the hope of running into her.

The meeting trudged on, and I hated every single one of them for existing. They were keeping me from fixing things with Andy and I hated it. I plotted methods to break Andy away from Matt for the morning but my creativity took a hit from the lack of sleep and mild hysteria.

"Hey, so, you guys aren't bringing dates to the wedding, right?" Matt asked as we started to adjourn. "None of you have actually RSVP'd."

"Did you doubt that we were coming?" Shannon asked. Matt

held up his hands and shrugged. "Are you bringing your dominatrix?"

Riley stretched his arms over his head and yawned. "Yesterday's news, Shan. That hasn't been happening for two months."

"Well now I'm disappointed." She turned toward Sam. "What about you, Stark? Or is a weekend with the same girl too long for you?"

"Shameless as always," he muttered. "I will not be bringing a guest, Matt."

"Okay, so..." I felt Matt staring at me but my eyes locked on Andy again. "Yeah. Just make sure you book your rooms. I don't care what you do, but I don't want anyone attempting to crash with me and Lauren."

We had a beachfront cottage reserved at the Cape Cod inn where Matt and Lauren were getting married. Andy's birthday landed two days after the wedding, and *we* planned to make a long weekend out of it.

Frowning, her eyes darted to mine.

It was either a breadcrumb or an indication I was going to be enjoying the Cape alone.

THE TASK OF GETTING ANDY ALONE COULD HAVE SERVED AS THE premise for the next *Mission: Impossible*.

She spent the majority of the day with Matt, visiting his properties. When they did return, they were busy geeking out over new environmental impact metrics. I loitered near the doorway of their makeshift office, eavesdropping on their discussion of solar panel return on investment thresholds.

They didn't notice me.

Much to Theresa's dismay, I pulled up a chair and took over the edge of her desk to keep an eye on Andy. She never looked up from her screen, and I was ready to go to war with Matt for burying her in work.

Late in the day, she sent a set of plans to the printer. The large format printer lived in a small, stuffy room near the garage, and it was my one opportunity, short of kidnapping.

Holding up the first page off the printer, she stood with her back to the door while my eyes traveled over her body. Her hair was everywhere, a thick, curling mass liable to suffocate me in my sleep one of these nights. I loved it. Navy pants hung low on her waist, and I abandoned all of my precisely planned speeches as my body was drawn to hers. I had to touch her.

My arms wrapped around her waist, and I sucked that first hit of lavender deep into my lungs. "Andy...you have to listen to me."

Her muscles tensed under my hands. She shook her head.

"You have at least thirty more pages. I know you're not going anywhere. You don't have to say anything. Just listen. Please." I swept her hair behind her shoulder, dropping my forehead there to assemble the right words. "I was wrong. So wrong. About everything. I didn't mean any—"

"That's not true," she murmured. "That's *not* true."

"Baby," I sighed. "I said stupid, awful things and I'm an asshole. That morning was terrible, the drive back was ridiculous, and I took it all out on you. Come home with me, and I'll fix it. I'll explain everything."

My lips brushed over the skin beneath her ear, and I felt my misery decreasing by the gallon. Loving her and needing her the way I did was crazy, but I wanted the craziness.

Andy twisted out of my arms and glared at me, her eyebrow

angling upward. "You let me believe I had a future here. You manipulated me."

Exhaling loudly, I crossed my arms over my chest and matched her hipshot stance. "Because you do. I wasn't lying when I said it was just bullshit paper, Andy."

"I understand it's bullshit paper to you, but to me? To me, it's proof that I let this—" she gestured between us, "—make decisions about my career, and they probably weren't smart decisions. You kept it from me while you knew I needed to be on a partner track. How am I supposed to feel anything other than manipulated and trapped? You had so many opportunities to tell me. So many."

I swallowed a sigh. "Andy, you should trust me, but you have to understand that I can't rewrite this today."

"Kind of like how I should know better than to be power-fucking?" I started to respond, and Andy held up her hand. "I get that you're not rewriting anything. That's fine, and that's not what I'm asking. But you expect me to believe it's all going to work out? I'm supposed to hang around for a few years and cross my fingers, hoping it falls into place? What happens when I'm left out all over again or your siblings decide they want to keep the partners' table exclusive to family? It might be bullshit paper, but I can't wait around with the hope that the bullshit paper changes. You need to get that I can't hitch my entire career to the possibility of something. I've worked too hard, Patrick."

"Andy, please. Just...let's go back to my place. We can talk this out. Or we can get dinner. I'm sure you're hungry."

"I can't do this. I'm going to finish my apprenticeship because I have ongoing projects, but I'm not letting this mistake with us ruin my career. It's only three weeks until the end of my time here and my exams, and then I'll be gone. This was all an enormous mistake from the start, and I let it happen, and I'm sorry."

There were at least nineteen things I could have said, and they were all better than my silence. Andy pushed past me. I leaned heavily against the wall as the door rattled shut.

NEGLECT DIDN'T BEGIN TO DESCRIBE WHAT WAS HAPPENING TO MY work. There was no convincing myself that it was my priority when Andy was planning to walk away forever.

"Are we doing anything today?" Riley asked when he strolled in late Tuesday morning. "Or are we watching these guys frame walls? I'm good with both."

I glared at Riley, and stepped aside him to collect a document from the printer. "Here are my current jobs. Come back with status reports mapped to the milestone trackers, and prioritize issues that you find. When you finish, check on the new investment properties. Establish cost estimates for aligning to code. When all of that is done, I'll talk to you."

"Great," he muttered. "Way to start the day as a dick waffle, Patrick."

Whatever the next level of dick waffling was, I reached it. Screaming at one of Shannon's advertising and PR assistants, Caley or Coley or Corey, after she left yellow card stock in the printer, was a low point. She cried, extensively.

I watched construction on the new offices. For the most part, I was pleased with the amount of demo, framing, and drywalling accomplished over the weekend. The painters got an earful when I noticed they were only applying one coat of paint over the primer, and when they didn't seem concerned, I fired them on the spot. A lower point.

Sam cornered me in the stairwell, and I inadvertently kicked one of his hornet's nests, fresh water supplies. He wanted to partner with a sustainable landscape designer, but getting excited about grassy roofs wasn't on my short list for the week. I told him I didn't care about the impact on insulation or net neutral footprints, and he dropped every water conversation talking point in his arsenal until I walked away. Even lower.

The real trouble started when I went to the kitchen. Tom was deep in conversation with Shannon's bookkeeping assistant. I flattened myself against the hallway and listened. By itself, a new low.

"So I heard that Sam goes to all kinds of weird natural healers, like acupuncturists," she said. "He drinks this horrible juice every day. It looks like frothy grass water. I think it's for cleansing or detoxing or something."

I knew that juice well. Lemon, ginger, cayenne, cucumber, and mint, and Andy was completely responsible for Sam's newfound obsession. The two of them could talk about herbs and bee pollen for hours.

"I've been here a long time, but I still don't understand Sam, or the way everyone tiptoes around him. Sure, he's a creative genius or whatever, but they act like he's really emotionally fragile. I think he has major mental health issues and they just don't want to see it. I don't think Shannon would ever admit it, either. But what's really strange is that he's a total manwhore. All while being the most fucked up guy in town. I've heard that he's all about anal, and never sees the same girl twice. He doesn't let any of his dates see his apartment."

Truth. On all counts.

"I knew that," she said. "Strange, considering he's such a germaphobe. What d'you think about Andy? She's really beautiful. Like, without even trying. They're always talking about bizarre natural stuff. Are they...do you think maybe they're hooking up?"

"That would explain why they hired her full time."

Furious, I sprinted upstairs to Shannon's office and slammed the door behind me. I waited while she finished her call, and by waiting, I mean I stomped across the office repeatedly and kicked her desk until she gave me the finger.

Shannon's phone crashed into place, and she turned to me with a scowl. "What the fuck is your—"

"I want you to fire Tom. And that assistant, the one who handles bookkeeping."

"Don't even start. Whatever it is, shut it down. We've had enough firings here today."

"They're sitting in the kitchen debating whether Andy has a job here because Sam's fucking her, and they're also discussing his psychiatric disorders and preferences for anal sex and fringe medicine. I. Want. Them. Gone."

Shannon scanned my face, her eyebrows lifting and lips pursing in response. "Tom is a valuable, trusted member of my team. He's been here for years. I'll agree that I want to limit that kind of conversation in this office, and I will talk to him about that. I can also discuss this with Danielle, but I'm not sure we're talking about termination-level offenses."

I rolled my eyes.

"I think you're sensitive about Andy, and overreacting. What the fuck is going on with you? This, Coley, the painters? And let me tell you, Sam is going to cash in on your little outburst about

Roof Garden Girl. We're calling her that now. I like it better than her name."

My hands fisted at my sides. "Make it happen, Shannon. I'm not asking you."

Shannon's mouth fell open, and I turned to go. "What did you just say to me?"

"You wanted it this way, Shannon. This was your call. You want me to be in charge, you want to be my second in command, then you need to find a way to get this shit done without argument. This is what you asked for, now deal with it."

The door bounced off the frame and banged against the wall, muffling Shannon's shouted curses as I stormed out. The walk to Café Vanille on Charles Street absorbed some of my nervous energy, and seeing Lauren's sunny smile brought me down a few more degrees.

"I ordered you a roast beef sandwich." She pointed to the table. "Sit down. Let's talk."

The bistro table was tiny, and I felt like a lowland gorilla as I settled into the wrought iron seat. "I don't know what to say."

"Start with why you decided to text me at four in the morning."

"Sorry about that." Another sleepless night. "Did Andy say anything to you this weekend? You guys went to the farmers' market, right? Is that where she got that necklace, the one with the matching bracelets?"

Lauren nibbled her croissant and shook her head. "Not how this works, pal. You need a friend right now, and I can be your friend, but I'm not trading insider information."

"I fucked up, Lauren. I fucked up everything, and she won't forgive me, and she's leaving."

"You do love a good exaggeration, Patrick." Lauren smiled

and sipped her coffee. "Yeah, you fucked up, but it probably wasn't everything. Maybe she's not forgiving you at this moment, but it takes time to walk away from anger and hurt. You need to let her be angry, be hurt, and process things at her pace. Don't deny her that unless you want her to stay a little angry and hurt forever, but be there when she's ready to leave those pieces behind. And maybe she said she's leaving. Is it possible she said that to lash out, to hurt you the way you hurt her?"

I stared at my plate and remembered the lunches spent with Andy. My stomach jolted with the realization I wasn't simply in love with her. Andy was for me, and I was for her. I could go on living without Andy, but I was going to be one miserable son of a bitch.

Just like my father.

ANDY'S HEAD WAS BENT OVER HER LAPTOP. THE WHIR OF NAIL GUNS obscured my footsteps and she didn't notice me in the doorway. I set the iced green tea beside her notebook and said, "I'm sorry. I'll do anything."

She edged the cup away with the back of her hand, and kept her eyes on the screen. Minutes passed without response while I stared at her, waiting. I couldn't access the memory of her skin against mine, and as I saw my Andy-less life unfolding before my eyes, an agitated, screaming howl formed in my chest.

I ran to the attic, ducked under the low, exposed beam ceiling, and burst through the door. With my hands braced on the roof deck railing, I gasped for breath. It was sunny and warm, and lilacs perfumed the air, but it might as well have been rain clouds. I was that miserable.

The door squealed behind me, and Matt appeared at my side, his knuckles white around his phone. "What are you doing up here?" he asked.

I crossed my arms over my chest. "What are *you* doing up here?"

He leaned forward and studied my face. "Your eye is twitching. If I had to guess, I'd say that's a problem."

A bitter laugh rumbled up from my chest. "Eye twitching isn't my biggest problem. I'm in the middle of some kind of mental collapse, and it's all I can do to not punch holes in walls."

"Oh, me too, that's great," he said dryly. "We can lose our shit together. I can't think of a better plan."

Matt was the calm one. If there was a bomb to diffuse, I wanted Matt doing it. He mediated the worst of Shannon and Erin's disputes, and every time Angus went balls to the wall asshat, Matt was our man. Seeing his head jerking in a spastic bob and his eyes erratic, I squinted in concern. His shit was long lost. "What's your problem?"

"Lauren's brothers are flying in Thursday night. The Navy SEALs. They've been off the grid for a few months. Top secret missions. Naturally." He gestured to his phone. "They're going to show up, and they're going to take one look at me, and they're going to know their baby sister is my little fuck doll, and they're going to make my body disappear after the greatest hits of black site torture."

That did sound bad. "Can't we just get them some hookers?"

"We do that kind of shit now?" Matt croaked, his hands running through his hair and tugging it until he looked freshly electrocuted. "When did we become the kind of guys who hire *hookers*? I don't even know where to *find* a hooker."

"I don't know, I figured Nick knew something about that," I said. "It was a bad idea."

"You think? And that's not the end of my problems. Erin's definitely coming. She's taking a red-eye flight from Rome, and arriving here Friday. I've been asking her for months, and I haven't seen her in so long, and I'm so happy that she's coming but the idea of Erin and Shannon under a tent at my wedding makes me throw up in my mouth. Shannon doesn't know yet, and when she finds out, she'll probably kill me, or ditch the wedding altogether."

I wish I could remember the argument that precipitated the schism between Erin and Shannon, but it was going on five years and the details were blurry. Shannon definitely had a point-by-point inventory of Erin's offenses. They were too much alike, and they pushed up against the wrong parts of each other.

Whatever it was, my sisters hadn't spoken in years and Erin required the distance of an entire ocean to cool off while she worked on her doctorate in Europe.

"I got it," I murmured. "Let's stick Erin and Shannon on Lauren's brothers. Make the girls responsible for keeping you alive."

"And Lauren can tell them to keep Shannon and Erin apart." He nodded. "Okay. That might work. Does that mean we're pimping out Erin and Shan?"

I pressed the palms of my hands against my eyes and groaned. "What they do with two SEALs on leave isn't my concern. It's not like they don't know how to rip off some testicles when needed."

Matt's fingers flew across his phone's keyboard while he asked, "So what's your problem?"

"I'm turning into Angus," I declared flatly.

"Unlikely. You're just a bitch sometimes. Doesn't mean anything." He glanced up from his phone. "Lauren's on board with her brothers keeping the girls apart, and wants to run point on that task force."

"I'd pay good money to see that. Now stop worrying about jumper cables hooked to your dick." I sighed before barreling ahead. "Would you tell me if I started turning into Angus?"

"Yes, and don't be a moron. You're not turning into Angus. Have you gone on any homophobic rants recently?" I shook my head. "Did you go on a pub crawl where you slammed every business partner that you have in town to anyone who will listen? Enslaved any children? No? You're not Angus."

Unconvinced, I stared out over the rows of roofs and toggled through memories of my father. Angus did unconscionable things, and most of those things defied forgiveness. But he didn't start out that way. If anything, he was a good father and husband right up to the day my mother died, and he turned on us because he believed we didn't do enough to save her. He broke, just like the rest of us, only those cracks deepened and spread over time whereas most of our cracks healed in strange, arthritic ways.

In a moment of perverse clarity, I understood Angus and his psychosis. I recognized the sound of his pain from the inside, and I knew its acrid taste. Andy was alive only three floors below my feet and merrily manipulating load-bearing walls. I couldn't imagine the gnawing agony of losing her to a horrific death, drowning in memories of her, or coming face-to-face each day with the six babies she gave me.

What was it that Hunter S. Thompson said? Something about no sympathy for the devil?

Thompson was wrong.

I wasn't forgiving, excusing, or justifying. I understood, and for the first time in my life, I sympathized with that particular devil.

"He chose to be a dickhead, Patrick. Don't forget that. He just didn't want to crawl out of the hole."

Step one to avoiding miserable bastardhood: stop being a dickhead.

Step two: get out of the hole.

I wanted it to be that easy.

I walked to the far corner of the roof, and stood beside Matt. We gazed to the east, and a thin shimmer of the Atlantic in the distance. "How did you know, with Lauren?"

He typed another message then pocketed his phone. "Are you asking because you're writing your toast for the reception and want a cute story? I don't think any of our stories are fit for general audiences."

Shit. Was that expected? Sam knew how to tell an eloquent story. Riley knew how to hit the bawdy humor. Shannon always delivered with the heart. Erin had the smart wit. Firm hand-shakes were my wheelhouse.

"There's no cute story," he continued. "It's hard work. It looks easy, but a lot of work goes into getting two people to that spot. There's never enough time, ever, and that's the most important thing. Time. Time to argue about keeping the peanut butter in the fridge, or whether we're raising our kids Catholic. And everything in between. We make each other crazy, but we'd also go crazy without each other." Matt propped his fists on his hips and shrugged. "I can't breathe without her, and I knew after one night. I picked out the ring less than a month later."

That sounded familiar.

"But really, why would anyone put peanut butter in the fridge?"

"That's absurd, and don't get me started on the hair in the drain," I muttered.

"Oh my God, so much hair," he groaned. Matt turned to face me. "Back up. What?"

I squinted at the ocean in the distance. "Judging by the amount of hair in the drain, women should be bald."

He glanced at his watch. "Let's not delude ourselves into thinking we're getting any work done today. It's presently beer o'clock, and I want to know whose hair is in your drain. It'll take my mind off waterboarding."

CHAPTER TWENTY-TWO

ANDY

My first year at Cornell, my roommate Myra's boyfriend from back home sent her a bouquet of flowers for their anniversary in October, and they arrived in a thin glass vase. As far as dorm rooms went, ours was petite, and flat surface real estate was at a premium. Myra made space on her desk for the flowers, but if she attempted to use her desk for anything else, the vase was always two seconds away from disaster.

Myra kept the flowers as long as possible—she even hung them upside-down to dry like a freaking prom corsage—and she kept the vase, too. Standing empty, it didn't serve a purpose, but it was a totem for their relationship—they survived college on opposite coasts after all, and if she couldn't see him every day, at least she could see the vase.

One day that winter, she was in a hurry to get to class and rushed past her desk in her thick puffer coat. She clipped the top of the vase, and it tumbled to the ground, shattering into a million shards. We found stray chunks and slivers in every corner of the room, and they appeared out of the blue weeks and months later. We agreed the suspicious gray carpeting was to blame for intermittently sucking in and spitting out the shards, and wearing shoes everywhere but bed was essential.

When springtime descended upon Ithaca and flip-flops didn't pose a frostbite risk, a chunk of glass roughly the size of a silver dollar carved up the head of my big toe as I walked across the room. I needed seventeen stitches—that's a lot of stitches for a toe, and it hurt like a motherfucker. How that piece of glass appeared, months later and smack in the center of our room, I will never know.

Patrick was my shard of glass on the first day of flip-flop weather. From the start he was dangerous, and even my best efforts at self-preservation failed. I knew nothing good could come from climbing into bed with my boss, but I went there knowingly. It ripped me open and branded me with the kind of thick, silvery scar that never faded.

And it hurt like a motherfucker.

PATRICK SEIZED EVERY OPPORTUNITY TO GET ME ALONE—WHICH wasn't easy, considering the Sam-Riley-Shannon-Patrick-Matt Show was packed into a couple of cramped offices and it was turning into a full-blown variety hour as the wedding neared—and he wrapped me up in tenderly whispered pleas for another chance. Between the office construction, the wedding, and all things Patrick, the week was overflowing with commotion, and I needed space to get my head on straight.

The wedding weekend finally started Thursday afternoon when two waves of Walshes loaded into Shannon and Matt's cars, and headed to the Cape. Patrick elected to stay in Boston to keep an eye on the construction—or stalk me, whichever let him sleep at night. Evading him and his perfectly timed teas meant bouncing between jobsites and dodging the office entirely.

Not a day went by that I didn't contemplate skipping Matt and Lauren's wedding. Backing out felt horrendously wrong and the thought surfaced Jess's raw critique, but neither killed the urge to stay home. Lauren and I texted about last minute preparations throughout the week, and she inquired as to my well-being one time too many. It was evident she knew what went down between Patrick and me, but she seemed to be the only one.

I didn't want to dump that on her this week. I also knew she'd have to choose between Patrick and me, and there was no contest. Before leaving for the Cape today, she insisted we spend her last single night together. It wrecked my plan to show up for the ceremony and leave after the cake cutting, but I agreed.

I carved out most of my afternoon for Wellesley with the goal of walking through every element on the design plan. That site required work straight through the summer and into the fall, and I wanted to leave detailed notes about the progress before the end of my apprenticeship. Unlike the rest of the Walsh Associates projects, I was the only one who monitored progress on the site.

Staring at the dining room fireplace, I cocked my head to the side in an attempt to determine whether the sconce was crooked. It was off by no more than five degrees. Caring about those five degrees was my job but a big part of me wanted to yank the fixture right out of the wall and replace it with something new. And straight.

Preserving the past now felt like an exercise in futility. It was all going to collapse eventually, right? What was the point in cleaning it up, preserving it, putting it on life support for another decade? We were tricking ourselves into thinking we could save anything.

Gripping the fixture, I inched it to the right and heard a pronounced click in the next room. My eyes scanned the library for the sound's origin, and I found one shelf in the built-in bookcase jutting out slightly. Just enough to be off.

I pressed the shelf backwards, and another click sounded in the hallway. Ghosts seemed the likely culprit after twenty minutes of running my fingers over every inch of the hallway and finding nothing.

A minimalistic modern house wouldn't pull this kind of shit.

I walked toward the front door to retrieve my notebook, and the hand-carved casing around the coat closet caught my eye. I saw an inlaid rosette in the upper right-hand corner standing out a bit too far. Not quite right. A firm push sent the rosette back into its inlay, and a gust of air blew the closet door open from the inside.

The shock sent me stumbling backwards and I stared into the open half-door at the back of the darkened closet. A narrow path illuminated by my flashlight led straight through the heart of the house.

I knew every hidden door and alcove in the house. Built-in bookshelves in one room connected to another, closets opened into other closets, and window seats revealed staircases to the rooms below, plus zigzagging laundry chutes and dumbwaiter systems. This wasn't one of them.

With a steadying breath, I was on my feet and headed for the front porch—I didn't need to make friends with any wall-dwelling creatures—and determined the situation called for Patrick's involvement.

Andy: You need to get out to Wellesley RIGHT NOW.
Patrick: Are you ok?
Andy: Yes but you need to get out here as soon as possible
Patrick: On my way

My legs dangled over the edge of the stone porch while I updated my project notes and waited for Patrick to arrive. He tore up the driveway within nineteen minutes, and dashed up the stairs to stand at my side. Patrick looked around, and reached a hand out to stroke down my back before snapping it back and shoving it in his pocket.

"What happened? You're okay?"

I beckoned him to follow me. "I'm fine but I found a secret tunnel in the middle of the house." I explained how I discovered the door, and pointed into the closet. "It might be Narnia. I can't be sure."

"What the fuck did you do, Angus?" Patrick knelt in the closet and examined the small door. The space was not much more than two feet wide, but it appeared to open up as the passageway deepened. He glanced at me. "I don't care how much you hate me right now. I'm not going into the secret room alone."

I rolled my eyes and followed him inside, between the walls where decades of dust and cobwebs billowed around us. Patrick reached for my hand and I let him—it was a creepy hidden hallway after all.

We approached a brick junction formed by the living room and dining room fireplaces, and a narrow staircase spiraled between them. "This is the stuff of horror movies, right?" Patrick asked as we climbed the stairs.

"Every time." I missed the warmth of our old routines. "Are

we expecting to find something in here, or are we just looking for trouble?"

"Look around. There's no better definition of trouble than this." Ten fire-safe closets lined the second floor, and we stared at each other.

"What could be in there?" I asked.

"Fuck if I know." Squeezing my hand, Patrick tugged the door open against its protesting hinges. We leaned into each other, bracing for the worst, but found it filled with neatly stacked boxes, all labeled *Abigael* in precise architect's lettering. Patrick rocked back on his heels, inhaling sharply.

"Who is Abigael?"

"My mother." He peered into a box, and retrieved a lace handkerchief. He turned it over in his hands several times, his fingers brushing over the delicate lace. "That crazy bastard."

The next two contained more of his mother's things—her wedding dress, jewelry, quilts, journals, photo albums, aprons, clothes—and it was clear Patrick hadn't seen any of it in ages. Shock and pain etched his features with each discovery. Carefully wrapped crystal and china filled the next three. Another closet held an assortment of large framed pieces interspersed with hand-painted portraits of the house and Patrick's family.

The final three closets housed boxes labeled for Patrick and each of his siblings. He sighed as his fingers brushed dust from the lids, the tense expression on his face telling me he knew what was hidden in each. Inside his box, he lifted a faded yellow photo album from the top, and a heartbreaking groan slipped from his lips as he opened it.

The first photo showed a stunning redhead proudly cradling a newborn baby, and her radiant smile jumped off the page. The baby's bright eyes gazed up at his mother from his spot on the slope of her chest. "Shannon looks so much like your mother," I said, shining a flashlight over his shoulder. "And you were a huge baby."

Patrick shut the book suddenly and returned it to the box. "We need to get out of here." Patrick collected a few items from the closets and secured the doors, and we retreated through the passageway and onto the porch. It was dark, and I couldn't believe we spent hours exploring that tunnel.

"I guess we know why the room dimensions changed," I coughed. I guzzled some water to wash away the thick coating of dust from my throat.

Patrick approached with his hand reaching for my hair. Warily, I stepped out of his grasp but he continued toward me.

"Andy, stop. There's a cobweb." He stilled me with a rough hand to my shoulder, and I stared at his royal blue polo shirt. "Didn't know how to get out of his hole," he muttered, his fingers sifting through my hair. "I get that he couldn't deal with it. Fine. But did he really need to build a cave and hide everything there? He couldn't have bought a fucking storage unit like normal people? This is officially psychotic."

His questions weren't meant for me, and I remained quiet. His hands stayed in my hair, and though I suspected the cobwebs were adequately dispatched, I didn't protest his touch.

"What kind of gamble was that?" Patrick continued. "What if we never found that door? What if we sold this place and never knew? That required years of work. That's what this does to people, Andy. It's insane, and destructive, but it's what this does."

Patrick's eyes met mine, his hands forming tight fists in my hair. "There are things that we'll never understand. People do illogical things that don't fit into neat columns, and we'll never know why."

"He told us he destroyed everything but he spent years building a secret shrine. That's what this does to people, Andy. Don't you see?" His hands loosened their hold on my hair and settled on my shoulders, his thumbs brushing back and forth against the pulse in my throat.

I wanted to wrap my arms around Patrick and protect him from his pain and everything locked in those closets. He was so much more than the sum of his scars.

Patrick's fingers tilted my head back, his eyes dropping to my lips. "Please, just...I don't know how to do this without you."

His lips touched mine, and that force drew my hands to his chest. His kisses started soft and cautious—asking permission. Patrick's hands held me in place, and his kisses turned deeper, slowly growing more demanding—asking forgiveness.

I pulled back, shaking my head as I put distance between us. "I used to think I could be everything you needed. I don't know if...I can't do this, Patrick." I grabbed my things and hurried off the porch. With one fleeting look before settling into my MINI Cooper, I met Patrick's eyes. "I'm sorry."

WAITING FOR ERIN TO ARRIVE IN CHATHAM WAS THE MOST difficult part of withholding news of Andy's discovery at Wellesley, but I had no intention of going through it twice. Erin was already excluded from too much. With everyone huddled around the patio fireplace, I paced back and forth with a box under my arm.

"Shannon, hurry the fuck up," I snapped. She leaned against the bar, gesturing animatedly with her beer bottle as she spoke to the bartender. She was doing everything in her power to avoid Erin.

"Yes, Optimus, we know it's your turn to talk." She sat on the arm of Sam's chair and waved her hand in the direction of the box. "Have you ventured into prop comedy now?"

"Shut up, Shannon," I muttered. "Andy was at Wellesley, at the house today and—"

"Who's Andy?" Erin asked.

"She's an architect working under Patrick," Matt supplied.

Riley broke into hysterical, gasping laughter. "You can say that again," he choked.

He dropped his head to Erin's shoulder while he rocked back and forth on the loveseat they shared, repeatedly snorting and slapping his thigh. I was ready to toss his ass in the ocean. Let the sharks deal with him and his inability to keep a goddamn thing to himself.

"Already time to cut you off, young man?" Sam asked. He drained his fourth gin and tonic and signaled for another. Right, because I needed to spend my night preventing him from passing out in a tide pool.

Lauren caught my eye and shrugged. The implication was clear, but that didn't make it any easier.

"Let me take this for you." Matt shifted Lauren to the other side of his lap. "Patrick's got a thing for Andy."

"You knew?" Shannon shrieked, wagging her finger at Matt before turning her attention to Lauren. "And you too? Patrick, you told me it was privileged! What the fuck? They've known?"

"Only for a few days," Matt said.

"Who here didn't know any of this until right now?" Sam asked. Erin and Nick raised their hands, and he laughed humorlessly. "Huh. Guess I know where I rank."

They broke into small discussions of Andy and me, and when and what they knew. A bullhorn would have helped.

"Goddamn it, people, I have something to tell you!"

"Are you asking her to marry you?" Riley asked.

I liked that idea. A lot. I never shook the image of Andy in a wedding gown. When I was delirious with insomnia, I saw her walking toward me in that white lace.

"Oh my God, another wedding to plan!" Shannon squealed.

Lauren put her hand on Shannon's arm. "Let's not get ahead of ourselves."

"Is she pregnant?" Riley asked.

I shook my head. I liked that idea, too. Not right now, not for a while, but maybe someday. A day when Andy wasn't walking away from me. My gut churned at the memory of her taillights fading into the night.

I reached into the box and held up a blue book with 'Riley Augustin' scrolled across the cover. That shut everyone up. "Ready to hear what I have to say?"

"Where did you get that?" Riley stood, the happy flush draining from his face, his eyes hooded as he retrieved the photo album. "Tell me where you got this."

"Wellesley. Andy found a hidden door in Angus's hall closet. It took twenty-nine other levers to open, but she found a door and there's an entire universe between the walls. It's all there. All of it. Everything."

Returning to the box, I distributed the items I grabbed yesterday. A pile of handkerchiefs to Matt. Mom's jewelry box to Shannon, and her last journal to Erin. The Irish knit scarf that still smelled faintly of her perfume to Sam.

As my siblings reverently ran their hands over the goods I distributed, I stared into the empty box and realized I didn't save anything for myself.

We passed around Riley's baby book, admiring our stunningly dated haircuts and clothes while attempting to count the rolls of fat on Riley's legs. Shannon's feathered hair and white fringed leather jacket won the night. Sam wrapped Mom's scarf around his neck and only grudgingly agreed to share it with the group. Mom's journals made their way to Shannon and her jewelry to Erin, but even the discovery of the century wasn't melting that ice.

"This doesn't make him less of an asshole," Sam said, the scarf wrapped tightly around his neck again. "This isn't the time or place for an Angus-hate tirade, and we should be happy that we have something of Mom's, but if anything, this a new level of assholedom, even for Angus. Really got the last laugh, didn't he?"

"I'll give you that," Riley replied. "It's right up there with hiding a body under the floorboards, and please tell me you didn't find any bodies in the bowels of the house?"

"Look at you with the Poe references," Erin laughed. "You're like a real boy now."

Riley rolled his eyes. "How have you not fallen into a volcano yet?"

"When you say between the walls, you mean...what?" Matt asked.

"I mean there are fire-safe cabinets between the walls of every room on the second floor, and a little staircase behind the fireplaces. That's why the plans didn't make sense."

"Yep," Matt replied. "I get that, but how's that shit being supported? It's not like he shifted load-bearing walls."

"I dunno, Matt, but it isn't coming down tonight," I sighed. "It was dusty as hell but Andy and I didn't notice any major structural issues."

"Can we go back to all that?" Sam asked. "All of this is incredible and Andy deserves a raise for getting to the bottom of Angus's last fuck you, but perhaps you could get the rest of us," he gestured to Erin and Nick, "up to speed on your impending nuptials? I noticed you didn't deny it."

With a groan, I dropped to the stone bench alongside the

fireplace. "Short version? We've been seeing each other since February. March if you don't count the bathrooms. But I was a dickhead and she's not talking to me, and she's probably leaving at the end of her apprenticeship. And I'm in love with her."

"How has no one noticed this until just now?" Erin asked.

I shook my head and studied my siblings. "No one except Lauren."

"I don't know about the rest of you," Sam started, peeling the scarf from his chin, "but I've had my own shit to deal with. Who handled fourteen green designs in that time, start to finish? Oh, yeah, me."

"Does it take both hands to stroke that ego?" Riley asked. "Or can you get by with just one?"

"Going out on a limb here," Erin said, her hand sweeping over the group. "I bet everyone wants the long version. Especially the part about the bathrooms unless that's some kind of weird sex thing."

I went all the way back to that heinous interview. I knew, even then. The second I saw her, I knew. I'm not shallow enough to say it was love at first sight, but something about the way she talked about history and preservation and restoration and sustainability struck a nerve. It wasn't about architecture, either.

Andy and me, we're a lot like those old homes. Steeped in history. Living in the present while bearing the weight of the past. Secrets hidden beneath the surface. She believed in histories and she believed they were a critical element in understanding the present. Andy showed me that it was possible for someone to know my soul.

The group fell silent when I finished. Their loaded glances pinged back and forth before everyone spoke at once.

Erin: "It's ridiculous that you all let him go through this shit by himself, and no one noticed anything. Way to be self-involved."

Riley: "So what are the odds you're going to cry in a corner like a little girl when she shows up?"

Shannon: "February totally counts."

Sam, passing a bill to Riley: "I'll take that bet."

Erin: "Am I going to get to meet this chick?"

Nick: "If it doesn't work out for you two, are you good with me asking her out?"

Lauren: "She should be here any time. I'm getting her drunk tonight and talking some sense into her skinny ass."

Matt: "Like I told you on the roof, you gotta find time to work your shit out."

Riley: "Would it be possible for me to watch from the closet? I'll buy the booze. I'll paint your toenails. Anything you want. Just let me watch. Maybe take a few pictures?"

Shannon: "Just ask yourself this: what would Ryan Gosling do?"

Matt: "You are one pervy son of a bitch, RISD."

Nick: "That's it. We're having a stag party tonight."

Riley: "The Gosling would build her a fuckin' house."

Shannon: "Build her a fuckin' house!"

Sam: "Bro, the only stag party we're having is with actual deer. Our boy's lost his taste for fresh tits and ass since getting engaged. And now this guy's licking his pussy-whipped wounds, too. Shambles."

Matt: "Dude, he doesn't have time to build a house right now. But," he pointed at me, "I'm betting she doesn't want something new."

Erin: "Still rocking the slimy player thing, Sammy?"

Riley: "Yeah, but if I know anything about Princess Jasmine and Optimus, PJ's buildin' the better house."

Sam: "I prefer slippery."

Shannon: "We'll do anything we can to help, Patrick. But if you ruin this wedding, I'll tear your balls off and feed them to you."

Nick: "Whoa. This escalated quickly. I'm really impressed by the full impact of the Walsh squad. Also, a little scared of y'all."

Erin: "May the odds be ever in your favor."

I already knew they weren't.

CHAPTER TWENTY-FOUR

FUN FACT: ELEVEN-THIRTY ON A FRIDAY NIGHT WAS THE BEST TIME to hit I-93 South and avoid holiday weekend traffic. My drive to the Cape was smooth sailing, and entirely motivated by a desire to avoid Patrick.

The Chatham Bars Inn on the far curve of Cape Cod was my kind of place—straight out of the 1910s, and recently updated with the best modern features while preserving the architectural integrity of the original structure.

On a better day, I would have photographed every nook, archway, and detail of the entire inn, but I was busy cleaving my brain into two separate and wholly unequal parts—the one focused on self-preservation and moving on from Patrick, and the one desperately in love with him.

It was always about Patrick. He was my ignition switch. I loved him years ago when I thumbed through the architecture school's grad student publications, and his thesis taught me how to cherish and honor the past, all while making it more efficient, more sustainable. Then, he was Patrick the craftsman and

Patrick the visionary, and without knowing it, he fostered my architectural spirit.

Working with Patrick changed my life. He changed everything but I didn't let other people plan my future. I was hurt, and haunted by the reality that he kept something enormous from me for so long. He shook every belief I had, and I honestly wondered whether I wanted to build anymore.

Or maybe I was too busy being wounded to realize I couldn't even enjoy Bikram yoga or goat's milk cheese these days, let alone feel passionate about sustainably preserved architecture.

I hoped my late arrival would free me from all Walsh interactions, but Shannon and Lauren were leaning against the front desk when I entered.

"Shan, chill." Lauren beckoned me closer, and wrapped her arm around my waist while I checked in. "I have a wedding planner, and we're paying her a fortune to take care of all of these things. If there's something we've missed, life will have to go on."

"I just want you to have an incredible day," Shannon said. "I'm annoyed about the gift baskets, and want to have a few words with the manager."

"I'm not annoyed. This is a party. That's all. Gift baskets are not required, are they, Curly Sue?" I shrugged and glanced between them. I didn't want to think about weddings—getting me here was a big enough challenge. "Go talk to Will. He was really excited to meet you."

Shannon glanced toward the bar area. "He's at the bar, and Wes is the one talking to my sister?" Lauren murmured in agreement. "Homeboy seems a lot more interested in kicking Matt's ass than talking to me."

"And if that happens, my day will be far less incredible,"

Lauren said. "Use some of that legendary Shannon Walsh charm, and keep him away from my Matthew."

Armed with a renewed sense of purpose, Shannon moved toward the bar, and settled beside Lauren's brother.

"I'm so glad to see you," Lauren said. "What took you so long? This has been a wild night. I've been running all kinds of covert operations to keep these kiddos under control. I met Erin! Talk about a blood feud. She brought me a lava rock from Portugal, because it's old and new, and I already love her. And I just heard about the tunnel at the house? How crazy is that?"

"It was crazy," I murmured. "I'm sorry I'm late. It's been a hectic week, that's all."

"I know, honey. Let's get a drink with the hooligans before we go upstairs." She led the way to the patio bar, and I willed the sound of crashing waves and the scent of sea air to calm me down.

Sam, Riley, and Matt were clustered on one side, while Patrick stood behind them facing the ocean, his hands in the pockets of his navy shorts with his back to the group. What I wouldn't give to wrap my arms around his waist, press my face against his back, and just drown in Patrick.

Matt and Sam were recounting a story at Riley's expense, interrupting each other and dissolving into hysterical laughter while Riley looked as if he was trying to swallow a goldfish. On one of those better days, I would have thrown some gas on that fire and asked about aunts who slept with alligators, and black-eyed meatloaves, but those stories no longer existed in my realm.

Shannon and Will struggled to kick-start a conversation at the bar, and she launched into a detailed accounting of her plan to work her way through locally brewed IPAs this summer. Another redhead was on the opposite end of the patio with Wes,

Lauren's other brother, and neither noticed our arrival. They were too busy staring at the sand dunes and looking like they were being held hostage.

I ordered a Riesling—everyone needed a real housewife—and let Lauren introduce me to her brothers. I couldn't fathom how curvy little Lauren was cut from the same genetic cloth as Wes and Will. They had Lauren's golden blond hair, theirs cut in closely cropped styles. They were shorter than Patrick yet huge, and I doubted their broad shoulders fit through standard, code-specified interior doorways. They represented a whole new branch of the Tight T-Shirt Brigade.

"Hey, Will, this is my friend Andy. She works with Matt," Lauren said, and patted her brother's shoulder. It looked like bone-in ham. "Andy, this is my oldest brother, Will."

"Will Halsted." He offered his hand, and it swallowed mine whole. "You're not part of them?" Will gestured at the array of Walshes scattered around the patio.

"No." I wasn't part of the inner circle anymore, and I'm not sure I ever was.

"Finally, an impartial witness. Sit down. I want the inside story."

"Are we not having a conversation?" Shannon snapped.

"Apparently she didn't take the hint. We'll talk another time, Andy," Will promised with an exaggerated eye roll, and he motioned to Shannon. "I don't spend nearly enough time listening to harpies. By all means, continue."

Lauren clutched my elbow and darted away from the bar as Shannon gasped.

Wes and Erin smiled politely at each other without speaking, and both looked relieved when we approached. "Wes, Erin, this is Andy. She's one of my very best friends, and an architect at the firm with Matt. Andy, this is my brother Wes, and Matt's sister Erin."

I gazed at Erin, taking in red hair and emerald eyes against alabaster skin, and I couldn't believe her resemblance to Shannon and her mother. "Hi," I managed, and fumbled to shake their hands.

For all of their similarities, Erin and Shannon were different in every way. Seeing Erin's skinny jeans and *Moby Dick* book cover t-shirt, I immediately wanted to befriend her—was there anything better than a *Moby Dick* t-shirt on Cape Cod? Seriously, no one would wear that without expecting a few ironic chuckles. I wanted to talk to the girl equipped with that kind of wit.

Shannon, on the other hand, was flawlessly pulled together in khaki shorts, a white tank top, and a breezy sweater that exposed one shoulder. She looked like a page from the Nordstrom catalog. Shannon was starlet waves, Erin was choppy side-swept bangs and shoulder-length layers. Shannon was smartly accessorized and Tory Burch espadrilles, Erin was a tiny, diamond nose ring winking in the darkness and simple leather flip-flops. In spite of it all, there was no mistaking them as sisters, and their resemblance to their mother was jarring.

Following a quick round of goodbyes and a steamy moment between Matt and Lauren—outside the attentive eyes of Will and Wes—we settled on the bed in my room with an exclusive bottle of tequila, a bowl of lime wedges, and two shot glasses. It was a recipe for mayhem if I ever saw one.

"To your last night as a single lady," I toasted, and we knocked the liquid back.

Tequila: my Mexican medicine man.

Or my chupacabra, depending on whether I survived the night.

"To your obnoxiously skinny waist," Lauren said as she poured another round.

"And your indecently perfect double D-cups," I added, and our glasses clinked.

Lauren lined up another round. "To barefoot beach weddings and no white dresses." She laughed, and our palms slapped together in a high five.

"To growly, bitey boys who love us so much they turn into cavemen," Lauren said.

I held my drink high but my chin fell to my chest. It all hit me at once, and the dam broke.

Lauren plucked the glass from my fingers, and her arms wrapped around my shoulders in a fierce hug while tears streamed down my face. "Why didn't you tell me?"

"You're marrying his brother! You're Team Patrick by default. And it's over. So over. Nothing to tell."

"There are no teams, Andy. It's not over. It seems awful right now, but you'll get through. You know that, right?" I shrugged miserably and she handed me some tissues. "You will. I need you. Who's going to help me when the next girl infiltrates these boys? It's a matter of time until Sam or Nick, or—mother of pearls—Riley finds himself with the girl who's going to change everything for him. The way you changed Patrick." She squeezed my knee. "I need you to help me talk them through it and get them to the other side when it all goes to hell because it always does. And I need you to help me rein in Shannon when she needs it. You picked out my wedding dress, Andy, and you're drinking with me the night before my wedding. You're my family now, and I'm not letting you get away. I'll mediate couples' counseling before I let you cross state lines."

I sniffled and glanced in her direction. I wasn't used to

having someone fight this hard for me, and I didn't know how to respond. I blew my nose loudly. "I hated you that day I met you at the farmers' market. I thought you were engaged to Patrick, and I hated you because I was already a little in love with him."

"Then don't let him go." She wiped the tears from my cheeks and handed me a glass. "Tequila," Lauren laughed. "Forget your problems, forget your man...hell, forget your name!"

I SWALLOWED, AND MY THROAT WAS LINED WITH SANDPAPER. THE groan that followed did not improve the situation.

"Here." Lauren nudged a cool plastic bottle into my hand. "Drink."

I guzzled the water, and shifted to lean against the headboard when I noticed Matt's arms anchored around her waist and his head on her belly. "How much tequila did we drink?"

Lauren smiled and ran her fingers through Matt's hair. "He wandered up here around three. He doesn't know how to sleep by himself, and he was worried that Will and Wes were going to abduct him from our cottage. They have a history of intimidating the guys in my life."

"Awesome," I muttered, and groped the nightstand for my phone. Nearly ten o'clock and another night without a single text from Patrick. I didn't know why I expected him to reach out to me, but I fell off the logic wagon late last week. I turned toward Lauren. "You're gettin' married today."

"That's my plan. I might finish that bottle before six tonight, though." She nodded at the tequila. "Are you good with me hiding out in here? I don't want to talk to anyone about flowers or bacon-wrapped scallops or gift baskets, and if someone tries to curl my hair, I will start throwing knives."

"Stay. I need to walk the tequila out of my system." After cleaning up and changing into slim yoga capris, a racerback tank, and a thin black hoodie, I emerged from the bathroom. "If there're any premarital, uh," I circled my hand between Matt and Lauren, "*activities*, put the Do Not Disturb on the door."

Escaping the long shadow of the inn reduced the odds of running into any Walshes but it forced me to address the questions intruding on the back of my mind. The solitude forced a look in an unforgiving mirror. I sifted through every uncomfortable notion about my work, my relationships, and myself while I walked. It was time to get on with my life.

My calves started burning after four miles at a near-jog, and it was a welcome distraction from my thoughts. My path back to the inn meandered along the beach, and I sat in the sand, watching as the empty tent for Lauren and Matt's reception transformed into gorgeously dressed tables dripping with seasonal flowers and sea grasses, and bitter memories of my over-before-it-started Pinterest wedding complemented my stinging muscles.

Eventually I stopped moping on the beach and gingerly climbed the stairs to my room, and an envelope waited at my door. I assumed it was my bill. Lauren was gone, more than likely tipsy, and most certainly killing everyone in her path with kindness in the final hour before the ceremony. I kicked off my running shoes and clothes, and started the shower before opening the envelope. A shiver wobbled through my shoulders as I read the precise architect's lettering.

Andy,

We can make this work.
We're not the kind of people who do anything half-assed. We never walk away when it gets difficult or we can't find the right answers.
We're perfectionists and we don't apologize for it because if there's anyone who can make something work, it's us.
We're not done now, and we won't be done tomorrow, or any of the tomorrows after that.
I love you and I need you. Come back to me.
Patrick

The envelope fell to the ground and I marched straight into the shower. My backside hit the cold granite tile of the floor, and I pressed my wrist against my mouth while the spray of the shower washed away my sobs.

THE RING TWISTED BETWEEN MY THUMB AND FOREFINGER, THE FINE mill-grained detail pressing into my skin and leaving a dotted trail on the pads of my fingers. Set in a delicate constellation of five diamonds, each one spat fire into the setting sunlight. Five probably represented something. Matt was meticulous like that.

Minutes to feel a connection. Hours to fall in love with her. Days to knowing they couldn't survive apart. Months since getting engaged. Kids they wanted.

"Why don't you let me hold onto that?"

After a quick glance at Nick, the pad of my thumb passed over the stones, and I handed it to him. He secured it inside its velvet box, and unbuttoned his suit coat to stow it in his pocket.

It was too easy for me to destroy everything I touched like a tractor in a fucking china shop to be responsible for Lauren's wedding ring.

It had been hours, *hours*, since leaving the letter at Andy's door, and nothing. No texts, no calls, no smoke signals, no sight of her anywhere. I left my spleen in that envelope, and if forced to choose between nail-gunning my hand to a wall and waiting for a response from Andy, here's to hoping my tetanus shot was up-to-date.

Nick's hand curled around my elbow, and he jerked me out of my seat while on my other side, Sam kicked my shin. "Where I'm from, it's customary to stand for the bride," Nick hissed.

A string quartet played Coldplay's "Green Eyes" and I didn't need to look at Matt to know he was beaming like a love-drunk fool, or his fingers were closed around my mother's handkerchief. I shuffled to my feet, turning to watch Lauren step out of the inn on her father's arm. Commodore Halsted wore the Navy's dress uniform well, and Lauren was beautiful in a cotton candy pink dress.

The dress Andy picked out.

I searched the crowd for her wild hair, finally spotting her on the far end of the back row. Big sunglasses obscured her face, and she was sitting ramrod straight with her chin tilted up. Spine of steel. Her hair was pulled into a knot that resembled a bagel, and it was mildly absurd. Given the location, a seagull was bound to attack at any moment.

She ordered the strapless indigo dress online during a late March snowstorm that trapped us in my apartment for a long weekend. Pockets were cut into the full knee-length skirt, and she found that appropriately quirky while I saw it as an opportunity to do filthy things to her in broad daylight.

By all measures, the perfect dress.

The perfect weekend. Not so unlike each one I spent with her.

The need to remind her of that perfection pressed into my sternum, and I swiped my phone to life. Warning her about dive-bombing seagulls was also a critical concern.

"Oh my fucking God," Sam seethed, and he snatched my phone away. "Not now, you moron." Sam leaned around me and met Nick's annoyed expression. "Can you get him a shot of chlorpromazine or diazepam?"

"Dude, it's weird that you know what those are, and I don't usually roll with Schedule IV substances."

"Operative word being 'usually.'" Sam locked my phone and tucked it inside his breast pocket. "And by that, I can deduce that you have enough drugs to take out the A-Team over there." Sam nodded toward Lauren's brothers.

"You mean Thor and Captain America?" I asked. "Unless you have a tranq gun, Acevedo, none of us are taking them anywhere."

We broke into poorly concealed laughter, and Matt killed us with his eyes six, probably seven times.

I wanted to gaze at Andy for hours, but Sam and Nick's hands on my shoulders forced me into my seat when Lauren arrived at the altar, and their jabbing elbows eventually turned my attention toward the ceremony. It was over quickly, or at least the parts I listened to were over quickly. Tuning out syrupy promises of love and devotion was elemental to my survival, especially when I didn't have a flask of whiskey on hand.

Andy dissolved into the crowd once Matt and Lauren were down the aisle, and Sam dragged me by the collar to pose for photos. After eighteen thousand different groupings and poses, I started to protest the activity but realized we were together, our new family, for the first time. There wasn't much else to hold onto without them.

I shut up, going along with every one of the photographer's mundane requests. Was anyone clear on why it was necessary for us to execute a synchronized jump?

"Where is Andy?" Lauren asked, standing on her tiptoes to see into the tent. She turned back to the assembly and met my eye with a smile. "I want her here, too."

The photographer's assistant scurried into the tent, returning moments later with Andy in tow. She shared a firm hug with Lauren, and nodded at something she said. Lauren gestured to the far end of the pose, where I stood with Erin on my right. "Right there, between these two."

Andy wedged between us, and my reaction was involuntary. My hands landed on her hips and into those devious pockets, my lips coasting against the exposed nape of her neck as I ducked to her ear.

"Do you remember that weekend?" I whispered. "Twenty-one inches of snow, *Order of the Phoenix* and *The Half-Blood Prince*?" My hand traveled over her bare shoulders. "And this."

To her credit, Erin locked her eyes on the photographer and stifled a knowing giggle. Whether she was laughing at my desperate attempts at Andy's forgiveness, or me watching *Harry Potter* movies, I wasn't about to inquire.

"I'm here for Lauren. And Matt. It's their day, and I can't do this with you right now, Patrick."

I pressed my hand to the small of her back and kept the other against her hip from the comfort of her pocket. Other than a slight inhale, she allowed no recognition she possessed all of me.

"YOU KNOW, IT'S FUNNY," SAM SAID, HITCHING HIS ELBOW ON MY shoulder as we stood at the edge of the tent. Matt and Lauren swayed together in the middle of the empty dance floor. Most of the crowd cleared out around eleven, the stragglers stayed until midnight, and now only family remained. "Everyone's spent the past few months worrying over my mental health, expecting a Hiroshima-level explosion, but it's been you all along."

"Hilarious." I rolled my eyes and sipped my beer, the swirling skirt of Andy's dress drawing my attention to the other side of the tent. She was with Erin and Thor, ahem, Wes, and they were embroiled in an animated conversation that appeared to require repeatedly refilling shot glasses. What were the odds it was peppermint schnapps?

"Write the caption for that." Pointing with his beer bottle, Sam chuckled. "A preservation architect, a volcanologist, and a Navy SEAL get drunk at a wedding. I'm putting fifty bucks on them staging a coup to seize control of Naples, and devising a plan to rehab and restore Pompeii before sunrise. Hundred bucks says they get it LEED certified."

He jutted his chin toward the bar. Red-faced, Shannon yelled and wagged her finger at Will while he laughed. Captain America had more balls than sense. Sam narrowed his eyes. "What the fuck is all that about?"

"It's the price of keeping Matt from taking a long walk off a short pier," I said. "We will owe her in ways we cannot begin to imagine."

"Fuck," he sighed. "At least the good doctor didn't need to sedate them into next Thursday."

Rooted on the tent's sidelines with the surf crashing a few feet behind us, we observed our people: Nick and Riley debating the quality of the Red Sox dugout; the hostile takeover of southern Italy by Erin, Andy, and Wes; Shannon and Will squabbling like political pundits; and Matt and Lauren whispering to each other, oblivious to the world around them. Our ranks were growing and celebration was in order, but it wasn't how I imagined this night.

From across the tent, Andy glanced over her shoulder and our eyes met. Our connection used to be so rare, so potent, but now dark awkwardness filled the space between us. My stomach slammed into my throat, and I shifted my eyes to the dance floor, forfeiting.

Following my line of sight, Sam produced my phone, holding it just beyond my reach. "Do not interpret this as permission to make unwise decisions."

I grumbled in response and went breadcrumb hunting. The lack of texts from Andy didn't discourage me. She needed me to go to her. She always did. Her Instagram featured new photos from inside the inn, the Chatham Lighthouse, and Chatham Inner Harbor. Facebook offered a handful of random likes, including Lauren's status, 'this girl's getting hitched today!' and Shannon's 'wedding day!!!! (keep your knickers on, not my wedding).'

It wasn't much. I didn't expect Taylor Swift lyrics in her status, but some evidence she was experiencing a fraction of my hysteria would have been nice. How long could I keep this up? It wasn't possible to live in this state of desperation for more than a week or two. My liver wouldn't survive this level of abuse for much longer.

Matt and Lauren strolled toward us, and he caught Sam in a hug before turning to me. "Your efforts at keeping my husband alive and unharmed are appreciated," Lauren said, her hand on Matt's chest. She smiled at him, and mouthed, "My *husband*."

"We'll see you in a couple hours, at the brunch," Sam said.

"No promises my *wife* and I will be there," Matt muttered, his lips meeting Lauren's.

Gifting Matt with a fond smile, she stepped out of his arms and motioned for me to walk with her toward the inn. "It's time to fix it. I know she wants you to. Whatever it takes. Throw her over your shoulder and tie her up if that's what it takes for you to get her listening, but don't let another day go by without fixing it."

"I tried!" I shouted, my arms spread wide. "I've tried everything. I don't know what else to do! I wrote her a letter to tell her that we'd make it work, and I tried to talk to her during the pictures today, and every day this week and...nothing."

"Try again." Lauren rubbed my arm. "Don't let her think you're giving up. She's expecting that. She's used to people walking away from her, abandoning her, and she's used to protecting herself because no one else ever has."

Matt wrapped his arms around Lauren's waist, announcing, "I'm taking you to bed, Mrs. Walsh."

"That sounds splendid, but I never agreed to change my name."

Matt laughed against Lauren's neck. "You don't have to, sweetness, but don't think I'll stop saying it." He smiled at me. "Whatever my *wife* told you to do, do it."

They walked toward their cottage on the far end of the beach, and I absently waved as my siblings took their cues and relocated the party to Sam's cottage.

Time ambled by while I sat in the sand and watched the waves as they met the shore. They never stopped. Some waves pounded the sand with force and fury, leaving trails of broken shells and seaweed in their wakes. Others merely lapped the shoreline. But they never stopped.

Forever intertwined and necessary for each other in ways only they knew.

A wave curled across the shoreline as it broke and I turned my head to watch its path, and there she was. No more than five feet away, Andy stood with her shoes hanging from two fingers. I blinked, stunned and speechless, and she nodded with an uneven smile.

"I'm going to sit down, if that's okay." She held my gaze a moment before dropping to the sand.

A breath away, with her toes dug into the sand, Andy sat gazing up at the night sky.

"It came to my attention that I'm an insufferable, self-important bitch," she announced after a long silence. My brow furrowed, and she elaborated. "My friend Jess, from Wiscasset. The one who likes all those smarmy clubs?" Eager to keep her talking but utterly confused, I nodded. "She dumped me last weekend. Cited my self-important bitchiness as well as my intolerance for smarmy clubs and idiots, even if they're nice. The idiots, not the clubs."

Her toes emerged from the sand and burrowed under again, and she shifted her gaze over the ocean. "I've been trying to feel bad about it, and I truly regret that I didn't take better care of her feelings, but I'm not sad we went our separate ways." Andy sighed and brushed the sand from her fingers. "We outgrew each other, and we didn't get each other anymore. I need to take better care of the people who are important to me. Much better care. All of this," she swept her hand in the direction of the ceremony area and the tent. "It's too short to spend with people that aren't right for me. It sounds cold and it sounds bitchy, but I'm not apologizing."

I wasn't right for her, and she was saying her final goodbye. "Does that mean you're...?"

"Sometimes, the worst decisions...they make all the difference," she said, her voice faltering. She tore a hammered silver cuff from her wrist and dropped the back of her palm against my knee. "Bruce drew it." She lifted a shoulder. "I like that it's kind of wonky."

The moonlight illuminated the delicate shape of a lopsided shamrock inked alongside her pulse. A breathless minute passed while I studied the thin lines.

I used to think Andy didn't give me much, that she only presented bite-sized morsels of herself when it suited her, that it was a matter of playing the long game. Tracing the ink as my heart beat a bruising rhythm against my ribs, it was obvious I was wrong. Andy gave me everything. Her everything never took the shape or color I expected, and she forced me to see it in places where I never intended to look. But it was everything I needed.

"Bruce?" I asked, my finger tracing the lines.

"Bruce. The bartender. He's studying graphic design. Good guy. He poured an excellent gimlet, and pointed out that Jess and I wanted our old relationship, and we never accounted for the fact we're different people now. We handled each other with too much passive-aggression, and that's why it all blew up. He also convinced me to stay even when I wanted to resign. And when I sat on the curb in Chinatown and cried about you after last call, he asked me what I needed to feel better. I told him I needed some Peking duck and a flawed shamrock, and he made sure I got both. Then he took me home and hid my phone so I wouldn't do anything I regretted."

I wanted to hug Bruce the Bartender.

She nodded at her wrist. "I risked it all with you, Patrick, and it kills me you never told me about the partnership structure. I'm a perfectionist and I freak out when I feel trapped in situations.

Finding out you never intended to have another partner, or partners from outside your family, that was a nightmare. I need you to be upfront with me about that stuff. Can you handle all that?"

I closed the gap between us and tipped her face toward me, away from the ocean. "I should have told you and I own that clusterfuck. I can't change the partnership structure right now. You know that and you know I was serious when I said I would." My eyes closed as my lips pressed against her wrist, offering a thousand silent apologies.

"I know, I know," she sighed. "I'm sorry I freaked out and it took so long to crawl out of it. I just...I felt like I needed to protect myself, and backing far away was the only option."

I nodded, recognizing Andy adhered to her own timelines, even if they were infuriating. Rushing her wasn't in the cards for me. "I figured out I won't turn into a sadistic bastard if I lose you," I said against her racing pulse. "But I'll do whatever it takes to keep you. I love you too much to let you walk away." Her fingers curled around my cheek and I leaned into her caress. "I don't expect this to be easy, Andy, but you're *it* for me. And I think I might be it for you."

Looking up, a tiny smile pulled at her lips and she nodded.

"I can handle you. I might Google half of what you say, but I can handle you." My fingers dug into her hair to loosen the knot and she promptly slapped me away to do it herself. "I'm telling you right now, I am far from perfect and I will fuck up again. You have to promise you'll talk to me, always. I love you, Andriel. Just don't shut down on me."

Her head snapped up. "You remember?"

"I'm from Boston *and* Irish. It takes a lot more to get me blacked out." She stared at me, confused. "I remember everything about that night." My arm wrapped around her waist and my lips pressed to her neck, I inhaled a wisp of lavender and felt my universe slide into its rightful place. "It's probably the only thing that's gotten me through this past week. What was that second middle name again? The long one?"

"Mazanderani." I met Andy's eyes. "There's more to talk about."

"Yeah, there probably is," I conceded.

"But right now..." Andy smiled, and speared her fingers through my hair. "This is terrifying and amazing," she whispered against my lips. "I love you, and you're mine. You've been mine since the start, and even before then. It just took some time to figure out. That seems to happen for me a lot."

I hauled Andy to her feet and claimed her lips as the last words vibrated between us. I tasted her tart cherriness and I knew I could make it to our cottage in a few strides if I kept all thoughts above the belt. I needed to feel her skin, needed to be inside her while she told me she loved me, and I wanted to hear it again very soon.

"And if something is terrifying and amazing, you should definitely do it, right?" I murmured, pulling her across the sand.

"Definitely, Patrick."

"REMIND ME WHY WE'RE DOING THIS."

Patrick stomped his boots on the doormat and shook out of his coat, leaving a small mountain of snow around him.

I glanced up at him from my nook beside the fireplace, watching as he dropped his outerwear into a soggy heap. He muttered about the cold and the snow in his socks while pouring a tumbler of whiskey, and then settled onto the sofa.

"Goddamn Christmas lights," he said to his glass. "Where the fuck do you expect me to put all those?"

He gestured to the knotted pile of lights in my lap and groaned.

"On the tree," I said. "When we get one."

"Of course," he sighed. "Of course you want a tree."

Oh, he was *so* grumpy, and there was nothing better than grumpy Patrick. It was irrelevant whether *I* intended to string the lights on the terrace, and he growled at me until I handed them over. Not to mention the mathematical precision he brought to the activity, starting with measuring every inch of the terrace and sketching a design, and ending with using a laser beam guide to ensure the lines were perfectly plumb. And he refused my assistance every time I peeked outside.

Setting the tangled lights aside, I crawled into Patrick's lap. "Thank you. They look perfect. They're exactly how I wanted them."

He moved his hands to my ass, squeezing and pulling me closer. "Remind me why we're doing this."

I shrugged and laced my arms around his neck. That simple gesture never failed to jolt me with the realization that Patrick was *mine*. Maybe it was absurd to assume that I'd wake up some morning and discover my feelings for Patrick were less intense, less electric, less overwhelming. If anything, the past six months seemed to prove the opposite. We weren't just living and working together; we were becoming an entity, our ends and beginnings blurred.

And I loved it.

"We're doing this because it's our first Christmas together," I said. My fingers passed over the nape of his neck, up to his hairline and down to his shoulders.

Patrick laughed. "Since when do *you* celebrate Christmas?"

"Since never! Since I was the only kid in town who didn't have a Christmas list or a letter to Santa or stockings. I had major Christmas envy, and it wasn't like we did the Hanukkah thing at all, either."

"I will never figure you out, kitten."

"This is not me being weird," I said. "Plenty of Jews have some degree of Christmas envy. The decorations. The songs. The movies. The food. The parties. Just not the whole wise men-manger-Virgin Mary thing."

"So now you want lights and a tree and...what? You want to roast a ham and listen to Bing Crosby?"

"I was thinking we'd have a Christmas Eve party here," I said. "We could start our own tradition."

Patrick ran his hands up and down my arms, his gaze trained on my hair yet faraway. He was sorting something out but I wasn't sure whether it was the notion of people invading our space, more decorations, or doing something other than drinking at Shannon's place on Christmas Eve.

"I want a holiday thing. Something we do with all of our people, something fun and weird, like us. But if you hate it, it's fine. We don't have to—"

"Tradition implies it would happen for many Christmases," he murmured. "That *we'd* have a party. At *our* house. *Every* year."

Right. He didn't want people in our space, and truth be told, I wasn't the biggest fan of entertaining either.

"I'm aware of that, Patrick."

I liked our apartment to be the one place we didn't share with anyone else. Memories lived on every inch of this place, and they were just for us.

The awkwardness we endured while learning how to live together.

The fight we had when Patrick found me sunbathing on the terrace. I still didn't see the problem with some naked tanning.

The way he fell apart on the anniversary of his mother's death.

The feel of the cool, metal door on my ass when he backed me up against it and fucked me before visiting my mother and step-family for the High Holy Days.

But the closer I got to Patrick—his siblings, too—the more I realized I wanted a family of my own. I wanted to be part of something that Patrick and I created.

"Does that mean you're thinking about being here next year?" he asked.

I leaned my forehead against Patrick's. "Where else would I be?"

Patrick laughed, his lips brushing over mine. "Stand up and take off your pants."

Eyebrows arched, I said, "Excuse me?"

"Be a good kitten. Do as you're told."

I complied, but left my socks on. I couldn't decide whether I was annoyed with his demands or massively turned on. I could be both, right? "Happy?"

He nodded and beckoned me closer. "Come back here."

A smirk pulled at the corner of Patrick's lips, his eyes sparkling. As much as I wanted to know what was going on in his mind, I was content being in his lap, his hands moving over me with urgent reverence, his cock hardening beneath me.

My sweater and camisole were discarded without delay, and Patrick folded my arms behind my back. With my hands gripping my elbows, he reached behind me. Before I could ask what he was doing, I felt the uneven texture of the twinkle lights snaking around my arms. His smirk grew into a bright, devious smile as he bound my arms together and crossed the strand over my shoulders and around my breasts.

His mouth dipped to my chest, and he sucked my nipple until I was grinding against him. "How do you feel about these lights now?" I asked.

"Baby, I will cover the entire building in lights if that's what you want," he growled.

In a few quick movements, his pants were down and he was

easing his cock into me. He was still for moment, his lips pressed to my throat and his body vibrating with tension. I used to think he stopped like this to gather himself, to restrain the beast that lived inside, but now I knew better. I got the side of Patrick that was fully wild and unchecked.

His hips started rolling, and he was sucking and biting my shoulders and neck. There was no finesse, no strategy, but I didn't need those things. It didn't matter that Patrick got lost in the sensations, that his thrusts were frantic and erratic. This was us: close and real and raw.

When his lips moved to my nipples, I was lost. The plastic biting into my skin, his growls and bites, the pleasure trembling through every ounce of my body, it was all too much.

"Just a little more, kitten," he groaned into my skin. "Just give me a little more."

And I always did. I'd give Patrick anything, always.

He came with a quiet roar, his arms locked tight around my shoulders, and everything in me tingled. My nose, my belly button, my toes, my lips. I felt the heat of us conducted through my cells, and if it were possible, I loved this man a little more.

It wasn't about the sex; it was never about the sex. Maybe it started with sex, but it was safe to say we loved each other as nerdy souls long before we got naked. No, it was about feeling infinite and invincible, and endlessly, perfectly possessed.

"No ham," Patrick murmured. "We can do better than ham."

I was too orgasm-drunk to understand a word he was saying, especially considering his cock was still twitching inside me. "What?"

"Our party," he said. "The Chrismukkah tradition we just invented. I'm thinking rack of lamb. Oh, no, wait—tamales!"

"That does sound good," I said. "But only if you really want to do this. We don't have to."

"I want to make traditions with you," he said. He loosened the lights from my body, slowly unwinding them from my arms and kissing every odd indentation and welt as he went.

"So do I."

Patrick's brow furrowed, and he laughed to himself when the strand fell to the ground. He massaged my hands and arms, gently urging the blood flow to return. "Can one of those traditions be that you wear red on Christmas Eve?"

"Sure," I said. "Does lingerie count?"

Thank you for reading!

Get exclusive sneak previews of upcoming releases through Kate's newsletter and private reader group, The Canterbary Tales on Facebook.

ALSO BY KATE CANTERBARY

THE WALSH SERIES

Underneath It All – Matt and Lauren
The Space Between – Patrick and Andy
Necessary Restorations – Sam and Tiel
The Cornerstone – Shannon and Will
Restored — Sam and Tiel
The Spire — Erin and Nick
Preservation — Riley and Alexandra

WALSH SERIES SPIN-OFF STANDALONE NOVELS

Coastal Elite
Before Girl

Get exclusive sneak previews of upcoming releases through Kate's newsletter and private reader group, The Canterbary Tales, on Facebook.

BEFORE GIRL

A sexy new standalone

She's the girl next door.
He's the guy who's loved her from afar.
They're in for an unexpected tumble into love.

She'll juggle your balls.
For Stella Allesandro, chaos is good. She's a rising star at a leading sports publicity firm. She's known throughout the industry as the jock whisperer—the one who can tame the baddest of the bad boys in professional sports without losing her signature smile.

But Cal Hartshorn is an entirely different kind of chaos.

He'll fix your broken heart.

This ex-Army Ranger and now-famous cardiothoracic surgeon fails at nothing...except talking to a woman he's adored from afar. Whether on the battlefield or operating room, he's exacting, precise, and efficient, but all of that crumbles when Stella is in sight.

Cal always knows—and gets—what he wants, and now he wants all of her.

His *forever* girl.

But Stella isn't convinced she's anyone's forever.

Kate Canterbary doesn't have it all figured out, but this is what she knows for sure: spicy-ass salsa and tequila solve most problems, living on the ocean--Pacific or Atlantic--is the closest place to perfection, and writing smart, smutty stories is a better than any amount of chocolate. She started out reporting for an indie arts and entertainment newspaper back when people still read newspapers, and she has been writing and surreptitiously interviewing people—be careful sitting down next to her on an airplane—ever since. Kate lives on the water in New England with Mr. Canterbary and the Little Baby Canterbary, and when she isn't writing sexy architects, she's scheduling her days around the region's best food trucks.

You can find Kate at www.katecanterbary.com

Made in the USA
San Bernardino, CA
03 May 2018